The Golden Glow

VOLUME ONE BOOK ONE

J L MARTIN

TIME TRAVELLERS PUBLISHING PTY LTD

SAMSARA

THE FIRST SEASON

The Golden Glow

Volume One Book One

J. L. MARTIN

Disclaimer

In reading the series 'Samsara', I ask you to consider the era in which this work of fiction is set. In these more enlightened times, elements of this story may be considered homophobic or morally corrupt — along with barbaric and downright ignorant. However; in 19th century Australia, they were not. Themes throughout the series are reflective of the times and are an accurate account of the attitude and bias a large majority of society held towards the LGBTQI+ community. In saying this, we no longer consider it appropriate for a fifteen-year-old girl to marry — forced or not — but 130 years ago, it was not uncommon.

The character of Leo is based on a real person. As outrageous, inappropriate and politically incorrect as he is — I love this soul. It is not my intention to stigmatise him or cause offence to anyone — only to remain authentic in my best effort to honour and immortalise a very dear man who left a significant imprint on my life — and who unfortunately was born without a filter and lacks all sensibilities; and can be very, very badly behaved. Although most of the buildings in this series did at one time exist — some still stand to this day — the author has taken creative liberties regarding some locations, floor plans, and design. A few scenes may disturb some readers throughout the series and include adult content and low-level violence.

Go to www.jlmartinauthor.com

Samsara- The First Season

The Golden Glow

First Edition published 2021

ISBN 978-1-925852-19-6

Time Travelers Publishing House

© Copyright 2021

J L Martin

Dedication

To my beloved grandchildren,

Samsara is the legacy I leave you

(Full Dedication At The End Of The Book)

A Personal Note from the Author

'S Samsara' — meaning reincarnation — was originally written as one enormous novel of 1.6 million words and spans from 1890 to 1968. The first series has since been broken up into twelve separate novels, resulting in a serial rather than a series. As we begin our new friendship, it's important you're aware of what you are signing up for, so there is no disappointment or feeling tricked into reading all the books to 'find out what happens next'...

These are not stand-alone books with a start, middle and end — instead, the story flows continuously from book to book — spanning an entire lifetime. I highly recommend that you read them in order.

This epic series was first available on Wattpad from 2016 to 2019 as 'The Golden Glow Chronicles', and for a brief time on Amazon. Since then, the story continued to develop as Volume Two (1790-1875) Volume Three (1968-2063) and Volume Four (2063-????) came into being, each containing up to 12 books per season. As a result, all twelve novels in Volume One have been revamped and published as 'Samsara- The First Season' in 2022.

The first BIG book in the series, 'The Golden Glow', is available to buy in paperback and audiobook from my website jlmartinauthor.com and leading online platforms and bookstores.

The prequel novella, 'That Fated Night', is my gift to you — a heartfelt thank you to those who have read everything in this series and still wanted more — and for those new to 'Samsara', who want to see for themselves what people are talking about without financial commitment. It is available (eBook) only from my website when you sign up for my newsletter, or for the free audiobook, subscribe to my YouTube channel. All titles in the series can be purchased in paperback, including the novella and spin-off books, to add to your bookshelf next to 'Samsara' for those like me who like to hold a physical book in your hand.

I ask that you leave a review for each book on your chosen platform or my website. This not only helps your favourite authors become more visible in the enormous world of publishing — it helps readers just like you discover books they never would have found. Thank you, and I really hope you enjoy your journey with Abigail, her friends, and the family she chooses for herself. If Samsara is not the series for you, I wish you well in finding novels that bring you joy and thank you for the time you invested. We cannot be everyone's cup of tea — or coffee, in my case — and life is far too short to drink dregs or read bad books. Much love to all, and I hope you enjoy Samsara xx.

A Few Reviews...

Margaret Pettet ~ I felt nothing but excitement waiting to see what was coming next as this series is so unpredictable and addictive. You could never call this author boring, and she has a wicked sense of humour and can be far from politically correct—a great story delivered in a beautifully authentic way. I haven't read anything as good as I don't know how long!

Ruben Dexter Panopio ~ I love it. It's raw—a genius style of writing. You won't be able to put it down once you've started reading this series. You almost feel you're right in there with the characters. Feel what they're feeling. A broad spectrum of emotions, from gut-wrenching loss to uplifting triumph. Humour. A lot of it. Magic. And a dash of naughtiness. It's an experience—a J L Martin experience, which is a unique one in itself.

Jenny Pickering ~ I am generally not a reader, but with this series, I couldn't put it down, wanting to know what happened next. It is the most intriguing series I have ever read and really hits its stride as you get further in. Worth the time invested, and I have been privileged to read 19 books in this series. It just keeps getting better the further you go. Love, Love, Love them, and I can't wait for the entire series to be published. I can see this on Netflix in the next few years.

Lena Sisk ~ Captures your attention from the first chapter to the very last chapter. Very intriguing on what's coming next; so many twists and turns. Can't stop thinking about the characters even after I finished series one. Anyone who wants to be transported on a roller coaster of emotions, it's a MUST READ. Very addictive.

And a Few More...

Hannah Cross ~ J L Martin transports you to a faraway place full of wonder, awe, and mystery. I have been here from the start, cheering, laughing, and crying, along with Abigail and her family. I was getting so caught up in the flurry of words that hours passed by before I realised it. I have never before been so abruptly taken by a book that I can literally feel myself living in Abigail's time and experiencing her life through her words, feeling like I'm right there with her. Each book will take you to a new place, full of life, love, and some unfortunate circumstances. You will laugh and cry and learn to love Abigail and her golden glow more than you ever thought you could. Don't hesitate. You won't regret it.

Scooter N Kris ~ I adored every part of this series. I neglected all my household chores until I read every available word. I was completely drawn into this story. J L Martin is a brilliant storyteller, and the details are amazing; how something she writes in book one comes up in book four and makes sense, then it's touched on again in series two and three and kept me so interested. I learnt so much about Australia and its history, too. By far the most exciting and unique series I have read, and I can't wait for all the books to be published.

Prologue

S HE CAME FROM NOWHERE. She belonged to no one.

Well, that was what she believed, a belief reinforced daily by the Sisters surrounding her; however, some knew this was far from the truth, choosing to remain silent for their own sake.

The unusually tall, slender girl emerged from an old stone barn, the heavy bucket she carried filled with water, while she held a scrubbing brush in her hand along with a bar of tallow soap, the skin on her hands appearing raw and painful. Her wavy red hair swung around her waist in two long plaits, while a blinding golden light surrounded her body and radiated from every part of her. It was not something anyone around the young woman could see, nor was she even aware the aura was there, but she had met people surrounded by a golden glow, only she did not understand what it meant.

She wore a calico bonnet, the ill-fitting, threadbare dress providing very little warmth as she shivered while trudging up through the mud towards the back entrance of what once was a private estate of a wealthy aristocrat.

The orphanage, a dilapidated three-story manor surrounded by twelve-foot-high stone walls built two centuries ago, sat on a substantial plot of land. The Sisters kept chickens and sheep, along

1

with pigs and goats — and an old horse named Tipple. Several cows produced milk for the children. Only half of the manor was in use, as the orphanage survived on charity from local parish donations, barely enough to feed the children, let alone keep the manor from falling into disrepair.

The young girl reached the door, placing the bucket on the ground before exhaling deeply. Lifting her arm to rub her shoulder for a moment, she then straightened up and narrowed her brilliant, emerald green eyes in amusement at a goat who raced across the yard, having escaped its enclosure, while making no move to chase after the beast. Her pretty face flinched for a moment, her mind returning to the fact that tomorrow, January 14th, 1890, she would turn fifteen, and they would push her out into the world from the only home she had ever known. She would leave without knowing the answer to hundreds of questions that had tormented her since she could remember. To be thrown out without kith or kin, knowing not a soul in the world beyond the walls that loomed above, frightened her to the core. She would leave without the security or comfort of knowing where she would go or what would become of her. The poor child had lain awake at night for months now, wondering how she would find the strength and courage to step out into a world they had sheltered her from her entire life, protected by these walls she hated so much.

She pushed the heavy door open before picking up her bucket and tools, making her way into the dark, wide hallway, continuing on until she arrived at the other end of the enormous building. She set down the pail of water near the front entrance, groaning loudly before sinking to her knees and picking up the scrubbing brush, knowing the sooner she started, the quicker she would finish. As she scrubbed the flagstones in the dimly lit hallway for the last time, she reflected on a past she knew all too well.

She had lived all her life at Emiliani House in Edinburgh, Scotland, so named for Saint Jerome Emiliani, the patron saint of abandoned children and the Order to which the Sisters belonged. In the winter of 1875, they discovered her on the doorstep in a wicker basket. The mother had wrapped the tiny wean in a blanket with a note inside, asking the Sisters to look after her and rear the child well, citing she had no means to care for a newborn. As if written as an afterthought, scrawled at the bottom of the expensive paper was one sentence, naming the child Abigail; however, they had not bestowed a surname on the poor wretch. While eavesdropping on the Sisters when she was seven years of age, Abigail had discovered she was only a few hours old when they had found her, was blue from the cold, and if left outside much longer, surely would have died that night. The Sisters had suspiciously noted her clothing, blanket and bonnet were expensive, and she wore an emerald stone on a gold chain around her tiny neck. The Sisters removed the precious stone immediately and, along with the clothes, stored them away for safekeeping — Abigail never having laid eyes on it in all the years since she had lived there. That was all the poor child knew about how her life began.

The Sisters, known throughout Scotland to take in unwanted girls, provide them with an adequate education, including instructing them how to behave, were hard taskmasters. All who lived under the benevolence of Emiliani House, no matter how young, were expected to master household skills that would stand them in good stead when they were of age to go into service for wealthy employers. The Sisters ran a tight ship, not allowing for luxuries of any kind. When Abigail was old enough to question the world, she often wondered if this came more from punitiveness than poverty.

The Mother House was in Inverness, where Mother Superior Mary Bernadette lived with the postulants and retired Sisters. As the head of the Order, it was her responsibility to oversee the orphanage's finances and operation and send replacement Sisters to teach and rear the children. The children saw her only during her annual visits, much to their relief. She terrified most of the orphans; with her wide mouth and flat nose. They laughed and made fun of her behind her back, comparing her to a toad — a toad that had let the power she held go to her head.

As Abigail grew, it became clear to the Sisters she was an exceptionally bright child, and this bothered several of them for reasons they never spoke of to anyone but each other. She could read by the age of three, knew all her letters and numbers, and could count beyond a hundred. What bothered most of them, though, was that she spoke with an English accent, despite rarely venturing beyond the orphanage walls and never having met a soul from England. Sister Mary Josephine became the closest thing to a mother the poor child had, and she loved her without limitations. She nurtured and lavished her with affection, often holding Abigail on her lap as she sat on her rickety old bed while reading to her and the other girls in their dormitory at night. She had slept in the nursery from the night Abigail arrived and then set up her bed in the dormitory for several years until she felt the child would not fret if she were not nearby. Surreptitiously, the kind-hearted Sister had provided her with books she found in a musty library in the unused portion of the manor, but occasionally presented her with new books she somehow obtained from an unknown source — whom she refused to identify still to this day. These books stimulated Abigail's mind, but most of all, her imagination. By the time she was twelve, she was reading the works of great philosophers and poets, art and history books, and anything else she could get her hands on, no matter who the author. She found great enjoyment within the pages of the small, tattered books with stories using language that was new and exciting to her, her inquisitive mind searching for words she could add to her vocabulary, while trying to understand the works of Charles Dickens and William Shakespeare.

The books provided a lifeline during her darkest days and confirmed there was a vibrant world beyond the orphanage walls, giving her hope one day she would have a life of her own, free from the harsh and lonely life she had endured so far in her short lifetime. By immersing herself in these fables, she was able to avoid what bothered her most — the golden glow — but little did the poor lass know, she would soon be unable to avoid it, even if surrounded by a thousand tomes.

Chapter One

A s I scrubbed the stone floor, one I had cleaned a thousand times during my lifetime, I giggled softly at a memory of my dear friend, Polly — who would complain from start to finish when ordered to scrub anything — while I wondered what tomorrow would bring. I heard footsteps drawing nearer, and I raised my head, my eyes slowly adjusting to the dim light. Sister Mary Josephine hurried along the hallway as if she had lost something, stopping several times to look on top of the many sideboards that lined the hallways, the paint peeling and yellowing, while several large cracks wound their way up the walls and across the ceiling. She looked beautiful in her black habit as she swished down the corridor, her rosary beads swinging from her pocket. When she noticed me in the alcove, she glanced across lovingly, then hurried to my side, coming to an abrupt halt in front of me before reaching down and gently patting me on the head.

'Get up, child. I'm eager tae speak wi' ye.' She patiently waited for me to set aside my brush, rag, and bucket so no one passing by would trip over them. I rose to my feet and followed her into the large parlour at the front of the manor, passing through the dim and shabby entrance. The smell of old leather filled my nose, the room

7

musty with dust floating in the air, illuminated by the light filtering through the two large windows. The Sisters rarely used the room, and then only when our parish priest, Father McLean, visited to partake in afternoon tea. 'Mo luaidh, have ye given any more thought about enterin' the convent?' She gazed at me, her striking blue eyes filled with genuine concern. She was a beautiful, sweet, and loving person and the only mother I had ever known.

'Yes, Sister, and no, Sister,' I answered. 'It is not my calling. You know me better than I know myself. Deep down, you know I would never be happy in a convent. I cannot commit to a life serving a God I do not believe in as you do.' I was calm, albeit defiant, as I felt I must be honest with her, along with myself. 'There is also the fact I see strange things you believe are not of God.' She fixed me with a hard stare, then shook her head disapprovingly.

'Haud yer wheesht. Somebody may hear ye, an' 'tis blasphemous.' She frowned, an expression I rarely saw, although even that could not dim her beauty — the golden glow surrounding her slight frame reminding me of an angel I often admired in the lead-light window of our church. I would never argue with her and always did as she asked, but this time was different. I wanted more for myself than they were offering. The Sisters had always considered me a determined child, and I continued to be despite some of them trying to skelp it out of me. I did not know what would happen to me tomorrow; however, I knew what I did not want my life to become. I moved towards the tattered chaise lounge and sat down at her request, silently waiting for her to continue. She sat beside me, placing her hand on my cheek, then shook her head at me again. 'Ye have always been so free wi' yer opinions, Abigail — but as I have telit ye afore, ye will have tae try harder tae curb yer tongue when yer in service, or ye will end up on the streets. It keeps me awake at night, leavin' me tossin' an' turnin' 'til dawn, a multitude o' thoughts runnin' through me mind, none o' them pleasant. I'm worried about what will ultimately become o' ye, mo ghraidh.' Tears filled her gentle, clear-blue eyes that stared into mine — unblinking and so full of emotion as a profound sadness settled on her face. She clasped my hands between her own, and I forced a smile, hoping to cheer her, despite having the same dark concerns myself. 'I've asked Sister Mary Monica where ye will go tomorrow. She telit me she is waitin' tae hear from a wealthy family in York that may need a new scullery maid. If this happens, yer future is assured, an' the burden taken from me. It hurts me heart I cannae do any more fer ye.' A tear escaped her eye that she quickly brushed away, appearing flushed and emotional, her hands trembling slightly.

'You have done everything and more.' I swallowed hard, willing the lump in my throat to disappear, but failed miserably, my eyes filling with tears. 'You are the only person I have in this world who truly loves me and cares I'm alive, and I thank your God every single day for giving you to me. They discarded me without a backward glance, no different from a piece of scaffy, and you made me feel valuable and worthy. You have been more of a mother than a nun to me, and I will always love you. I will always remember and be grateful for all you have done for me. The nights you came to tuck me in and kiss me, always encouraging me to be a kind person no matter what my circumstance. You always made sure I did a good deed before a bad one and guided me — then there are the wonderful books that saved me in so many ways. You are the one who taught me how to be the person I am. I couldn't have asked for a better mother than you.' I burst into tears and let my body crumple into her side, placing my head on her shoulder while I sobbed. She slipped her arms around me and stroked my hair while stroking my cheek.

'Oh, mo luaidh.' She dug into her habit and pulled out a linen handkerchief, quickly wiping her eyes and then mine, before smiling sadly. 'I feel a part o' me will be leavin' wi' ye. Ye are such a special wee child tae me, an' ye are the closest I will ever have tae a daughter of me own. Ye have always been so strong-willed an' always ken yer own mind, always readin', absorbin' everythin', ye clever lass. Ye could never let me down or disappoint me, Abigail — nae ever, naw matter what choices ye make in life, good, bad, or stupid — or if ye make decisions that lead ye straight up that evil path tae the gates o' hell, I will still love ye. I'm ever so proud o' ye, me girl, an' I ken ye will be sensible whatever yer choices. Whatever happens, I would like ye tae write tae me when ye can.'

'I promise.' I sniffed, then blew my nose loudly into her handkerchief, feeling overwhelmed with grief at the thought of parting from her forever. She hugged me tightly as I cried onto her shoulder for what seemed like the longest time.

She was such a pretty woman, short and plump, with big, blue eyes. I knew she had brown, curly hair under that wimple, only finding this out when taken ill with fever just after I turned ten. In her dressing gown with a nightcap on her head, she had rushed to my bedside. Her hair was fighting to get free from under that cap, and it was winning, its tight curls pushing their way out so I could see them for the first time since I had known her. She was in her third decade now and was barely grown herself when they took me in, only living at the orphanage for a few weeks before my arrival.

She often told me I had the memory of an elephant. If I read or experienced something once, it imprinted in my mind, just waiting to be called upon at some inappropriate moment — causing me to be chastised by many of the Sisters a thousand times over who were not so fond of me.

They well knew Sister Mary Agnes for her sharp tongue and quick temper, but remained silent on the matter and rarely intervened. I was fortunate to have Sister Mary Josephine to love and care for me — and blessed to have her protection from the Sisters who found great joy inflicting misery and pain on their charges — but there were many who suffered immensely under their care. Sister Mary Josephine embraced me, memories filling my mind of how she had loved and protected me during my childhood, keenly aware I would not have survived without her intervention.

'Sister Mary Monica wants tae see ye,' she said at last. 'I've been sent fer ye. Please mind yer tongue when ye meet wi' her, mo ghraidh, as she is yer last hope o' findin' somewhere tae go. Ye ken very weel if ye upset her, she will likely push ye out the front gates tomorrow herself, leavin' ye on the streets. Hurry up now, as she says 'tis o' an urgent nature.' Releasing me from her tight embrace, she helped me to my feet before leading me out of the parlour. We walked side by side down the long hallway towards Sister Mary Monica's office before I stopped abruptly and embraced her again.

'You will always be the mother I would have chosen for myself,' I whispered as she broke down and wept openly while hugging me tightly in return.

Sister Mary Josephine composed herself before knocking on the office door.

'Enter,' I heard in a sharp tone. She turned the brass handle and held the heavy door wide for me as I took several tentative steps before stopping in front of the authoritarian nun. The latter stood by the door, eyeing me with disdain, while Sister Mary Josephine remained outside the door. 'Sit down,' she barked, causing me to jump in fright before hurrying to the worn leather chair and sitting down heavily. I gazed around the room and observed once more how shabby and neglected it was. A wooden desk with a broken corner, some shelving behind it in disrepair, stood in the middle of the room. The smooth plaster that once lined the walls was missing in large patches and exposed solid bluestone walls. A worn leather-upholstered chair stood behind a faded desk, while a sideboard held a crystal decanter and four sparkling glasses that glittered in the light that streamed through the window. They had been on the cabinet ever since I could remember and, having spent a lot of time in this office due to being wilful — as the Sisters politely called it — I realised I had never seen them moved. I assumed their only purpose was for when Father McLean visited. He was a hard man, and the children avoided him at all costs. The bookshelves behind the desk bulged with many tomes, mostly ecclesiastical works I was certain I would have found loathsome to read. Then there was the gruesome crucifix that took up nearly the entire wall of the room. Whenever summoned to this office, it had always frightened me. I found it extremely disturbing having to stare at a life-sized Jesus with blood dripping down his beastly wounds inflicted by evil people. 'Thank ye, Sister Mary Josephine. Ye may go,' Sister Mary Monica ordered my beloved Sister, who nodded politely and quietly closed the door behind her. Sister Mary Monica appeared puzzled as she strolled past me and around her desk to sit in the imposing chair. 'This box arrived this mornin'.' She stabbed her pudgy finger in the air several times at a wooden object on her desk, screwing up her face in disdain, the grey glow that surrounded her body only making her appear even eviler than I believed her to be. 'It contains some interestin' documents. I dinnae consider it tae be in yer best interests ye are informed o' the contents, but have nae choice in the matter. This could significantly affect yer future, scabby bassa, an' I expect ye tae take this seriously. Ye are nae tae treat it as a joke, as ye do wi' everythin' else,' she added, the contempt in her eyes clear as she glared at me while I observed what seemed to be a very expensive-looking wooden container in front of her and ignored her hostility.

She had never liked me, and I was certain it thrilled her each time they sent me to her to be flogged for misbehaving, which was usually just for opening my mouth with an opinion. Nausea settled on me without warning, my insides shaking while my heart pounded so hard it thundered in my ears. I had no time to recover before she continued.

'First o' all, there is a document in here namin' ye as Abigail Delmont. If ye are connected tae Isabelle Delmont in any way, the de'il's own blood is runnin' through yer veins. She never had the right tae even use that name — the maleficent trollop — an' should have reverted tae Howard decades ago,' she spat before regaining her composure while I stared at her in confusion. 'It gives the name o' yer mother, a Mary Campbell, a hedge creeper naw doubt, an' yer father is naw listed at all, as I have always suspected. This strumpet Mary is likely spawned from Isabelle somehow. Important information if ye plan tae find this family ye think ye now have — a family I would be ashamed o' if the truth be known. Do ye think ye will seek them out, ye scabby bassa?' She glared across the desk, her eyes silently challenging me. She was such a spiteful cow and clearly resented any news I might receive of my family or any information about where I came from, which she knew full well was vital to me and always had been. I paused, needing time to get over my shock and disbelief.

'I — I don't know,' I finally stammered. I felt dizzy. It quickly dawned on me that, if true, I had a surname and could now find my parents. I would belong somewhere and be part of a proper family now — or at least soon. Pure happiness surged through my entire body, even as I sat in her office overcome with fear — that fear now mingled with a growing sense of excitement.

'Weel, ye have tae remember they left ye here fer a reason, an' the likely reason is they dinnae want anythin' tae do wi' ye in the first place,' she simpered, blood rising to my face while my stomach felt as if she had struck me. 'It will cause ye much distress an' heartbreak should ye go an' find them — an' tae find they have started new lives wi'out ye would be wretched for ye.' She stopped for a moment and smiled to herself. 'They obviously dinnae want tae be in contact wi' ye, or they would have returned tae claim ye — but they never did.

An' they have plenty o' time tae do it. Naw. Mark me words, our wee bassa, ye are better off tae get on wi' yer own life an' go intae service for a nice family that'll look after ye in tae yer old age.' She paused, allowing her words to hit me, and they did. Harder than if she had slapped me with her own hand. 'Ye could consider dedicatin' yerself tae God. 'Tis nae a bad life here. Ye work hard from the dawn 'til the dusk tae make sure the bairns have what they need — though we have fallen on hard times in the fifteen years since we lost our benefactors, may they burn in hell — an' then our kirk closed an' became attached tae the larger parish. We are scrapin' by tryin' tae ensure churlish lasses like ye have a chance in life. Naw, ye obtuse blaigeard. If ye want tae stay here, ye would have tae shut that big mouth o' yers. Ye are more than aware we spend four hours a day in silent contemplation an' prayer. It would be very hard on ye should ye ever join the Order, as ye are a disobedient ingrate who I dinnae believe will make anythin' o' yerself. I'm o' the firm belief that ye should nae look fer yer parents, as they dinnae want ye then an' they will nae want ye now. Dinnae ferget they left ye here for us tae raise ye in poverty. They dinnae care about ye an' never did,' she spat with icy contempt as the smile faded from my face, while her lips turned up into an insidious smile, appearing to take great pleasure from my confusion and pain. My heart sank. Maybe Sister Mary Monica was right — perhaps they would want nothing to do with me if I just turned up and disrupted their lives. 'The second document,' she continued briskly, 'is a letter addressed tae me instructin' I hand ye this sealed envelope an' ensure all instructions are followed.' She deliberately hesitated before passing the envelope across the desk, prolonging the suspense.

I reached over and politely took the letter with a shaking hand, avoiding her gaze. As I held it between my fingers, the beautiful paper smooth and crisp, I noticed it was of a quality I had never had the privilege to use or even lay eyes on before. I slowly broke the wax seal and opened it, realising this was the first letter of my own I had ever received — only reinforcing the fact I did not have anyone in the world other than Sister Mary Josephine who even cared if I lived or died. Inside, I found a five-pound note, a train ticket, and a message directed to me personally, written by an experienced and creative hand of some education. Five-pound was as much as I would have earned in a year, slaving away as a maid for some entitled and often cruel master — and more money than I thought I would ever see at once. Yet here I was, holding it in my hand. I found it hard to believe someone out there somewhere cared enough to send it to me. I scanned the brief message before passing the letter and money back to Sister Mary Monica, who held out her hand expectantly to read the contents herself. I had never held money before, and it felt good, so it was with reluctance I handed it back to her. Money meant freedom and choice, and that was what I wanted. I knew well I would never fit in or be just ordinary — I was female, alone, and I struggled to bite my tongue and comply without question. This was not how women behaved, especially in service, where even the menfolk were expected to be submissive and agreeable. Every waking moment. I watched in amusement as Sister Mary Monica's face darkened, appearing even more unimpressed as she read the note. She grimaced before she placed it to one side of the desk, gazing across at me intently.

'I heard back only yesterday from a family in York who have kindly offered ye employment as a scullery maid on their estate.' She looked up from the letter she was reading and narrowed her gaze across the desk. 'Surely ye are bright enough tae ken ye would be better off takin' this position on the chance this solicitor, Mr Malcolm, an' his motives are inauspicious? Why has this arrived only the day afore ye are tae leave here forever? An' I must say, thank goodness ye'll be leavin' on the morrow! I'll be celebratin' seein' the back o' ye. The Lord God has finally answered me prayers. After readin' these documents several times, we have nae idea what this is about, who is behind it, or what could happen tae ye travellin' tae London all alone, nae knowin' if there will be anybody at the other end waitin' fer ye. Naw that I care, but we do have Sister Mary Josephine tae consider, who has openly favoured ye the entire time they forced us tae tolerate yer existence. I am weel aware o' how concerned she is fer yer welfare — an' she's favoured an' protected by Mother Mary Bernadette. Therefore, I must ensure ye are at least safe on the day ye leave here. What happens tae ye after that 'tis none o' me concern.'

I felt the bitterness that dripped from her voice as I held her stony gaze. She would never want or expect anything good to happen to me, and now it appeared I might have a slim chance of finding my parents, she couldn't stand it. She was doing all in her power to discourage me — her dour face even more so today — revealing just how much she disapproved and resented this turn of events.

'May I have permission to leave, please, Sister? I would like to be alone to consider what this all means. I now have another option other than going into slavery for the rest of my natural life,' I whispered defiantly, my voice faltering as I tried to resist the urge to cry before leaning back in my chair and crossing my arms. She pursed her lips, her eyes glinting dangerously.

'Oh, so it seems ye will nae be needin' the scullery position, then? Ye are above that kind o' work now, are ye? Why? 'Cause some solicitor in London wants tae see ye? Has it made ye feel important fer the first time in yer pitiful life?' She scoffed, attempting to humiliate me, a place she consistently went to when not winning an argument, or the rare times when those brave enough would refuse to obey her without question. I shook my head a little too vigorously.

'No, I will not accept the position until I have had time to myself to consider my future, but please thank them for their kind offer of employment.' She widened her eyes in disbelief before grunting loudly, her face a mottled red. Whatever was going to happen, I believed it could not be worse than working eighteen hours or more a day, and it was pure luck if your master was decent and you were fortunate to have a kind employer. Even then, those in service worked from dawn 'till dusk carrying out the most menial and back-breaking tasks, then falling into bed to only have to rise hours later to do it all over again. If my parents did not want me, I had already made up my mind to use the five pounds to book passage to France and see for myself the things I had only read and dreamed of while shivering in my bed on those cold winter nights that seemed to go on forever. If Paris turned out to be all I expected, I would seek employment there — Find a decent job that was interesting, and I enjoyed doing. I could make new friends and start a new life — one I could choose for myself.

'It says in the letter ye will be collected at the end o' the train journey at London Station an' taken tae yer lodgin' afore meetin' wi' that solicitor the followin' day. Have ye considered the genuine risk o' gettin' stranded in such a dangerous city wi' nae hope o' work or help if this comes tae nought?' She grimaced as if she had just sucked on a sour sweetie, her displeasure clear.

'I will take my chances, Sister.' Bravely holding her gaze, I grunted again, then shifted in her worn leather chair. Needing to be alone to contemplate what all this meant for me, I was growing impatient. I knew I was risking nothing by taking the train, a novel experience for me, given I had rarely gone beyond the walls of the convent since arriving all those years ago. I felt I would regret it forever if I did not find out what the solicitor wanted and any information he may hold regarding my family, reigniting my longing to find my parents. Now there was a glimmer of hope, no matter how small, and I planned to take it with both hands and claim my birthright. I would go, and nothing was going to stop me — especially not this machete mouthed bitch who, despite being married to Jesus, only behaved as a Christian woman when people were watching on a Sunday in kirk.

I walked back to the sparse dormitory I shared with nineteen other girls from my age down to four years old, finding as I stepped into the room someone had neatly placed a calico bag on the end of my bed. Reaching out to pick it up, the cloth was rough in my hand, while neatly sewn by the Sisters with a strap to slip across the shoulder to carry it. Taking several steps towards my side drawer, I took out a brown woollen shawl and set it aside — my only warm winter outerwear — knitted for me by Sister Mary Josephine with love. I placed one of the two new dresses the Sisters had allowed me to make for the outside world, smoothing the coarse fabric down neatly as I looked around the empty room. I had copied the styles out of a magazine retrieved from a scaffy pile while walking home through the village from church one Sunday. Big hats were in fashion, but I did not own a hat or even know how to make one. I would have to wear my bonnet when I left tomorrow, if only to appease the Sisters, although I had every intention of throwing it on the street as soon as I arrived at the station without looking back. I did not like hats anyway, so I was more than happy to sacrifice wearing one, although I would not fit into this brand new world where being accepted was important to me. The dresses I had sat up into the night making were high in the neck with slim sleeves, a cinched-in waist, and a plain skirt that fell to the ground, one a deep shade of brown that complimented my hair, the other a dark, emerald green I found lovely. I felt confident I would blend into the crowd, although I was not a gifted seamstress. Modestly styled, they were decent enough to walk down the street and not stand out, which was the last thing I wanted. I hated being the centre of attention, finding when people stared at me, I felt embarrassed and self-conscious. The dresses might not have been the height of fashion, but they were new, and they were grown-up, which was all I wanted.

I stood by the bed, gazing at myself in the tiny hand mirror Sister Mary Josephine had smuggled to me, given mirrors were not permissible for girls in a Catholic orphanage should they encourage the sin of vanity. My eyes seemed overly large, and my dark, long lashes made them look so much older than they were. Despite being shut away in an orphanage, I had read far too much of how cruel and unfair the world I was about to enter could be. A world I was cynical about — and that frightened me a great deal. The most important thing to me was finding my parents and belonging to someone, knowing I would find peace only once I discovered where I came from and who my people were. I needed to look at tomorrow as the start of an adventure and a day closer to them holding me in their arms.

I lay in bed with a thousand thoughts running through my mind. I would die if my life turned out to be mundane. If my fate were to do the same things over and over every day like the Sisters or as a servant, I would wither inside and lose hope and end up as bitter and twisted as Sister Mary Monica. No. My life would have meaning, and no matter how poor I was, I promised myself I would find joy in every situation. I did not know how, but things would work out — especially when I reunited with my parents.

My thoughts turned to Sister Mary Josephine, and suddenly my heart hurt and I felt miserable. I would never forget her for the rest of my life. I was fortunate enough to have in my possession a miniature portrait of her taken several years ago by a photographer. He had come to the orphanage to take a picture of all the Sisters for a newspaper article. His visit had caused a great deal of joy and much banter between them as they practised their poses. Sister Mary Josephine had slipped it to me during our hallway embrace, and I had added it to my meagre possessions in my calico bag.

I felt ready to face tomorrow and accept my fate, whatever that may be, knowing I had one special person in the world who would always love me unconditionally — even though separated in body — possibly forever. She would always be at the forefront of my mind wherever I was in the world. I lowered myself down onto the hard, rickety bed and pulled my threadbare blanket up to my neck, my body shivering for a time until sleep engulfed me. I dreamed of a ship, a dark cellar, and Paris — but darker dreams crept in as the night drew deeper on towards morning, leaving me tossing and turning while they tormented me to the very core of my soul.

Chapter Two

T HE PALE LIGHT FILTERED through the cracked pane glass window as I turned over before slowly opening my eyes, feeling excitement mixed with fear well up inside me, knowing this was the first day of my new life, whatever direction it may take. As I lay in my uncomfortable, creaky bed for a moment longer and listened to the winter birds singing their morning chorus, I realised today would be a day of lasts — the last time I would hear the birds chirping from outside, perched up in the oak tree that had grown for over a hundred years outside the dormitory window. The last time I would see all the children I had watched grow alongside me. The last time I would be in the presence of the Sisters. The last time I would have a secure roof over my head, no matter how lonely or void of love, I did not have to pay for myself. The last time I would be a child — for today, they would throw me out into a world I was unfamiliar with and expected to behave as an adult, no matter my tender years.

I tossed off the blanket and rose quickly. 'This is the last time I will get out of this bed; thank the Sisters' God,' I mumbled to myself. The ancient, squeaky structure made of cast iron had rusted long ago and would not be missed — the mattress so thin I could feel the hard base underneath. There were some lasts I was relieved I would never experience again, and I smiled to myself.

I quickly stepped into my new green dress, my thin shift underneath, and secured the tiny buttons one by one up to my neck, then slipped on my new shoes. The Sisters provided a new pair of boots the day before leaving the orphanage to carry you through until you began employment and could pay for your own necessities. It was an extraordinary feeling to have new shoes, providing us with one pair every year that had to last, even if our feet grew. The Sisters would cut out the toes of the shoes or boots for children whose feet grew too quickly if a used pair in their size was unavailable. As I grew, I seemed to always have the toes cut out, leaving my feet dangling over the edge by the middle of the year. I hated my enormous feet. All the Sisters had tiny feet, but then, I stood a full head taller than most of them. These new boots fitted me perfectly and, although not fashionable, they were undoubtedly serviceable and quite comfortable.

I smoothed the blanket into place on the bed, then placed my bag on my small table before making my way to the dining hall, where I had eaten every day for most of my life. It was a vast space containing tables and bench seats, with no effort or thought to provide a comfortable or attractive environment for the children to enjoy their meals. It was clean and efficient, but far from homey, no different from the rest of the orphanage. The Sisters did their best with what they had, but there was no money ever left over for anything other than essentials. I crossed the room to collect my breakfast from the elderly cook, making my way over to an empty table where I could eat alone before sitting down to a barely warm bowl of porridge. The lumpy consistency and gluey taste often caused me to gag, but I would force it down, given my limited options. I was accustomed to terrible food, eating it without another thought while daydreaming. I mindlessly gazed up at the high ceiling and the intricate stonework on the walls and floors of the dining room. I wondered what the room would have looked like in all its glory — imagining flag-draped walls flanking an enormous table groaning with exotic foods eaten by cavaliers and fine ladies; while a string quartet played in the background, filling the room with beautiful music. I looked around at the other children in the room, some young while others were closer to my age. It would hurt my heart to say goodbye to them all today. Even though the younger ones sometimes annoyed me and those near my age had little in common with me, I still felt a sense of fond attachment, safety and belonging being amongst others in the same situation as me.

My one and only friend, Polly, had left the orphanage more than a year before me. We had been like sisters our entire lives, growing up side by side. They had placed us in the nursery together for our first three years with the other babies, and we had slept in the same cot. Polly was a year older than me, but because the Sisters could see the bond between us, and poor Polly was small for her age and sickly, they allowed her to remain with me until she was four. They could not see the golden glow that surrounded Polly, although I never spoke of auras to anyone as I matured, given the reactions I received when I was too young to understand the repercussions. Talking of it openly placed me at risk of being accused by zealous religious followers of being a witch, or even worse, the spawn of the devil. When the time came to move to the larger, colder dormitory where the older children slept, they placed our beds next to each other, and we became inseparable.

The Sisters would tease that if they saw one of us, the other would arrive shortly thereafter. I would help Polly with her writing and numbers, as she found it challenging to keep up with the other children during our lessons. At night, as we lay in our beds, I would teach her to count and go through her letters with her, then move on to spelling, explaining the meaning of all the unfamiliar words we had to learn; and some I had discovered myself through my love of reading.

As we grew, we would talk about the things I had read in books, trying to imagine the impossible things they spoke of. It seemed as probable as going to the moon for it to be true there were candleless lights, and hot water would come out through pipes into a bath just by turning a tap. Some of the wealthy had a privy inside their homes, flushing their sewage out, I assumed, to some unknown pit below. To Polly and me, to have anything like that was thought impossible unless you were of noble blood and born into great wealth. With no one in the outside world who cared what happened to us, we felt lucky to have a roof over our heads, no matter how often it leaked.

Long after we were meant to be sleeping, Polly and I would whisper to each other in the dark about the boys we would see at kirk — arguing over who had the loveliest smile, wondering who we would marry, and dreaming of how our lives would be perfect. We fantasised about eating whenever and whatever we liked and dreamed of smooth, sweet, hot porridge I had read about in books. We told each other everything and were often in trouble together, constantly summoned to Sister Mary Monica's office, where she reprimanded us and assigned extra chores. Depending on what evil we had committed, our punishment nearly always included the strap, or cuts as we called it; the skin on our palms lined with bleeding welts by the time she had finished. If a task took the two of us, we would spend the whole time talking and laughing, as Polly had a gift for impersonating the Sisters, Father McLean, and our gardener, Mr Potts. She was so gifted she spoke like a proper English woman, having copied my own unexplained accent since we were small. A year ago, the day came when they forced Polly to leave. Sister Mary Monica secured a position for her as a scullery maid in England, and Polly resigned herself to the fact it was the only option available to her. The Sisters advised her in no uncertain terms it was an excellent opportunity for her to make something of herself and dedicate her life to the service of others.

We had spent her last night talking, laughing, and crying. Huddled together in my bed, we reminisced about our childhood, knowing deep down we would never see each other again. We promised to write and find each other in the outside world, but we both knew that was unlikely to occur. When I was five, we swore an oath that when we grew up and left the orphanage behind us, we would live next door to each other and have babies at the same time, who would also grow up to be best friends. It was all we wanted in our hearts, although we knew real life never turned out as you hoped and dreamed, and we were clinging to a fantasy that would never be within our grasp.

Tears trickled down my face as I remembered how we had clung to each other at the bottom of the steps at the entrance to the orphanage, sobbing our hearts out just before she was so brutally ripped away from me. The Sisters stood on the stairs watching us, some with stony expressions, while others appeared slightly saddened they were forcing us to part.

Mr Potts had come into view, with Tipple pulling the old wooden cart behind her. The old man pulled gently on the reins as he drew up beside the grand entrance, once immaculate, the manor hosting kings and queens in its previous life, now looking sad and neglected. He glanced down, his weathered face softening for a moment, watching intently as we held each other tightly and sobbed before straightening up in his seat, mumbling to himself as he gazed out over the fields. He climbed down and picked up Polly's bag without a word and placed it in the back of the cart, then returned to the bench seat, impatiently waiting for her to join him so he could take her to the train station before returning to carry on with his chores.

Mr Potts was not one for human interaction, the only reason I believed he was still working at Emiliani House long after he should. He had been here for many long years before I was born and was the oldest person I had ever seen. Responsible for growing and tending to the vegetables and grain, he fixed anything broken and in need of repair, along with keeping the outside of the orphanage spick and span. He would go into town twice a week to collect necessities for the Sisters. Then, when the time came, he would transport us to the train station. He had never said more than two words to me the entire time I had lived at the orphanage. I often thought he enjoyed working alone and had become so used to it he had forgotten how to talk and interact with others.

As Polly and I clung together that day with neither wanting to let the other go, Sister Mary Josephine had hurried down the stairs and gently whispered, 'Polly has tae leave now. Let go o' each other, girls, afore the Sisters become impatient wi' ye.' Then, she had pried our arms apart and ordered Polly into the cart while holding onto me, so I would not follow.

Polly slowly pulled herself up and sat next to Mr Potts, her black hair gleaming as she placed her head in her hands for a moment, then turning to me, hiccupping and crying, called out she loved me and would somehow find me again in this lifetime. I would never forget the sound of her sobbing, her heartbroken wails often filling my ears while I slept. I was so overwhelmed with grief, knowing our friendship was lost to me forever, I couldn't speak or say anything back to her. As they passed through the enormous gates and disappeared, it physically hurt my heart. For the first time in my life, I knew what it was like to lose a person you truly loved.

Promising myself I would never again become close to anyone, I tried to push Sister Mary Josephine away. However, she would not let me, gently reassuring and allowing me to love and trust her again in my own time while I slowly recovered from my loss. Once Polly had left, I immersed myself in every book I could get hold of, terrified of what would become of me when my time came to leave. Now that time was here.

What a difference a day could make. While this time yesterday, I was frightened about what would happen to me. Now all I felt was anticipation and excitement, as I knew in my heart — I just knew — I would soon meet my parents.

I hurried towards Sister Mary Monica's office, which she had rudely told me to do this morning by sending a note to my table during breakfast, carried by a sweet five-year-old of whom I had become fond. The door was open as she stood up from her desk and beckoned me inside, appearing to be in a bad mood the moment she set eyes on me, sitting down heavily as I closed the door and waited for her to permit me to sit.

'I take it ye have naw seen sense an' changed yer mind?' Her tone was sharp as she glanced at me, waving her hand towards the old leather chair that sat in front of her desk before looking down at a pile of correspondence that required her attention. I tried to smile as I looked back at her suspiciously, shaking my head ever so slightly while she continued to ignore me.

I sat down before she reached across, her eyes glittering dangerously, and passed me the envelope with my ticket, the money, and the document that gave me my parents' names.

'Ye will catch the nine o'clock train. Ye leave in an hour.' She shook her head in disbelief before sighing deeply, narrowing her gaze before fixing me with a stare. 'Ye do favour Isabelle Delmont, an' I would nae be surprised if ye are spawned from her lineage. I lay awake most o' the night, an' the morn', thinkin' o' it, an' the more I think, the more sense I make o' that terrible night ye arrived here. A night I continue tae try an' ferget, but it haunts me, an' likely will till' I take me last breath. If, in fact, it is true ye have Isabelle's blood, it pleases me greatly, as ye have a family curse ye will carry fer the rest o' yer life 'cause o' that woman. What she did tae me great-grandfather will never be forgiven or forgotten by anybody who kent him, includin' their descendants, who all despise that sorceress tae this day. Her soul

27

naw burns in the fires o' hell, just as ye will.' I sat back in the chair, my eyes wide as she spun away and gazed out the pane glass window, clearing her throat. Who she was referring to, I had not a clue, but it sounded like a nasty family feud that, unsurprisingly, she still carried a grudge over. I would not have expected any less from her, given how hateful she was and had always been. Despite attempting to upset me, I knew I could be related to hundreds of people based on my looks and surname alone and had always been deaf to her opinions.

'I ken ye was an imp o' Lucifer himself an' would bring trouble tae our door that night I first saw ye in the nursery. An' I ken ye were the spawn of a pythoness. Me fears were confirmed as soon as ye started tae talk wi' an accent not from these parts. If it had been me that found ye that execrable night, I would have left ye out there fer the cold tae take ye, but Sister Mary Josephine got tae ye first an' has never left ye since. Ye bewitched her that night, ye did, an' the sooner ye leave here, the easier we will all rest.' After what felt like an eternity, she turned back to me, her face showing no emotion. 'An hour gives ye plenty o' time tae say yer goodbyes tae all here an' arrive at the station shortly afore the train is scheduled tae leave Edinburgh. The older children an' the Sisters will say goodbye at the entrance o' the orphanage. I hope ye are sure about what ye are doin' as I'm against this path ye have chosen, only fer the sake o' Sister Mary Josephine, but, as ye pointed out so stubbornly yesterday, it is ultimately yer own decision. I wish ye the best in yer endeavours, an' I hope ye have fond memories o' us wherever ye end up.' She showed no emotion and spoke in polite tones as though I was a lost stranger she had just met on the street who had asked for directions.

She handed me the little wooden box. I opened it and saw it now contained the tiny gown I had worn when abandoned on the doorstep all those years ago, along with a knitted blanket and bonnet made from the finest wool. An emerald necklace lay nestled among the fabric, while the fawn-coloured garment appeared well preserved.

Sister Mary Monica rose to her feet, then stretched out her arm expectantly, waiting for me to kiss her hand. I hesitated only slightly before standing and politely taking her cold, unattractive fingers in mine and reluctantly submitting for only a moment, pulling away and straightening up while preparing to leave. I would not miss her. The only attention she ever gave me was when barking orders relentlessly, multiple times a day, every day or punishing me harshly and cruelly without conscience over the slightest misdemeanour. Not once had she ever shown me even a drop of kindness, empathy or compassion; however, this was another last and one that brought me great joy mingled with relief. I felt an overwhelming sense of satisfaction as I crossed the room, ignoring her as she sat back down behind her desk and picked up a brown ledger. I stepped out into the hallway, leaving her office for the last time with the small box under my arm and my head held high. I quietly closed the door behind me and did not look back.

I slowly made my way down the long hallway towards the nursery, or the weans' room, as we all called it. I had spent my first three years in that room, kept in a cot alongside the other infants day and night, unless in need of bathing or a clout change, or when the Sisters would take the children outside for an hour on the rare occasion when the sun was shining. When it came time for feeding, the Sisters would move from cot to cot, carrying a large ceramic jug with a tiny funnel, pouring warm milk into the babies' mouths. Then, once you were a little older and strong enough to stand, you would pull yourself up and hold the railing while the Sisters went from cot to cot, spoon-feeding the children from large bowls. More often than not, they filled them with porridge for breakfast and vegetable stew for lunch and — if you were lucky — some unappealing concoction with meat for dinner.

I had been fortunate, though. Sister Mary Josephine was one of the Sisters assigned to the weans' room, and she had taken it upon herself to care for me, often found holding me in the crook of her arm as she went about her duties. She had a special fondness for me; she believed because she was the one who had found me abandoned at the door of the orphanage. When the time came for me to move to the larger dormitory, Sister Mary Josephine requested a transfer, and permission reluctantly granted, enabling her to continue to care for me.

By the time I turned ten, I was in the weans' room each day, picking up the children, playing with them, and watching them grow while helping the Sisters care for them. The Sisters made it a priority, especially in winter, to keep the nursery warm, much warmer than the rest of the old manor. I would teach the older weans words and numbers and tell them stories of distant places I had only read about. The Sisters were glad of my visits and told me often how grateful they were for the help. It gave them time to do other essential chores while I kept those sweet, innocent souls entertained and happy.

The bairns annoyed me at times, but I tried to hold my temper and remember what it was like to be their age. They would come to my bed during the night seeking comfort when they were having nightmares or had soiled themselves. I always relented and allowed them to sleep with me in my own tiny bed. Although I found it inconvenient and sometimes irksome over the years, it was also something I would dearly miss now — that close contact with other human beings and the comfort of being surrounded by those in the same situation as myself. I reached the end of the hall and knocked on the thick, imposing door of the weans' room.

'Come in,' Sister Mary Marion called out cheerfully, then enthusiastically took me by the arm and began addressing me in her typically frenetic fashion. 'There was braw banter in the Sisters' quarters last night wi' the mystery o' the London solicitor. Do ye have any idea what any o' it means? O' course, ye dinnae. How could ye ken? But 'tis all very titillatin', isnae? Aye, it certainly is, but ye will find out soon enough, that's fer sure. We all wish ye weel, me bonny lass. We all wish ye weel.'

She was tall compared to the other Sisters and possessed a plain face, her speech nonstop and rapid. She was never at a loss for words, and I found it hard to imagine how she could be silent for four hours a day while in deep prayer and contemplation. Poor Sister Mary Marion possessed ill-fated eyes — one turned outwards, so you never knew which eye was looking at you or which one to look at when speaking to her, always making me uneasy I may stare into the wrong one. Even before the day they found me on the steps, she had worked in the weans' room, and I remembered how kind she had always been to me.

She led me over to the four newborns who had arrived all within a week of one another. The room was large and warm, with high ceilings and rows and rows of old rickety cots that held one blanket for sometimes two children. At least with the newborns, the Sisters had placed knitted caps on their tiny heads and made their gowns from thick muslin, making it less of an issue the threadbare blankets barely added to their warmth.

I picked up a wee girl with curly, black hair and held her in the crook of my arm. She slept peacefully as I kissed her tiny cheek, turning to place her back in the crib gently. None of the newborns had names, given their parents had abandoned them at the doorsteps of the orphanage without care or identification. The Sisters would not name them until their baptism next Sunday, only I wouldn't be here to witness it. I touched each of the infants, silently saying goodbye, then went to the rows of cots to say my farewells to the older babies.

It saddened me that the Sisters of Emiliani House struggled to live on the donations they received from the religious community, the village shops, and the local farmers — all impoverished themselves — the pittance given barely supplementing what they grew and made themselves to feed and clothe the children. I had heard rumours since I could first remember things had not always been so grim. They once had a wealthy benefactor who supported them well and ensured they had all they needed, often providing additional luxury items they could not afford. I had heard the stories of long ago when they served meat every night and had access to an abundance of food and cloth, a time when every room in the mansion was in use and filled with happy, thriving children. Now that was no longer the case. They did their best, but sometimes it was just not enough when you were a child shivering at night because the only blanket available to you was so thin it barely provided any warmth. You learnt as you got older to put on your nightgown first, then a dress, followed by the thick socks knitted by the Sisters. I knew sleeping cold was another last. The first thing I was going to buy was a warm blanket to ensure I was cosy and warm every night for the rest of my life, no matter what other necessities I would consequently sacrifice.

I stepped into the dormitory, a room filled with so many memories and a refuge where I had slept for most of my life. An invisible weight lifted from my shoulders as I glanced across at the bed that no longer belonged to me, taking several steps closer to check the drawers of the small side table before opening my calico bag. It contained a nightdress, my new brown dress, a change of bloomers, and two pairs of socks. I had packed a solid silver hairbrush and matching hand mirror, a gift from Sister Mary Josephine, who told me it had belonged to her grandmother. I placed her photograph inside the small wooden box with the tiny clothes and precious stone, then slipped it inside the bag, causing it to bulge and strain the stitching. The cook, Mrs Murphy, had packed me a bag of parritch and several bannocks filled with cheese and pickles to take on my journey, along with a jar of barley water, all of which I also tucked away in the now full bag. I was grateful, but Mrs Murphy had to be the worst cook in the world, and the Sisters knew it, given they too were forced to suffer in silence along with the children. They kept her on out of loyalty, as she had been there forever and was now older than the dinosaurs I had read about, and far more and cantankerous. We learnt not to complain about the cold, greasy, tasteless food. I slipped on my bonnet and tied the strap securely under my chin, then picked up the bag, walked with purpose to the door, and paused, turning back to take one last look at the room that had been the only sleeping place I had known. With one last glance, I strode out into the hallway, promising myself I would never look back.

They stood together in the front garden, from the very young to the aging Sisters, all patiently waiting to say goodbye. I hugged several of the children, kissed the hands of many of the Sisters and then went to look for Sister Mary Josephine. I found her standing alongside the castle wall, away from the others, trying to catch her breath from the sobs racking her lovely frame. As I approached, she appeared highly distressed, and I felt a sudden pain tear at my heart. It was the most distraught I had ever seen her. I reached across and placed my hand on her shoulder, embracing her as I whispered in her ear.

'Sister, I'm leaving now.' She stared into my eyes, anguish clear in her own.

'I cannae let ye go, mo luaidh. I feel like me heart is bein' ripped out ever so slowly.' Tears streamed down her face, her body shaking as she sobbed, unable to be comforted. 'I ken I cannae keep ye, but I want tae, even though I ken 'tis wrong. I want ye tae have the best life possible, but if anythin' bad should ever happen or ye need help,

I beg ye tae come back, an' I will find a way tae look after ye. I will ensure ye are safe, naw matter what I have tae do, even if it means contactin' me family after all these years an' beggin' for their help.' I broke down as I hugged her tightly.

'I love you, Sister, and I promise all will be well. I will write to you as soon as I can, and I'll miss you every day we are parted, and someday I will find my way back to you.' She embraced me forcefully before we dried our tears, linking her arm through mine as she led me back to the front of the manor to wait for Mr Potts and his cart. As he approached, she held my hand tighter, and with fresh tears in her eyes, kissed me on the cheek for what would likely be the last time. Mr Potts placed my bag on the cart as I squeezed her hand just as tightly, the finality of it all hitting me hard. 'Thank you... thank you for every single thing, and all the love you lavished on me without asking for anything in return. I love you to the moon and back a thousandfold,' I whispered, kissing her one last time before I stepped up and sat next to Mr Potts on the uncomfortable bench seat of the old wooden carriage that had seen better days.

As we slowly pulled away, I looked back and saw them waving to me. Sister Mary Josephine stood at the front, sobbing while flapping her arm in the air in farewell. I waved back with tears trickling down my face. I would never forget this place, my home, for fifteen long years. It had provided me with shelter, food and love, and now the only security I had ever known would soon disappear forever. I knew not a soul in the world, a world that loomed around me like a formidable giant.

I had not a clue what would ultimately befall me beyond the walls of the orphanage, but I knew I now had something to hold on to, a glimmer of hope of being reunited with my parents, which was more than I had yesterday. What this solicitor, Mr Henry Malcolm, wanted from someone like me had me flabbergasted, but whatever it was must be of some importance to summon me all the way to London.

I knew I could drive myself mad by dwelling on all the possibilities, sighing deeply as I pushed my unwanted thoughts to the back of my mind.

I gazed across the peat fields for the last time as Mr Potts guided Tipple slowly toward the train station, the soft ground making it difficult for the poor horse as he snorted, sweat lathering around his neck and shoulders as he continued to strain. The road soon became firmer, much to my relief. He slowly made his way towards Edinburgh on the winding dirt track, picking up his pace. Turning my face up towards the dark and threatening sky, I promised myself I would not lose hope, no matter what lay ahead of me. I raised my chin further and closed my eyes, the icy breeze cutting into my skin like razor blades. Pulling my shawl a little tighter around my shoulders, I let out a deep sigh, leaving behind all I had ever known.

Chapter Three

M R TIPPLE STOOD QUIETLY beside the station house at the rear of the elaborate building, lathered in sweat. Mr Potts jumped down from the rickety carriage, then extended his hand up towards me. As I passed my bag to him, my dress caught on the seat, and the hem tore. 'Typical,' I muttered. Mr Potts' mouth twitched as he handed back my one possession in the world the moment my feet hit the ground.

'Weel then, lass. Guid luck tae ye,' he said gruffly, avoiding eye contact before tipping his woollen cap politely then climbing back up on the cart. It surprised me he had spoken at all.

'Thank you, Mr Potts, and good luck to you, too,' I replied, smiling up at him. I lifted my bag and headed toward the platform where the train waited, following behind several people headed in the same direction, not one of them noticing when I quickly undid the strap of my bonnet and threw it on the ground without hesitation, not glancing back even once as I continued on. I held the ticket in my hand, and as I rounded the corner of the ornately decorated building, I caught sight of the passenger train with its enormous steam engine. It was overwhelming to see one up close, let alone the thought of riding inside all the way to London Town. The black body of the train with red trimming gleamed as the whistle's shriek caused me to jump in fright while nearly rupturing my eardrums, prompting me to pick up my pace as I moved forward. A pleasant-looking man dressed in a conductor's uniform stood beside the train, glancing down briefly as he held open the door to the second last carriage.

I entered, quickly sitting down next to a substantial woman who took up half my seat, holding a large basket on her lap. The seats arranged in rows of wooden benches, all facing the same way toward the front of the train, were hard and uncomfortable. My companion was sweating profusely under the weight of her thick winter coat and, eyeing me suspiciously, gripped her bag even tighter, perhaps expecting at any moment I would run off with it. The carriage reeked of chicken faeces, sweat, and various stenches I could not identify. I attempted to hold my breath as I eyed the passengers who carried their livestock with them. Judging by the mingling odours that continued to violate my senses, I concluded many of them had not washed in a very long time.

Although we bathed only once a week at the orphanage, they expected us to wash daily. I was grateful to the Sisters for caring and taking the time each day to make sure we presented ourselves at our best. They would always say we may have been poor, but there was no excuse not to keep our bodies and clothes clean and smelling nice, just like the Lord intended. We didn't have perfumed soap, but a coarse substance the Sisters made themselves, lard being the primary ingredient. From today forward, I would no longer refer to any of the Sisters formally by using their generic name of Mary, as they had forced us to do. I could now call my beloved nun just Sister Josephine and would do the same for all of them, suddenly feeling empowered by the mere thought.

The conductor approached me, his face thoughtful. 'May I see yer ticket please, lass?' I handed it to him, surprise crossing his face as I felt my stomach drop. 'I'm sorry, but ye are in the wrong carriage.

If ye care tae come with me, I will take ye tae the right one,' he informed me cheerfully. I managed with some difficulty to squeeze past my large companion, who grunted at me for the inconvenience. I picked up my bag, the conductor politely taking it from me with a warm smile, before I followed him up the aisle through the next three carriages. The last carriage contained spacious compartments with large padded bench seats facing each other, roomy enough to accommodate six adults in comfort.

He escorted me inside, where I found a young man and woman about my age sitting on one side, and on the other, a pretty child with ringlets tied with pink ribbons, whom I quickly sat beside. They all possessed the most beautiful blonde hair, their fine clothes immaculate, and were lovely to behold. The young woman emitted a soft, golden glow around her body. It had shocked me initially, as I had seen that glow before, but I had assumed it was only because of the deep love I held for Sister and Polly. The first time I had observed such a glow was around Sister Josephine when she held me as a baby. It was a faint glow surrounding her body, which became stronger as I grew older. I once told her about it, and she said it was never to be spoken of again and was of the devil himself. Polly's glow did not differ from the one I saw around Sister Josephine. I did not know what it signified, but looking back, they were the two people who meant the most to me. Although Sister Monica had an aura, it was not golden. It was a dark, dirty grey that swirled around her when she was angry with me. It confused me and I could only assume a grey aura was sinister based on how it made me feel; the opposite feeling of joy settling on me when in the presence of the golden glow surrounding the two people I cherished most, the thought of Polly making my heart hurt.

For the first six months after Polly had gone, I remembered how I hoped for a letter from her as she had promised, but nothing ever came. I cried myself to sleep many a night, praying Polly was happy and safe, and she had warm blankets and a comfortable place to live and sleep.

I wondered what role this young woman with the golden glow would play in my life, as we were only going to spend today together. I shifted on the plush seat and made myself comfortable, turning to gaze out the window as the train started to move, soon watching the buildings slowly disappear and the countryside come into view. As time passed, the silence in the compartment became too uncomfortable to bear.

'Hello. My name is Abigail. Abigail... um... Delmont.' I addressed the young man while assuming his companions were his sisters. The young woman, who could have been a little older than me, looked shy. She sat motionless, her head lowered, her straight blonde hair falling down the sides of her face, while avoiding eye contact with everyone present. Their younger sister was around ten and returned my greeting, her sweet smile easing my nerves ever so slightly. The young man glared across at me and scowled, causing my stomach to drop while making me feel awkward and defensive all at once.

'What makes a person like you think you can travel with people like us? It is as obvious as the grimy nose on your face that you have never travelled first class before. You do not even have a hat or bonnet to cover your hair.' Widening his eyes even further, he screwed up his face in disdain.

'I have never travelled on a train in my whole life, let alone first class.' My voice was surprisingly calm and steady, although my face became warm while anger and humiliation rose inside me. 'Nor have I come across anyone as rude or as arrogant as you, Sir. Where I come from, we don't judge people based on their appearance or the clothes they wear, but by their character, and the kindnesses they show through their words and actions.'

This was all I needed on my first day in the real world. It was just my poor luck that the first person I was forced to become acquainted with was a snobbish boy who appeared intent on making me feel bad about myself. I felt frightened and intimidated by the changes that were occurring through no fault of my own, and I found it overwhelming. I was suddenly responsible for myself when I still felt like a child.

The young man gazed across at me, his long nose still wrinkled in disdain. 'Do not even try pretending to be like your betters. It's offensive,' he barked, eyeing the ragged tear in my dress before glaring back at me. 'You're well spoken, I'll give you that, and English I see; however, you look like you come from a workhouse. Look at your hands, and your dress is torn. Surely you know how to mend? You look as if you have lived as a scullery maid since the age of five.'

My temper continued to rise, but embarrassed, I hid my work-worn hands from view. I knew I should keep quiet, but this privileged young man did not know my history. Although sheltered, I had seen and heard people talk roughly outside the taverns in the village many a time, and quite enjoyed it. He continued to glare at me, the anger I felt finally exploding into pure rage.

'You are no gentleman — and are certainly not my better — in character or manner. Trying to make me feel bad about myself just because my clothes are not as fine as yours reflects on you rather than me. I suggest you bend over backwards and slip that ignorant head of yours up that refined arse you so proudly sit on — no doubt rarely getting off it to do anything for anyone other than yourself — you may well locate a brain somewhere in there if you look hard enough, but I doubt that very much, you condescending funt.' He jerked back as if I had slapped him, glaring across at me, hatred filling his eyes. He remained silent, his mouth opening and closing several times — the fact he appeared speechless only brightening my mood. I turned and stared out the window, making myself comfortable as I prepared for the long journey ahead in silence.

Silence hung over the compartment, the train rocking comfortably as it glided along the tracks at great speed until the young woman lifted her head and looked directly into my eyes. She smiled at me; her smile becoming wider before she giggled, a faint sound that turned into a musical laugh.

'That was an obvious message to be nice, William,' she remarked to the young man before turning to me, her smile still radiant. 'I don't think I've ever heard anyone talk to Mr. Self-Importance here like that before. My name is Catherine, and this mean fellow is my brother, William. And here is our younger sister, Beatrice.' She was beaming, her golden-blonde hair falling just below her shoulders, her beautiful, pale-blue eyes reflecting her mirth. Finely built and pretty, she had the loveliest smile. 'We are travelling to London to catch a ship and migrate to Australia to be with our parents. Where are you going?'

I explained I was meeting my parents in London and how we planned to settle there. My explanation seemed to appease them, and they relaxed with me, despite William giving me the odd look of disgust from time to time. Of course, I knew it was a white lie, but it could still be possible this solicitor business was about meeting my parents and, until I knew for certain, that was what I chose to believe. I pulled my bag onto my lap and dug around inside before I triumphantly produced the cheese-and-pickle bannock. The only thing I would miss about the orphanage food would be the fresh bread filled with cheese the sisters crafted themselves, pickles they would simmer for days into a sauce, all wrapped up in the fresh flatbread. I offered half to William, who turned his head away from me dismissively and stared out the window. Catherine, however, took the half with great pleasure and broke some off for Beatrice, who thanked me.

As the three of us enjoyed our morning tea, Catherine told me about herself and her family. They lived in Scotland at their grandparents' estate for the past year, as their parents had sailed to Australia to start up a fashion business in Melbourne. Their father had become wealthy by pursuing his passion and becoming a tailor, who discovered he enjoyed creating dresses for beautiful women, given he had more opportunities to use his creative flair than make boring menswear. He imported the most glorious materials from all over the world to make into exclusive and very fashionable gowns. He had owned a store in High Street, London, named Montague's, to which women would come from far and wide to purchase his stunning creations. Mr Montague was what they called in Paris, a designer; he prided himself on producing exquisite gowns just as good, if not better than those found in France, and one-off creations for those in society who could afford his prices.

He wanted to give his children a better lifestyle away from the hustle and bustle of London, Catherine had told me proudly. A friend advised him there were no businesses like his in Australia, where there were many wealthy women who would pay any price to have the latest fashions at their fingertips rather than send to Paris for them — a costly, months-long experience. Their father had purchased land near Melbourne and was building a grand house; however, their parents were living over his large shop at present. In his letters, he informed them, although not extravagant; the quarters were spacious enough for their entire family until they completed their new home.

While she talked, Catherine noticed her brother had fallen asleep. She shared how William was reluctant to immigrate since he viewed Australia as a place filled with convict spawn and second-class citizens. This, she whispered secretively, had contributed to his bad temper and rudeness, for which she apologised repeatedly. She believed, but had no proof, William secretly had a sweetheart, and this was the real reason he did not want to leave. Catherine and Beatrice were noncommittal about the move, leaning toward muted excitement. They had heard stories of the great ocean and the sunshine, beautiful mountains, and the friendliness of Australians.

'That should take William down a peg or two, going from a castle to an apartment above a shop.' Catherine giggled wickedly as she brushed a loose strand of hair from her eyes. 'Don't take it personally what he said before. I think you look lovely and you are beautiful. I have never seen eyes of such a deep green before or hair of that colour. It's as if you have ten different shades of red and copper in your hair, and it's so thick and long. I would give anything to be blessed with curls like yours.'

I felt ashamed for what I had said to her brother in anger, but thanked her and advised her I was in no way damaged by William's words. Catherine moved closer and settled herself beside me so we could talk, while Beatrice moved across to sit by William. She confided they had been raised by nannies, as their father and mother were far too busy with their business and social calendar to spend much time with their children. Living on an estate just outside London their entire lives with a house full of servants that included maids, nannies, tutors, a gardener, and Rover, their beloved red setter they were forced to leave behind, they had been provided with private tutors and were taught the correct way to behave in high society. Catherine expressed embarrassment over the fact William so obviously relished his privileged life, and the status and wealth of their parents, and believed he was better than others. As she described her life, it surprised me that her childhood resembled my own, the only difference being she had warm blankets, food, and a surname.

I could hear rattling coming closer, a loud knock sounding before the door was flung open. I turned towards the door to see a server standing next to a trolley laden with food and drink, the sudden interruption rousing William from his sleep.

'Guid afternoon, an' a bonny one 'tis at that. I hope yer all peckish as here's yer lunch. Would ye also like puddin'?' She smiled as she waited patiently. We nodded and thanked her as she served us beef stew with mashed potatoes and Cranachan for dessert. The meat melted in my mouth, and the creamy potato had so much butter in it, I felt like I was in heaven. At the orphanage, we were rarely given butter, as they served it to the Sisters first, and if any remained by the next morning, only then was it given to the children, which was rare. I loved butter and would eat it on anything and everything when I had the chance. There was something about its creamy texture, subtle saltiness, and lovely creamy flavour that set my taste buds dancing.

We had finished our lunch and were about to start our dessert when the woman returned, just as suddenly as when she first appeared. 'What kin I get ye tae drink, ma wee bairns?' She rattled off our options one by one, smiling fondly at us. As soon as I heard her mention coffee, I knew I must try it. I had read so much about it — how it grew in far-off lands, was harvested, dried, and then transported all over the world. I placed my order and turned back to the window. The countryside was flying past, and I could see blurry cows and trees, and it appeared an icy wind was blowing. I was so grateful to be warm and cosy in this compartment, enjoying Catherine's company.

As I sipped the glorious beverage called coffee, Catherine and I talked all afternoon while Beatrice and William slept. It was the first time I felt drawn to another person my age since Polly had left the orphanage. Catherine still had that soft, golden glow around her, and I wondered if I was right — that people I saw with this glow became close to me. I hoped so, as I liked Catherine. The golden aura that surrounded her was a mystery to me, yet one I wanted to explore.

I could tell she was a kind girl, with a childhood not unlike my own, and although talkative, she appeared nervous and did not seem to have a great deal of confidence. Although appearing relaxed with me, she would often drop her gaze and not hold eye contact for long. I wondered at what stage of her life she had come to believe she was less of a person than others, and I found her situation saddening, as she truly was one of the nicest people I had met.

I soon felt the need for a nap, and as I drifted off to sleep wrapped in a thick blanket the lovely lunch lady had provided, I thought about how blessed I was. Despite my upbringing, I had blossomed into an outspoken, confident person. I had Sister Josephine to thank for that, for she was always telling me I was special, that I would continue to be unique even when I grew up, and I was worthy of love. Most of the Sisters had kind hearts; however, there were those who took great pleasure in mistreating the children they were obligated to love and protect. I shoved the awful memories to the back of my mind, as I always did when I didn't want to think about something.

As sleep came, the last thing I remembered was a feeling of being encased in warm, soft leaves and laying in the sunshine in a far-off land, gazing at a sky so blue you only ever saw it in dreams.

Chapter Four

I AWOKE TO THE sounds of Catherine and William arguing, the train swaying to the left as we travelled around a bend in the track, the farms passing in a blur.

'You have been positively awful to her, and she is the sweetest girl I have ever met. Try to be nice, William. I know you can be. I don't want her to think we were poorly raised.' Catherine was clearly upset with him, my mouth twitching in amusement as I remained as still as possible.

'Why should you care what she thinks? She is a peasant, an insignificant nobody who has the foulest mouth I've ever witnessed, and you should be ashamed for even attempting to defend the likes of her and her kind. Our parents would be mortified if they knew you were in the presence of someone as rough and ill-bred as her. Why should I waste my time trying to be nice, as you say? We will never see her again, anyway.'

'Whether you approve or not, I plan to write to her and remain friends.' I could hear the tremor in her voice, her pitch several octaves higher than earlier. I smiled to myself, touched that she was standing up for me despite being unmistakably intimidated. It was obvious she rarely spoke up to him, or anyone else, for that matter. I felt a sense of peace settle on me, realising I had met my first real friend in this new world, and it was a pleasant feeling. I yawned to alert them I was awake, slowly opening my eyes and stretching before straightening up in my seat and smiling politely across at William.

'Hello. How long do you think we have left until we arrive in London?'

'Maybe an hour, possibly two,' William remarked politely, turning to look at the passing countryside, the sky dark and threatening.

'Thank you. Where are you staying tonight, if I may ask?'

'They will accommodate us at *The Savoy Hotel* for the next week,' Catherine replied as she moved a strand of hair from her eyes, settling herself back next to me.

'Then we take a ship to Australia if the seas are calm enough. My brother seems to think we will sail in a week, but we have another six weeks of winter, and I'm reluctant to travel by sea if it's rough and stormy as I might get horribly seasick.'

Poor Catherine could not afford to lose much weight, as she was fine-boned and dainty, her chest flat as a board. I had read The Savoy was the first luxury hotel in London with electric lights and hot-and-cold running water. I would have to pay a visit to Catherine if only to see the electric lights with my own eyes.

'Where are you staying?' Catherine pulled me out of my daydream, my mind having wandered to thoughts of my parents.

'Hm, that's where it gets a little complicated. I'm not quite sure. All I know is my parents' solicitor, Mr Henry Malcolm, has dispatched a coach for me that will wait at the station to take me to my lodgings tonight. Then I meet with him in the morning to discuss my plans.'

'Oh, that sounds vaguely mysterious.' Her face broke out into a warm smile as she reached across and took my hand in hers.

'I am confident your lodgings will be satisfactory enough for you, even if they are in a dingy tavern on the docks,' William muttered.

I wondered what I had done for this boy to hate me so intensely. I could almost feel it vibrating from his body. Nevertheless, I believed I was a kind and decent person, and I had been friendly to him beyond what he deserved. I did not bother to respond. I had decided at this point, William was the rudest person I had ever met, or he was just an arrogant youth who no one had ever taken the time to teach how to behave appropriately.

'Would you like to come and visit me at The Savoy and dine with us, maybe the day after tomorrow? We would love to see you and hear about your plans once you see your parents and know more.' Catherine's face was positively flushed, and she looked embarrassed at her own invitation.

'Of course, I would love to come — if it meets with William's approval?'

William looked down at his hands, remaining silent for some time before raising his head and glancing across at me, an insincere smile crossing his face, clearly for my benefit alone.

'It would be our pleasure to entertain you.' His body was tense, and he immediately looked away as I rolled my eyes.

'All right, then. It's agreed,' Catherine said, her lovely face lighting up in a beautiful smile.

As we pulled up at the majestic station in London, I was again overwhelmed. It was beautiful. I could see four steam engines had just arrived to either unload their weary passengers or load those eager to start their journey. It appeared to be backbreaking work, loading cargo to transport to the outer towns of England and Scotland, while other railway workers were unloading produce and items sent to London to sell.

I strolled alongside Catherine, William a short distance ahead of us holding Beatrice's hand while dragging a trolley with their trunks loaded high behind him. He stopped to beckon a railway employee to assist him, then haughtily instructed him to take the trolley to the station's front entrance. We made our way along the platform, then into the extravagant foyer, carefully descending the stairs before stepping out into the street in front of the grand building. The carriage for The Savoy stood waiting for them at the front of the line. Catherine turned to me as William waited for their trunks to arrive, while Beatrice excitedly climbed up the steps and into the carriage.

'Our surname is Montague. I feel like I have found a new best friend, and I want to make sure we see each other again. Please, please say you will come.' She gazed intently, her eyes pleading as a thousand thoughts ran through my mind.

'Catherine, I give you my word I will be there by five o'clock,' I promised, hoping I would not regret my decision. Catherine embraced me as the driver loaded their trunks onto the carriage, William calling out impatiently for her to hurry.

'I must go, but I will see you on Wednesday — and thank you for being so lovely to me.'

She ran to the carriage where William was irritably waiting while gazing across at me, an odd look on his face. Although tall and handsome, he was undoubtedly a strange boy. I had observed him with Beatrice and could see he was caring toward her, yet he could be so nasty in the next instant. As they pulled away, Catherine slipped her arm through the carriage window and waved, while I raised my hand and waved back with a smile on my face. Although my body shivered, I was warm inside and intensely happy.

I ambled back to the entrance of the station with my little calico bag. It was so cold. I only had my dress and the shawl around me for warmth. I scanned the row of carriages, finding one with *Henry Malcolm Esquire & Sons* painted on the door and underneath in gold lettering, *Solicitors and Barristers*. I approached the carriage just as the driver was getting down.

'Mistress Abigail Delmont, is it?'

'Yes, sir..'

'Here, love, give me your bag, and I'll help you in, then I can get you to your lodgings for the night.' He assisted me up into the carriage before quietly closing the door behind me.

The carriage, lined in red velvet with shiny wood panels, the seats so soft they engulfed your entire body, was like nothing I had ever seen. The carriage suddenly jolted as the horses moved forward, taking us over cobblestone streets and down alleys, the clip-clop of their hooves filling my ears. I gazed out the window, feeling so overwhelmed by all the unfamiliar sights, smells, and sounds, and for a moment, I wanted to run back into Sister Josephine's arms. I felt frightened, having never been alone before and without someone watching over me. I had never seen so many buildings and lights, but I still had no clue where I was or my destination. At least they had collected me from the train station, but I still did not know where I would stay or with whom, leaving me sick to my stomach.

I felt the horses slow, but I could see nothing in the dark. Finally, after a few minutes, we turned into the wide driveway of a towering building. The driver pulled the horses up, and I felt him dismount as I sat frozen in my seat, wondering where I was. At that moment, the only thing I was certain of was this was the largest building I had ever seen. The driver appeared out of nowhere and opened the door before helping me down from the carriage with my bag. I inhaled sharply as I looked up at the spectacular structure, the black sky fading insignificantly into the background, while light sparkled from every window.

The orphanage had been three stories high, but this looked more like ten, possibly more. The driver finished tethering the horses and sauntered back over to me. He seemed to be a friendly man of middle

51

age, with greying hair. He was polite and had a lovely face when he smiled.

'Mr Malcolm warned me you might get confused by it all. Me name is Miller, an' I drive for him. I'll collect you in the mornin' at nine o'clock to meet him at his office. All you need to do, Mistress Abigail, is walk through them large doors at the front, go to the man at the desk, an' tell him your name. He'll explain everything else. I'll see you in the mornin'. Good evenin' to you.'

After thanking him and bidding him farewell, I crept up to the entrance. As I climbed the stairs, I could see electric lights burning that reminded me of twinkling stars, then noticed a man in a uniform and top hat at the entrance as I drew nearer.

'May I help you with your bag, Miss?' I looked up at him in surprise and clutched my meagre possessions protectively to my chest.

'Thank you, but no. I am quite able,' I answered politely. The man held the door open for me, and I reluctantly entered, looking around for someone to help me. There were several men, along with a woman, all standing behind a long counter that circled half the room; while the ceiling was so high, I had to crane my neck to see it. An enormous chandelier hung in the centre of the elaborate reception, the room brightly lit, so brightly, in fact, it hurt my eyes. I had never seen an electric light, and I was unsure how to feel about it. I stared open-mouthed at everything around me, feeling awkward and knowing I did not belong here. It was so much to absorb. There were things I had never seen before and did not know what they were, along with others I had appreciated only in books. The room looked magical, and my eyesight suddenly blurred, trying to take in everything at once as I slowly approached the enormous desk.

'Can I be of service, Miss?' asked an elderly man with greying, curly hair from behind the counter. I pulled myself together and smiled as confidently as I could.

'Hello, yes. My name is Abigail... err... Delmont.'

'Yes, Miss Delmont. We have been waiting for your arrival. My name is Mr Grant, and I am here to help you. We have reserved the master suite for you. If you would please come with me, I will accompany you to your room.' He bowed low, then walked away without a backward glance.

I followed Mr Grant to the end of the room, where there were several identical doors. Well, they looked like doors, only they were wider and had metal grates in front of them. Mr Grant slid open one grate, opened another door, and entered the tiny room behind it. I stayed where I was, staring at him curiously with my hand on my hip while making no effort to move.

'Have you been in an elevator before, Miss?' he asked as I stood frozen.

'No, I haven't. I have never seen the Otis elevator in real life.' I felt the blood rise to my face as he looked back at me with a mixture of surprise and sympathy while I remained where I was, refusing to move.

'You're a brilliant girl. Just brilliant. I would have to say you read a lot of books to know that. It's all right, Miss Delmont. I promise you it is very safe, and we have not experienced a moment's problem with them since the hotel opened,' he reassured me as I nodded thoughtfully.

'Well, how long has the hotel been open?' He gave me a kindly smile before winking mischievously.

'Six months.' I grimaced and remained where I was.

'That means there is still plenty of time for people to fall screaming in terror to their deaths,' I told him as he chuckled to himself.

'We can take the stairs, but your room is ten floors up.' He waited patiently for my decision as I considered my options. I already knew there was no way I was climbing all those flights of stairs when I was cold, tired, and hungry. I finally admitted defeat and stepped into the box-like structure. Mr Grant smiled to himself before closing the grate, then the door, reaching over to press a button. I felt myself being pulled upwards, and my legs shook, forcing myself to stand up straight while holding onto a brass rail that lined the walls of the little room. My stomach dropped as we lurched up into the air. It terrified me that the cables holding the car would snap as it drew me upwards at an alarming rate, feeling this would never end. Finally, there was a heave as the contraption came to a stop, and Mr Grant opened the doors. I quickly exited and gratefully stood on solid ground again. I felt a little dizzy and reached out and placed my hand on the hallway wall to balance myself while waiting to be shown to my suite.

After several moments and a few deep breaths, I regained my composure and followed Mr Grant, who had been observing me patiently with a sympathetic look on his face. As we proceeded down the hall, I wondered why he had said the hotel had been expecting me or if they said that to all their guests. I felt ignorant. I could not understand even fundamental interactions between people or the new objects surrounding me. I did not know the first thing about what the world expected of a young lady, and I had no idea how I should behave.

We arrived at the suite, Mr Grant politely opening the door, swinging it wide as I thanked him. I stepped inside and gasped in surprise, unable to believe my eyes — to the right of the elaborate entrance, the bedchambers contained an enormous bed, the largest I had ever seen, covered in the thickest and loveliest quilts and blankets in a rich tapestry of colours. The pillows were large and soft, and there appeared to be dozens of them piled up neatly against the velvet bedhead; the matching curtains surrounded the bed hanging from the canopy above. I stepped back into the hallway and continued on to a large sitting room that contained several lounges covered in the softest fabric I had ever felt; the autumn tones of sage-green, cream and touches of burnt orange and tan I found indescribably beautiful, with a charming, low table sitting in the middle. Two wing-backed chairs sat near the fireplace with a small side-table next to each; the soft, brown leather, although a different colour, complimented the lounges perfectly. The rugs on the floor made me want to take off my shoes and walk on them barefoot to feel the luxurious fibres massaging my feet. To the right, in the far corner, was a small kitchen table overlooking the window; I assumed where they expected me to take my meals, the thought of food reminding my stomach it was empty. Mr Grant entered the suite, placed my bag in the wardrobe, and then joined me in the sitting room, smiling warmly.

'Through that door is the washroom and privy, as we call them at home. There is a bath that has water piped straight into it, along with a basin and a thing called a flushable toilet. Apparently, they call it a bathroom these days.' He chuckled, pointing to a closed door close to the entrance to the suite. I felt excitement well up inside me at the thought I would have my very own private washroom — at least for tonight, anyway. I had only seen them described in books. When we needed to relieve ourselves at the orphanage, we had two options; the chamber pot or a long walk outside into the often freezing cold of the night to use the smelly outhouse. I always knew I would eventually get to clean a real bathroom if I went into service; however, I never dreamed of ever getting to use one.

'I feel like I've died and gone to heaven, Mr Grant. I can't even put into words how I'm feeling.' I smiled, eyeing the doorway to the magnificent room I was going to be sleeping in, before glancing longingly at the closed door, which I now knew led to the washroom. A real bathroom, just like I had read of in novels set in grand homes, castles and palaces. My bathroom.

'You are a refreshing girl,' he remarked, chuckling again. 'Most of the people who stay here act as if they have seen places like this every day of their lives, and I know they haven't, as this is one of the finest luxury hotels in the world. Only finished last year, and it has everything. All the luxuries. Hot water that comes out of a tap straight into the basins to wash the dishes and bathe. I never thought I would see the day. Here — may I show you how to use the bath?'

I nodded and followed him into the bathroom, gasping as I caught sight of the enormous bathtub in the centre of the room. The privy closet with the flushable thing Mr Grant called a toilet sat in the corner, and to the left was a large sideboard that held a small basin. A gold tap hung above it that appeared permanently fixed to the solid wood bench-top, so highly polished I was sure if I bent down, I would see my reflection. On the wall was a looking glass as long and as wide as the sideboard. I had never in my life seen a mirror so big you could see nearly all of yourself in it at once.

I surveyed myself and, after studying my dress, face, and hair, I realised William was just a vicious bastard for criticising my appearance, as I didn't look any better or worse than the people I had met or seen in passing today. On the sideboard sat bars of soap, along with bottles filled with unknown substances, and a jar, round and stout. I had used nothing but plain soap on my body and hair. I noted that today, although initially frightening, had been one of many firsts for me, and they had not all been unpleasant.

Mr Grant bent down, turning a gold knob, joy filling me as I watched water pour into the bath before he turned it off. He placed a round gold thing on a chain he called a plug into the drain hole and turned on the tap again. The water flowed hot and strong as I ran my hand under it. I turned it off again, for now, feeling disappointed I could not fill the bath and slide in at this moment, drawing comfort from the fact that soon I would be immersed in warm water that didn't first have to boil over hot coals. It had been a Saturday night ritual; the girls waiting in turns to bathe and wash their hair in a small, metal tub.

Not that you were guaranteed a warm bath by the time everyone had been in there, and it was your turn last. The tub we used at the orphanage only fitted an older child if they sat with their arms and legs hanging out, forcing them to wash in stages.

Sister Josephine would come in after I had helped all the younger children bathe and would throw out the dirty water, then fill the tub for me with warm, clean water, washing my hair by the firelight. She was always doing special things for me, only one reason among many Sister Monica despised me. She felt I was favoured and had put a stop to Sister Josephine letting me have clean water. Instead, she forced me to take the last bath in the water left cold and dirty. She had always been a cruel soul; however, she especially disliked me, which I could never understand. I had always tried my best to treat her with respect, but I could clearly remember her animosity towards me even when I was an infant. Even the sight of me irritated her, and as I grew, she would walk past me and reprimand me, giving me chores to do without cause when I hadn't uttered a word or misbehaved. There were many times when I was going about my tasks and behaving myself when she would appear from nowhere and hand out some form of punishment, never explaining what sin I had supposedly committed. I soon learnt not to ask. There was absolutely nothing I could do to protect myself from her other than stay out of her way as much as I could.

Sister Josephine had always done her best, but there were times when she could not assist me because she was under the authority of Sister Monica, who ruled the Sisters just as she did the children — with an iron fist and not a drop of compassion or kindness. She had made my time there as difficult as possible, always watching me like a hawk, waiting for me to make a mistake so she could humiliate and castigate me.

Sister Josephine loved me without limits and took many risks to ensure I was well cared for, often going behind Sister Monica's back to provide hot, clean water for my weekly bath. The cruel bitch was in bed by that time of night and never found out, thinking I was still washing in disgusting water every week, which I knew delighted her. Well, tonight, for the first time in my life, I would soak in a proper bath where I would not have to share the water and could wash my body and long hair with lotions and things I had never seen before. I looked longingly over at the thick towels I could see folded up on a chair; however, I did not want to be rude after the kindness Mr Grant had shown me. I followed him out of the bathroom and back into the sitting room, scanning the room curiously. There were several boxes on the lounge, all piled one on top of the other. He stood a polite distance away, taking great pleasure in my reaction to everything so new around me that everyone else took for granted.

'These are for you, Miss Delmont. A Mr Malcolm sent them today with a note. Here it is; it must have slipped under the box.' He reached down and kindly handed me the envelope, which I politely placed on the table to read later. 'If you would like anything to eat or drink, I can bring it up for you. You can have anything you could wish for and more. All I have to do is ask our head chef Hannigan,' he said, smiling at me, almost in a fatherly way.

'Thank you so much; that is very kind. I would enjoy most anything tonight, and will allow you to choose a meal and dessert for me, accompanied by a non-alcoholic beverage, please.'

I felt embarrassed. The only reason I had asked Mr Grant to order for me was I did not know how to order for myself. I didn't know what food they would have on the menu or the names of anything other than the basic fare provided at Emiliani House. I pictured the grey, lumpy porridge from my past and certainly hoped they did not serve that here.

I now realised I had much to learn, more than I expected. I felt I could only do so by allowing myself to experience life, even if I occasionally humiliated myself. Of course, it helped that I knew a little from books, which I was extremely grateful for now. Still, I had muddled my way through so far, only embarrassing myself a few times, although it made me cringe as I thought of all my mistakes.

With that, Mr Grant excused himself and left the room. I slowly approached the boxes and counted them, finding seven packages of all shapes and sizes. They all looked of high quality and very expensive, just by the feel of them. One was extraordinarily flat and large; the rest were slightly smaller. I was curious to look inside them, but first picked up the letter from Mr Malcolm, sat down on a lounge and opened it, quickly scanning the page.

Dear Miss Delmont,

I have taken the privilege of purchasing some essentials I felt you might require.

Please accept them with my best wishes. I look forward to meeting you tomorrow.

Kind regards,

Henry Malcolm, Esquire.

I wondered what was going on and why I would receive these parcels at all, crossing the room to where the boxes sat before opening the first. It stunned me to find a pair of shoes in soft, green leather that looked like they would fit me. The next box contained a thick winter coat in soft green wool, tailored at the waist and ending below the ankles, with a thick lining of fur around the collar and hood. It felt beautiful, and I put it on over my dress. It fit me perfectly, and I questioned how this stranger knew my size.

I was not of an average build, being so tall. Clothes that would fit me, I was sure, would have to be made especially for me. I was feeling a little scared. What if this man was not a gentleman and had enticed me to London under false pretences to have his wicked way with me? What if he planned to hurt me and then kill me to keep me quiet? My mind spun, and my imagination was running wild.

I opened the third box and found a beautiful nightgown and matching dressing gown in a soft blue that complemented the colour of the sky. Again, this looked like it would fit me, and as I held it up against my body, I found it was even long enough and fell past my ankles. I felt I was in a dream I couldn't wake from as I continued to open the boxes. Inside was a plain, white serviceable corset; a large, green hat; a soft, green, fancy day dress in the most exquisite material; and a matching reticule. When I put everything together, it was all beautifully complementary, and every single piece was close to or in my exact size. Well, at least there had been no bloomers in there. If there had been, I indeed would have run away from the hotel, got straight back onto the train to Scotland, and entered the convent as a postulant; Sister Monica be damned.

I placed the nightgown and dressing gown over my arm and made my way into the bathroom. I bent down and turned on the taps, adjusting the temperature of the water before turning to hang my nightwear on a hook as I waited for the tub to fill. We had only ever been allowed to have our metal tub no more than halfway full. Ever. Tonight, I was going to have a full bath, as full as I could get it. I had never seen such an enormous bathtub in my life, and I could hardly wait to get in.

As the water deepened, I wandered over to the sideboard and inspected the bottles. One said *Bath Soak* on the label, and I opened the lid and gingerly sniffed the contents. It smelled like roses straight out of the Sisters' garden and made me feel wistful for a moment, making me wish for a fleeting second I was back there in their safe embrace. I walked over to the bath and poured in half the bottle. The other bottles were liquid hair wash and a scalp conditioner, along with a large jar of what appeared to be pink salt, but I didn't know its purpose. I decided I would wash my hair with these products, which I had never known existed before. I picked up a bar of soap and sniffed it. Lavender and sweetgrass filled my nose, reminding me of a day in the garden. The other bar of soap had a honey fragrance and roughage in it. I assumed it was for scrubbing your body, but I wasn't sure.

I felt the temperature of the bath and turned the taps off. I inhaled again deeply, the air heavy with the scent of roses as I stripped off my dress and shift before I eased myself into the deep bath. It felt like heaven as the fresh, warm water engulfed me. The water came up to my neck and immersed my entire body. I tied my hair on top of my head to soak and wash my body before washing my hair. I lay there for what seemed like forever, finally realising the water was losing its heat. I pulled out the round gold plug and drained half the water, then turned on the hot tap and filled the tub again.

It was pure bliss. I had experienced nothing like it before, except for the times in summer when the weather was warmer and the Sisters would take us down to the loch to swim, but even that did not compare to this. To have your body fully immersed in fragrant, warm water that relaxed every part of you was my idea of heaven. These simple things were life-changing for me, and I was thoroughly enjoying myself — as long as I did not think any farther ahead than tonight. I had no words to describe exactly how I was feeling.

I took my hair down and submerged myself under the water, letting my hair float underneath me as I lay with just my face exposed and my eyes closed. After a while, I sat up and used the liquid hair wash, washed my hair twice with it, then rinsed it in the water. It had made my hair smell like lilies of the valley, and I breathed in all the new fragrances in the room, making me heady. Next, I opened the scalp conditioner and ran it through my hair to the ends, making sure it was well covered, then piled it all on top of my head and relaxed back in the bath up to my neck as I waited for the conditioner to be absorbed.

After nearly an hour, my skin had shriveled, so I rinsed my hair out with fresh, warm water. The scalp conditioner had transformed my hair into silk, and, given how long and thick it was, there wasn't one tangle. I got out of the bath, wrapped my hair in a towel, and then wrapped another around my body. My skin was soft, and my breasts were full and round with sensitive nipples that would sometimes go hard whenever I would see a young man with a nice physique or think about being kissed by a man. It would shoot warm tingles throughout me, leaving a pleasant feeling in the pit of my stomach. Despite learning the basic facts of reproduction through the written word, I had never found a book that explained this. I slipped on my new nightgown and dressing gown, which were a little loose, although comfortable, and felt like I was Queen Victoria herself as I waited for my dinner.

Soon there was a knock on the door, and I jumped, all the unfamiliar sights and sounds causing me some anxiety. I was uncertain if I should allow a strange man to see me in my nightclothes, no matter how respectable. I hesitantly opened the door to find Mr Grant standing in front of me with a tray. I smiled at him and gestured with my hand, inviting him into the room. He placed the tray down on the table near the window, the two matching chairs sitting neatly on each side.

'I will send the ladies' maid up in the morning after breakfast to assist you to dress,' he said kindly. I looked at him blankly, feeling my cheeks flush as he realised I was uncertain of his meaning. 'Oh, I'm sorry. A ladies' maid is a special maid who only looks after her Mistress, or in our case, the female guests who stay here without their own. Ladies' maids organise her for the day and help her dress in the morning. They carry out any repairs needed to her wardrobe, while also being here to help in any way they can. They help bathe and style hair and will come immediately if summoned should you require anything at all.'

'Thank you for not making me feel stupid,' I confided, smiling shyly. 'I only turned fifteen today.' I relaxed as I explained about the orphanage and how awkward and scared I felt. Surprise mixed with sadness crossed his face, turning towards me as he stood near the door, ready to leave.

'First of all, happy birthday, Miss Delmont,' he said with sincerity. 'I once worked at Emiliani House, you know? Quite a long time ago now. What a fortunate coincidence,' he exclaimed before continuing. 'You are a lovely young lady, although I thought you were a few years older. You're not alone in the world at all. Obviously, you have your solicitor looking after you very well, and I'm sure it will take no time for a young lady like you to make friends. I understand it must be frightening to feel you are on your own after being raised and protected by the Sisters, but I assure you, it will become easier as time goes on. You will meet more people and see and do things in life you could never have imagined. You have your life in front of you, and take my word for it — time leaps ahead of us before we know it. Enjoy each day and make yourself happy at least once a day for the rest of your life. We only have one life to live, and this isn't a dress rehearsal, so grab it with both hands and make something fantastic out of it. Never live it for other people, as why should they have ownership of your life along with their own? You are a sweet lass, and I can see you'll do well wherever life takes you.'

I focused intently on his words, committing them to memory while appreciating his kindness. Mr Grant seemed to be such a wise and lovely man, and I admired his attitude about life. Well, if he could be so positive, then I could take a leaf out of his book and do the same thing. There were good things in front of me. Whether it involved my parents, I still wasn't certain, but I would do everything in my power to ensure my life went in the direction I wanted, and not the way others expected it to go. I still hadn't ruled out running away to France and living in 'gay Paree' with my five-pound note.

I thanked Mr Grant, who showed himself out, remaining at the door as I waved him off. He had been the third nice person I had met today who I had genuinely liked and who seemed to like me back. I sat down and uncovered the hot meal in front of me, looking at the sheer size of the serving. I slowly cut into something I didn't recognise; it looked like a roll of bread fried in breadcrumbs. But, from the first delicious bite, I knew I was mistaken, instead tasting chicken with some sort of creamy sauce inside.

The cook had prepared the vegetables using a method unfamiliar to me. However, I knew what they were, having wanted to taste them ever since I first smelt the roasted meats and vegetables many families would eat on a Sunday. My stomach would rumble, and my mouth water as we passed through the village on our way home to eat slops — and now in front of me sat a plate filled with roasted root vegetables. At the orphanage, the vegetables were all served mashed or boiled. These vegetables were so sweet and crunchy. Everything tasted different, even though I had eaten chicken and vegetables in the past. It had never crossed my mind someone other than our cook at the orphanage could take the same ingredients and create something that tasted as wonderful as this. It was the best meal I had ever eaten in my life, and I was thoroughly enjoying myself, as food had always been my downfall. I loved it. The more I could have of it, the happier I was. Given my enormous appetite, I was always hungry at the orphanage. The cook, despite her crankiness, would often give me extra at each meal when asked to by Sister Josephine, who also would sneak me pears from an ancient tree near the walled garden, and leftovers during the day to stop my stomach from rumbling. I had heard there had once been a gardener solely employed here just to grow pineapples for the dinner parties held in the grand castle; however, I had never even seen a pineapple, let alone tasted one.

I cleaned my plate and started on dessert. It was dark brown and tasted like nothing I had ever eaten before. It was sweet and vaguely reminded me of something I had tried a long time ago. I scooped up a little more and placed the spoon in my mouth, thinking hard as the velvety custard titillated my tongue. Then it came to me. I was three years old, and at Christmas, a parishioner had brought all the children some treats made with chocolate. I had only ever eaten it once, but had never forgotten the incredible flavour. This tasted like sweet chocolate custard; only it was light, silky, and divine.

I picked up the glass bottle sitting on the table beside my meal and twisted the cap. The liquid inside fizzed violently before I could pour some into a glass, bubbles shooting up to the top so fast I had to sip from the top of the bottle before it emptied all over the table. The flavour exploded in my mouth. Sweet lemon water, something I had never experienced before. At the orphanage, we only drank water, milk, and occasionally barley water if it was a special occasion, and I had never heard of or tasted anything like this in my life.

This had been the best meal I'd ever eaten, and it was embarrassing to me, almost shameful, I didn't know the names of the dishes served to me. However, I vowed to make the best effort to learn all the different things I didn't know as, until today, all my learning had come from books and experiencing life from a very limited and sheltered upbringing.

It was time for me to go to bed — not because I was tired — but because I could no more delay the experience of what it would be like to lie under all those warm blankets, in that enormous bed, than I could stop the moon from shining. I hurried to my bedchamber, removed my dressing gown, placing it over the chair for the morning. I listened intently as a booming bell chimed nine o'clock from an enormous tower nearby, which I had read in a book they called Big Ben.

I wondered if I would have time to visit the places I had only read about while I was here in London. There were so many interesting sights in the city described in novels I had read. I felt obligated to visit as many of them as possible while here. As Mr Grant had wisely told me, I should get out and experience life, turning it into exactly what I wanted it to be.

I pulled back the thick, satin quilt and squirmed my way into the beautiful bed, somehow certain I would never again have to sleep in a tiny, creaky version with a wafer-thin mattress and threadbare blanket — I would make sure of that. No matter what happened, I would only move forward and not backward, and I would take every opportunity offered to me.

I cushioned my head on a down-filled pillow that felt like floating on a soft cloud. The bed encompassed my whole body, right down to my feet, and as I sank into it slightly, I felt myself slowly relax. I knew I was going to sleep well tonight, at least physically. My mind raced, and I felt confused, unable to make sense of any of it, nor did I understand what it was all about.

'Well, tomorrow morning, I will know one way or the other,' I muttered to myself before slowly drifting off into a deep sleep, where a limestone castle, a black horse, and chicken in a delicious cream sauce all figured prominently.

Chapter Five

I NOTICED THE SILENCE first, then the absence of birds singing their morning songs as I slowly woke, the room becoming brighter, and I wondered what time it was. There was a knock at the door, causing me to jump, and within moments, a maid let herself in and was standing next to me with my breakfast tray. I sat up and smiled at her.

'Thank you very much.'

'You're welcome, Mistress. The ladies' maid will be here in an hour to help you get dressed.' She nodded her head in a no nonsense fashion before exiting the room to place my breakfast on the table. She was a short, solid woman with a look of determination on her face and an efficiency about her I admired. The golden glow surrounding her body fascinated yet confused me. The nameless maid quietly let herself out, and I quickly sprung out of bed, ravenous and eager to try this new food, while deep in thought about the auras only I could see.

I slipped my dressing gown over my shoulders and raced to the sitting room, quickly sitting down at the table while hungrily looking down at two eggs sitting on the plate, unsure if they were poached or fried, then admired the crispy bacon on the side. On another plate were pancakes with butter and honey. I found a large mug of coffee with cream and sugar and a tall bottle of orange juice. I felt like I had indeed died and gone to heaven — wherever that was. I had eaten bacon and eggs before, but never like this, and the pancakes were delicious. They were fluffy and dripping with honey. As I chewed, I wondered what today would bring.

Within a few hours, I would know about my parents and why I had to meet with this solicitor, who had already made it his business to dress me for the day. The more I thought about it, the more confident I was that this was about my parents. What else could it be? I was an unwanted orphan, yet someone was paying for all this. I wondered if my father was rich and was coming back to claim me. Maybe he didn't know about me until now and had trodden the four corners of the earth to find me and bring me back to him. That was all it could be, something to do with my parents. I had such a deep desire to know where I came from — I wanted it so much — my heart physically ached.

The carriage door opened, Mr Miller holding it wide as he grinned at me. I could see the large writing on the glass of the shopfront, *Mr Henry Malcolm, Esq. & Sons*, and underneath that, *Solicitors and Barristers*, the same as displayed on his carriage door. I remained inside wearing my new outfit and an oversized hat secured to my head, not wanting to move. I had never worn a corset before, and thanks to the ladies' maid, the laces were pulled so tight I could barely breathe. It cinched my waist in even smaller than it was and pushed my breasts up towards my chin. I had stood looking in the full-length mirror for a long time, surprised I now looked like a lady from a respectable family with means and appeared several years older than I was. If only William Montague could see me now, I thought darkly, still stinging from the insults he had directed at me. Suddenly, I realised Mr Miller had been holding the carriage door patiently while I daydreamed and quickly apologised. I hurriedly exited the carriage and started up the stairs to the front door of the office.

'Good luck, Missy,' he called out. 'Whatever happens, let it be good news. You're a sweet girl, and you deserve it. I hope it's about your parents, lass. Good luck again.' He smiled and crossed his fingers for me while I crossed mine as well, showing them to him as I smiled back. I turned and rang the bell near the door of the solicitor's office, my heart racing and my hands trembling.

'Come on in, it's open. Just give it a shove,' I heard a woman's voice call out. I entered, closed the door behind me, and turned to find myself in a large room with chairs lined up around the walls and a lady sitting at a desk. She was an attractive woman — who appeared to be in her mid-thirties — her blonde hair pulled back tight into a bun at the back of her head, and, as her dress stopped just above her ankles, the strangest shoes I had ever seen. They had the highest heels on them and, as she walked over to me, it surprised me how easy she made it look.

'Are you Miss Delmont?' she enquired, looking me up and down approvingly.

'Yes, I am,' I replied, my hands unconsciously straightening my skirt as I looked around curiously.

'I'm Miss Delaware, Mr Malcolm's secretary. I do pretty much everything around here except sit in the courtroom. You can go straight through, as his nibs is ready to meet with you. Stop looking so confused and come with me; I will show you.' She laughed loudly at her own joke as she led me down a narrow hallway to a large room lined with books and holding an impressive desk. She offered me a chair. I accepted gratefully and sat down heavily, feeling both anxious and excited at once. 'He will be with you soon, love. He shouldn't be long. I will get you a cup of tea while you wait.'

Miss Delaware left me to my own devices. I scanned the room, noticing a framed law degree from Oxford on the wall, which impressed me. I had read about the university, so I knew this man must have some credibility. The desk was grand, with intricate designs carved into the expensive wood. There was a large folder sitting in the centre of the desk, with surrounding appurtenances in perfect order.

Miss Delaware brought my cup of tea on a metal tray and handed it to me, which I gratefully accepted. It was intense and sweet and the perfect temperature. I tried to sip it slowly while I waited, feeling as if it were taking forever. Would my parents walk in with him? My poor stomach felt like it had hundreds of butterflies flying around, and I couldn't calm myself down. My hands were clammy, and I felt shaky inside. I placed my rattling teacup and saucer down on his desk before they shattered on the floor, my hands trembling wildly while my heart felt as if it would pound out of my chest.

I heard footsteps coming towards me before the office door swung open, and my stomach dropped. Could I be meeting my parents at any moment? I stood up to greet a tall man with greying hair and a grey moustache who appeared to be in his early fifties. He had lines around his dark brown eyes that looked as if he laughed a lot, and a sparkle in them when he found something amusing, a fact I would discover within moments. He approached me, then took my hand in his.

'Miss Delmont, it is an honour to meet you,' he said generously, shaking my hand. I felt a sense of familiarity overwhelm me, as though I had met him before.

'What do you mean, an honour?'

'You get straight to the point, don't you? Much like your great-aunt, Lady Isabelle Delmont, did when she was alive, God rest her soul,' he replied, observing me intently as he stepped back.

'What are you talking about?' I asked, feeling rather alarmed. He made his way around the desk and sat down in his oversized leather chair, then looked at me with a kind expression on his face.

'I will explain from the beginning, as the matter is complex and of a sensitive nature. Please relax, as I see you are feeling uncomfortable. I completely understand — being summoned here must have come as quite a shock, given no one has informed you of the purpose of this meeting.' I liked him already; he was friendly, and he seemed to take a fatherly interest in me already. I sat back in my chair and tried to do as he said. He opened the file in front of him and raised his eyebrows, staring across at me and appearing ready to begin. I took a deep breath as he riffled the thick pile of papers that looked weighty and serious. 'All right, I will begin, Miss Delmont. I understand the suspense you have been in, and I apologise, as there were far too many details to send by letter. However, I felt it was better you met with me here rather than at the orphanage, surrounded by Sisters wanting to know your private business.'

'Thank you. I appreciate it very much, whatever news you have to give me, good or bad.' My stomach was in knots, and my hands continued to shake.

'Well then, just settle back and try to relax, as I have a great deal of information to provide to you.' He smiled across at me before clearing his throat and focussing his attention on the documents in front of him. 'Fifteen-and-a-half years ago, Lady Isabelle Delmont came to me and dictated her last Will and Testament. She brought along with her further legal instructions that she made through a solicitor unknown to me. This second document was in a large, sealed box, along with other documents she did not disclose to me. She requested I send the said box to a solicitor in Geelong, Australia, with her last instructions when she passed away. Lady Delmont was, in fact, your great-great-aunt on the paternal side of your family. She told me my grandfather, Mr Gilbert Malcolm Esquire, represented

71

her in a criminal matter when she was a young woman, and she had never forgotten his kindness to her. Sadly, he had passed by the time she required the services of a solicitor, so she came to me. She made several stipulations in that Will and appointed you as her sole beneficiary, which is why you are here today. The instructions, as outlined in this document, state all of Lady Isabelle Delmont's worldly possessions are to be transferred to you on your fifteenth birthday in their entirety, should you agree to abide by the conditions of the said Will.' He paused, gazing across at me as I felt the blood drain from my face. I gasped aloud, unable to breathe. I had family and even a great-aunt who knew about me and had made me her beneficiary, although I knew nothing about them.

'Why was I left at an orphanage to grow up without parents if I had a family that cared enough to leave me some money?' There had to be some mistake, as none of it made sense to me at all.

'Well, that is all a very unfortunate business.' He shifted in his seat, avoiding my stare. 'I will tell it to you as it was told to me by your great-aunt Isabelle the only time I met with her to draw up this document.' He looked up from the papers he was holding and smiled, kindness in his eyes. 'Your mother, Mary Campbell, was young and very poor and worked in a tavern just outside of Edinburgh. Your father, Lord Christopher Howard, passed through her village, took one look at her, and fell in love.' He appeared embarrassed as I continued to maintain eye contact with him, the rage growing inside me, ready to explode.

'Why are you telling me this?' I felt my heart race, pounding in my ears as I attempted to slow my breathing. He made a placating motion with his hands.

'I'm sorry for the descriptive nature of the information,' he apologised, smiling in an attempt to soothe me, 'but your great-aunt specified you know all the details as she relayed them to me. She had me document everything, as she knew the time would come where you would want to know your origins. I will go on. Your father stayed several nights in the village trying to gain your mother's affections. However, I believe she spurned him. A few weeks later, he returned to the village, and she soon became like clay in his hands, believing everything he told her and that he would come back to marry her. He would pass through her village at least once a month, stay for several nights, and disappear again. On his third visit, your mother told him she was with child. He promised poor Mary he would look after her, and you, and they would be together. He left the village the next day and never came back.'

'Do you know why?'

'Sadly, yes. Your father was already married with a family who lived with him in the north of England.'

'I still don't understand why I am the one sitting here in your office. How did my father's aunt find out about me?' Tears welled in my eyes, but I brushed them away before he noticed.

'Well, unfortunately for him, and fortunately for you, your great-aunt Isabelle heard through a friend what had occurred and took great offence at his behaviour. She told me she was so disgusted, she banished him from her home. Your great-aunt set out to meet with Mary and soon found her at the tavern where she worked. Serendipitously, she knew of your mother through her elder sister, Anna, with whom she was well acquainted. Your aunt explained she was there to help her, given the situation her nephew had created. Your mother made it clear to your great-aunt she didn't want to keep you, as she had no husband and no provisions or skills to raise a child, and she was only eighteen. The baby would be a constant reminder of her broken heart, her humiliation, and she was adamant that, although she wanted you cared for, she could not raise you.' I could hear a hint of sadness in his voice before he went on. 'Lady Isabelle was too old to raise an infant. You show a striking resemblance to her as, despite her age, she looked decades younger than she was.

An attractive woman she was, about the same height and build you possess. I have been told by several people who knew her, she was considered one of the most beautiful women of her day. I know there was some family scandal no one talks about to this day that involved her, and I believe it related to my grandfather's dealings with her close to ninety years ago. He never spoke about her, and your great-aunt certainly didn't elaborate, so I have no further information.' He placed his document back on the desk and studied me for several moments.

'I resemble her, then? I actually look like someone else who had the same blood as me?'

'Young lady, you more than resemble her,' he replied, his body now relaxed as he gazed across at me. 'You look like a younger version of her. She still had her natural hair colour, not a silver strand in it, the precise colour of your own glorious hair. She wore it long; however, she had it up under a hat when I met her. You have her eyes, which are the most unique colour I have ever seen. It startled me when I first met you to see how closely you favour her. The eyes come from your paternal side of the family, without question.' As he spoke, I raised my fingers to my face and traced the outline of my eyes. 'Shall we keep going, or would you like another cup of tea?' I shook my head as I tried to absorb all this information, information about a family I had only ever dreamed of finding.

'No, thank you. I would rather we continue.'

'As you wish. Lady Delmont arranged with your mother that, as soon as you were born and your mother strong enough to walk, she would take you to Emiliani House, where she had a friend whose daughter was a nun there. Your mother stayed with her in a private house on the grounds of an estate called Merinda Manor in Scotland until she gave birth. She was present in the room when you were born and was certain you would be a girl. I was told that shortly after you arrived, Lady Delmont sat down on a chair to hold you, and it was she who named you Abigail, after someone dear to her heart. She handed a note to your mother to leave in the basket with you for the Sisters, before giving her an emerald necklace to place around your neck.'

'Do you know what happened to my mother?'

'No. Your great-aunt died not long after you entered the world, I am sorry to say. I met with your mother and her sister at Lady Delmont's funeral, and she disclosed the circumstances of your great-aunt's death to me; however, I have had no contact since and do not know her whereabouts. I know you want answers, and unfortunately, I don't have them. Sadly, the situation is the same regarding your father. I have never met him, and although I am aware of his whereabouts, your great-aunt did mention he was not a man she would want you ever to have contact with and hoped you would not search for him or your mother.' His voice was gentle, but I felt tears slipping down my face against my will. He paused for a moment and handed me a handkerchief, looking across at me with such sympathy I wanted to hug him. 'Lady Isabelle had already organised her last Will and Testament before you were born. For the past fifteen years, a trust fund has been operating in your name. All property she owned in England and Scotland was sold soon after her death, and the proceeds, along with all money held in the bank in her name, were transferred into this fund. It has doubled in size from the interest earned and income from businesses in which you have a stake. You have inherited several properties outside of England and Scotland, which I will explain at a later time. The trust fund in England is not available to you until you attain thirty years and will continue to be managed by this firm until then. I am under no obligation to disclose the amount of money in your fund; however, I assure you we only take a small amount each week to cover the work we do and to ensure we meet the stringent conditions in the Last Will and Testament of Lady Isabelle Delmont. Do you have questions? I am aware it is a lot to digest.'

I sat unmoving, my thoughts scrambled. I had parents; only they had no interest in me to this day. My father had cruelly left my mother alone and pregnant without a second thought or offers of help when he was obviously a man of means, although my great-aunt's warning about him had struck me like a knife through my heart. My mother had never returned for me and it seemed my aunt's opinion of her was no better. I felt a huge lump building in my throat, but I tried not to lose control and break down completely. I could no longer be a child, so I refused to make a fool of myself in front of a stranger.

'Yes, I do. Many. So, you don't know where my parents are or how I could find them?' I asked him again, stifling a sob and feeling pain rise in me at the rejection I had not only suffered once at birth, but was now experiencing a second time. I realised they never wanted me at all and, as Sister Monica had said, were unlikely to want to know me now. He shook his head, indicating he did not. 'And I have been left an inheritance I'm not allowed to touch, and some businesses and property, but we are not discussing that today? Have I got that right?' I asked curtly, squeezing my hands together tightly in my lap.

'Well, when you put it like that, it sounds mysterious and suspicious. Maybe I haven't explained myself clearly.' He appeared worried, glancing down to recheck the documents to see if he had missed anything.

'No, I understand what you have told me, but I'm confused as to why this great-aunt has left me anything. I don't understand any of it.'

'How do you like the hotel where you are staying?' He was a kind man, attempting to cheer me, although it made little difference to my heavy heart.

'It's wonderful; I have seen nothing like it.'

'I'm glad to hear that, as you are staying in The Delmont Hotel. Your great-aunt designed the building and arranged for it to be completed by your fifteenth birthday, with all the modern fittings of

76

the time, of which I am proud to say I think we have achieved. You are the sole owner of the hotel, by the way and will never have to worry about money again, but you need to be aware of all conditions attached to this Will.' He leaned back in his chair and exhaled, grimacing for a moment before continuing, somewhat reluctantly. 'You will stay in London for another six weeks at The Delmont, and then you will migrate to Australia on a steamship. During the coming weeks, my family and I will help get you organised by arranging a ladies' maid to accompany you to Australia and provide the necessities you will require for your travels. You will meet with a solicitor in the city of Geelong, Victoria, where a home for you has been arranged. He will explain further conditions of the Will required to be met before you can access your inheritance. I have nominated my son, Richard, to be your chaperone while you are in London because, compared to where you have come from, London can be a perilous place for a young woman on her own. I hope you will accept this with the best intentions on our part.'

'Am I to stay in Australia? And may I ask, why Australia?'

'Lady Isabelle spent a great deal of time in the State of Victoria and had a number of business interests there.'

'I really do not understand any of this now at all. I need to think. What if I don't want to go?' I crossed my arms as he leaned back in his chair, narrowing his gaze as if I were a child who needed a stern lecture.

'Under the conditions of the Last Will and Testament of Lady Isabelle Delmont, if you do not follow the guidelines and requests as set out therein, you will forfeit all claims you have to any property or monies you were entitled to, in England and Australia. All of it, every last penny, will pass on to the next in line Lady Delmont named — a distant cousin of yours, I believe.'

This was the last thing I expected to hear. In fact, I had never dreamed of anything remotely like this. I suddenly felt I had a whole new set of people in charge of my life, and I felt sick to my stomach.

'Don't I have any say in my own future?' My face burned as resentment rose in me.

'You have every say in what your future holds, Miss Delmont. You could let fear ruin this opportunity, or it could excite you good fortune has shone upon your life. Given the start you have had, the options available to an orphan of no means, with no family or friends, are almost non-existent. I promise I will do everything in my power to ensure we protect you and all your needs are met. You seem to forget I am here to act in your best interests,' he advised me, not unkindly. I remained silent for a moment, thinking over what he had said, and I felt my body relax a little and my mind ease slightly.

'Thank you. I appreciate that very much. This has come as a great surprise to me, and I would like to know what the conditions are before I agree to anything.' Calmer now, I uncrossed my arms and tried to smile at him. I knew he was only carrying out instructions and doing everything he could to help me in every way.

'Understandably so, my dear young lady — understandably so.' He sighed, leaning back in his chair and putting his hands behind his head. 'In all honesty, I can only tell you what I have already disclosed. Not because I am hiding anything from you, but because of how your great-aunt structured her Will. It appears she gave a certain amount of responsibility to me, with the rest bestowed on the solicitor, a Mr McPhee, in Geelong, where she lived for a time. I don't actually know what the conditions of the Will are after you arrive in Australia.' Although I hadn't known this man very long, I believed he was telling me the truth.

'Where is Geelong, by the way?' I asked, suddenly curious.

'It is to the west of Melbourne. From what I hear, it is a large town with a well-established community. A friend of mine described it as a beautiful country with great open spaces and breathtaking countryside beside the ocean. I'm sure you will find the place quite appealing. Thousands of people are immigrating to Australia each year to get out of our overcrowded cities and away from the rising poverty, seeking new opportunities the colony seems to offer without discrimination. It's not just a place for criminals anymore.' He chuckled, and I saw the sparkle in his eye. He seemed a man of gentle nature and good spirits. I liked him, and I believed I could trust him. 'We have plenty of time to discuss the finer details,' he went on. 'For today, I have arranged for you to go to an upmarket women's clothing store. A very dear friend of mine, Madame Felicity, owns the store and she is aware you will visit her premises today. They will take your measurements and make the wardrobe you will require for your travels. The shops I send you to will charge your purchases to my firm, and I will pay your bills each month from the interest in your fund. I have procured four trunks to take on the ship to carry your clothing and personal items. I will have them delivered to your suite today. Two of them have false bottoms for you to hide anything precious you own or acquire before your travels. After the dress shop, my driver will take you to the Cobbler to order what you need to go with your gowns. Is this all too much for you, Miss Delmont? You are looking quite pale.' He seemed concerned as he stood to open a window.

I felt dizzy and sick to my stomach. Yesterday, I was so excited to meet my parents. Yet, within minutes today, that dream had been shattered into a million pieces, only to be replaced with the notion I was potentially wealthy — or at least I thought that was what Mr Malcolm was trying to tell me. It just wouldn't sink in. I was having trouble piecing it all together, and I truly believed I had gone into a state of shock.

'I am just feeling a little faint, Mr Malcolm. May I have a glass of water, please?' I asked as I tried to stop my hands from shaking. He quickly left the office to attend to my request. I could not process what I had heard with my own ears while my head had started to ache. He returned within moments and handed me the water, which I drank appreciatively. It was cool and crisp and made me feel much better. 'Can I ask you how you knew my clothing size when we had never met?' I asked curiously, and he smiled.

'I took a guess based on your great-aunt Isabelle, as she told me all the women in her family were of a similar build. I was of the hope you might take after her likeness, and I see was correct. Even then, it has surprised me how strikingly similar you are to her. She was right that the women in your family have powerful genes. I hope you were not offended,' he explained, appearing concerned.

'No, just surprised, Mr Malcolm, but I appreciate it very much.' His purchases had been so very thoughtful, knowing I wouldn't have much to wear, considering my past, and I was grateful to him. Smiling, he sat back down behind his elaborate desk and smiled across at me.

'Well, I believe that's enough for today, Miss Delmont. I have more to discuss with you, but I think we can leave that for another day. You look exhausted and somewhat distraught, for which I must apologise. I will arrange the carriage for you. It would be my pleasure to invite you to my home tomorrow night to introduce you to my family and have dinner. You must meet Richard, my son, as he will be your chaperone and your guide around London for the time you are here.'

'Thank you. That would be lovely,' I said, and truly meant it. I knew no one here, and it was nice to have a connection to another person who seemed to have my best interests at heart. He opened his desk drawer and took out a wad of money, which he handed to me across the desk. I looked at him, wide-eyed, then stared at the enormous amount of money he had placed in my hand, poised in mid-air, not knowing what to do with it or where to put it.

'That is for you to buy anything you may need that cannot be billed directly to my office,' he explained. 'You can now purchase what you would like to take with you to Australia. I have never been there myself, so I don't know what is available once you arrive. Which is why, to be on the safe side, I've arranged to have your wardrobe made here by Madame Felicity. Additionally, you can purchase personal items you believe you may need while here in London. My carriage will collect you tomorrow at half-past five to bring you to my home for dinner. Well, you should be going — you have a full day of shopping ahead of you.'

He stood, smiled brightly, and shook my hand. I quickly put the money into my reticule so I wouldn't lose it. Most people earned much less than a pound a week for working six days, twelve hours a day. This money made me feel extremely rich.

'Thank you again, Mr Malcolm. When I can clear my mind, I will have more questions. Is that all right with you?' I asked shyly, feeling awkward.

'Of course, Miss Delmont. Now go and enjoy yourself, and I will see you tomorrow evening.' He escorted me to the front door, where he shook my hand fondly again before I quietly left with my thoughts racing and my reticule held close to my chest.

Chapter Six

I STEPPED UP INTO the carriage; the door clicking shut behind me, the sounds of the street floating in through the small window. The carriage lurched forward while I settled back in my seat and tried to relax. Finally, I was alone. How did one even begin to comprehend something like this? In a matter of just thirty minutes, a long-dead aunt had turned my life upside down. I tried to deal with the shock of my parents' heartbreaking story and the unexpected fact I would be a wealthy woman. That seemed possible only if I obeyed every direction. I would give back the money and all the things that came with it just to be reunited with my parents and have them love me and want me, but this seemed highly unlikely after what I had discovered today. I needed some time on my own to sit down and think instead of being forced to go shopping.

The bills in my reticule seemed impossibly heavy; I felt as if I was now guarding a brick of solid gold. I had never had money before and remembered how rich I'd felt with the five-pound note I still had in my possession. Mr Miller had been provided with Madame Felicity's address and firm instructions to take me there post haste, but had taken his time, slowly guiding the horses through the streets. I was lost in my own thoughts when I felt the carriage come to an abrupt halt and noticed we had arrived outside her shop. With a deep sigh, I decided perhaps this shopping trip would help cushion the emotional turmoil I was experiencing.

'There you go, Missy. I will wait here, then take you to buy shoes,' the kindly coachman said as he opened my door and helped me down. With that, I entered the shop and immediately felt out of my depth. I had never seen so many beautiful dresses. Dozens in all styles and colours were hanging on racks to be finished, although I immediately realised most of them were far too short for me. I spotted a woman sewing a ribbon onto a garment on a dressmaker's dummy, walked over, and introduced myself as confidently as I could. An assistant was working on another garment in the back of the shop, eyeing me suspiciously.

'Bonjour, my dear girl,' she said briskly. 'I am Madame Felicity. Mr Malcolm sent me a note yesterday explaining your situation and the need to make you an entirely new wardrobe for your travels. Now, come here and stand in the light so I can see you and decide which colours will be best.'

I moved near the window, where Madame Felicity looked me over, front and back, up and down. She was petite with black hair and dressed in the finest outfit I had seen in ochre with ribbons and beads adorning the bodice. She was a handsome woman who appeared to be in her forties.

'You have a perfect figure, despite being so tall, and your face is captivating. I have never seen such eyes before — green like emeralds, and hair the colour of flames. I will measure you first, as I have many ideas for your dresses. I hear Australia is sweltering hot, even in winter. Some dresses I design will be in lightweight material; then, I will create some for the cooler weather. My dear friend Henry has requested I make evening gowns for you to wear on the ship and matching hats for all the dresses. A proper lady wouldn't leave her home without wearing one. It will all be fabulous and oh, so much fun. I love when I start with a clean slate. Your figure will carry my designs perfectly and do them justice,' she added with the enthusiasm of an artist impassioned by her work. 'Tell me, what colours do you favour?' She led me into a back room, where there were hundreds of rolls of very fine material. I went through dozens of them, picking out what I liked — the patterns and colours that appealed to me most. 'Exquisite taste, my dear — yes, we can do a lot with what you have chosen.' She patted my waist, turning me around while she continued to look me up and down. 'I will have them ready in two to three weeks. Do you have only this dress I sent over yesterday?' She appeared concerned, as though that would be the worst thing that could ever happen to a woman.

'Yes, and two dresses I made myself.' Despite the pride in my voice, she rolled her eyes and threw up her hands in apparent disgust.

'Those will never do. Come over here with me.' She grabbed my arm and guided me across the room to a rack displaying longer dresses. 'This is my special-order area. I keep odd sizes in stock for robust and tall women. There has to be something here that will fit you until I can get your dresses made.'

She sounded confident and started pulling several gowns from the rack, then ordered me into the change room to try them on. She was the type of woman who expected obedience without question, so I did as I was told. I hurried inside and closed the door, then removed my clothes down to my corset. She brought over several dresses and hung them on a hook for me to try. With the help of her assistant, the first I tried on fitted as if they had made it for me. Made of the softest velveteen, a material I had never touched before in a glorious deep orange, it impressed me. Clinging to my waist, it fell in a bell shape to the floor, snug around my torso, breasts, and arms, but very comfortable. I stepped out of the change room and showed it to her.

'Oh, you look so beautiful. Yes, that one was made for you. Try them all and take your pick,' Madame Felicity instructed as her assistant stood nearby, silently watching me.

I tried on each one, deciding to take the orange dress, a midnight blue dress, and two others with lovely patterned material in various colours that fit me perfectly. They were all day dresses; however, far fancier than anything I had worn. I wondered what an evening gown would feel like, for it was something I had yet to experience. The only time I had ever seen evening gowns was in magazines. I quickly put my green dress back on, with the help of her assistant, and readied myself to leave. Madame Felicity disappeared again into the back room and returned with matching hats for the four dresses I had taken with me today. I could not believe the size of some hats. They were oversized and ostentatious, but who was I to question what was in style, given my lack of exposure to the fashion world?

'You are an exquisite woman and will be even more so in my gowns. It is truly wonderful when you find customers with the perfect figure to do your creations justice, rather than these fat, wealthy women who have the appearance of a plum pudding dressed up to attend the opera. They make my designs look dreadful,' she complained while wrapping my garments in tissue paper and putting them in boxes. It was apparent she thought a great deal of her creations and even more so of herself. However, she was far too uppity for my liking, and I could not wait to get out of her shop. She seemed fake and superficial, character traits I detested. Nonetheless, I thanked her profusely, then collected several of my packages and hurried outside to the carriage.

'Are there more still inside?' Mr Miller enquired, and I nodded. He sprang up the front steps to the shop and entered to collect the rest of my parcels. I waited on the street, watching the women dressed in their finery, not one resembling a plum pudding in fancy clothes at all. Finally, Mr Miller returned, placing everything in the carriage before offering his hand to assist me inside, quietly closing the door behind me.

The carriage jumped forward as the horses trotted up the street and around a corner. They slowed to a walk, then stopped within moments as I looked out of the window. I could not believe my eyes when I saw the shop, its window filled with shoes of all styles and colours. I jumped down from the carriage before Mr Miller had moved from his seat, feeling a tiny bit of excitement for the first time since I had left the hotel this morning. I had only ever owned one type of shoe. They were the same every year and never in a colour or style other than plain, sturdy, and black — sensible, flat shoes that were comfortable to walk in, but not what anyone would call fashionable. For the first time in my life, I was about to get several pairs at once, and I felt as if I had died and gone to heaven. I pushed open the door and entered, a tiny bell tinkling above my head. A short, stocky man came out from behind his counter.

'Can I help you, Miss?'

'Yes, Sir. Mr Henry Malcolm sent me here to select some shoes.'

'I, yes, Miss Delmont. My name is Mr Higginbottom, but you can call me Higgy. Now, please come with me and sit down so I can measure your feet.' He skipped ahead of me, his face creased in a brilliant smile as he cheerfully directed me to a chair. When I had settled and removed one shoe, he took out his measuring tape and ran it along the bottom of my foot, then around the width of it while writing numbers down in a small pocket notebook. 'Well, you do have enormous feet, don't you?' he remarked, his eyebrows raised. 'They are quite slim in width, though, but no matter, as I cater to all sorts here. We may have something in stock in your size. I will have to see, given the size of these. They probably feel like large boats attached to your ankles, do they not? The rest I will have to make especially for you. It will take me several weeks if that is all right? I make them all myself with my own two hands. You will never have a more comfortable pair of shoes than what I will create for you.'

The more I looked at him, the more he looked like a proud, overgrown bullfrog, which made me burst into giggles. At least he didn't resemble that toxic toad of a Mother Superior back in Scotland. Thankfully, he ignored my laughter and went to the storeroom, returning with several boxes.

'Try these on, and I will look for more out back, as I know I have some in your size.' He struggled back up to his feet, taking a moment to catch his breath. 'I had another woman come in about a year ago who had enormous feet like you. She ordered twenty pairs of shoes and, from my recollection, she did not buy them all in the end. I detest customers like that, so I have made sure they will pay your order in full before I even begin to make them for you. The problem I have is if you change your mind, I won't be able to sell them to anyone other than a man who likes to wear ladies' shoes.'

I wasn't sure if he was serious or possessed an odd sense of humour. I was well aware I had large feet, but he made them sound like flippers on a sea monster that were imperative for it to swim. I felt embarrassed and was relieved there were no other customers in the shop to witness my humiliation.

He hurried away as I leaned forward and removed my other shoe, then tried on the shoes in the boxes. Three pairs were made from leather and fit me perfectly; however, one pair felt like velvet. I asked Mr Higginbottom when he returned empty-handed. He looked at them and proudly held one up.

'I made these from a new material called suede. It is all the rage in Paris right now, and I managed to get my hands on some to make them here in England.' He then added, as if to himself, 'Very hard to get; very hard to get.'

After he had wrapped my three pairs of shoes, we went over all his styles, and I chose another three pairs for him to make, all in different colours to match my new dresses. He promised to make me a pair of long sturdy boots he said were for riding horses. I had never ridden a horse before and didn't know if I ever would, but I liked the boots. I requested all my shoes be made with a very low heel, to which Mr Higginbottom agreed.

'We don't want you to look any taller than you are now, do we?' he said, then mumbled to himself, 'You would look abnormal; you would be a yard taller than most men, and we don't want that, now, do we? No, we don't want that.'

I looked at him sharply, wanting to smack him across the head as the blood rushed to my face. Already I was sticking out like a sore thumb because of my height, and I was getting sick of hearing people comment on it. I didn't know what to say to this strange little man, who was good at what he did, but his mind seemed to wander off at times into his own little world. Of course, I did not mind people who were a bit strange in their ways — I liked them, even — as it was better than being just like everyone else.

I arrived back at The Delmont Hotel feeling drained and worn out, and it was only nearing midday. I bid farewell to Mr Miller, who reminded me he would collect me at four o'clock to take me to the Savoy Hotel for dinner with Catherine. I felt I needed to clear my head after this morning's events and decided to take a walk. Everything went by so quickly when riding in a carriage and you saw nothing for more than a fleeting moment. I set off with my five-pound note, wondering what I would buy. Lunch would be the first thing, but I did not know where to go or what to have, so I walked on. I had only ventured two streets from the hotel when I stumbled across a tiny shop that smelled divine. I entered and ordered one serving of fish and chips. When I handed the five-pound note to the proprietor, he looked perturbed.

'Love, I don't earn this much in a month, so I don't have change to give you. Stay with my wife here so I can go over to the shop across the road to exchange it for you,' he said generously, his brown eyes kind as his wife appeared from the back and smiled at him before approaching the counter.

'Thank you, I will,' I replied as I stood enjoying the warmth of the shop. Outside was overcast and, although it hadn't rained, the sky appeared threatening with looming black clouds low on the horizon. The people I had met so far were relatively friendly to me, and I had started to relax a little now I knew Mr Malcolm's intentions. The shopkeeper's wife was sweating over the hot oil, and I watched in fascination as she cut up potatoes into long, thin chunks, then dipped some fish into a creamy white substance and dropped it into the oil with the potatoes. I had only ever eaten potatoes mashed, except for my first meal at the hotel, so did not know how this dish would taste. The times we had eaten fish at the orphanage, it was broiled and dry.

The proprietor returned and handed me my money. I still had four pounds left, with lots of coins. I had no idea how money worked, what anything cost, or how much I was supposed to receive back when I bought something. I was relying on the honesty of the shopkeepers until I could work it out and understand it all. When I met him the following evening, I would ask my chaperone, Mr Richard Malcolm, to teach me about money when he showed me around London, so I didn't feel so stupid or helpless.

My order was soon ready, and I watched in fascination as she drained the oil from the food, then sprinkled a generous amount of salt on top and wrapped it all in a sheet of newspaper. Finally, I thanked the couple, took my rolled-up parcel and a large bottle of lemonade and headed out the door.

I had noticed a park near the hotel during my carriage ride, so made my way there to find a bench and watch the ducks swimming in a pretty pond. I found an empty wooden bench and sat down heavily before unwrapping the steaming package. I bit into a golden chip, finding it crisp on the outside and fluffy inside, the saltiness biting into my tongue as I soaked up my surroundings. The fish was like nothing I had ever tasted, with a crispy shell and sweet, white flesh inside that melted in your mouth. Everything I ate became my new favourite food, and each meal seemed to get better than the last. I ate almost everything and enjoyed my cool drink while watching the ducks swimming around. I tossed them some leftover chips, which they excitedly devoured.

What was I going to do? The choices I would make in the next few weeks would ultimately decide my future happiness. There was nothing for me in England, and now I knew I had to travel to Australia to finalise this Will, I felt like I had hit a fork in the road. It was such a long way, but I knew I must see what life held for me there. Knowing the story surrounding my birth, I realised my parents were ambiguous and did not care whether I lived or died, so it was pointless to stay and try to find them. I could not face being rejected by them for the third time. It was painful to know I had a family who had the financial means to look after me yet had left me in an orphanage for fifteen years, where I dreamed of them every day in the hope they would come back and claim me. It had never happened because they did not want me to begin with, and in time, I knew I would learn to accept that; however, it was ripping my heart apart now, and I could think of nothing else.

I had waited so long to have someone who would call me their own after being alone my entire life. As I did every day of my life, I thanked the universe for Sister Josephine and that she had been sent to love and care for me. I would not have turned into the person I had become without her. I knew it would take me some time to process everything, but for now, I had to concentrate on the things I did know for certain. I knew I had a house in Geelong waiting for me, so at least I would have a roof over my head. Catherine would be living in Melbourne with her parents and her frightful brother William. Given that, I would migrate to Australia and see what the rest of the conditions of great-aunt Isabelle's Will were, then make a final decision.

Now I had made up my mind, I stood up and started back to the hotel, ambling along and smiling at the people who passed me, many of whom smiled back. It felt so good to be free, to choose to go for a walk and interact with people I had never seen or met before, just to have them smile at me or say hello in passing. It made me feel not so alone.

I arrived back at the hotel, walked up the grand stairs to the front entrance, and then made my way across the reception area to the staircase. I did not care they had put me in the fanciest suite on the top floor; I would climb thirty flights of stairs if necessary to avoid that Otis elevator, vowing never to ride in one again. It had terrified me so much on my arrival last night that, shaking and hyperventilating, I thought I would pass out. Back in my room, panting after my long walk, I sat down on the lounge to catch my breath and suddenly felt an overwhelming sense of grief. I began to cry, which soon turned into heartbroken sobs. I was sobbing for everything I had lost — Sister Josephine, Polly, and, now I knew the truth, my parents and the family I could never have. I knew I had to pull myself together as now they expected me to behave as an adult whether or not I liked it, but for now, I wanted to be the child I was.

I met Mr Miller down in the grand reception room at the agreed-upon time. I was spending most of my day getting in or out of his carriage and the rest of my time riding inside it. I felt excited at seeing my friend again; however, I was worried about the reception I would receive from William. After the day I had experienced, I felt emotionally vulnerable, and I didn't know whether I could keep my temper under control if he were rude to me again.

'How are you, Missy? I hope it was good news this morning, as you look like you've been crying. You don't have to tell me the details. I'm just askin', as I'm worried about you, young lady,' he said, concern in his eyes as he opened the carriage door. I remained standing where I was as I stared back at him.

'Help me up next to you, and I'll tell you about it on the way.' He grinned at me, then shut the door and boosted me up onto the front bench so I could cry on his shoulder.

We arrived at The Savoy, and I climbed down by myself, so Mr Miller didn't have to get down. 'Now, chin up. Things will get better, I promise,' he said kindly.

'Thank you for being such a good listener. You're the best,' I told him with a smile, which he shyly returned.

'I will collect you at nine o'clock if that suits you?' he asked, his face becoming serious as if suddenly remembering his job and supposed social position.

'Yes, that would be wonderful and thank you for everything you are doing for me. I really appreciate it.' I stepped away from the carriage and waved, smiling as he waved back.

'Well, thank you, too, my dear girl. It's nice to be appreciated. You have a lovely night with your friends, and I will see you later.'

As he trotted off, I strode toward the entrance and entered the reception. It was just as grand as The Delmont and just as awe-inspiring, with its elegant entry and modern decor. I walked up to the front desk and waited for someone to notice me, as I had no idea where Catherine would be. Soon, a young man approached me from behind the counter and raised his eyebrows inquiringly.

'Hello, I'm Miss Abigail Delmont. I am here to see Miss Catherine Montague.' I ran my hand over the countertop as I waited for him to respond.

'Just one moment, Miss Delmont. I will send word that you have arrived. Please take a seat until Miss Montague comes down to greet you.' He directed me to a lounge, pointing his finger before dismissing me with a wave of his hand. I obeyed him and made my way over to a plush lounge that looked extraordinarily comfortable and sat down, wishing they had the same lounge at The Delmont. It relieved me I didn't look out of place here, thanks to my new pale-green dress and matching hat, even though I didn't feel like I belonged. I thought I would never be as good or keep up the façade of being a well-bred lady. I would just have to do it my way and be myself. I noticed Catherine hurrying through the reception at great speed with a wide grin on her face.

'Oh, I didn't think you would come.' She smiled down at me before reaching out for my hand. 'Not that I thought you would lie to me, it was just that ...' Her voice trailed off as she blushed, although the smile remained and her joy palpable.

'Oh, don't worry about it, Catherine. I know what you mean. Do you mind if we take the stairs?' I asked, my stomach clenching. She nodded mindlessly before leading me by the hand to the grand staircase. I followed her up the two flights of stairs as she chattered nonstop about her day and how she had hoped so much I would come tonight. Finally, we arrived at their suite, and Catherine opened the door to a large room. My eyes widened as I stepped inside to find their suite was sophisticated and luxurious and quite different from The Delmont but equal in its extravagance. William was sitting in a leather wing chair near the window, barely taking notice of my presence. His face suddenly changed as he looked at me for what felt like an eternity, and familiarity crossed his face. He rose to his feet, his eyes wide as he came towards me, then took my hand in his.

'You look so different, Miss Delmont. It's like you were Cinderella yesterday, and today you are a princess. I mean, you can't blame me for my behaviour, given the way you were dressed, can you?' He stared into my eyes as I snatched my hand away from his.

'Well, actually, yes, William. I do blame you. No one should be treated as inferior, no matter what they wear or how much money they have. Even the way you look at me tonight differs completely from the way you looked at me on the train.'

'Should we get ready for dinner?' Catherine chimed in, attempting to silence me.

'I'm ready. Whenever you want to leave, we can.' William continued to gaze at me, an odd look on his face as I felt fury rise in me.

'Catherine, I'm sorry, but I refuse to eat if William is there.' I waited silently for her response, turning away from William to stare out the window at the darkening sky. Catherine looked blankly at each of us, her face starting to flush. I could see she was trying to muster the courage to say something; however, the silence became unbearable.

'I am happy to dine alone with you, Abigail,' she said finally, directing a withering look at her brother. He stared back, appearing confused, not understanding for a moment how offensive he had been. With that, Catherine led me to the door and ushered me down to the hotel restaurant, leaving him standing in the room open-mouthed.

We sat at a lovely table next to a large window that overlooked an intricate garden that, even in winter, was immaculate and beautiful. 'At least we can talk properly without William here,' Catherine remarked, smiling shyly. 'How funny it was when he saw you, with his eyes bulging like he couldn't believe you were the same person.

What an absolute idiot he is. It's so embarrassing to have him as a brother.' She giggled softly as I took a deep breath. I knew I could open up to her and tell her the truth about myself.

I confided in her of my childhood, what had occurred since that wooden box arrived, and the events of the day. She sat back in her chair, thinking hard.

'Well, although it is all a bit mysterious, it's good fortune on your behalf. The best part is we will not live far from each other.' She leaned over and hugged me tightly, her excitement clear. 'It's as though it was meant to be, Abigail. Meeting on the train and getting along so well right from the start, and now the both of us moving to the same country is just pure luck. I mean, yesterday morning when we boarded that train, who could have guessed that this would happen?'

'I know. I don't believe in coincidences. We met for a reason, and that is to become best friends and sisters,' I told her sincerely, as that was how I felt about her. She squeezed my hand across the table in acknowledgement.

'I promise, as sisters, I will tell not a soul of your plight before I met you, and that includes William, who would only use it to his advantage and make fun of you.' I smiled, grateful for her loyalty, as she shifted in her seat, then leaned back and made herself comfortable. 'Do you realise now you can become whoever you choose to be and have all the freedom you like? No one knows you in Australia, and you can be anyone, especially if you have lots of money and no parents to boss you around,' she said wistfully.

I could see she was thinking about herself and how trapped she felt living with her family. She couldn't wait until she was an adult to be free to do as she chose. She had an adventurous spirit like me, and I knew that was part of the reason we felt drawn to each other. A big part was the golden glow and how, for some unexplained reason, I somehow felt connected to those who had it. I thought about what

Catherine had just said, and she was right. I did not have to conform, and I could be the person I had always dreamed of becoming once I no longer had to live under someone else's authority. I did not have to rely on anyone, and I could follow my own path in life, although I knew I was likely naïve due to my limited life experience. I confided everything in Catherine, trusting her absolutely with my darkest secrets, and she did the same and sadly told me how I was her first real friend. She had never been allowed to go to school, so she had never had the chance to mix with other children, unlike me, who had been surrounded by them every minute of my life.

We talked and talked from our hearts for hours. I hadn't felt the joy of being this close to another person my age since Polly. We had a wonderful dinner and stayed late until the restaurant closed when we were politely asked to leave, starting the night as friends and parting as sisters with an indescribable connection.

I lay staring at the ceiling, tucked up all snug and secure in the softest bed in the world, as I thought of how marvellous it was you could meet someone and know right away your souls would always be connected, that you would be friends forever. In Catherine, I found a true sister, and it made the most sense to me this was what the golden glow meant. I had a future, and for now, that would be in Australia. I could always return here if I hated it or if things did not work out, even though I had nothing here apart from Sister Josephine. I slowly descended into sleep, my mind filled with images of a ship, green shoes, and a man with curly black hair.

J L MARTIN

Chapter Seven

I SAT MOTIONLESS IN Sister Monica's office, feeling nauseous as she gave me a stern lecture about going to London, chastising me harshly over the poor choices I had continued to make since I could walk. She reprimanded me over and over for the mess the entire situation had turned out to be, sneering at me, shouting how I was a disobedient, wilful girl who had the devil's own soul. Then, there was a knock at the door; however, she ignored it and continued to berate me, glaring hatefully at me the entire time. There was another knock, only this time slightly louder. She acted as if she could not hear the banging, when it was all I could focus on. The knocking continued, becoming louder and longer until her harsh words faded into the background, and I woke up with a start, feeling disorientated and wondering why I would dream of that wicked woman.

I hurried out of bed and through to the entrance of the suite, opening the door to see Mr Miller standing in the hallway, trying to catch his breath.

'Hello, Miss Delmont. Mr Malcolm would like to see you immediately,' he panted, slowly regaining control of his breathing. He was sweating profusely, and I guessed he had avoided the elevator and taken the stairs, my mouth twitching in amusement as he turned and looked down the hallway at a guest who was being escorted to his room by the bellboy. 'I will meet you downstairs at the carriage, Missy.' He tipped his hat politely before turning and making his way back down the hallway towards the stairs, still panting softly.

I stared after him, amused, before gently closing my door and making my way to my wardrobe. I took out my new orange dress, excited to put it on for the first time. It was one of my favourites so far. There was another knock at the door, and I sighed, placing the dress on the bed before crossing the room and returning to the front door to open it again. The maid, surrounded by a beautiful golden glow — a determined woman who had attended to me several times — stood patiently in the hallway, waiting for me to invite her in.

'The man says you need a maid to help you dress, Mistress?'

'Yes, I do.' I waved her in before returning to my bedchambers, bending down to smooth the fabric of my dress as it lay across the elaborate quilt. She entered the room, shut the door, and came to my side, assisting me in slipping out of my dressing gown and nightgown. My new, silky bloomers I had purchased from Madame Felicity felt soft against my skin as I stood before her, half-naked, feeling self-conscious.

'My name is Bessie, and I am here to help you in any way I can,' she said. 'Here is your corset, Mistress.' As she took the intimidating garment from the drawer and held it up in her hands, I could not take my eyes from her — the golden aura surrounding her body was truly beautiful. I had felt since our first encounter I knew her, but had no memory of where we had met.

'Thank you,' I managed to say, although my throat was tight.

'Now, turn yourself around. Not that you need the corset, you are already so tiny — but not at the front.' She looked up at my face and grinned. 'You will make some man a very happy husband one day. Here, let me put it on you.' She promptly turned me around next to the bed, instructing me to hold on to the bedpost. With that, I was bound, trussed, and dressed in minutes.

'Thank you, Bessie. You are excellent at your job, even though I didn't know what that job was until the other day.' I giggled, and she smiled at me.

'I'm not qualified to be a ladies' maid, Mistress; however, I do help when times are busy. If all the so-called ladies I looked after were as lovely as you, I would enjoy my job a lot more than I do,' she said with a wink.

I liked her; she was friendly and straightforward, something I adored in others. Possessing a lovely face with big brown eyes and curly brown hair, I found her interesting, and somehow felt comforted in her presence. She was short and stocky; however, this did not hinder her in her job, as she had been quick as a flash getting me ready this morning. We walked side by side to the front door, and I thanked her before she departed; then shut the door behind me and hiked down the unending flights of stairs, through the reception, and out onto the street, where Mr Miller was waiting for me, dozing in his seat.

I quietly approached the carriage, opened the door, and helped myself up, sitting back to catch my breath. I suddenly felt movement at the front of the carriage, and it took a few moments, as I had expected it would, for him to find his bearings.

'Now, you can't be doing that again, Missy. People will think I'm not a proper coachman and will report me to Mr Malcolm,' he called out loudly from above. Given he had been in a deep sleep when I had approached the carriage, I had just taken matters into my own hands and climbed in myself, not wanting to disturb him.

'All right, Mr Miller, I promise I will wake you up next time,' I called out the window, smiling to myself. His silence spoke loudly of his consternation, and I continued to smile as we headed to Mr Malcolm's office, clip-clopping briskly along the cobblestone streets.

As I gazed out the window, fascinated by all the unfamiliar sights and sounds surrounding me, I noticed a large, grey building with people milling around out front, and I wondered what it was. I would have to find somewhere in London that had books to buy. Books that explained the city's history and where everything was located, along with more books, including one that would tell me the average cost of a dress, a blanket, and the day-to-day items I needed to purchase. I was feeling so lost and dumb in a world so big and knowledgeable.

We arrived at the office, and the horses came to a halt. Mr Miller called out from his seat up front, 'Now, don't you move a muscle, Missy, I'm coming down to get you. Not one muscle — I mean it. In fact, don't even breathe until I get there.' I heard him land heavily on his feet, then waited with a smile for him to open my door. I quickly thanked him for helping me disembark. His eyes twinkled as he winked mischievously. 'You're very welcome, Missy, but don't try pulling a swifty on me again.' I smiled and turned to walk up the office steps, giving him a wave before opening the door, the little bell above the door chiming as I entered.

'Hi, love, are you back again?' Miss Delaware smiled from across the room.

'Good morning, Miss Delaware. How are you? Yes, Mr Malcolm has requested to see me.' I tried to smooth my hair as I smiled at Mr Malcolm's secretary.

'I feel like I've been shagged backwards through a hedge. I'm so tired, but I'll get through the day. Thank you for askin', you kind girl. I'll take you through to Mr Malcolm.' I burst out laughing at her imagery as I waited for her to come out from behind her desk. She walked ahead of me and knocked on the door a few times in quick succession, not unlike during my dream this morning.

'Come in,' a muffled voice called out. She ushered me inside before closing the door, her footsteps becoming softer as she returned to her desk. Mr Malcolm, who was standing at his bookshelves looking for something, motioned me to sit. I lowered myself into the comfortable leather chair opposite him and smiled politely when he sat down.

'How are you today, Miss Delmont? Are you having a pleasant time in London?' he enquired courteously, standing again and placing a large book back on the shelf before returning to his seat and leaning back, making himself comfortable.

It was still sinking in that I was not homeless and living on the street and actually had a house — my first proper home — waiting for me in Australia.

'I am fine, thank you. I would like to express my gratitude for the new clothes you organised and paid for.'

'There is no need to thank me, as you have paid for it from your own funds.' He leaned back in his chair, his face softening as he stared at me. 'The reason I called you in is I wanted to talk more about how you are feeling after our discussions yesterday. I know it must have come as an enormous shock to you to hear you have inherited a great deal of money, but to have all these constraints placed on you must have also had an impact. So I thought today could be about answering any questions you may have,' he said, kindness in his voice.

This was only the second time we had met; however, I found I liked him more and more. He was professional but treated me as a person, and I found him caring and considerate. I had many questions running around in my head, but I did not know what to ask first. I worried they would sound stupid once spoken aloud.

'When you met my mother, did she look like me?' I asked, tears immediately stinging my eyes. I quickly pulled myself together, refusing to cry in front of a stranger.

'A little; however, nowhere near as much as you resemble your great-aunt,' he replied patiently. 'I would say you are so similar that if you could find a portrait of her at your age, I wouldn't be surprised if you are identical. I think you must favour your father's side of the family in appearance. Your features resemble Isabelle Delmont's very closely, and you have her eyes.' I could see he somehow recognised I needed to know as much as possible before making any decisions concerning my parents or siblings in the future.

'Did my mother say whether she ever wanted to find me when I was grown or even mention me at all?' My throat had closed while my hands trembled, finding I could no longer stem the tears that flowed freely down my cheeks.

'I'm sorry, no. I got the impression she was moving forward with her life, that she had put the situation behind her.' He handed me a clean handkerchief across the desk, deep sympathy in his eyes.

'So, by the situation, you mean me?' I replied through my soft sobs. I did not understand why she had thrown me away like that without even trying to love me. She obviously had no feelings for me at all. She would have known she had fifteen years to claim me or even come and see me, and once I left the orphanage, there would be no record of where to find me. I could not believe a mother, even one such as she, would forget the age of a child she had given birth to, her inactions clearly proving she did not intend to have any contact with me then or in the future once I was free of the orphanage. I continued to wipe away my tears that refused to stop flowing.

'Yes, and I'm so sorry, child. She was young, and if I happen a guess, she loved you but wasn't mature enough or had the economic security to keep you,' he mumbled, trying to soften the blow and make me feel better. I wiped my face and decided I would not shed another tear over either of my biological parents, as I doubted they had given me much thought over the years. Instead of holding onto a dream of belonging to a proper family, I would let it go and focus on creating a life for myself without them. I pulled myself together and changed the subject.

'What do you know about this Isabelle?' I enquired, given she was the one with whom he had spoken in-depth.

'Yes, Lady Isabelle.' He sighed, relaxing back in his chair while making a steeple with his fingers as he spoke. 'She was a lovely woman. Kind and generous, and very caring, despite what you must think of her leaving you in that orphanage for all this time. Before you were born, she came to me to complete her last Will and Testament, as you know. She named the unborn child of Mary Campbell and Christopher Howard in the Will, giving instructions for us to contact you on your fifteenth birthday, with Emiliani House listed as your place of residence. At no time did I think you were in an orphanage, as I would have sent money for your care at the very least, and I would have attempted to find a family to bring you up. Unfortunately, I was not given the opportunity for reasons I do not quite understand. I thought it was a grand residence that brought up girls from wealthy families to be young ladies, although I found it strange when I only recently discovered nuns ran the place. I never thought to question your aunt or even your mother when I met her. No, things would have been very different for you if I had known,' he said sympathetically, sadness in his eyes. I smiled and reassured him my life had not been all bad, to which he smiled back with apparent fondness.

'How do I get money in Australia if I can't access this trust fund?' I asked as the thought suddenly occurred to me.

'An excellent question, young lady.' He straightened up and slipped on his spectacles before ruffling through some paperwork, finding the document he was seeking and scanning it closely. 'You have several businesses in Melbourne and Geelong that generate a substantial income for you. Lady Isabelle spent many years in Australia building her wealth through property and a shipping company, I believe, or so the rumour goes. That is all I know, and, like I said yesterday, I am telling you the information as it was relayed to me directly. The way the instructions were written, your great-aunt appears to have split her wishes into two parts, providing me with only enough knowledge to get you to Australia and manage your affairs in England. After that, I am as uncertain as you are as to what will come next. I would love for you to write and inform me of the details, if you find the time, just to satisfy an old man's curiosity.' He stopped to shuffle some papers before continuing. 'Your aunt was an elderly woman when I met her,' he went on. 'She was quite — how would you say it? — eccentric. A striking woman with an air of authority about her who came across as someone not to be trifled with. She left me instructions to sell her estates and any property she owned in England and Scotland upon her death and place all monies into a trust fund for you. There were no stipulations to send money to your place of residence, which I greatly regret now, and I wish I had discussed a monthly allowance for you; however, I cannot change the past. We transferred any money she had in the bank into the trust fund after her death. I do not know how your great-aunt made her fortune here in England and never asked her, but a fortune it is. I suspect it is all family money, but again, it is only a guess. I know very little about her personally, as I only ever met her once,' he explained thoughtfully as a memory crossed his face. 'There were future requests made at the time, with The Delmont Hotel to be built according to plans she had designed herself, on a large piece of land she owned in London. All the profits will feed money into your trust fund, which will become even more substantial now the London hotel is operational. She also left you properties on several continents; however, I do not know what or where they are. That is up for discussion with your Australian solicitor, who has all the details. I will remain your barrister in England, handling all business matters and keeping a protective eye on your trust fund. We take two pounds a week to cover our expenses in relation to overseeing your fund. It may seem like a large amount of money; however, with the amount of time and work spent on keeping everything in order, it justifies our fees; of that, I give you my word. The fee was agreed upon by the late Lady Isabelle Delmont before her death.' He looked a little uncomfortable as he gazed across at me to ascertain my reaction. I thought two pounds must be a large amount of money, as he was looking somewhat abashed. If I were reading him right, his firm must work day and night on the trust fund, with several people assigned solely to manage my fund for it to cost that much. As far as I was concerned, it was okay if it worked and kept them honest in their dealings with me. I nodded my head in response and agreed I was happy for the same arrangement to continue.

'If I want to send money to Emiliani House each year, could you do that for me?' I asked, feeling nervous and as if I were asking for charity for myself.

'Yes. I can and will be happy to do so,' he replied, a broad smile breaking out on his face. I had been eyeing him a little anxiously, but I was starting to trust him.

'I'm going to embarrass myself now since I don't know the value of money, and I need your help to decide how much to send each year to them. I want enough money given to the orphanage to buy the children new beds, blankets, and quilts. Enough so they can hire a new cook who will make smooth, sweet porridge — meals the children can eat until their stomachs are full; and dessert every night so these children know they are not second-class citizens. I want them to have two pairs of shoes and stay if they choose until they are eighteen, and they must be guaranteed employment before they are forced to leave. I want new workers to help run the place alongside the Sisters. The children should be able to spend more time in lessons and play. There are too many things to list right now that I want for Emiliani House.' I stopped to catch my breath. I felt I was ordering him around and behaving as if I were better than him.

'I can imagine some of the other things you would want them to have. I think one thousand pounds per year would not be objectionable. If you think it would help, maybe two-thousand pounds for the first year and one-thousand pounds every year after that?' He noticed the confusion on my face and smiled gently. 'What it means is that they will have all those things you mentioned and more. Not even half that money would be spent annually on what you outlined they require. The rest of the money will buy all the extras, like coal for the fires to keep them burning all winter in every room of the house, extra money for food, and many other things they couldn't afford before, along with restoration of the building. Is there anything else you wish to talk about before you leave?' He seemed eager to end our meeting, indicating he had other plans for the day, our discussion coming to an abrupt end with a wave of his hand.

'No, thank you. I appreciate all you have done for me, and please call me Abigail,' I replied politely, rising to my feet and smoothing my skirts.

'Oh, one more thing, Miss... I mean Abigail. I wanted to confirm you are coming to dinner tonight at my home. I think it is important you meet my son Richard, given he will be your chaperone.' I nodded, thanking him before striding out of the office and onto the street, feeling as if I were floating on air.

I returned to my suite and took off my new shoes. They made me slightly taller than I would have liked, and the idea I would look abnormal and be the size of a man still stung, causing the blood to rise to my face at the memory of Mr Higgingbottom. These shoes also pinched my feet, and it relieved me to get them off.

I relaxed on the lounge and rubbed each foot gently, easing the deep ache as best I could. Unfortunately, it looked like I was getting a blister on my small left toe, which irritated me. I planned to do a lot of walking in the next six weeks and needed shoes that wouldn't leave my feet covered in sores and blisters.

Catherine would arrive soon to take luncheon in my suite, which I was looking forward to, and knew she would not mind if I left my shoes off during her visit. I felt so comfortable with her, as if I had known her for years, and we had only met twice. It was strange. I had met four people in my life who had that golden glow, that beautiful aura that radiated from their bodies as a mesmerising, transparently golden light surrounding them. It was not just about how the aura looked, but its magnetic quality — I was drawn to the people with it, and they seemed drawn instantly to me, my new ladies' maid surprising me the most. I wondered how often I would see it again in the future with those crossing my path.

Now I was aware of this pattern, I wondered if my future husband would have that glow. Of course, it would only make sense if it meant what I thought it did, but whatever it was, I now knew it was a good thing, not something to be ashamed of or frightened about, or only talked about in hushed tones with the likes of Sister Josephine. Thinking of her reminded me of my promise to write, so I took some stationery from a nightstand drawer and began penning a letter.

I sat at the table with the hotel notepaper and outlined all my news, from the train trip to the fact I was travelling to Australia to what it was like in London. I knew it would gladden her heart and shut Sister Monica up to hear everything was going in my favour. If I sent it today, I might be lucky to receive a letter back from her before I departed, given I missed her so much already.

I slipped the letter into the envelope and then began writing a list for Mr Malcolm of all the things I wanted him to purchase for the children. I made a special note that there was to be a strict condition that if Emiliani House accepted the money, the current cook had to be retired, and someone who showed skill in the art of cooking hired to replace the cantankerous old goat. There was no point in supplying good food to the orphanage, and lots of it, if it would be turned into something horrendous by a cook who had to be the worst in Scotland. I felt purely happy for the first time in my life — I was making a difference to so many little lives and taking the load and worry off the Sisters so they could comfortably live and focus their attention on the most important thing in their care, the children.

I stipulated they had to open the rooms in the building that had been closed because of their dilapidated condition, have them repaired and put into use as classrooms, smaller dormitories, and double bedrooms for older children over the age of twelve.

Emiliani House was a decrepit building after years of having no funds for its upkeep. Mr Malcolm could now hire labourers to restore it to its former glory, and new maids and kitchen staff could be employed. I thought about the children Emiliani House was forced to reject due to having no beds, the poor things sent to the workhouse. Although the orphanage was not the most nurturing place to grow up, I knew they always did their best, except for the few evil Sisters who hated children and put no effort into disguising their vile souls.

I pondered whether I should put in a stipulation to have certain Sisters removed to minimise the cruelty at the orphanage. If it made things better for the children, was it wrong to use the power of money to issue direct orders to people over whom I had no actual control? Finally, I decided to go ahead as I would be unable to sleep at night, knowing some of the Sisters were cruel to the children in their care. I dipped my quill in its pot of ink before writing it down and listing further conditions they were required to abide by over the next year for the money to be paid annually.

My thoughts again turned to Mr Malcolm. He seemed to show genuine concern for the children and the orphanage itself. I believed he would be the perfect person to oversee such an extensive project, monitor the institution financially, and make sure the funds were used to benefit the children. If he agreed, I would give him new instructions for changes each year, based on his recommendations. As an enticement, I would add another two pounds per month to his fee. I smiled to myself in satisfaction as I continued to write.

There was a knock on the door, causing me to jump as I quickly placed my notes for Mr Malcolm in a drawer with the letter for Sister Josephine. I rushed to the door and opened it wide to find Catherine standing before me, smiling brightly. We embraced, and I asked her how she found my room.

'Well, I remembered you said you were staying in the master suite, and I thought if I was running this business and the owner came to stay, where would I accommodate them? Then it came to me that they would put you on the top floor, so I took that beastly contraption up, and the elevator operator pointed out your room. I feel positively bad in a good way.' She laughed, her face lighting up mischievously.

'Come in.' I grabbed her hand and pulled her into the sitting room. 'I have ordered food. I don't know what we're getting, but I told them I wanted the best things on the menu and a selection of delicious desserts. I felt like I was ordering them about, but I made sure I said thank you.' She burst into giggles, her body shaking as she laughed at me.

'Oh Abigail, you are so sweet. That is their job, and if you did not ask them to do things, they would not be employed and could not feed their families. The fact you are so nice to them is a change from most of the snobs they have to deal with daily, so I'm sure they appreciate how kind you are and won't spit in our food.' I laughed a little nervously as she grinned wickedly.

'Do you honestly believe they would do that to guests they don't like?'

'Who knows? But I would if I were treated the way I see some servants get treated, especially when they work in private homes. If I had to go into service, I would much rather work at a large hotel like this. You know you can give the maids a tip when they do something nice for you?' She put her feet up and lay back, relaxing on the soft lounge.

'What's a tip?' It surprised me just how much I had to learn.

'Money, silly. Go today and get shillings so you can give them one each time they help you.' I smiled. Without Catherine or Mr Malcolm to guide me, I had no idea what I was meant to do or how I was supposed to behave. I could use my money to help people, starting with the orphanage and now the servants at the hotel.

I had been thinking about funding an orphanage in Australia in the future if I had enough money, as I did not know just how much I was to inherit. I would have to check with the Geelong solicitor if I had the funds to go through with something like that. There were so many conditions from my great-aunt, making my life go in directions that frightened me, all of which I had no say or control. Although having access to money was enjoyable and opened doors, I realised it did not shelter one from suffering.

'I heard your hotel has a swimming pool on the roof. Is that true?' Catherine startled me, bringing me back to the present.

'I don't know. I haven't asked anyone.'

'Well, let's get them to take us on a tour. It is the perfect opportunity to see what you actually own. Come on, Miss Delmont of The Hotel Delmont in London,' she said, grabbing my hand firmly and dragging me barefoot from my room, down the stairs and into the grand reception room. We approached the marble counter, where I was acutely aware of other guests and hotel staff staring at my bare feet.

'Excuse me. Would someone help the owner of the hotel, please?' she asked in her clipped, upper-class voice with her dainty little nose pointed up in the air. Three people rushed toward us.

'Can we help you, Miss Delmont?' a tall man enquired, who arrived at the counter within moments.

'Well ....' I was mortified and unable to speak, my face burning and the urge to run strong.

'Yes. Miss Delmont would like a tour of the hotel.'

'We would be delighted. Absolutely delighted. This is Mr Dorset, our manager. He will take you around, and if you have any questions, don't hesitate to ask.' A short, balding, obese man I assumed was Mr Dorset emerged from behind the desk, not the handsome, young man who had also tried to help me I was secretly hoping was Mr Dorset. He stood in front of us, his chest puffed out proudly. All the employees of the hotel were looking at him admiringly, which he seemed to enjoy. I just wanted it over because now we had everyone's eyes on us, and unlike Catherine, I hated being the centre of attention.

'Come with me, ladies. Now, as you already know, this is the reception, the entrance to the hotel, so it must look its best. The hotel itself was built from stone, while the marble is only the finest imported from Ireland at substantial cost. Astounding, isn't it?' I looked at the creamy texture of the marble and the glistening streaks of red, gold and silver that ran through it, touching it gently with my fingers. It was one of the most beautiful things I had ever seen, the way it was smoothed into columns and shaped around the front desk, only adding to the luxury of the place. 'The Delmont was finished six months ago and is the largest hotel in London, or, to be more precise, in England, boasting more than a hundred rooms, not including our master suites. It has electric lighting and hot-and-cold running water. Since opening, we have been swamped with guests, with many a night having a full house,' he told us, sounding so proud it was as if he himself owned the hotel and had built it with his own hand.

As we trudged up the stairs, I could hear him start to wheeze. I knew he wanted to take the elevator, but word had already spread about my dislike for the Otis. We stopped on the fourth floor for him to catch his breath as Catherine and I exchanged glances. Then, to buy himself time, he took out his keys and let us into one of the rooms.

'This is our standard room. As you can see, there is a large double bed with luxurious bedding, a small sitting room, and a bathroom. The views are better the higher up you go.' His breathing was relatively normal now.

I looked out and could just see over the tops of other buildings. In the distance, I noted another large park and decided I would go there when I had the time. We walked to the top floor, where there was indeed a swimming pool. There was a small, round, bathtub-like pool next to the larger pool that looked highly enticing. Mr Dorset appeared as if he would have a conniption, so we had left him leaning against the wall gasping for air and went to have a look at the facility, which was thankfully empty of guests.

I bent down and placed my hand in the deep, round tub and found the water was hot — not an uncomfortable heat, but a pleasant warmness that would encompass you like a hug. However, the water in the larger pool was lukewarm, and I decided I had to buy bathing garments tomorrow to experience what it was like to go in a swimming pool for the first time.

Mr Dorset had left without saying goodbye, and we made our way back to my suite, making ourselves comfortable on the lounge as we gossiped.

Catherine confided that once she arrived in Melbourne, she had every intention of becoming a designer like her father and would not be pressured into marrying into the most eligible family. It surprised me when she said family, not man. She explained each upper-class family had to meet with another's approval, as they saw marriage as the formation of one large, extended family. It was rarely about how the couple felt towards each other. What was most important

114

was how the families would get along and how they would use the union to better their social status and increase their assets and social standing. I decided I did not want to be a member of high society for any reason.

A polite knock on the door interrupted our conversation. Shortly after that, our lunch was laid out on the kitchen table by the maids. I nodded my head and made some agreeable noises as Catherine chatted about her life plans while thinking about how innocent she was. I was aware people in her social circle did not take young women who wanted to work outside of the home seriously and often openly ridiculed them. I believed she would have a rude shock when she arrived in Australia, as even someone as naïve as I knew women of Catherine's station did not seek employment. Instead, they married wealthy men who were seen to be good husbands and upstanding members of society.

Catherine and I moved over to the little table to eat our lunch. They had brought us mouth-watering brisket that had been slow-roasted until it was falling apart and boiled vegetables covered in a cheese sauce. We had both begun eating, and I had just commented on how delicious the meal was when there was another knock on the door.

'Oh, shite,' I said crossly, slamming my knife and fork on the table as I stood up. Catherine looked shocked at my cursing, but I ignored it. When I opened the door, I found William standing outside, his face white as a ghost. 'Are you all right, William? You look terrible.' I swung the door wide for him.

'I need to see my sister — ah, there you are. Have you seen Beatrice?' He seemed anxious and extremely worried, pacing back and forth while running his hands through his blonde hair.

'No, why? What happened?' Catherine appeared frightened, placing her cutlery down gently before rising to her feet. William

115

continued to pace up and down in the sitting room, trying to calm himself.

'The new governess was supposed to be watching her. When I came back, Beatrice was nowhere to be found, and that useless woman was asleep on the lounge, so I told her she was fired and came straight here.' He tugged his short, blonde hair frantically with both hands, appearing intent on ripping it from his scalp. Shocked, I looked across at Catherine, who shook her head in disbelief.

'No, we haven't seen her.' Her voice was barely audible as the colour drained from her face.

I felt sick to my stomach, as she was only ten, and London was a big city that was not safe for a child to be roaming about in alone. Catherine began to shake and started to sob. William placed his hand on her shoulder, his face softening.

'It will be all right, Catherine. I just know it will. I'll go now and talk to the police and then start looking for her myself.' William kissed her on the top of the head before leaving without another word. Catherine remained with me, and I did everything I could to comfort her, knowing in my heart nothing would help until we found Beatrice.

Chapter Eight

CATHERINE CONTINUED TO CRY as she sat on the lounge, her body shaking. I moved closer and embraced her, speaking in soothing tones. After some time, she managed to calm herself, and I handed her a handkerchief to wipe her face. When I suggested she finish her meal, she declined, and I asked her if she would be offended if I sat and finished mine, as my stomach was rumbling.

'No, of course not. There is nothing we can do other than wait.' She stared out the window, unblinking and in despair, while tears occasionally ran down her face, which she tried to hide. I finished quickly, took our drinks over, and sat close to her.

'Is there anything I can do?' I asked, hugging her while feeling helpless.

'No, all we can do is sit here and be the last ones to know anything.' She burst into tears again as I realised I was only making things worse. No matter what I said, it seemed to set the poor thing off into more uncontrollable crying. I felt sorry for her and was certainly deeply concerned for Beatrice's well-being, but the desserts were calling to me now, and I was not doing much good with my mouth empty and blabbing ineffectually.

Eight sweet delicacies beckoned me from a silver tray. Since leaving the orphanage, I had discovered proper food, and I had a strong desire to scoff all eight first — then hug Catherine afterwards. I knew I was a terrible friend, but I couldn't help myself.

'Well, as you said, there is nothing we can do right now, so come over here, Catherine.'

I led her over to the table and placed the desserts in front of her. She chose what looked like a strawberry cake with thick cream in the middle and a swirl of icing on top. I selected a creamy custard that tasted of cinnamon with tiny, crunchy lumps of sugar throughout, which was pure bliss. I thought about all the new things I was experiencing, good and bad, which brought my thoughts back to Beatrice. I sat next to Catherine and tried to comfort her while we waited for news as she began crying again.

'It's all my fault; I should have been there with her,' she sobbed. 'But I was being selfish, wanting to spend time away from her, as she can be very irritating, and I so wanted to have a fun afternoon with you without her around to annoy us. I should have brought her with me, as I didn't trust that Nanny, but I ignored my suspicions.' I rubbed her back while she sat forward and sobbed harder.

There was a sharp knock before the door swung open, and William hurried in, appearing upset and flustered.

'They have sent the local police out looking and, I hope you don't mind, Abigail, but I left this address as a way for them to contact me with any information,' he said curtly, and I nodded.

'Yes, of course, that's fine. Would you like some tea when the maid comes back?' I asked him as gently as I could.

'Thank you, that would be nice.' He sighed deeply before sitting down next to his sister. We waited in silence, with no one knowing what to say or do, so we just sat. To occupy myself, I looked out the window and traced and retraced with my eyes the outline of the buildings below while I watched the tiny figures of people I didn't know walk the streets.

Time elapsed, with us saying only the briefest things to each other, each of us lost in our own thoughts. Finally, the maid came and left quickly to get our tea when she saw how distressed Catherine was, even though she didn't know what was wrong.

She returned shortly with another tray of refreshments and placed them on the low table in front of us. The three of us took tea silently, all worried sick about what might have happened to Beatrice. Then, after what seemed an eternity, there was a knock at the door. William jumped up and admitted two police officers who looked extremely serious.

'I'm sorry we are here under these circumstances, but we have found your sister,' the older officer stated without emotion. 'She is alive but at the hospital receiving treatment. It seems Beatrice wandered away from the hotel and went to nearby Coventry Park, where she was playing alone. An unknown man snatched her and hurt her, but she somehow managed to escape and was found fleeing the park by the police. Because of her hysterical state and some cuts and scrapes, she was taken to the hospital by ambulance. If you would like to see her, we can take you there now. It's not far.'

He sounded sympathetic, and his face had softened. William approached him, speaking quietly while Catherine and I rose to our feet, holding each other for support. I slipped my shoes back on, grabbed my coat, and followed them downstairs to the carriage.

We arrived at the hospital within minutes, although it seemed to take forever. I noticed it was an imposing building as we rushed through the entrance and into a very efficient-looking waiting room. I had never been to a hospital before, so I didn't know the correct names or even what some things were as I looked around. There was a nurse in a little office and people with a number of ailments waiting to be attended to by a doctor. William quietly enquired about Beatrice.

'Yes, she is on the first floor. Head up the stairs, and you will find someone there who can help you,' the young nurse advised him with a polite smile. We did as we were told and were led to a bed with curtained screens around it. I followed Catherine and William as they rushed to her side and kissed her, holding her tightly; however, she did not utter a word or show any sign she recognised them. They asked her several questions, but she did not respond, only laying motionless and looking back at us, her face void of emotion.

'Who's responsible for Beatrice Montague?' a doctor asked as he walked in and eyed each of us with suspicion.

'I am,' William replied. He stood up from the bedside, took a deep breath, and followed the doctor into the hallway. Catherine and I spoke softly to Beatrice as she lay there while Catherine gently stroked her head, murmuring sweetly in her ear. After several minutes had passed, William returned, appearing shaken. He approached the chair next to Beatrice's bed and sat down heavily.

'I cannot talk about it,' he murmured to himself, shivering as he wiped away a solitary tear that trickled down his cheek. The blood had drained from his face, and he swayed slightly, as if he was about to faint. I quickly wrapped a blanket around his shoulders and stepped away, not wanting to upset him further. He appeared to be in a state of shock; whatever the doctor had said must have been serious. We sat with Beatrice, holding her hand until dark, until she finally drifted off. No sooner had she fallen asleep, she began sweating and thrashing about. Within moments, she woke up, her screams piercing my ears and echoing out into the hall. Catherine continued to hold her, trying everything she could think of to comfort her but failing miserably.

'There, there, my precious sister, you are safe now. We're here,' she whispered soothingly, trying to calm her. William called out to the doctor, who promptly entered the room and advised us to go once he administered chloral hydrate, explaining it would help her sleep through the night. We stayed with her until the drug took effect, and she appeared groggy. We kissed her good night, remaining by her side, and within minutes, she was in a deep sleep. We slowly made our way downstairs, passing many sick and injured patients who lay on beds waiting to be examined and treated. When we arrived outside, we found Mr Miller waiting patiently atop his carriage, as I had sent word from the hospital to Mr Malcolm advising him of the situation.

'Is everything all right, Missy?'

'Yes, thank you. Everything is fine now, Mr Miller,' I replied, summoning a false smile to my lips. Unfortunately, I didn't feel like smiling, and if what I suspected had happened to Beatrice were true, she would have many more sleepless nights ahead of her. 'Can we please take my friends to The Savoy, Mr Miller?'

'Yes, we can, only because you asked so nicely,' he teased, then laughed aloud. We climbed into the carriage, making ourselves comfortable in the awkward silence, no one willing to speak first.

'I think something terrible has happened to her.' I felt awful saying it, but I felt someone had to.

'Like what?' William asked defensively, narrowing his gaze as he crossed his arms against his chest.

'I think she has been raped. She appears extremely traumatised, given they initially said she was only frightened by the man and he was seen by someone taking her into the bushes.' I felt terrible for putting words to what was such a private matter for them.

'Don't you ever say that again, do you hear me?' William shouted, turning his nose up in disgust before looking away. I nodded my head, shocked at his response, before sitting back and firmly closing my mouth. I knew all I had been doing all day was making things worse the more I said. Catherine had been unusually quiet; however, her face had begun to flush as she glared at William.

'I think we have to concentrate on Beatrice now and help her get better. It doesn't help if we fight amongst ourselves, does it?' she said sternly, glancing across at me before returning her attention to William. I nodded in agreement and apologised to them both; however, William ignored me. At last, the carriage stopped at their hotel.

'I will see you tomorrow,' I whispered as they stepped down from the coach.

'You will. I will be at the hospital from nine o'clock onwards if you would like to meet me there?' Catherine was visibly upset as she reached up and embraced me tightly before stepping away.

'Yes, I will be there. Thank you so much for today, and I am deeply sorry for what happened to your Beatrice. I will see you in the morning. Good night.'

I felt numb throughout the journey back to my hotel and terrible about not showing up at Mr Malcolm's home for dinner. I would have to send my apologies in the morning, but when it came to something like this, there had been no choice.

I thought about what I believed the man had done to Beatrice, and I felt anger rising within me. How could someone do that to a ten-year-old little girl so innocent of the ways of the world? Rob her of something so precious in a violent and hateful act?

I departed the carriage, saying good night to Mr Miller, after arranging transport to the hospital in the morning. Back in my suite, I sat eating the leftover desserts while pondering Beatrice's chances of a full recovery. I didn't know what it was about me and food, but I was eating everything in sight, taking such pleasure in all these new tastes and textures and going to bed with a full stomach. I was hungry all the time, and if I kept eating all this rich food, I knew I would end up the size of the Delmont itself. But, at that moment, I didn't care. I would deal with it when my new dresses no longer fitted me.

I woke to the cushioned silence of my room. At times, I missed the orphanage and the sounds it made just before everyone arose, and you could not hear yourself think — the rooster crowing his morning song, the house creaking and groaning as though it, too, was waking from its slumber. But, it was the birds I missed the most, singing their songs as if only to me as I lay in my cold bed and listened. As I lay in this cosy, warm bed, thinking what the day would bring, there was a polite knock at the door.

'Please enter,' I called out loudly. When a young maid marched in with my breakfast, I sat up quickly, requesting she take it to the kitchen table, before making my way into the sitting room in my nightgown. I sat down to eat, but not with my usual vigour. On the contrary, food was the last thing on my mind, and I felt downhearted after a night where all I had dreamed about was what I believed happened to Beatrice. When the maid returned for my tray, I asked her to assist me with dressing, to which she obliged.

'Where can I buy ladies' things?' I asked, feeling hot in the face.

'What do you mean, ladies' things, Miss?' she enquired.

'Personal things we need every month,' I replied, my face now on fire.

'Oh, those. Well, I make my own, but for ladies like you, we recommend Jeanne's. It's a shop not very far from here; you could even walk. I will write down the name and address for you.' I would go there as soon as I had finished at the hospital, slight twinges in my uterus warning me of what was impending.

Once dressed, I made my way downstairs to find Mr Miller waiting — my comforting steed, always there when I needed him, and happy to lend an ear to my problems.

'Good morning, Mr Miller. Thank you so much for collecting me,' I said as he helped me into the carriage.

'It's no problem for me, Missy. You are the nicest passenger I've ever had. Mr Malcolm can get a bit grumpy if you catch my meaning?' He winked before closing the carriage door and climbing back up into his seat. I did, but I could not imagine Mr Malcolm being impatient with anyone. He had been so lovely to me, ensuring my needs were met, and I was comfortable.

I was going to dinner tonight at Mr Malcolm's house and would meet Richard, my new chaperone. I hadn't been told a thing about him, other than he was Mr Malcolm's son. I would find out this evening and was confident he would be just as charming as his father.

I arrived at the hospital, quickly climbing the stairs that led to Beatrice's room, and found Catherine sitting at her bedside, holding her hand. Catherine turned to me and started crying as I embraced her tightly.

'She won't talk to me. She won't talk to anyone,' she exclaimed, her eyes swollen and red. 'They think it's the shock, but they can't tell me when, or even if, she will ever recover. What will our parents say to us about letting this happen? We have sent for our old Nanny, Miss Trippity, who had been with us since William was a baby. She decided she was too old to immigrate to Australia, but she will surely come once she knows the circumstances. That is our only hope. We don't have time to hire anyone new, as we sail in three days. I only hope that Beatrice can travel. We need someone she knows, like Nanny, to care for her. She is living in London, so we should hear from her today.'

Miss Trippity was in her forties and had been with the Montague family since she had started as a scullery maid at the age of fifteen. However, the Montagues saw something more in her, and they promoted her to a maid, then to Nanny when William was born. She had single-handedly raised the three children and was more of a mother to them than their own. Maybe that was why Catherine was so confident she would indeed come to them.

Beatrice lay on the bed, staring listlessly at the white fabric screens surrounding her bed. Catherine continued holding her hand and talking to her with no response. I motioned as I prepared to leave, and Catherine stood. I went to Beatrice and kissed her, telling her everything would be all right. I left the room, with Catherine following me.

'I need to talk to you if you have time?'

'Of course. Anything for you, Catherine.' I looked into her eyes and waited for her to speak.

'The doctors don't know why she isn't talking.' She sniffed loudly before continuing, her pretty face pale and tear-stained. 'I'm frightened she will never recover. Our parents are going to be furious with William and me for not watching her more carefully. I do not know how I will look our parents in the eye when we arrive in Australia if she remains in this state.' She looked around to ensure we were alone before lowering her voice to a whisper. 'You were right last night in the carriage. About what happened to Beatrice, I mean. That she was raped. William told me this morning the doctors advised him she was found in torn clothing with no underwear and was bleeding from her ... you know ... down there.' Catherine pointed vaguely below her waist, her face bright red, and I felt my stomach clench into knots. 'William doesn't want anyone to know. He says it would bring shame on our family, as well as Beatrice, and if people found out, she would have no hope of marrying into a good family. The doctors here think moving to Australia will be a good start for her — to forget what happened and start a new life'.

'I can't imagine you would ever forget something like that happening to you,' I said. Several metal dishes crashed to the floor in the next cubicle, the beleaguered nurse cursing under her breath. 'It is not your fault you had a slothful Nanny who didn't know what she was doing. You and William have done nothing but love and care for Beatrice in your parent's absence. Please don't blame yourself and feel bad; you can't be held responsible in your heart or your mind.' Catherine cried harder, embracing me tightly.

'Thank you, Abigail. You are such a great friend to me. I hope we are sisters for a lifetime. You are my first real friend. I am only fifteen. I was not allowed to attend school, and I am too young to attend dances and outings. I never asked how old you are. You look about eighteen.'

'I turned fifteen just a few days ago, and I'm even less socially experienced than you. I would like to stay; however, I must take my leave now, as I have to attend a dinner with my solicitor's family this evening. Will you be all right?'

'Oh, I think so. What else can I do? I will stay with Beatrice until tonight, and they are releasing her in the morning, so I hope Nanny comes.'

'I'm sure she will. Do not fret. Everything will turn out all right in the end,' I reassured her, wishing I fully believed it myself. I kissed her on the cheek, then quietly left the room.

The horses trotted up the street, the carriage rocking from side to side when I was unexpectedly thrown forward from my seat as we came to a sudden and complete halt. I could hear shouting and turned to look at where the ruckus was coming from. I stuck my head out the carriage window to see two men in a fierce fistfight in the middle of the road. I became excited and quickly opened the door and stepped down onto the street to take a better look. They were yelling obscenities at each other, some I recognised and some I didn't.

Still, I enjoyed every moment and tried to memorise the epithets that were unfamiliar to me.

'Get back in that carriage, Missy. Now!' Mr Miller roared at me. I quickly obeyed, not wanting to be on the wrong side of him. I could still hear wonderful cursing going on outside as we moved on past the battle. I was on my way to Jeanne's to obtain some personal items, and this little brawl had thrilled me. I giggled to myself as we moved on, still laughing as we pulled up outside an upmarket shop front.

As I entered, I could not believe my eyes. On display were corsets, undergarments, items of a more intimate nature, and other items that I had no idea of their use. Then, a woman, who appeared to be the proprietor, approached me. She was short and thin, wore an evening dress and hundreds of feathers in her hair, her ageing face covered in thick makeup. The largest diamond earrings I had ever seen were dangling from her earlobes, and she was smoking a cigarette in a long, slender holder that made her look elegant and wise. She led me around the shop, explaining her products, and I advised her of what I required. Then, she showed me to a small corner of the shop where numerous unfamiliar items were on display.

'Could you help me, please? I don't know which is which, and I would be eternally grateful if you could explain them to me.'

'Yes, of course. We have those basic materials, and then we have the luxury ones over here. Feel the difference. They come in light, which is not too thick; medium, which is of average thickness, and the thickest you can get for those poor sisters of ours who suffer the most,' she remarked, appearing sympathetic as she looked me up and down.

I picked up one of the basic thin ones. It was well-stitched and padded and made of an acceptable material. I felt the expensive ones and knew they were what I would buy. The material was superior and soft to the touch. Even the stitching was of a higher standard. I ordered dozens to take with me to Australia, as I didn't know what I would find there — or even if they had shops like this.

I shyly asked if I could try on some corsets. The woman smiled and told me to wait while she went and got a selection in my size. So far, I had only seen white corsets, but here they had pink, red, and even black ones, which I thought were so wicked I smiled to myself. I strode over to the changing room when the woman summoned me, feeling self-conscious under her gaze.

I was stunned. The different colours and styles of the corsets were beautiful. I tried one on, and it was almost comfortable. I decided right away I had to have them all. I selected one in black to wear under my dark dresses, feeling positively naughty — in a good way, as Catherine would say. I asked for matching undergarments and stockings for them and walked up to the counter. I took out my thick wad of money when the woman came to charge my order, handing it all to her.

'Good lord, my dear, you don't want to go flashing that amount of money around. Oh, my poor darling, you don't understand our money, do you? What country do you come from?' she asked loudly. I was too embarrassed to respond, considering whether to run or remain where I was to complete my purchase. 'Now, look, my poor, sweet, little naive girl. I will take out the money — are you watching? — and give you back the rest,' she said, very slowly and loudly, so I could understand. Then, she handed me my change, more coins I did not understand, and the remaining money in notes. 'Next time you buy something, you only take out one note, and they will give you change,' she advised, continuing to speak to me in a raised tone, implying I couldn't hear or understand English, and not just the nation's currency.

I thanked her and collected my parcels, hastening toward the door. The smell of cigarettes clung to my hair and clothes, and I wanted to be out of her presence. She assumed I was stupid or could not comprehend what she was saying, which deeply hurt my feelings. It was all because no one had taught me about money. I knew it was not malicious on her part or that she meant to be unkind, but I felt humiliated and vowed again I would remedy this deficit in me as soon as possible.

Mr Miller relieved me of my items and placed them on the seat in the carriage. Now I had to get back to the hotel to get ready for dinner. I climbed up to the driver's seat and sat with Mr Miller, confiding in him what had happened to Beatrice. He slowed the horses' pace to a walk so he could listen. He said little, but I felt better getting it off my chest, and he was such an excellent listener.

I could not decide what to wear — a pale pink dress with lots of ruffles on the bodice, or a peacock dress with lots of feathers in the hat. I took a last look at them, picked up the two hats, and mixed them up on the bed. I then closed my eyes, extended one hand, and the first one I found was the one I would wear. I felt feathers, opening my eyes to see the peacock held firmly in my hand. I worried a bit, as that dress had a lower neckline than I was used to, but I could not back out now. I had made a deal with the hats, and the hats had won. The peacock gown was my destiny.

Chapter Nine

I RELAXED BACK IN the carriage as it made its way to the Malcolm home through the narrow streets. I felt like a sinner and I would be sent straight to hell if anyone could see under my dress. I could feel my lacy, black corset, along with the new undergarments rubbing the inside of my thighs, and I smiled to myself at what the Sisters would think if they could see me now. I would undoubtedly be sent to Sister Monica for punishment if any of them knew I had bought anything like this, let alone was wearing it at my age.

Despite feeling so small and naïve in an enormous world, I was losing my fear of the unknown and enjoyed making my own decisions. However, it still surprised me when I politely asked someone for help at the hotel, and they would do whatever I wanted without question. No one had ever listened to me before — except for Sister Josephine.

I had sent flowers this morning to Mrs Malcolm as an apology for missing last night's dinner. I had only known to do this because a maid at the hotel had advised me of the proper etiquette when apologising for some unintentional faux pas. That was the problem. There were millions of things I didn't know yet, down to the simplest things that would always leave me feeling humiliated when I made a mistake in front of someone.

I hoped Mrs Malcolm wasn't so upset with me she would poison my soup or put laxatives in my dessert, as I had never met her and didn't know what to expect. 'What's wrong with you, Abigail, thinking thoughts like these?' I muttered, feeling cross with myself. However, I was sure she would be extremely gracious, just as her husband was. They were already opening their home to me and doing everything they could to keep me safe by providing me with a chaperone, for which I was grateful.

I had never been around a man, other than Mr Potts, who really didn't count. Their son was only five years older than me, so I hoped he was more likeable than William, because if he were haughty and arrogant, I would get rid of him in a heartbeat. It was bad enough I had to put up with William for the sake of my friendship with Catherine.

The carriage slowed, then stopped as we arrived at a well-kept house in an affluent-looking street. Mr Miller opened my door, and I walked as elegantly as possible up to the enormous front doors of a double-story home that was graceful and tidy, despite not being overly large compared to other mansions I had seen in books. I knocked on the door and was greeted by a maid, who smiled brightly and invited me inside as though she were expecting me. She took my coat and led me to the dining room, where there was a large table with beautiful, ornate dining chairs surrounding it.

A crystal chandelier hung high in the centre of the room, and I assumed this was where they entertained. I imagined they would have a less formal kitchen with a table where the family ate their meals together without all this fuss. Mr Malcolm stood up from his seat at the head of the table and welcomed me, smiling broadly. He came to my side and gently placed his hand on my back, introducing me to

Mrs Malcolm, who asked me to call her Jenny as she stood and came over to embrace me.

'You are a lovely young lady. I can't believe you are only fifteen. Oh, Henry, we are going to have to keep the boys away from this sweet one,' she said, then giggled like a young girl, covering her mouth while her eyes sparkled. I liked her immediately. She acted as if she already knew me and appeared friendly and outgoing.

I sat down next to Jenny, with an empty seat on the other side of me, which she explained was for her son, Richard, so we could get to know each other before he showed me around London. Jenny offered me wine, to which I eagerly agreed. As far as I was concerned, they expected me to behave like an adult, so people should treat me like one. I lifted the glass to my lips and sipped gracefully, drinking in the flavours that exploded in my mouth. The wine, a Cabernet Sauvignon I later learnt, made me feel light-headed. I decided at that moment I would drink wine every day for the rest of my life, and lots of it. I felt it go straight to my head, then spread its warmth throughout my body, and I felt instantly at ease.

A man I assumed was Richard entered the room, pulled out his chair, and sat down next to me. In his early twenties, he appeared comfortable in his own skin and was easy on the eye. He turned to me and introduced himself as I gazed at him in fascination.

'So, you are the famous Miss Delmont?' He smiled, revealing beautiful straight teeth as I blushed.

'What do you mean, famous?' I asked, a little too sharply.

He chuckled, picking up a glass of wine and taking a long drink. 'My father has told us all about you and what a lovely girl you are. Don't worry. He hasn't told us all your secrets,' he teased as he smiled at me.

Each time I looked at him, he would stare unblinkingly into my eyes, making me a little uncomfortable. I was not romantically attracted to him, despite the golden glow surrounding him.

Although I felt drawn to him, I didn't feel what I would have expected when meeting the first man who had that glow.

I wasn't sure if this was how all men behaved towards women or if he somehow liked me. I was unsure how to read the signs, but I noticed my effect on men, seeing how they looked at me when I walked down the street or went into a shop, and I found it embarrassing. Richard did not set my heart racing or release butterflies in my stomach, which from the novels I had read suggested would happen when I met my one true love.

Mr and Mrs Malcolm got up from the table and excused themselves, advising us they were expecting several more guests and they would await their arrival in the parlour. Richard asked how I was enjoying London so far. I explained how it frustrated me not knowing the streets or the buildings or where I was. I confided in him that I didn't understand how the money system worked, and he promised he would show me and not tell anyone, including his brothers.

'You don't have to feel embarrassed, Miss Delmont. No one would expect you to know any of these things. I promise we will sort out all the problems you are experiencing and, by the time you take ship, the other passengers will wonder where this sophisticated young woman has come from,' he reassured me, grinning broadly.

I relaxed in his company and enjoyed some of the stories he went on to tell me about the university where he was studying law. I assumed he would go into his father's law practice once he completed university, aware he had two elder brothers who had completed their law degrees years before and were now working with their father. I saw them in their offices when I had visited Mr Malcolm, but I hadn't spoken to either of them or been formally introduced.

He confided in me he did not plan to work for his father, much to my surprise, planning to practice criminal law out on his own. He believed everyone had a right to a fair trial, including decent legal representation, and that is what would keep his conscience clear. I asked him how his father would react to the news. He grimaced as he stared into my eyes.

'Not well. But he won't know about it until I graduate two years from now, so I still have plenty of time to enjoy my life,' he chuckled. Richard believed it would outrage his father when he found out, as he had always prided himself on the fact he would have three solicitor sons to continue the family business. However, I thought surely his father would accept his choices and love and accept him because he was his son and said so, much to his surprise. 'No. Once my father has his mind made up, that's it. You can't change it. I'll bet you he's convinced you to do things you don't want to do. He has, hasn't he?' he said, laughing softly. He could see from the look on my face he was right. 'Don't worry about it. He can get around the best of us.'

I completely understood what Richard meant. It had taken a lot for me to agree to go to Australia, but Mr Malcolm had gently pushed me in that direction and obtained my consent. Not too many people could have achieved that, given my stubbornness. However, he had managed it without me even realising. I felt sorry for Richard, with all the pressure placed on him.

'So, how did you get stuck with me?'

'My father told me you were in London on your own, and, since I have some spare time, I offered to show you around. Is that acceptable to you?'

'Yes, perfectly. I couldn't imagine a more charming chaperone,' I replied, and I meant it. He was a gentleman, and I felt I would enjoy my time with him, feeling relieved we were getting along well so far. Of course, being as handsome as he was did not hurt either. I studied him closely as he sipped his wine and realised how much like his father he was. He was tall and powerfully built, with dark brown hair and lovely blue eyes. His face broke easily into a smile when he spoke to you, and when he did, you felt like the most interesting person in the world because he wanted to know all about you.

'Your necklace is exquisite. It looks old, although the emerald is of a high grade,' he remarked as my hand went to my neck, clasping the emerald in my fingers.

'I do not know its history as my great-aunt gave it to me,' I explained, the necklace feeling as if it had only ever belonged to me.

Jenny and Mr Malcolm returned, escorting a couple into the dining room. Richard turned to me, raising his eyebrows inquisitively, and I shrugged my shoulders, indicating I didn't know them either.

'This is Mr and Mrs Clive Appleby. They are long-time family friends, and they have come here tonight because they knew your great-aunt and wanted to meet you. I hope you don't mind?' Mr Malcolm informed me, pouring more wine into my empty glass and a large drink for himself. He filled Jenny's glass and kissed her on the cheek, which I thought was lovely. It was clear to all in the room just how in love they were by the glances exchanged between them and the easy affection they shared, impressing me how thoughtful he was toward her.

Here he was, already a little tipsy from the wine, asking me in his own home if I minded who his guests were, which was gracious, given it was none of my business who he invited. Mr Malcolm sat down after introducing his friends and drank the rest of his wine. He was extremely cheerful and appeared to have drunk quite a few glasses before this, of that I was certain. He poured another and raised his glass to toast the group. Richard leaned over toward me and lowered his voice to a whisper.

'I'm sorry my father has put you in this situation. I saw your face when you found out why they were here and they knew your relative.' He looked at me sympathetically, shaking his head in disbelief.

'Yes, well, I did not know my great-aunt, so I don't know what to say to them,' I whispered back. 'She was the one who chose to leave me in the orphanage, despite having enough money to find me a family. I do not even know what I think about this woman. Although she hurt me, she did save me. I just don't like the attention placed on me.' My face was burning and my tongue-tied as I looked across the table at the Appleby's, who were staring at me, appearing fascinated. Their dim grey auras radiated softly from their bodies, although they were calm and not swirling around them like a storm as it did for Sister Monica.

'Ah. A bit shy, are you? Well, that's all right. Spending a few weeks with me will get you over that,' Richard said with a laugh, and I laughed with him.

We ate our meal as he and I chatted quietly between ourselves. I did not have a clue what I was eating — some kind of fowl; I believed — and felt too embarrassed to ask; however, I could have eaten twice as much. It was so delicious. Jenny kept looking fondly over at Richard and me as we talked, and I got the feeling she would have liked to see us become more than friends in the future. I caught her several times, giving Mr Malcolm a look that was clearly about us.

The main meal was something called pheasant, which I learnt when I heard Jenny ask the maid to praise their cook. It tasted a little like chicken, but as if they had rolled it in the dirt first and served it with roasted vegetables and steamed green vegetables. Dessert was banana cream pie, which had a flaky crust filled with a gooey, sugary caramel topped with bananas and whipped cream.

'You have a rather enormous appetite for such a slender woman,' Richard remarked, eyeing my empty plate and chuckling.

'Time will tell, believe me,' I replied, a smirk touching my lips. However, I wondered if the new dresses I had ordered and would receive in several weeks would still fit me.

The evening passed with no outstanding conversation, except for Richard, who saved the night for me, gently trying to guide the conversation away from talk of great-aunt Isabelle, who was becoming a big problem in my derriere. However, Mrs Appleby, or Regina as she asked to be called, would not be swayed from sharing her history with Isabelle for all at the table.

'She was a lovely woman, our Aunt Isabelle. May God rest 'er soul. We was shocked about 'er Will; leaving it all to an unknown child was all we was told. We was a tad upset, you know, with 'er not rememberin' us, what with all the help we gave 'er in 'er last years. Yes, we was very 'elpful, and rightly so, even though she was a cranky old biddy. But we loved 'er and got no credit for it,' she said, looking at me as if expecting me to thank her and possibly compensate her for their time.

'I'm sure,' was all I could bring myself to say as I swallowed hard and tried to compose myself. 'In what capacity did you know her?' I swallowed again, trying to dislodge the lump in my throat.

'Oh, me Clive 'ere once worked at Merinda Manor. She would come and go over the years, dependin' which country she were living in. She 'ad been close friends with old Lady Harrington since they were young centuries before and spent a lot of time there. Mind you, some rumours were 'ard to ignore, but me and Clive 'ere remained steadfast friends to 'er despite that old skilamalink Dowager. She somehow convinced the master to sack Clive only days after Isabelle's death, and we still 'ave no idea why to this day.'

It was clear they had known my great-aunt in her later years, realised how wealthy she was and befriended her to gain financial favour when she died. I was already aware she was not a frail woman, even up to the day she passed. Therefore, I doubted she had required any support from anyone. Whatever their motivation or plan, it hadn't appeared to have worked out for them, and there had been no mention of them in her Will. The financial reward they had been expecting on her death in exchange for their friendship — if they had indeed known her as well as they claimed, never eventuated. Now they were trying it on with me, attempting to make me feel sorry for them, and it wasn't working. I had no intention of giving them a penny. I realised I didn't like either of them as I narrowed my gaze.

'How do you know Mr Malcolm? I mean, it's such a coincidence, knowing my great-aunt and also knowing her solicitor.' I glanced at Mr Appleby suspiciously, his eyes darting away. I heard Richard snort beside me, then try to regain his composure.

'Oh, we aren't close friends, are we, Mr Malcolm, Sir? We never would 'ave expected an invitation to 'is own table, but knock me down with a feather; Clive comes 'ome this afternoon and says we are invited to the grand house. All pomp and ceremony and all that, and I was to wear me best dress and 'at. No, darlin', Mr Malcolm represents my Clive 'ere. Clive is what they call an investment broker, you know? 'Is only crime is some investments for 'is clients got away from 'im.' She addressed me with such a sense of pride before turning and gazing at her husband adoringly.

Was she talking about that scheme in the newspapers recently? I wasn't sure and preferred not to know. They were a strange-looking couple. She was tall but thin and reminded me of a bird with her sharp features, while he was a short, obese man with a shifty-looking face. I felt like I would burst out laughing, feeling it bubble up inside me until I could no longer contain it, and I did. Wine spurted out of my mouth across the table, splattering all over Clive Appleby as he looked back at me in shock. It started a coughing fit I could not stop, with Richard pounding me on the back while trying not to laugh.

Everyone was staring at me silently. A solicitor invited his shady, possibly criminal, client to dinner to meet a wealthy client. That did not seem like a well-thought-out plan to me, and I wondered if he was tipsy when he had come up with this bright idea. I apologised for my outburst and contained my laughter, wiping my mouth with a linen napkin. I was showing my age and not acting like the adult I was expected to be. However, the Applebys' did not seem to mind and laughed along with the others. The party appeared to be a success, but the time had come for me to excuse myself and leave. Richard indicated he would walk me out. I said my goodbyes to all and thanked the Malcolm's for their hospitality.

'Now, you make sure you come again. You are welcome anytime, even on short notice,' Jenny said, embracing me.

'I will, and then you won't have to go to so much trouble. We will be able to eat in the kitchen.' She looked at me, appearing confused, as Mr Malcolm shook his head at her warningly, Jenny raising her eyebrows at him but remaining silent. I wondered what I had done wrong as I walked with Richard to the front door, and he kindly opened it for me.

'That was the most amusing dinner party my parents have ever held,' he said, chuckling as we stood in the driveway. 'I thought my mother was going to have a conniption when you told her we could eat in the kitchen. Only servants eat in kitchens, Miss Delmont. Please do not feel embarrassed. I will teach you all the things that seem so small that everyone forgets to tell you.' He looked at me with kindness, and I again felt humiliated.

'So, people eat like that every night? In extravagant rooms with plenty of servants?'

'Well, not everyone, but the people you will associate with do, and you will end up doing the same thing when you have your own home,' he explained. I smiled at him, grateful he hadn't made me feel like a fool.

'No, when I have my home, I will eat in my kitchen with my friends,' I replied, and he laughed. We talked and laughed together about the unusual dinner guests as we waited for Mr Miller to arrive.

'It was lovely meeting you, Miss Delmont, and even more of a pleasure to be assigned as your chaperone,' he said, and I could tell he meant it.

'The pleasure was mine. I am looking forward to seeing London while I'm here, and — I need to know where I can find books and a blanket.'

'Your wish is my command. Should I collect you in the morning to take you to find what you need?'

'Well, actually, no. I am visiting with friends tomorrow, and I wish to see them the day after, as they leave for Australia. Would Monday be more suitable? Then you could accompany me to where the boats leave and meet them before they embark.' I was already demanding, placing my hands on my cheeks as my face began to flush.

'Sounds perfect. I will see you on Monday then at nine o'clock?' He really did have the loveliest smile.

'Yes, that would be wonderful. Goodnight,' I replied as Mr Miller stopped the carriage beside me. Richard helped me in, then waved goodbye, and I was soon on my way back to the hotel. Unfortunately, I could not call it home, as I hadn't found my home yet, and I had no idea where that would be.

When I arrived at my suite, there was a note sitting on the table. I opened it, confident I knew who it was from, and quickly scanned the page, my heart racing.

Dear Abigail,
Nanny has arrived, and Beatrice is back with us at The Savoy. Please come tomorrow.
Catherine

I felt relief flood my body. The hospital had released Beatrice early, so surely that was a good sign. At least I could go to sleep knowing their Nanny was there looking after them, and I would see them in the morning. I drew a long, hot bath and soaked in the rose-fragrant water for an hour before reluctantly drying myself off and slipping into my nightgown. I had experienced an interesting evening, meeting new people, which my goal had been on leaving the orphanage. I wanted to get to know as many people as possible, and it seemed to be working.

Chapter Ten

THERE WAS A KNOCK on my door and a cheery, 'Hello, it's me,' as Catherine came skipping into my bedroom. I had been leaving the door unlocked since the day after I had arrived. So many people came in and out; I was sick of answering the door. It must have been early. The sun was only starting to emerge; however, the room was dark and gloomy, the day already overcast and grey. I drew my attention back to my visitor and smiled sleepily as she stood by my bed, looking down at me. She giggled happily and jumped up next to me, bouncing me up and down as I laughed at her.

'Hello, Catherine. How are you, my friend?' I asked, smiling as she climbed under the covers and took my hand in hers. Her smile slowly turned to a look of trepidation.

'I'm well,' she replied, 'although Beatrice is showing no signs of improvement. She has not spoken a word, although, at night, she screams in her sleep. I do not know what to do to help her, but Nanny is looking after her. She goes to her in the night when the screaming is at its worst and holds her until she goes back to sleep. Nanny has agreed to come to Australia with us, and if she does not like it, she can return to London, and we will pay her ticket home. It's so good to have her back, Abigail. It feels like home again, and she is wonderful with Beatrice. We do love our parents in our own way; however, Nanny is like our mother. I know you understand that better than anyone because of your Sister Josephine. I hope she stays on, but if she cannot, at least she is with us to get Beatrice through the worst of it. Are you coming over today? I brought the carriage from The Savoy to collect you. I thought you could have breakfast with us — to see what the competition is like?' She talked non-stop, not allowing me to get a word in edgewise.

'Okay, okay. I'm getting up. What kind of friend are you, dragging me out of bed at this god-forsaken hour?' I moaned and pretended to swipe my hand at her head. She ducked and giggled.

She helped me dress, and we were back at The Savoy within a half-hour. These days I bathed and washed my hair every night, finding it much easier to get ready in the mornings, as my hair had dried into loose waves, and I did not use make-up on my face. Of course, the most time-consuming chore was the corset, since you needed someone to help you put it on. Catherine had flushed when she saw the new pink one she had helped me put on today. It would be considered risqué, I would think, based on the standard white corset we were accustomed to wearing.

We jumped out of the carriage without assistance and raced each other inside like schoolgirls, getting into trouble with management for misbehaving and disrupting the staid decorum of the place. The manager caught us at the bottom of the stairs, where I had tripped over my own big feet and ended up sprawled flat on my face on the floor, with Catherine looking down at me in fits of laughter. We had darted through the reception area, nearly knocking over several people who were too slow to get out of our way.

After his stern lecture, we both apologised to the manager, who helped me up and ever so slowly escorted us to the Montagues' suite. We tried not to burst out laughing at being chastised like children just for having a bit of fun. Instead, he left us there with a final disapproving look. As we entered, I was met by a large, white-haired woman whose face crinkled into well-worn wrinkles when she smiled.

'I have heard so much about you, Miss Delmont. It's a pleasure to meet one of Catherine's friends,' Miss Trippity said, looking directly into my eyes with her warm, hazel ones, which were so full of kindness and concern.

'Thank you. I am pleased to meet you too. I have heard only wonderful things about you,' I replied, smiling back at her.

'Well, don't believe everything you hear, cherub, as only half is ever true, and the other half wasn't anywhere near as fun as it should have been,' she said, making herself laugh, and I knew immediately I liked her. She had genuine warmth and a sense of humour, which was essential in anyone I wanted to spend time with. She was a stocky woman, with the most enormous bosoms I had ever seen; however, she moved quickly and efficiently across the sitting room, excusing herself to attend to Beatrice, who was in her bedroom still sleeping. Nanny would stay beside her in case she woke from a nightmare and be there to comfort her immediately.

The maid knocked at the door to take our breakfast orders, and I self consciously ordered what I wanted. By this time, William had joined us, and we all sat down on the lounges and made ourselves comfortable, with Catherine sitting next to me and taking my hand in hers again.

'So, how are you enjoying your time here, Miss Delmont?' William asked me formally, politely for once.

'I'm enjoying myself very much, thank you, William. Are you ready to sail?'

'Ready, but not willing,' he replied with a scowl. 'I can't believe the people in Australia have enough money even to buy one of my father's creations, let alone wear them every day. It makes me so angry we must suffer because of his flimsy dreams that will never come true.

145

He does not care about the money, which is the entire problem. If he did, he would regret all the rich clients he is leaving behind to service a bunch of poor people in a colony of criminals and their offspring. He believes these Australians should have the right to wear only the best. I completely disagree. None of this makes sense to me.'

William appeared deflated while Catherine tried to brighten the mood. 'Would you like to see Beatrice? She is much improved since Nanny has been here.' I indicated I would, and Catherine rose and escorted me to the bedroom. Miss Trippity was sitting by the bedside, stroking Beatrice's forehead as the traumatised girl stared into space. When she saw us, Nanny rose and assured her charge she would be back soon. I sat down by Beatrice and held her hand.

'Hello, sweetie, how are you?' I asked as she continued to stare unblinkingly ahead. 'It's all right now, Beatrice, the wicked man cannot get you here,' I told her gently and stroked her face.

With that, she sat bolt upright in the bed, emitting a high-pitched scream that nearly burst my eardrums and became hysterical. Catherine looked at me, her eyes wide in horror. Nanny and William came bursting into the bedroom as Beatrice continued to scream.

'What did you do to her? What did you say?' William roared over her piercing shrieks as I backed away from the bed, feeling awful.

'No one said anything, William, and Abigail certainly did nothing wrong,' Catherine defended me. William looked at both of us while the screaming continued, not believing either of us.

'I think it best Abigail leaves now, as this is a family matter, and strangers should not be a part of it,' he said firmly to his sister while ignoring me. Catherine started to say something, but I turned to William.

'I am perfectly fine with leaving. You are right. It is a family matter and best dealt with in private. Thank you for having me. I will see myself out,' I told him, and smiled weakly at Catherine. I left the bedroom while Catherine chased me out.

'Are you all right?' she asked, catching up with me as I gathered my things.

'Yes, I'm fine. I just need to go from here. Look how much trouble I caused, and look what I've done to Beatrice,' I said, angry and upset with myself as I straightened up and hurried to the front door.

'It's all right. Everything is setting her off. I hold on to the hope the poor child will improve day by day. You said nothing wrong. You were just trying to comfort her,' Catherine said kindly as she drew up next to me and opened her arms wide, pulling me into a warm embrace.

'I know. I've just now realised how selfish it is of me to be thinking of only myself.' I shook my head, slipping my arms around her and hugging her back. 'I haven't offered you any support for what you're going through. If you need me, I am here; you can call on me whenever you need me for anything, Catherine, as I see how hard this is for you. If you would like to come to dinner tonight to have some relief, you are very welcome.'

'I actually will come as I need a break,' she said before kissing my cheek and bidding me farewell, closing the door quietly behind me.

I felt like a terrible friend. I did not feel like going back to my hotel this early in the day, arranging for the driver to take me to Mr Malcolm's office. When we arrived, I saw Mr Miller sitting in his seat atop the carriage, looking like he had just awakened from a long sleep. I climbed out of The Savoy carriage and walked up to him.

'Hey, there. I was wondering if you were busy?' I asked, smiling sweetly up at him. He heard my voice and looked down at me fondly.

'Not at all. Where do you want to go?' He grinned widely as he climbed down.

'Well, I need to go back to my hotel to collect an item I require, then I want you to take me to the most fashionable street in London if you don't mind?' I said in a voice mimicking all the very upper-class people I had met at the hotel. He laughed at my charade.

'Sounds good to me. I will help you in.' He opened the door to the carriage and promptly lifted me inside. I sat back and relaxed, staring out the window from my comfortable seat at the interesting people who passed me by. After checking with Mr Malcolm's office first, he made his way to The Delmont. When we arrived, I quickly hurried inside to get the money I needed. Then I ran back downstairs, jumping into the carriage without Mr Miller's assistance and gasping to catch my breath.

'Missy, I have warned you about sneaking up and doing that, but I swear, if you do it again, I will make you wait five minutes longer for my services each time.'

'I'm sorry. I forget sometimes, and I was in a rush. Kick those horses into action, my dear man,' I yelled out, and within seconds, we were on our way. Mr Miller had done his research and later told me he had asked the hotel staff where to find the most expensive street in London, and they had advised him of several places to take me. He knew where he was going, the carriage flying through the streets at a speed that seemed to excite him, with me along for the ride.

We arrived in a beautiful, cobble-paved street with handsome shops along both sides. I waited for Mr Miller to get down and open my door. I knew he did not make empty threats, and if I kept jumping in and out of the carriage unassisted, he would add five minutes each time to the period I had to wait for him. He knew I was an impatient girl who wanted everything done right now. Finally, he opened the door for me, smiling.

'Now, you go and have a wonderful time, and if you cannot find what you need here, I will take you to Harrods. Buy something special for yourself,' he said, as if he were an indulgent father pampering his daughter. 'Don't just spend money on others, Abigail. You need to spoil yourself, too, and buy some things that will always remind you of this time in your life when you were young and free. Believe me, lass, time goes fast, and before you know it, you're old like me and looking back, wondering why you didn't do half the things you had the opportunity to do. Don't make the mistake so many others have before you. Live each day to its fullest, with no regrets, and you will make yourself a happy life, my girl.'

I would follow his advice and promptly entered the first shop I saw — an elegant place displaying hundreds of glittering jewels. While browsing, I spotted a stunning pair of diamond earrings with gold posts. I had never had my ears pierced, and I had heard it was quite painful, but earrings like this were unusual. I had noticed most earrings worn by upper-class women were clipped-on, but these brilliant baubles were silently calling my name. Mr Malcolm had provided me with the money to spend on items I thought I would need for my journey, so I did not see the harm in spoiling myself a little.

As the shopkeeper was wrapping them up, I readied myself to pay. He looked at me expectantly, and I handed him one note and waited for him to give me my change. He continued to look at me, and I handed him another note. His look was unchanged, so I grabbed all the money out of my purse, feeling humiliated, and slammed it down hard in front of him.

'Take the amount it costs,' I ordered, feeling embarrassed while using all my strength not to shout at him. He raised his eyebrows, took two more notes from the pile, then pushed the rest of the money back to me without saying a word and handed me my parcel. I avoided his curious gaze before turning and hurrying out onto the street.

When I had calmed down enough to continue my shopping, I looked around and noticed a small shop that had blankets displayed in their window. I quickly crossed to the other side, worried the horses that frightened me so would knock me down if I didn't hurry. I stepped inside, finding myself in a place I had dreamed of visiting my entire life. As I closed the door behind me, I could smell animal skins and the sweet smell of wool. The shopkeeper approached and asked if he could assist me.

'Yes, I need a lot of help. I want to place an order to be delivered to The Delmont Hotel, under the name of Abigail Delmont.' He nodded, smiling brightly as he realised I might be there to spend a lot of money. I stood before the blankets and felt them all. Some were so soft, with wisp-like hairs tickling your hand as you ran it over them, while others were smooth and tightly woven. I chose ten of them in different colours and then ordered a beautiful quilt on display. This time, as I put my pounds on the counter, I told the sales clerk I needed help because I did not understand the currency.

'Of course,' he said, graciously taking the correct number of bills and handing me my change. I was finding the process easier the more I practised. Most people understood and, once I explained my need for assistance, were always polite and kind. I decided after that experience to continue shopping until Mr Miller returned to collect me.

Back in the suite, I kicked off my shoes and lay on my bed. I would walk around barefoot day and night if I could get away with it. I loved the feeling of the luxurious carpets and rugs on the floor and adored the sensation of grass between my toes. I had just eaten a lovely lunch and felt full to the brim. I was certainly enjoying the food on offer to me any time of the day and night. I was eating at least five times a day, not including small snacks of fruit or cakes.

I wondered how I would fill my time until Catherine arrived while pressing my hands on my bloated stomach. Finally, I decided I would wander over to the swimming pool and try it out for myself. At one of the many shops I had visited this morning, the assistant, a French woman, had informed me the swimsuit I was trying on was the 'height of fashion', so I'd bought it — mainly because it covered me, I needed a swimsuit, and it had been the only one small enough to fit me.

I struggled to my feet, collecting the swimsuit from my wardrobe on the way, then stepped into the washroom and undressed. When I donned the swimsuit, I ran my hand down the soft material. It had capped sleeves and a high neck, covering my breasts completely, which I had been mindful of when choosing what to buy, and the pantaloons stopped just above my knees. The fabric was dark blue with white trim and, although made of thick material, the sales assistant had assured me it would keep me cool, even in the harsh Australian sunshine.

I slipped my dressing gown around my shoulders, pinned my hair on top of my head, grabbed a fluffy towel from the washroom, and headed up the stairs to the pool. Apprehensive, I halted at the door when I found, swimming in the pool, the most handsome man I had ever seen. I had hoped no one would be here, as I had never been in front of a man in a swimsuit before, and I wasn't sure I had the confidence to go in now.

I considered returning to my room but then realised he wasn't paying attention to me, so I took off my dressing gown and quickly got into the small, round dipping pool before he could see me. It was just like having a bath with your clothes on, and I did not see the appeal. I would much rather be in my tub alone and relaxing without worrying about who was around and looking at me. I was about to get out and dry off when the man stopped swimming and bobbed over to me with a wide grin on his face.

'Hi, my name is James. Who do I have the pleasure of meeting?' he asked, studying my face intently.

'I'm Abigail. It's nice to meet you.' I leaned forward and shook his hand, which seemed to surprise him. I was realising women were not supposed to shake hands.

'Nice to meet you, too. I'm here on business, but I'm also making time to visit my family, the ones who still live in London.' I nodded thoughtfully, my hand going to my neck and unconsciously caressing the emerald through the thick material of my swimming costume.

'Where did you move to?'

'I took a position working for a family in York several years ago. They breed exotic horses and, as they knew my father, offered me a job training their Martarinos.' I nodded, surprised a stable hand would have the means to stay here. He smiled again before continuing. 'So what are you here for, if you don't mind me asking?'

'I'm here on personal business,' I answered, smiling back at him. We chatted for a time, and he asked me out to dinner, offering to bring his mother to chaperone.

'I am sorry, but I cannot.'

'Tomorrow night, then?' he asked hopefully, and I shook my head. 'Any night?' he insisted, staring at me with a grin. I shook my head again. 'I'm sorry if I offended you. You aren't married, are you? Please help me out here, as I'm drowning.' He chuckled to himself, my mind racing with a thousand thoughts.

'Yes, I'm sorry. Unfortunately, I am seeing a young man; otherwise, it would have been a privilege to have dinner with you.'

I was learning how to say no in a kind way. Catherine had helped me with that. We had talked about men approaching us, and she was just as uncomfortable as I was. It was a new world for her, too. We had concluded it was best to say we were already being courted. Although I was attracted to this young man and would have enjoyed spending time in his company for the remainder of my stay, he did not have the golden glow — the uncanny thing that kept tripping me up. I would have loved to have gone to dinner with him and maybe let him kiss me at the door, but I could not, with a clear conscience, involve myself with someone I knew I had no future with. It was not fair to them or me.

The golden glow had to be important for it to keep happening to me. I didn't understand why I was the only person I knew who could see it, and I was hoping to meet others in the future who had the same ability, who might then explain to me what it all meant. I had decided to wait for what I believed to be the real thing — true love with a man surrounded by the golden light people dear to me possessed.

I was now alone in the pool area. James had left to attend a meeting with a man wanting to purchase four horses from the estate where he worked, and we had said goodbye warmly with no talk of seeing each other again. I decided to swim since no one else was there. The water was much colder than in the dipping pool but warmer than the river where we used to swim in summer. I waded deeper until the water was up to my neck. It was a beautiful feeling, and not one I had experienced often, to have my body encased in water and feeling completely weightless.

I wondered what I would find to do in London for the five remaining weeks after Catherine had sailed. Of course, I was looking forward to getting to know Richard and spending time with him; however, it wouldn't be the same without her here, and the weeks would drag on until I boarded the ship that would take me to her. She was already a big part of my life, and I hoped that would continue when I saw her again.

I got out of the pool, wanting to bathe and dress before Catherine arrived. I wrapped my towel around me and hurried down the stairs to my room, holding my dressing gown closed before anyone could see me.

'Looser, please,' I begged the maid, who was roughly yanking at my corset. 'I want to be able to eat.' She pulled it tighter as I hung onto the four-poster bed for support. Bessie had gone home for the day, and left me with a maid I found very similar to Sister Monica, who I thought I had left behind at the orphanage.

'I've got to pull it nice and tight to hold everything in its right place, Mistress, so stay still,' she ordered, holding me there firmly, unable to move.

'No, I think I will leave it off for tonight,' I replied, sick of being trussed up like a sausage and not being able to breathe properly. Being strapped into one prevented you from running or doing much at all physically, including eating and drinking, and I was not prepared to sacrifice the new love of my life.

'Mistress, excuse me for saying so, but you can't go without. No lady goes walking around the streets, let alone from The Delmont Hotel, without her corset, and you will not be the first,' she said determinately. She let go of me for an instant, and I whirled around and glared at her.

'Well, I am for tonight. Please take it off at once.' She stared back at me wide-eyed and open-mouthed, but reluctantly turned me back around and did as I asked.

I pulled my dress on, and she proceeded to do up the buttons, muttering to herself. Once she had finished, she turned on her heel and abruptly left the room, slamming the door behind her, which made me smile. Many of the maids were still not aware I was the owner of the hotel, and I found it amusing how differently I was treated by the ones who knew. People often made minor things into enormous problems when there was no need to do so. I wasn't hurting or offending anyone by going without a corset. The damned torture devices were only intended to make women's bodies appear smaller and their breasts bigger, pushing them up towards your face until they appeared deformed and unnatural.

I studied myself in the full-length mirror, finding it was barely noticeable I wasn't wearing one. I didn't look any different, except my breasts weren't holding my chin up. The dress fit me perfectly, and it was so much easier to breathe. I closed the door to my bedchambers behind me just as Catherine burst in through the front door.

'I'm here,' she called out in her musical voice.

'Yes, I know you are. I'm right here too. Come and tell me how Beatrice is.' She followed me into the sitting room and joined me on the lounge while I reached across and pulled my new woollen blanket over our legs.

'William is being hideous, as usual, and won't leave our suite in case Beatrice calls him, always ready to tell her he is standing by to protect her from strange men. He is mean to everyone, especially me, and the closer it gets to us departing, the worse he is. But, as usual, Nanny is being her lovely self and looking after all of us like a proper mother would. She stays with Beatrice day and night and refuses to leave her side, even to sleep. We asked the hotel manager to put another bed in the room for Nanny, as we do not want her to wear herself out. She sleeps in her room, comforts her when she has nightmares, and still looks after William and me. She is the most wonderful woman I know, and I truly love her.'

Her eyes glowed with pure affection for the woman who had not married and was now too old to have children of her own. She regarded them as her own and treated them as such. Miss Trippity's devotion made me think of Sister Josephine. I wondered how she was and imagined how she would feel when my letter arrived. I could feel how happy she would be to know I was safe. I hoped I would receive a reply before my departure. I wrote her a letter almost every second day and planned to continue writing, even on the ship. I would post all the letters at once when I arrived in Melbourne.

Catherine was still prattling on about William and his bad moods when our dinner arrived. Over our meal, we chatted about boys and her upcoming journey. I told her about what had happened at the swimming pool. She began talking about the current fashions and how her father predicted something called mutton leg sleeves would be prominent in the future. While she spoke, I daydreamed about Australia.

Beatrice was getting worse instead of better, and Catherine was worried sick. She told me Beatrice had not spoken a word to anyone, and all she did was scream. She would go into a trance-like state, where she was quiet for hours, then would suddenly become hysterical, screaming unendingly. No one knew what to do, and the doctor came three times a day. He had given Nanny some tonic to keep her calm, but nothing was working. They were to sail the day after tomorrow, and Catherine was worried about how Beatrice would cope with the voyage.

'I must go. I have stayed far too long and should have returned to Beatrice hours ago.' We walked arm in arm towards the front door.

'I will see you mid-morning tomorrow, and, just so you know, I'm taking you out to lunch, Catherine. You have been cooped up like a chicken in a cage for far too long, so put on your finest dress. We're going to dine in style.' My lips twitched mischievously as I stepped into the hallway and turned to embrace her.

'I will see you in the morning, then. Thank you for being such a dear friend and caring so much.' She closed the door behind her.

Later, as I lay in bed, I thought about how much my life had changed in a matter of days. This time last week, I was hungry and cold, shivering in a bed so hard it did not differ from sleeping on the ground. Now I was floating on a cloud of feathers with crisp, white linen surrounding my freshly bathed body and the heaviest of quilts pushing me down deeper into the feathered mattress. All I knew at this moment was every child at Emiliani House would now have only the best beds and linen. No longer would they have to curl up into tight, little balls under thin blankets, shivering night after night, year after year. That knowledge made me feel truly happy for the first time in my entire life. I smiled to myself, and, basking in that glow, I finally slept.

Chapter Eleven

I OPENED ONE EYE for a brief moment to find a young maid standing over me, calling out her morning greetings in an irritatingly loud and cheerful manner. The room was brighter than usual when the maids arrived at eight o'clock, unless ordered otherwise, and I realised I must have overslept. My breakfast was waiting on the table by the window where the young woman was laying the cutlery. She placed a small vase of white roses in the centre, nodding to herself in satisfaction, before returning to my bedchambers, hurrying me out of bed. After she had slipped my dressing gown over my shoulders and tied it securely at the waist, she then marched me into the sitting room and over to the table, clapping her hands at me to eat. I noticed the chef had prepared something different this morning. It was crisp, flat, and looked like worms all stuck together. I raised my fork to my lips and tasted it, finding it to be the best breakfast dish I had the pleasure of eating so far. When I asked how it was made, the maid advised me that grated potatoes were mixed with egg, then fried like a pancake until golden brown and crisp.

'Mmm, thank you, it's delicious.' I yawned widely, forgetting to cover my mouth. 'Is Bessie not attending to me this morning?'

'No, I'm sorry, Mistress. She has been delayed with other duties and sends her apologies.' I nodded politely and started on my breakfast, devouring the potato pancake and drinking my orange juice in a flash. Today was the last day I would spend with Catherine before seeing her set sail tomorrow, and then I would be all alone again. Well, I told myself, there was time enough to feel bad when they had gone. I was determined to enjoy today with her, and lunch would be a surprise. I wiped my mouth, belched loudly, and rose to my feet, ignoring the look of surprise that crossed the maid's face. I rushed across the room and followed her into my bedchamber. She was waiting near my bed with her hands on her waist, her foot tapping impatiently on the floor. I obediently stripped off my nightgown, donned the undergarments she held up for me, crossing over to the door where the dress she had chosen for the day hung on the back, suspended by a brass hook. I took it down, then stepped into it before pulling it up to my waist, preparing to slip my arms through the sleeves. The maid watched me intently, clearly horrified, as she held out the stiff white corset, her hand trembling slightly.

'Mistress, I can see your breasts moving.' She widened her eyes further, her face flushing.

'At least they are not flattened and pushed up so high I can touch them with my tongue.' I was defiant, my eyes glittering as I glared at her warningly. She continued to stare back, clearly speechless; however, she hurried to my side and attended to the back of my dress. I glanced in the mirror as she made some minor adjustments at the back while shaking my head at how parochial many of the hotel employees were, knowing if they wanted to continue working here, they would be forced to remain so. Finally, she left the room without uttering another word to me, the door clicking shut behind her.

I hurried up the stairs and into the wide hallway, screams filling the entire floor. As I drew nearer to Catherine's room, the spine chilling shrieks became louder and frenetic. Finally, I knocked sharply on the door, pounding harder to be heard over the commotion. After several moments, Catherine opened the door slightly, her face white, while her eyes anxiously scanned the hallway. She swung the door wide, turning to glance down the hall for a moment before ushering me inside.

'Come in, Abigail. You will have to excuse me — we have the doctor here.' She turned and hurried back to the bedroom. I closed the door behind me and followed her, as I was never one to be left out of anything. I stood against the wall in Beatrice's bedroom, not wanting to intrude, but needing to know she was going to be okay. The doctor attempted to examine Beatrice, but she would have none of it, thrashing around in the bed, clearly terrified of him, while Miss Trippity sat lovingly by her side, attempting to calm her without success. Finally, he stepped away, seemingly defeated, before fumbling through his leather medical case and removing a bottle containing a dark liquid.

'This will help her sleep. Until she is calmer, that is all I can do for now. She won't let me close enough to conduct a proper examination, and I don't want to distress her any more than she already is, the poor, dear child.' He appeared close to tears as he gazed down at Beatrice, thrashing around as Miss Trippity held her tightly and murmured in her ear. 'That man is a monster, and I hope he swings for it,' he remarked to himself before handing the tonic to Catherine.

'Thank you, Dr Whitney.' She smiled gratefully at him, the doctor bending down to collect his bag before nodding at her politely. 'We'll send word if she gets worse.'

William nodded in agreement while Nanny took the bottle from Catherine and promptly left the room, appearing distressed, only making my heart ache for them all the more, especially Beatrice and her endless ordeal. Nanny soon returned, holding a glass, the dark liquid mixed with apple juice. She got Beatrice to swallow it, surprising us all. William and Catherine kissed Beatrice before making their way to the sitting room while I followed behind. We sat down and made ourselves comfortable, Beatrice's screams filling every room of the suite.

'That should calm her down. Nanny got it all down her throat, every last drop, so we will see how long it takes to work — if it does,' William remarked, staring out the window, his shoulders slumped.

He appeared despondent and exceedingly pale. He was certainly not the self-assured boy I had met on the train only days ago and of late had been civil to me. I worried neither of them were taking care of themselves and only looking after Beatrice. We all spoke quietly for a time, and I listened sympathetically but was acutely aware of the growls emitting from my stomach and worried they were, too.

'Come on, Catherine, we are going out. Collect your reticule and get ready to enjoy yourself.' I smiled brightly; however, I only received a weak smile in response. Mr Miller had told me of a street across from Hyde Park where people sold food from small stalls, where they cooked everything fresh, and the cuisine was from all over the world. I thought it would be fun to take Catherine there and see what exotic food and drink we could taste, given they subjected us to fancy fare morning, noon and night. Not that I didn't appreciate it more than a bag of diamonds, but I wanted to go where ordinary people went to eat, to see things everyone else took for granted. I could hardly wait to buy food from street vendors and eat it with my hands.

'Do you wonder what it's going to be like, starting our new lives in Australia?' Catherine asked dreamily as we stepped out into the hall and made our way down to reception side by side.

'I can't stop thinking about it. I asked Mr Malcolm how far away from Melbourne I will live, and he said it's only a couple of hours by train, so I will be able to see you often. I'm fortunate I have a house to go to Catherine, as I would be a scullery maid even as we speak if this miracle hadn't occurred.' The concierge held the door open as we greeted him before hurrying to the waiting carriage.

'Well, if anyone deserves it, you do,' she said. 'You are the sweetest and loveliest girl I have ever met, and you are officially my best friend in the world. It's like it was all meant to happen for some reason, meeting on the train like that, and then finding out we are both going to the same place halfway around the world.'

I nodded in agreement as I glanced at her before stepping up into the carriage, Catherine following closely behind me before the driver loudly closed the door. We settled back, smoothing our large skirts as the horses took off at a trot, jolting us around as we laughed. She had changed since we had become closer, becoming so much more confident and open now than when we had first met. We enjoyed each other's company, and we had similar views about the world, no matter our limited life experience.

The driver stopped at Hyde Park and hurried us out of his carriage. Catherine firmly advised him of the time she expected him to collect us and thanked him when he agreed. As we crossed the street from the park, Catherine looked around suspiciously. I noticed a cart with a woman standing beside it, selling what looked like small pastries. I dragged Catherine by the hand and smiled brightly at the vendor as I took a deep whiff of her delicious-smelling offerings of meat and vegetables with curry. She smiled back, raising her eyebrows questioningly.

'I will have four, please,' I said, reaching into my bag and taking out six coins. I held them out in my palm for the woman, who had the longest black hair I had ever seen and a red dot on her forehead. She took two pennies, thanked me, and handed over the food wrapped in butcher paper. Catherine and I walked a short distance down the road, eyeing the wares the many vendors were selling as we passed by, many calling out cheerfully in an attempt to attract us to their carts.

'You don't mean for us to stand here on the side of the road in our finest outfits and eat with our fingers in front of everyone, do you?' Catherine appeared horrified as I handed her a pastry.

'Yes, I do. Come on, Catherine, we have never done this before.' I nudged her on her arm and winked, my mouth twitching in amusement.

'And likely never will again.' She bit into the delicious delicacy, glancing around suspiciously to ensure no one was taking notice.

After eating the pastries and wiping our fingers on our handkerchiefs, we strolled further along the street, sampling bits and pieces from carts and trays offered to us. I bought two bread rolls and tucked them into my purse. Finally, we stopped at a small restaurant. I inhaled deeply, the smell of such sweet and savoury aromas flowing from inside filling my head, making my stomach rumble and my heart sing. Despite being bitterly cold, we chose to sit at an outside table and waited for the server to come and take our order. We continued our discussion of Australia — what we imagined it would be like and the things we would do once we were there.

We ordered our drinks and a large slice of cake each. While we waited, I studied the people in the park and those walking past on the street. Different heights, sizes, body shapes, skin and hair colours, and people's unique faces, even down to their distinct voices, life experiences and accents, all fascinated me. What a wonderful world of differences, I thought as I smiled to myself. This new world intrigued me, and I wanted to do everything at once; meet everyone in it, and hear their stories, much like my passion for gaining knowledge from books. I wanted to learn why people did the things they did and felt the way they felt.

'Why do you want to be a designer like your father?' I asked, taking a forkful of my delicious cake the server had so kindly placed on our table.

'Oh, Abigail, when I look at a lady's dress and how it moves when she walks, I can't wait to buy some material and create something with my own hands, something I know will look even more beautiful. I see dresses on the street, and I think to myself, I could make that look so much nicer. I think it is in my blood, and it is what I see myself doing for the rest of my life. I do not care if I get married — I know I will always be able to earn my own living as a seamstress. I plan to open my shop when I am older and design unique and beautiful gowns for the women who come to me. It has been my dream ever since I was small and passing pins to my father when he was working on one of his creations.'

I watched her face intently as she spoke. I wished I were as passionate about something as she was. Unlike her, I did not know what I wanted to do when I arrived in my new homeland. I sat there looking at her, so full of life and feeling a little jealous she knew exactly what she wanted to get out of it.

'Will your parents support you?' She rarely spoke about them, and I assumed they were not close.

'I doubt it. They only want me married off to a man from a wealthy family and for me to bear hundreds of grandchildren. It makes me furious because William can study at any university of his choice, have a prominent career and marry if he chooses. It is completely unfair, and I have decided I will do it my way, Abigail. You just watch me,' she promised, and I did not doubt her for a moment. She was determined, and I could see she would become whatever she chose to be.

We finished our desserts, then slowly made our way back to Hyde Park to have a look around. We walked for a bit, then found a lovely teak bench, sat down together, and talked while glancing at the sky. I noticed clouds like fluff twisting and turning into distinct patterns. I could see a horse soaring gently above me, and it reminded me how I had never ridden one and hoped I never needed to. I was terrified of the large, sweaty animals. They had always scared me and I was fearful they would bite or kick me, so I made sure I always stayed away from them. I had never even touched one.

Catherine continued to talk about Australia, and what it would be like while I thought about my future. I had every intention of taking the helm from the solicitors, who seemed determined to plan my life without my consent. I would take a leaf out of Catherine's book and become the one steering my ship in the direction I wanted to go. But, for now, I felt as if the tiny wooden boat they forced me onto was being pulled in all directions, rudderless, with no sail, floating aimlessly on a stormy sea.

We watched several families playing with their children during a quiet moment, both bursting out in unison.

'I never had that.' We turned to each other and just about fell off the bench, laughing.

'Was it terribly lonely not to have parents?'

I nodded. 'Yes, at times it was, but I was fortunate to have Sister Josephine. She would cuddle me at night when I was small and sing songs to me. Whenever I was sick, she would come to my bedside and stay all night with me. Sometimes, I felt I had my mother with me. She was a stand-in for her, and from what I now know, a far better mother than the woman who gave birth to me.' I knew if anyone understood, it would be Catherine.

'You are blessed to have her. It is more than my mother ever did. I do not remember a single time she came to my bedside. It was always Nanny reading to us at bedtime and singing songs to soothe us to sleep. We were marched down at breakfast to eat with our parents, and then again, in the evening, after we were bathed and dressed for dinner, not a hair out of place, to be inspected by them like we were little soldiers. If we were ever sick, it was Nanny who came to us. In a way, you were luckier than me. I mean, unlike you, I had everything a child would need, but I never had that love, not from anyone who was not paid to love me. No one has ever really loved me.' She wistfully watched the families playing together as I reached across and clasped her hand in mine.

'Well, I love you, Catherine. You are the loveliest, sweetest person I have ever met, and we will be friends forever.'

'Thank you. I love you, too, Abigail, and you are the first friend I have ever made in my entire life,' she replied, embracing me. 'Just make sure you come to see me in Melbourne as soon as you get there so we can continue our friendship.'

'Of course. Your shop will be the first place I visit,' I promised. 'Now, it's getting cold, so I think we should go. Come on now, cheer up as it is time to feed the ducks in the pond.' I handed her a bread roll, and we tore them into small pieces and tossed them to the grateful, quacking birds.

We slowly climbed the stairs to Catherine's suite, deep in conversation about William, before stepping through the door and hurrying into the sitting room. Beatrice was unusually quiet, so I assumed she had fallen into a troubled sleep. William and Nanny looked dreadfully tired, and I wondered how they would cope on the long voyage to Australia with the amount of care Beatrice required. We chatted for a time about their impending journey before I said my goodbyes. Finally, Catherine rose elegantly to her feet and escorted me to the door.

'Thank you for a wonderful day today,' she said. 'It was so nice to get out in the fresh air... and those pastries. Have you ever tasted anything like them before? I cannot believe we ate them with our hands. I felt so unladylike, but what fun.' She giggled and hugged me tightly.

'I'm sure that, in time, you will recover,' I said wryly. 'I will see you at the docks tomorrow morning at ten o'clock, is that right?' I felt my stomach clench at the thought of her departure.

'Yes. I will look out for you, so do not be late. We will be at the first-class entry.' She bid me farewell as we waved to each other before she closed the door, and I rushed down the hall before bursting into tears.

Now that the rest of the day was mine, and I had nothing to do. I asked the driver to take me to my solicitor's office. Mr Miller was outside when I arrived, a good sign Mr Malcolm was inside. He dozed in the driver's seat as I passed, so I decided not to disturb him for now. I walked into the waiting room, where several other people were sitting. I took a seat to wait for my turn.

Miss Delaware noticed me right away. 'Oh. Hello, Miss Delmont,' she said. 'You don't have an appointment, do you? No, you don't. Is it urgent, love?'

'Not urgent, but I do need to talk to Mr Malcolm as soon as he is available,' I replied with a polite smile.

'I will go and ask him. Excuse me.' Miss Delaware toddled off on her enormous heels as I looked around the room. I glanced at the woman to my right. Brightly dressed, she had her face painted and her breasts pushing out the top of her blouse. Well, her occupation was not too hard to guess, I thought, suppressing a smile, then kicked myself for being so judgemental. Returning down the darkened hallway, Miss Delaware stood in the doorway, directing her attention at me. 'Mr Malcolm will see you now, Miss Delmont.' She guided me through, and on the way to his office, she offered me a cup of tea, which I gratefully accepted.

'Go on in, and I will bring you the tea,' she told me kindly. I knocked and stepped into Mr Malcolm's office. He stood up from behind his desk and motioned me into the soft leather chair opposite his own.

'Good afternoon, Miss Delmont. How are you feeling today?' he asked cheerfully, beaming at me like a Cheshire cat. Judging by the clients in his waiting room and the couple I had met at his home, I prayed there was nothing nefarious behind that grin; although, I did not believe that to be the case from my recent, although limited, dealings with him.

'I'm well, thank you. I appreciate your hospitality at dinner the other night. It was wonderful, and I enjoyed myself immensely. I thought you agreed to call me Abigail?'

'Only when we are not in my office and you are very welcome. Now, what can I do for you today?'

'Have you worked any more on the documents for Emiliani House? About the conditions and restrictions we are placing on them to receive the money? I feel bad about myself at the moment, demanding changes and threatening that they will get nothing if they do not comply when the same thing is happening to me,' I spat bitterly, taking a deep breath as I tried to calm myself. He ignored my frustration, holding my gaze intently.

'Yes, but the restrictions — or conditions, I should say — are in the best interests of all the children of Emiliani House, are they not?' I nodded. 'Well, then, you don't have to feel guilty at all, as you are doing something generous and kind.' I felt relief wash over me and smiled across at him before outlining further conditions I wanted and repeated some of the previous requests I had mentioned before.

Mr Malcolm was to buy as many good quality beds as Emiliani House needed, and they must have thick mattresses. Work on

Emiliani House was to begin immediately to restore it to its former glory and open the unused wings. Labourers were to be employed from the nearby village, as many as required, to complete the job well and quickly. The extra rooms were to be made into smaller dormitories and shared rooms for the children. More bedrooms and dormitories opened up for the Sisters to expand their Order and provide more teachers and caretakers for the children. A library Mr Malcolm would provide with books he selected and sent from London; and more schoolrooms.

Women from the village were to be employed to clean, help in the kitchen, and make the children's clothes. The children were to spend their days in school or playing, while the old cook was to be retired on a pension, and a new, younger cook who showed skills in the kitchen was to be employed. The food was to be of high quality, with large amounts at every meal — allowing the children to have as many helpings as they needed to fill their little bellies — and dessert was to be served every night to every child. Mr Malcolm agreed to purchase all the items listed for Emiliani House and large pots and pans for the new kitchen that was to be installed as soon as possible.

One condition I wanted was for the children to be accompanied once a week into the village to buy sweets, and another, bedtime stories were to be read to the younger ones every night. In addition, I asked they be placed in the smaller dormitories with children of a similar age, and they would require a Sister to sleep in each dormitory should they be needed during the night.

'I have documented your wishes and will add the new ones we have discussed,' Mr Malcolm advised, nodding his head and appearing satisfied as he placed his quill down next to the dark pot of ink. 'I have added my own stipulations, the first being that more teachers are to be employed, and the children are to be divided into classes according to age groups. There is also the condition that the children can remain at Emiliani House until the age of eighteen, when

employment must be guaranteed before they leave, as you requested.'
He looked up from the document that lay before him and smiled
across at me. 'We will supply enough cloth to Emiliani House to
make four dresses for each child, twice a year; one set for the cold
and another for the warmer month, along with two pairs of shoes
that will never have the toes cut out under any circumstance.' He
looked up and nodded reassuringly, noticing my uncertain smile. 'We
will replace all shoes with new ones when outgrown; again, as you
so wished. In addition, each child will be provided with a warm,
woollen coat for winter, and enough wool for the workers to make
scarves, hats and gloves for each child will also be assured, along
with cloth for the Sisters to make their own habits and winter capes.
Then there is the condition that the children take music and French
lessons. Is that still required?'

'Yes, I think it's important. Don't you?' I asked, uncertain again.
I wanted them to have the prospects that being fluent in a second
language would give them and the opportunity to enjoy and
appreciate music of all types.

'Well, yes — yes, I do,' he agreed, smiling to himself before picking
up his quill one more time.

Back in my suite, I lay on the bed, wondering what to do with
my evening. Finally, a thought came to mind that sent me racing
to open my closet door. I struggled to remove my dress without
help, grunting and puffing until it dropped to the floor and pooled
around my feet. I stepped out of it and reached for a simple, albeit
tight-fitting, bronze dress that buttoned at the front and quickly
pulled it on; not taking the time to look in the mirror before hurrying
out the door and downstairs to find a carriage as I continued to secure
the tiny buttons.

I arrived at The Savoy just as it was getting dark. 'Please wait here as I will need you for the next few hours if that is suitable for you?' I asked the driver, who opened my door and helped me out.

'Anything you say, Miss,' the young man replied, averting his eyes from my uncorseted breasts. I ran through the hotel and up the stairs to Catherine's suite and knocked on the door, leaning forward with my hands on my knees as I tried to catch my breath.

'Come on, get dressed. I'm taking you somewhere. It's a surprise,' I panted when she finally opened the door, her eyes wide.

'Oh, Abigail, it's time for bed, and I have to be up early tomorrow,' she complained, inviting me in with a smirk as I straightened up and smoothed the skirt of my dress.

'You can't say no. It's our last night together,' I pleaded, taking her hands in mine as she led me into the sitting room.

'Oh, all right, then. But you had better not get me into any trouble,' she admonished as I sat down on a lounge to wait while she dressed. William and Nanny were nowhere to be seen, and Beatrice was quiet, most probably asleep. I struggled to my feet, my dress heavy, before strolling across the room. I gazed out the window at the skyline of a London I had barely seen. Catherine was going to be more than surprised at where I was taking her.

Catherine's expression turned from serene to one of shock when we pulled up in front of The Green Dragon in High Gate.

'We are going in there? Into a tavern? By ourselves? Without a chaperone?'

'Yes, and it's going to be so much fun. Come on,' I said, grabbing her drawstring reticule and placing it in her hand. She reluctantly stepped down from the carriage and held her tiny bag close to her chest. We gazed up at the white, double story building. A friendly young man opened the tavern's heavy wooden doors for us as I dragged Catherine up the steps and through the entrance.

I entered with my head up, looking around, while Catherine clung to me, looking down at the floor, her cheeks flushed. I walked over to a large round table where two men and two women sat and asked if we could join them. They appeared happy to oblige, given they looked as if they had been imbibing for most of the day into the night.

Once seated, Catherine lifted her head and slowly gazed around the busy tavern. There were women dressed in no more than their underwear sitting and talking with patrons, groups of men, all sharing drinks together, along with sweaty female servers, who just looked worn out and sick of life. Our server, Maggie, was warm and friendly, appearing happy to be attending to us and not the drunkards at the next table.

'Me aunt told me 'bout a new concoction from France. Ya feel as if ya are in 'even — only the 'morrow, yer gonna feel like ya dead and been sent ta hell, dependin' 'ow much you 'ave.' She chuckled loudly, making her way back to the bar to make our drinks before we had even agreed. I laughed aloud while Catherine giggled quietly, gazing into the single candle that illuminated our table in the tavern's darkness. While we waited, two men sauntered over to where we sat, watching the wax drip down and onto the freshly scrubbed oak table, both dressed in clothes the colour of dust.

'May we sit down?' one of them asked.

'Yes, of course.' I gestured toward the two seats next to us.

'I'm Ian Rafferty, and this here is me brother, Colin,' he said as he smiled down at us. They were tall and solid, both possessing bright blue eyes and flaming red hair. I introduced ourselves, and we started to chat. They spoke of working on the railways to send money home to their family in Scotland, although Colin was due to immigrate to America any day now. They were ruggedly handsome twins with sparkling eyes that lit up when they laughed. Yet I was looking for the golden glow, and there was nothing.

Catherine seemed to enjoy the banter going on between the brothers, joining in the laughter. She was the happiest I had seen her since before Beatrice was attacked, which gladdened my heart. What if I never met a man who had the golden glow? Although the beautiful light surrounded Richard, I didn't know him well enough to be certain if the friendship forming between us would turn to love or the comfortable affection I already held for him would go no further. I knew I was young, but I wanted to be married one day, and I wanted my husband to have the golden glow.

I took a sip of my drink. It tasted like mint and was creamy and cold. It was so enjoyable I gulped it down then ordered two more. I was starting to relax, and my body had begun to feel heavy and warm. Ian and Colin were paying Catherine a great deal of attention, and I was happy for her. I wanted her last night in London to be special and all about her. We spent the rest of the evening talking and laughing with our new friends, continuing to down the many, many minty drinks, our server promptly delivering the next one before we had finished the last. Catherine was now my only friend in the world, and for that, I was grateful.

Chapter Twelve

I WOKE THE NEXT morning feeling slightly under the weather. In fact, I felt if I moved too quickly, I would empty the contents of my stomach all over the bed. I lay as still as I could so as not to make my throbbing head worse. I didn't know how many drinks Catherine and I had consumed last night, and I also did not remember getting back to my room, yet here I was, dressed in my nightgown and tucked up in bed. I heard someone come through the bedroom door. My eyes were sealed shut and would remain closed as far as I was concerned, as I was feeling far too wary of opening them in case it hurt my head even more.

'Wakey, wakey, Mistress. I'm here to help you feel a hell of a lot better, scuse' my French,' a voice called out, and I groaned. It was Bessie, the only hotel employee who spoke normally to me. With everyone else, it was, 'Yes, Mistress. No, Mistress. Anything you want, Mistress.' I had only recently discovered her full name was Bessie Smyth. Although she had attended to me numerous times and emitted that beautiful light, we rarely spoke of anything personal, including her last name. She was medium in height and plump, although her size did not hinder her work, and she could move as quickly as me. She possessed lovely chocolate brown eyes and brown hair always tightly bound back at the nape of her neck, leaving me curious to know how far it fell down her back.

We had become almost like friends, and I felt comfortable around her because we were similar in many ways. I was drawn to her not only by her golden glow but because she couldn't resist speaking her mind and was a fighter in life, which I admired. She had been raised in an orphanage and had gone straight into service at fifteen as a scullery maid. She had worked too many hours a day to count and never given a day off the entire time she worked there — despite being advised when she first arrived she was entitled to a half-day off every Sunday. Within months, she feared she would drop dead of exhaustion if she stayed her entire life in that position. However, she didn't die but was promoted to housemaid two years later. Another eight years had passed when she noticed an advertisement in a newspaper the Master had discarded — the front page announcing a grand new hotel in London was hiring maids. She sent in her references, not believing for a moment she had a chance of successfully securing employment in London; however, much to her surprise, she was contacted a month later and asked to attend an interview. Her life had swiftly changed for the better once they hired her the day of her interview. She now lived in a small flat near the hotel, relieved she only worked twelve-hour days, and she had one day off each week. It was all thanks to The Delmont, she would often say. It made me feel good that a business I now owned was helping people in its own way.

I opened my eyes slowly to find her standing by my bed, looking down at me without an ounce of sympathy. I would have expected at least that, given I felt so terrible and was certain I didn't look much better.

'Here. Drink this. All of it,' she ordered, holding up a full jug of cold water in front of me. I slowly sat up and obliged, drinking the entire contents as quickly as my stomach allowed, all the while thinking it was silly. Finally, I lay back in bed, my head pounding, wondering how I would stand upright. Bessie returned shortly after and handed me a second jug of water. I drank it slowly this time, not wanting to bring it back up, as my stomach was lurching around like a dinghy in a squall.

As time passed, I felt the water was helping. I began to feel slightly better and struggled to my feet, holding the bedpost for support as the room spun. I had drunk a little alcohol only a few times in my life, without any ill effects, until last night. I hoped I hadn't consumed poison, as I could think of no other reason to feel so poorly. I continued to hold the bedpost for several minutes until the spinning stopped, and I could stand unsupported. Bessie had wandered off to organise my outfit for the day. The thought of having to get dressed and go down to the docks scared me, given how terrible I felt.

'What's this I'm hearing about a lady sashayin' 'round the hotel and streets in nothing but her dress?' Bessie remarked, the smile gone from her lips.

'I've decided I'm not wearing corsets anymore. I can't eat as much as I would like to in them, and they do stupid things to my breasts,' I replied before sighing deeply. The thought of food triggered a wave of nausea, which thankfully passed quickly.

'Well, if you keep eating the way you do, you will be the size of me by the time you get to Australia, and we won't find a corset to fit you,' she retorted cheerfully, laughing to herself.

'I don't care how big I become; I am not wearing them anymore.' I watched her suspiciously from across the room as her face darkened and she fixed me with a stare.

'You are not going down to the docks with no corset, looking like a lady of the night!' She held the white corset in her hands, and it dawned on me she appeared as if she were ready to chase me and tackle me to the floor if I tried to get out of the room without putting it on.

'But I like my breasts better without a corset,' I huffed at her.

'You may like them better, but so will the hundreds of blithers hanging 'round them docks. Now, come over here so I can lace you up and get you into this dress. The sooner you get it done, the sooner you will be back in bed.' She would not budge an inch. I could see she was even more stubborn than me, so I reluctantly admitted defeat and gave in. Bessie had me dressed within minutes, then led me into the sitting room, and towards the table where my breakfast was carefully laid out, the plates covered to keep the food warm.

I sat down, hoping I could keep the food down, while Bessie took a seat across from me at my insistence and poured herself a cup of tea. I was glad it was pancakes. Lord, I could not face eggs this morning. After a moment, I focused my attention on Bessie.

'I have a question to ask you. Would you consider becoming a ladies' maid and immigrating to Australia with me?' I was nervous even suggesting it, but felt I needed to as we had a connection I couldn't explain.

'For you? Oh, sweet Mary, Jesus and Joseph, yes, I would. I have always wanted to go to Australia, and to work for you would be a privilege and a pleasure. But, if you're serious, I must go and give my notice at once and prepare to vacate my apartment.' She jumped up and clapped her hands before leaping up and down excitedly, then stopped suddenly and looked across at me, appearing embarrassed. 'Are you sure it's me you want? You could have the best ladies' maid in London, not someone who's the dog's body for both the guests and management.'

'I definitely would like to offer you long-term employment and a place to call home.' I chewed a mouthful of pancake, trying to swallow as quickly as I could. 'We can discuss the conditions at a later time. I'm feeling dizzy, and I have to go and lie down for a while.' Bessie nodded before guiding me to the lounge, making me promise to drink another jug of water before I got up again. She could not stop smiling as she covered me with a blanket and left me to rest. Richard wasn't due to arrive until nine o'clock, and I had some time to relax 'till then.

Two loud knocks at the door startled me awake. Richard let himself in, and within moments, was standing over me. He looked bright-eyed and full of energy as he stared down at me, lying as if dead on the lounge.

'God, you look tired. What did you get up to last night?'

'You don't want to know.' I struggled to my feet, groaning loudly, then politely excused myself for a moment to use the washroom. I returned several minutes later to slip on my shoes, straighten my dress and hair, then finish the last of the water, a dark cloud of regret hanging heavily above me.

The carriage came to a halt at the docks, and I abruptly looked up from the newspaper I couldn't concentrate on. I turned to glance out the carriage window, surprised at just how many people were there. I could see, from a distance, the enormous steamship, RMS Victoria, waiting for its passengers to board. I had never seen a ship so big in real life before, and I stared up at it in awe. I soon would embark on a similar vessel, and I wondered what it would be like. I could not take my eyes off the monstrous hull as Richard opened my door.

'Come, Miss Delmont. I will escort you over to say goodbye to your friends,' Richard said kindly, his handsome face grinning.

'Richard, can we please stop with the Miss Delmont scaffy? Abigail will be fine.' He chuckled as he reached up and offered me his arm.

'All right Abigail, I will walk you over now.' He assisted me down from the carriage, pushing his way through the crowd, with me following close behind as he cleared a path. Finally, we reached the first-class boarding entrance, where I saw Catherine and William immediately. Beatrice was standing still as a statue, her head bent as she stared at the ground. Nanny stood beside her clasping her hand tightly and murmuring to her, Beatrice appearing terrified, refusing to look at the men around her. They had obviously been forced to sedate her, as she appeared groggy and blank. I embraced each of them, including William, and wished them safe travels, leaving Catherine last. I was going to miss her desperately.

'I had so much fun last night, more than I have ever experienced in my entire life, but, oh my, what was in those drinks? I feel dreadful today,' she croaked softly. We giggled, then held each other tighter for what would be the last time before she sailed.

'I will miss you, Catherine. You are my first friend in the real world, and I thank you for opening up to me. I will miss you so very, very much.' I felt I would burst into tears. We held hands and said goodbye as the others climbed the ship's gangway. 'Good luck, everyone. I will stand here to wave you off,' I shouted as Catherine ran to catch up with them. I watched them slowly board. When they turned to wave goodbye, I waved back — a little urgently due to the fact I was desperate to relieve myself, my kidneys forced to process a ridiculous amount of water since I woke. I turned to Richard and enquired where I could find a privy. He suggested we go to a nearby tavern until it was time for the ship to depart.

He held out his arm for me, and we walked past rows of taverns that lined the streets beyond the docks. Finally, we entered a large, two-story establishment that looked rough; however, I didn't care as long as they had an outhouse. He led me to a table where we sat down. Richard ordered for us, saying the hair of the dog that bit me would cure my hangover, whatever that meant. I asked the server where the privy was, and she led me through the crowd, down a hallway and out the back door.

I ran as fast as I could and only just made it, feeling such relief my bladder hadn't burst and I hadn't wet myself in front of everyone. When I returned, I sat down next to Richard and drank my cider while observing the people in the room. There were a few women dressed in their undergarments, and several of the patrons, all of them men, were taking them one after another upstairs for what I guessed was a sexual encounter paid for in full.

'This probably wasn't the best place to bring you, but it was the closest, and you said it was urgent.' Richard sounded apologetic. He, too, looked around and noticed the ongoing business transactions taking place. I smiled to reassure him I was not feeling uncomfortable.

'No, it's perfect. Your father has sheltered me since I arrived in London. It is so kind of him, but it's nice to be in a place with everyday people like I grew up beside. The places your father has sent me to are lovely, but they are very upper class. In my wildest dreams, I never knew places like this tavern existed. I mean, I do — I have read about them and seen them while walking in the village near the orphanage, but being in one is so different from just reading about them. We went to one last night in Highgate, although it was more of a club and very middle class, nothing like this.' I shifted in my seat. 'I must excuse myself again before we leave.'

I rose to my feet and rushed towards the hallway that led to the privy, needing to empty my bursting bladder again. The jugs of water, and now the cider, had gone straight through me, although I felt a hell of a lot better than this morning. I slammed the privy door and repeated my last performance.

Several minutes later, I stepped back into the hallway and turned a corner to re-enter the tavern, colliding with a small girl, winding me. 'Oh, my God, Abigail,' I heard. Stepping back as I gasped for breath,

I looked down at her, my eyes widening in shock. It was Polly. She was staring up at me, her face beaming with happiness as the glorious golden glow shone around her. She jumped into my arms, both of us laughing, crying and screaming, all at once. I let go of her and realised she was in her undergarments and looked terrible. She was so emaciated, I could see her bones in the centre of her chest. Her thin top was low, exposing one of her nipples, her lace skirt transparent, and it mortified me to see she had no undergarments on.

'Oh my God, Polly.' I took her gently by the arm and led her back down the hallway.

'Abi, please stop. I have so much to tell you and no time to do it. They are going to wonder where I am. I will send a note to your table.' She spoke frantically, her voice barely audible, hugging me again before turning and running down the hallway to the main room in the tavern. I returned to our table, my heart racing and my hands trembling, while the urge to vomit had returned. I felt sick at the thought of what must have happened to my dear friend to lead her here.

'Richard, I have to tell you something, and I need your help,' I whispered in desperation. 'It's a long story, and you will have to trust me until I have more time to tell it, but I need you to buy a girl for a week.'

'What are you saying? You want me to buy a girl? A prostitute, you mean?' He appeared shocked and sat back in his chair, alarm crossing his face as his eyes widened in disbelief.

'Yes. She is a friend of mine, who grew up with me. I don't know what has happened to her, but she needs my help. I need you to buy her for a week so I can get her out of here.' I stared into his eyes pleadingly and saw his expression soften. He glanced at me, and although still in shock, seemed to regain control of himself.

'Which girl is she?' He looked over to where several women were sitting with patrons, some drinking ale with them, while others sat on their laps and pandered to their egos. I pointed her out to him in the corner, where Polly stood with an overweight, greasy-looking man who made my skin crawl. 'Let me think about this for a minute. You want me to buy your friend for a week, and then what?' He narrowed his gaze suspiciously, studying my face for what felt like forever.

'I don't know. I haven't thought that far ahead yet, but all I know is I can't leave her here.' Tears stung my eyes as he leaned over the table towards me, lowering his voice to a murmur I could barely hear.

'I want you to go back to where we were standing next to the ship. Go and wave your friends off while I handle this,' he whispered. I remained where I was until Richard stood and approached a man I presumed to be the owner after asking the barkeep a question I couldn't hear. He then slowly ambled over to Polly and took her by the hand, raising it to his lips and kissing her palm. He whispered in her ear, and she walked away from the fat, greasy man who, until then, had his hand on her bottom. Richard led Polly back to the owner, who looked pleased and nodded his head as the two men talked. Money was passed over the bar, and they shook hands, the barkeep appearing extremely pleased with himself. Richard leaned down and whispered in Polly's ear, a slow smile spreading across her face before she then disappeared up the stairs.

I stepped out of the dark and dingy tavern and onto the docks. My heart was thumping, and I felt so many emotions — joy I had found Polly but distraught over her condition and surroundings. What had happened to her to make her do this? Whatever it was, she must have had no other choice.

She held similar values to me, and I knew her better than she knew herself. I had no doubt this was killing her inside, and her suffering was immense, both physically and emotionally. I looked at the ship in the distance, my eyes welling up with tears as I made my way towards it. I returned to the place where I had said my last goodbyes to Catherine and her family. Craning my neck, I couldn't see them among the hundreds of people waving down at us.

Finally, Catherine came into view on the top deck, along with the others. She was waving and calling my name. I waved back vigorously. The ship began to move, and I could see her face glistening with tears, although she was smiling. Seeing this caused me to burst into tears, too. I thought how alone she was now and the awful situations she was forced to deal with all at once. I continued to wave until I could no longer see her. Richard and Polly found me as the crowd was dispersing. Polly was now in grimy street clothes, but I didn't care. I embraced her again, not wanting to let her go.

'Come along,' Richard ordered briskly. 'We need to get away from here. We can talk in the carriage and at the hotel.'

I wiped the tears from my face; some shed for Catherine mingled with tears for my darling Polly. There were still great hordes of people milling around, and we needed to return to our transport. The problem was there were so many people, it was hard to see where we were going. Polly and I held hands as we followed Richard through the crowd. We finally found our carriage, or more accurately, Mr Miller found us by standing up on his seat and calling out, attracting our attention. We made our way over to him, with me holding Polly's hand tightly the entire time. Once in the carriage, it was hard to hear each other as we both talked at once. We were crying and laughing, and Richard didn't seem to know where to look or what to say for the first time since I had met him.

'I thought you were working in a grand house?' I asked when she finally stopped for breath.

'Well, that's a long story, and one I would rather tell you only in private,' she replied, glancing sidelong at Richard but clearly addressing me. 'What's happened to you, looking like a lady and all? Do you have a rich man taking care of you?'

'No, of course not. I will tell you in private, as well.' We smiled lovingly at each other. Surrounded still by the golden glow she had always had, the beauty of her aura and herself, as a person, hadn't altered. We sat side-by-side, holding hands in silence for the rest of the journey. We both realised there were hard questions to be asked and answered, and we had plenty of time now we had found each other again.

At the front desk, I ordered lunch with extra portions. I knew Polly would be hungry; she looked like she hadn't eaten in weeks. When we arrived at my suite, I opened the door and watched them shuffle in and through to the sitting room, where I joined Polly on the lounge; however, Richard chose to stand, gazing out the window.

'You first, Polly,' I said, raising my brows, knowing she knew exactly what I meant. 'Richard is a friend and soon-to-be solicitor, so you don't have to be afraid to talk in front of him.'

I noticed just how frail Polly had become, how her dress was loose on her tiny frame, and she looked tired and defeated. Her head came just to my chin, her being so much smaller than me. She possessed long, black hair that hung straight as an arrow, although it was now matted and appeared as if it hadn't been washed in weeks, just like her body, which showed signs of dirt. She smelled dreadful.

She told me how she had gone into service at a Duke's grand residence, working until midnight every day, yet had to be awake when the cock crowed. Although tired, she was happy there until she caught the Master's attention one morning as she cleaned the hearth in his dressing room. After that, he would make it his daily habit to be there when she came to perform her morning ritual, chatting with her while she laid the fire before the sun had even risen. His presence hadn't overly bothered her. Not until he began to comment on her breasts and backside, and shortly after, touched her.

At first, he would brush against her breasts with his hand, apologising profusely, which in time led to him grabbing her and passionately kissing her, then progressed to him lifting her skirts and having his way with her. Polly had felt unable to stop him, as he was her employer, and had threatened to dismiss her if she told anyone or stopped coming to his dressing room.

Finally, after several months, Polly had enough and ran away to London, where she begged on the streets for food. Soon after, she met Leroy, an African man from America, who told her she was beautiful and how he would look after her. And he did — for a little while. Then he claimed he was in trouble and owed a debt, and she would need to work so they could pay it; otherwise, he would surely be killed. Polly would have done anything for him by this time, as she saw him as her saviour. He had taken her from the streets, fed and clothed her and provided shelter, and she had fallen deeply in love with him.

He introduced her to a select group of men initially, telling her they were his friends, and there was no harm in her going to bed with them for the money he needed. Soon she was ordered to frequent the taverns by the docks, eventually being installed in the one where we had found her. Leroy would come each week to collect most of the money, and the owner of the tavern rented her a room and took half of what remained of the little she earned. Despite the countless men she slept with, she never seemed to get ahead or have money for herself.

She often thought of me, daily in fact, and she wanted to write, but she was so ashamed of where her life had ended up she didn't know what to say to me. She hadn't wanted to frighten me from going into service, which seemed to be my only option, since she knew I would never become a nun. Polly convinced herself she would find me when she had a respectable job or married Leroy, whichever came first, but I had found her before either of those unlikely things could occur.

Bessie entered the room with two maids to lay the table, placing several trays down on the sideboard before carrying the plates over and setting them down. I discreetly asked her to stay behind and assist me, to which she agreed. I helped Polly to her feet and guided her to the table. We ate our delicious lunch of quiche and chips with a salad, followed by ice cream and fruit. Polly ate like she was starving and hadn't seen food in a long time, eating two wedges of quiche and all her chips. She turned her nose up at the salad, but I insisted she eat everything, which she finally did. Richard sat quietly beside her, eating slowly, contemplating the situation I had dragged him into. He had realised I had no intention of returning Polly to the tavern after the week was up, and he looked worried. When we had finished eating, I asked Bessie to take Polly's measurements. She agreed in her usual cheerful manner and guided Polly to my bedchambers while I followed.

'Look at you, all skin and bones, you poor luv. But don't you worry, we will fatten you up at The Delmont, and you will look as fit as a fiddle in no time,' Bessie reassured her kindly. Polly glanced shyly at Bessie, who efficiently took her measurements and wrote them down. I decided to give them privacy, leaving the room quietly and returning to the sitting room, letting myself drop heavily next to Richard on the oversized lounge.

'I need a big favour.'

'Whatever you need, you only have to ask,' he replied, his face serious.

'Would you go to Madame Felicity's and purchase several nightgowns and matching dressing gowns in her size? They must be soft, warm, and comfortable. I also need one dress for Polly so once she is recovered, I can take her there myself and get her fitted out, but

I think she will need at least a week in bed to restore her to her former self.'

Richard nodded sympathetically. He took the piece of paper with Polly's measurements, calling out to Bessie, asking her to measure Polly's feet. He stood to leave, poking his head into the bedroom to write down the measurements so he could purchase shoes.

'I will be back shortly, Abigail,' he called out, remaining at the bedroom door. 'Polly, it has been a pleasure to meet you. I will bring what you need, but then I will have to inform my father of these developments,' Richard advised as she emerged from the bedroom and made her way to my side, nodding wearily before thanking him. She sat down, placed her head in my lap, and immediately fell asleep.

Chapter Thirteen

I RAN THE BATH for Polly while Bessie undressed her carefully. The emaciated girl had bruises to nearly every part of her body. 'Just part of the job,' Polly murmured, noticing my stare, pain tearing through my heart as I tried with all my strength to keep the emotion from my face. I had never imagined she would suffer as she had, or I would find her in this state, even though I had feared for her every day since we had parted. She reacted no differently from an animal beaten into submission who had lost its spirit. I felt pure hatred for the first time against the men who had done this to my soul sister, and I wanted to hurt them — badly; however, I remained silent as I scattered the fragrant salt into the bath, breathing deeply as the room filled with the scent of a thousand roses.

'It's like the Sisters' garden.' Polly smiled at me, and I smiled back.

'I thought the same thing the first night I was here. I used the liquid but was delighted when I discovered they could infuse salt with a strong fragrance. I read somewhere that bathing in salt is good for you and keeps the Russian flu away. It's lovely, isn't it?' I asked her softly, unable to dislodge the lump in my throat before quickly brushing the tears from my eyes before she noticed. She nodded wistfully while Bessie supported her gently under each arm and guided her towards the luxurious porcelain tub that sat in the middle of the large, elaborate room.

We eased her into the bath, where I began to wash her dull, matted hair while Bessie gently cleaned her body from head to toe, removing what seemed like months of grime. Polly stood, a towel wrapped around her as I held her close while we emptied the black water and refilled the tub, Bessie scattering the rest of the infused salt into the fresh, warm water before we helped her slide back in. I gathered her wet hair and scrubbed it twice more with the hair cleanser, rinsing it well each time before applying the scalp conditioner.

I took the brush and started brushing the cream through her hair gently, from the top through to the ends, working out the knots as I went. Bessie had cleaned her feet by the time I finished and scrubbed the grime from under her nails, both fingers and toes. Her face was now a rosy pink; the parts of her body that did not carry bruises of varying colours were now grime free and glowing. Tears continued to sting my eyes each time I looked at her. Finally, Bessie politely excused herself, removing Polly's tattered clothes before closing the door behind her. I sat down on a stool next to the bath, deciding to tell her everything that had happened since leaving the orphanage and how I would soon leave England.

'Polly, I want you to come with me to Australia.'

'To Australia?' She arched her eyebrows before rolling her bright blue eyes.

'Yes. Why not?'

'They will kill me if I try to escape.' She abruptly turned away from me, gazing up at the small chandelier that hung in the centre of the elaborate room, the black and white chequered floor tiles complementing the solid oak used throughout, the mirror over the hand basin, the largest I had ever seen.

I reached over and gently touched her on the shoulder, causing her to jump; however, she did not push me away. 'Yes, you can. We will have all that sorted out, I assure you. Just promise me you will come. There is absolutely nothing here for you.'

'I want to come with you, Abi, but I don't want to involve you in my problems.' She continued to stare up at the light as I shook her gently by the shoulder.

'Polly, I'm here for you, and I want you to start a new life with me. I have a surname now. Did you know that?' Her eyes widened before she turned back to me and smiled slightly. 'I am still surprised by it myself.'

'Really? That's every orphan's dream.' She gazed at me quizzically, a knock on the door interrupting us for a moment before Bessie strolled back in with a cloth and bucket, preparing to clean the floor and straighten the room.

'Yes, and I want to share it with you. You can travel with me and start a new life as my sister — Polly Delmont.' I felt excitement overwhelm me, my heart pounding hard at the thought of the life we could create together. If she agreed to come with me, I would not only have Catherine waiting there for me but my sister Polly beside me on this brave new adventure that would take me across the ocean. Polly remained silent, appearing to take a moment to gather her thoughts, the room quiet for several minutes as she gently splashed the water over her chest and neck. Finally, she struggled to sit up, and I quickly leaned over to assist her.

'Yes. I will come with you, but I will have to hide until we travel because if Leroy finds me, he will hurt me.' The fear was clear in her eyes as my heart broke again. The situation was pitiful. Through no fault of her own, she had ended up a prostitute within twelve months of leaving the orphanage just to stay alive. It hurt my heart to see how gaunt my dear friend was and hoped she would recover with some rest and good food before we sailed. Bessie hurried to her side and helped her out of the bath, then wrapped her in towels. I left them and made my way out to the sitting room, finding Richard had returned with several packages.

'Thank you so much, Richard; you are truly my saviour. What were you able to purchase?' I asked as he grinned at me. He handed me the parcels and followed me to the table, where I sat down to open them. I found a gorgeous, thick nightgown made of pure wool and a matching dressing gown, a soft apricot colour I was certain would complement Polly's complexion. I hurried to the washroom to give the nightwear to Bessie before returning to Richard and thanking him again.

'Could you please tell your father what has happened in person? I will need to meet with him fairly urgently, when it is convenient for him, of course,' I added.

'Yes, certainly, I will. I have sent word, and he is expecting me, no doubt.' Richard nodded politely before backing away. 'I will leave now and give you your privacy. Please give my regards to Miss Polly.'

He seemed much more relaxed now we were away from the docks. I walked him to the door, thanked him yet again for all his help, and embraced him. If I had been blessed with a brother, I was confident I would feel the same way towards him. When I was in Richard's company, I felt like a younger sister he cared for and kept entertained. When I returned after seeing him off safely, Polly was in the sitting room looking refreshed and clean and back to how she used to look, only pitifully thin. She was a picture of loveliness in her new nightgown and snuggled under one of my recently purchased blankets.

'Did you plan to take me with you as soon as you saw me in that place? Is that why Richard told me to bring along anything precious to me? That's what I have in this bag.' She picked up a tattered carpetbag from the floor and reached inside, showing me a photograph of us together, taken at our first communion, one of several items she had stolen from Sister Monica's office before she left.

She also had a stone I had polished and given to her days before she departed Emiliani House and a multi-coloured scarf I had made for her. 'The scarf reminds me of Paris, and the things we used to talk about, so I kept it with me, always hoping one day I would wear it there while sipping espresso with you at a café. That's what kept me sane when things got bad, thinking about us finding each other and doing all the things we said we would.' Tears filled her eyes as I felt them sting my own, but I gathered all my strength and suppressed them.

The last thing Polly needed was my pity or for me to shed tears in front of her. I knew she would hate it. I led her to my bed and tucked her in, then lay down next to her. She was sound asleep within moments, her soft snores bringing a smile to my lips. I gazed down at her as I stroked her cheek, so peaceful and small, snuggled up in that enormous bed and still the beautiful soul she had always been. I realised at that moment that although she had been restored to me, her innocence was lost and would never be found again.

I let her sleep until the sky had started to darken, deciding to wake her for dinner, given she could not afford to skip even one meal. I passed the meal to her, Polly weakly reaching for the tray as she lay propped up on pillows in the enormous bed. I sat down beside her as she ate very slowly, falling asleep halfway through. I woke her again, fed her the rest of the meal myself, and forced her to drink some juice. She fell asleep almost immediately when she had finished everything, and I took her tray back to the table.

I took myself off for a bath and organised myself for bed. What a day it had been. I had lost one dear friend for the immediate future and found my lifelong childhood friend abused and bruised. I hoped Mr Malcolm would allow her to immigrate with me. I could pay for her ticket and had enough money to keep her healthy and safe until we secured employment in the new land. At least I knew I had a house there in which Polly could live with me, and we could start a new life, just as we had always dreamed. I did not know what awaited me in Australia, but at least I knew I would be surrounded by people I loved and who loved me. Polly, Catherine, and Bessie — three people more than I had in my life just a week ago — and I was grateful.

Polly slept all night and into the late morning. I had asked Bessie to stay with her while I left the hotel to visit Mr Malcolm and to ensure she slept and ate every few hours, along with providing her with plenty of broth and milk to build her strength. While passing the front desk, I spoke to the manager and requested they train Bessie to the same standard as the ladies' maids they employed at The Delmont over the next five weeks until it came time for us to depart to Australia. He appeared surprised they would soon lose a maid; however, he agreed immediately and advised he was confident she would be trained and ready by then, which sent a thrill of accomplishment through me.

I arrived at Mr Malcolm's at eleven o'clock and entered his building. Miss Delaware wasn't in, so I sat down and waited. Finally, Mr Malcolm strolled out to the front desk, saw me, and invited me to join him in his office.

'So, I hear you had some excitement yesterday and rescued a prostitute with Richard?' he said, his eyes twinkling as we walked down the hallway together.

'Well, yes we did, but I rescued my friend, not a prostitute,' I replied, a little too sharply.

'I'm sorry, I didn't mean to offend.' He appeared embarrassed as we entered his office. I sat down on what was becoming my regular chair while he made himself comfortable behind his imposing desk.

'I'm not offended, Mr Malcolm, but I would prefer you refer to her as Polly.' I explained what had happened to her over the past year and that she was poorly, both physically and mentally.

'And you want her to travel with you to Australia?' he asked simply, and I nodded.

'Yes, I do, as my sister. However, since she doesn't have a surname, I want to give her mine, and I am asking you to do the legal paperwork.' He gazed across at me; his shoulders slumped before exhaling loudly.

'Have you thought about taking her on as a ladies' maid?' he suggested, shaking his head wearily.

'I have already arranged for a ladies' maid, and I would never ask a friend to work for me — it would be degrading to them and me.' I felt my face flush as anger crept up inside me. I swallowed hard and repressed the urge to stamp my foot and demand he followed my instructions without question in this circumstance. Polly was none of his business, as far as I was concerned. He chuckled in an attempt to take the edge off my reaction, but failed miserably. I told him about Bessie, and he appeared pleased I had found someone I was comfortable with, an adult who could keep a watchful eye on me. He agreed to prepare the paperwork to give Polly the surname of Delmont, although he appeared unhappy about it.

'Once you consider her your sister and give her your name, what if she takes steps to claim part of your inheritance or use you for money? I hope you are aware she would win in a court of law.'

I rolled my eyes at him. 'Polly would never do that to me. I trust her completely, and we have been closer than biological sisters our entire lives. I know for certain if our positions were reversed, she would do the same for me.'

'All right, then. If you are convinced this is the road you mean to take, I will complete the paperwork for Polly to sign; and I will book passage for her and your ladies' maid. Does that please you?'

'Yes, thank you, it does,' I replied, feeling relieved. I stood to go, but he raised his hand to stop me, asking me to stay a few moments longer.

'How are things working out with Richard as your chaperone?'

'He is wonderful and couldn't be more of a gentleman if he tried. You have raised an upstanding, moral son, and I have found him to be lovely.'

'Yes, he is a good boy but stubborn, much to my chagrin; however, I am glad things are working out between you both as I know he enjoys your company. I will need you to attend my office with Polly when she has recovered and bring Bessie along to finalise the arrangements. Do you think Polly will have the fortitude to come with you to my office by the end of the week?' he asked politely, and I nodded.

'Yes. I will give her a day or two to get her strength back, then bring them both in. Thank you, Mr Malcolm. I will see you again in a few days.' I smiled at him warmly before hurrying out of the office, feeling the happiest I had ever felt in my life.

I stepped into the grand reception, spotting Bessie speaking shyly with the hotel manager. I was uncertain if she had been informed of her promotion, although she beamed at me when I passed her, waving discreetly. She was only twenty-five years old, but she was grabbing this new opportunity with both hands, and it was shining through, even in the way she held herself now. I climbed up the stairs to my room, smiling to myself, and quietly let myself in. Polly was sound asleep, so I proceeded to the lounge and sat down, deep in thought. Shortly afterwards, Bessie arrived with a tray of food, smiling across at me before entering the bedroom, while I struggled to my feet and followed her.

'And you're looking better, Miss Polly,' Bessie called out, her eyes shining as Polly slowly opened her eyes and pushed herself up, leaning back on the pillows, yawning widely as she stretched before smiling shyly at Bessie. 'You are getting some colour back in your face and looking a little brighter. See, it won't take long until you are back on your feet and strong and healthy again.' She served her some hearty meat and vegetable stew and remained by her side until she finished every mouthful while I lay silently beside Polly, staring at the canopy above.

'Thank you, Bessie. I am already feeling much improved,' she replied. She polished off a rich, creamy custard after finishing her full bowl of stew, then lay back down in bed and fell asleep almost immediately. It was clear to me she had not slept for a very long time. She needed to rest and sleep as long as possible to allow her body and mind to heal. I slowly rose from the bed and tiptoed silently into the sitting room, where I sat back down on the chaise lounge. After Bessie quietly bid me farewell and closed the front door behind her, I lay down on the lounge again under the blanket, waiting for Polly to wake. I began going over all that had happened in the past week, falling into a deep sleep within moments, not waking until late in the afternoon. I organised myself then made my way down to reception to enquire what was available for our evening meal. I was able to speak to the chef, Hannigan, asking him to send up something special, to which he politely agreed. By the time I arrived back at our suite, Polly was awake and sitting up in bed, looking much like her old self.

'How are you, my dear sister?' I went to her side and embraced her, feeling her bones through her nightgown.

'So relaxed, but still tired. I feel like I am being lazy and need to get up.' She placed another pillow behind her and leaned back, closing her eyes for a moment; her shiny black hair plaited neatly and pulled back, thanks to Bessie. 'This has been wonderful, being able to sleep and feel warm and safe. Oh Abi, thank you so much for taking me in and loving me as you do.'

'It's my absolute pleasure, Polly, and nothing could ever diminish my love for you. You can eat your dinner here in bed and then go back to sleep, as I want you to rest now. We will see how you feel tomorrow and decide then if you have the strength to get up and dressed. We need to meet with Mr Malcolm, depending on how you feel, but we don't have to attend the appointment for a few days.' There was a knock at the door, and Bessie stepped in carrying an enormous tray, appearing especially animated.

'They have assigned me to you, and are training me separately from the other ladies' maids. I feel special for the first time in my sad and lonely life,' she sang cheerfully, placing the tray on the bed before she sat down to feed Polly.

'That's wonderful news. I can't wait until we sail for Australia, knowing you are both coming with me,' I replied, kissing Polly goodnight before rising to my feet and making my way to the sitting room to allow Polly to eat without distraction. Once finished, Bessie marched into the room and promptly sat beside me on the comfortable lounge.

'I'm so happy, Mistress.' Her grin was wide as she turned to me and gazed into my eyes, reaching for my hand and squeezing it for a brief moment. 'I want to thank you for giving me this opportunity. It has changed my life. I have no one, and nothing, left in England. I know now that, with your kind help, I will make a new life for myself.' Tears filled her warm, brown eyes as I wrapped my arms around her in a tight embrace before she pulled back and brushed away the tears that trickled down her cheeks. She shifted in her seat, moving away from me as she straightened the skirt of her new black uniform, her white lace apron crisp and without a mark on it, while her white cap lay on the low table in front of us. She looked beautiful in her new outfit, her freshly washed hair gleaming, always bound tightly back at the nape of her neck and not a hair out of place, her happiness palpable as her face glowed.

'First, you have no idea how relieved I am that you have agreed to come with me,' I told her honestly. 'I don't know what we will find there, but I'm sure it couldn't be worse than the three of us being back in an orphanage, or God forbid, joining the Sisters.' I screwed up my face in disdain as she giggled. 'Second, I know for certain I would be terrified if I were forced to immigrate to Australia on my own, knowing not a soul, and for that, I am truly grateful. To know you and Polly will share this experience with me and I won't be alone, fills me with excitement. Third, I do have an issue regarding your employment I need to bring to your attention.' Her brown eyes widened while her hand trembled slightly before she nodded, silently urging me to go on. 'From now on, I want you to call me Abigail, not Mistress. I consider you a friend, as well as a trusted employee, and I prefer the familial term.' She nodded thoughtfully before shaking her head.

'No. I apologise, Mistress, but I cannot agree to your request. You will always be Mistress to me until the day I am no longer under your employ. There are certain traditions when you are in service that must be respected and continued for the next generation of servants, and I take my position with you very seriously. I don't want any of the young ones blaming me when they become idle or disrespectful, thinking if it's good for the goose, it's good for the gander.' I bit my tongue, nodding several times as she winked at me, giggling to herself.

Polly had drifted back to sleep, her snores echoing through the suite as Bessie smiled affectionately and patted my leg before rising to her feet and hurrying to the washroom to draw my bath. After she had bid me goodnight and departed, I completed my nightly ritual of bathing and washing my hair and readied myself for bed.

I slipped in beside Polly, falling asleep almost as soon as I lay my head on the pillow. Images of iron bars and mangoes ran through my mind before I looked skyward, finding a storm approaching, the black clouds above frightening me as I lay trapped in a dream I could not awaken from, no matter how loud I screamed.

Chapter Fourteen

I SLOWLY OPENED MY eyes to find Polly wasn't in bed beside me. Throwing the covers off, I jumped to my feet, panic rising in me as I hurried across the room and out of our bedchambers to find her. I immediately noticed her standing by the window in her dressing gown, gazing thoughtfully out into the gloomy sky. She smiled when she saw I was no longer asleep.

'I can't believe the view you have from here.' She smiled slightly before shaking her head in disbelief. 'I can see the Thames and that big clock tower, and the buildings down below are so small from up here. Remember when we used to talk about how the wealthy lived, Abi? How we couldn't imagine what it would be like to have everything we wanted? To not be hungry or cold? I have eaten more here in two days than I have in the past month, and I'm feeling so much better for it. I am in such a deep debt to you.' She shook her head again in wonderment, holding back tears.

Of course, I was fortunate to have had some time to get over the shock and bewilderment I felt over all these new things, the new and sometimes frightening experiences of a completely different way of life, but Polly hadn't. She had only experienced hard times. I was so relieved we had found each other again — I shuddered to think what could have become of her. I sat down in the lounge, placing several cushions behind me, and leaned back against them.

'Polly, we will have a glorious life like we used to talk about, even though we don't know what awaits us. That is the best part of going on an adventure, the not knowing. But you can be sure it will be better than the lives we have here, and we will be together.'

'Yes, I know, but I'm finding it all too hard to believe,' she replied, appearing perturbed. 'I loved Leroy, and a part of me still does, but I know he doesn't love me, or he wouldn't have let me become a prostitute. I just wonder what my future holds, as no man will want me once he knows what I am.' She looked so miserable at that moment my heart broke for her again.

'Polly, what they forced you to do, you did to survive, and it is all in the past now,' I told her, my throat hoarse as I lowered my voice to a whisper despite no one else being present in the room. 'No one ever has to know about it. You will be, for all intents and purposes, my sister. No one will suspect a thing, as they will regard us as proper ladies now. The power money holds is immense, and you can be anyone you want to be when you have wealth to fall back on. You don't owe me anything — we have truly been sisters since we were babies, and I couldn't love you any more than if we had been born of the same mother.'

Her face softened into a small smile, and she turned and jumped into the lounge beside me.

'I love you too, Abi, and one thing I do know for sure is that as long as we are together, everything will be all right. We have each other.' She leaned over and gave me a big hug.

Mr Malcolm turned away from unlocking the front door of his office to find Bessie, Polly, and me pulling up outside his law firm, the carriage halting abruptly. 'Come in, young ladies. It's so nice to see you all, and you look extremely well on this fine day,' he called out warmly, his eyes twinkling while we clambered down ungracefully from the carriage with poor Mr Miller's help. We obediently followed him inside and were shown into his office. Mr Malcolm placed another chair next to the two that sat opposite his desk, indicating for us to sit while he went to make us a cup of tea. I wondered where Miss Delaware was, as he had never made tea personally for me before. Bessie appeared nervous while Polly gazed around the room in awe.

'I don't think I have ever seen so many books,' Polly remarked, her eyes wide as she scanned the bulging bookshelves.

'Yes, Mr Malcolm has been lending them to me, and I have read many of them already.'

'Yes, I remember how fast you can read, Abi; it's not normal,' she laughed. Bessie glanced at me, appearing confused, leaving me to explain.

'From the time I knew my letters, I was blessed with the ability to read very quickly. I could run my finger down a page, no matter how big the book or how small the print, in seconds, absorbing every word and committing it to memory. Polly used to say it was impossible. She did not believe me until, when we were older, she took the Bible I was holding and made me read one page. She then asked me what it was about, and I recited the page I had read word-for-word back to her.' I smiled to myself at the memory while Bessie listened intently, her nerves appearing to have vanished. 'Polly's eyes became wide as she read along, and I accurately repeated every word. Then, to see if I had memorised the page beforehand, she tested me on the second to last page, which I hadn't read yet. I obliged and read the page she held up before turning the book back to herself, making sure I couldn't see it, and I repeated it again word for word. She warned me not to tell the Sisters, or they would cast me out as a witch.' Polly giggled as I smiled across at her. She had worried about me for as long as I could remember, a long time considering I held vivid memories from when I was a tiny infant. Polly saw herself as my protector and, as the eldest, my big sister. Now I had the chance to return the favour.

Mr Malcolm entered the office with a tray holding our tea and biscuits, bending down to place it carefully on his desk in front of us. He sat down in his oversized chair and smiled.

'Well, this must be the Polly and Bessie I've heard such nice things about.' He smiled again, looking at both in turn. Polly nodded her head, too shy to speak, while Bessie leaned over and shook his hand politely; although she appeared quite overwhelmed. 'We have a lot to discuss and go through today, so where to begin? I think we should address Polly's name change first. I have the completed documents here, and all that is required to finalise the matter are your signatures. You are welcome to read over them first, which I would always advise as your solicitor, Miss Delmont, especially if you find yourself in a similar position again,' he remarked, peering at me over his reading glasses with some consternation. I understood the look in its entirety.

He handed us each a copy, and I read mine in seconds. It stated Polly would hereby be known as Miss Pollyanna Delmont, a descendant of The Delmont Hotel founder, Lady Isabelle Delmont of London, England. Mr Malcolm placed the document down in front of me, which I signed immediately, then slid it across the polished desk to Polly. I noticed her hand tremble as she signed at the bottom, placing her new surname alongside her given name. I saw her quickly wipe away a tear that had trickled down one cheek, and she turned and smiled at me.

'We're really sisters now, Abi. Legally. I can't believe I have a surname,' she said, appearing as excited as I felt for her. Mr Malcolm placed the document in the file and turned his attention back to us, smiling fondly.

'I have a Contract of Employment here for you, Bessie, which states your passage will be paid to Australia, and you will work from March the 2nd 1890, starting the day you board the ship to sail. Your terms of employment state you will work solely for Miss Abigail Delmont as her ladies' maid. You must attend to her every need without complaint and be available to her at all times. Your food and accommodation, along with your uniforms, will be supplied. You will receive the sum of two pounds per week, to which I must interrupt here and tell you, Bessie, will make you the highest-paid maid in the Colony. This was at the request of Miss Delmont, against my better judgment, as it goes against all aspects of running a successful business.' He appeared slightly perturbed, shuffling the documents that lay in front of him before turning his attention back to Bessie. He cleared his throat before continuing. 'Are you happy with the arrangements, Bessie?'

'More than happy, Sir. I am counting the days until we leave this stinking hole of a place if you would scuse' me, sir.' She stopped abruptly, realising where she was. I smothered a smile — not only because of what she had just blurted out but the fact where it stated in the contract she would have to meet all my needs without complaint.

'If you can please sign here, and you sign there, Miss Delmont, we are in business,' he said efficiently. I noticed Bessie's hand shaking as she signed Bessie Smyth on the document and realised she was more nervous than she had been letting on, despite outwardly appearing happy and excited about leaving London. When Mr Malcolm stood, I remained seated.

'Mr Malcolm, may I speak with you for a moment, please?' I asked politely.

'Of course. Ladies, I will escort you to the waiting room, and Miss Delmont will be with you shortly.' He completed the task and arrived back, appearing exasperated. 'Miss Delaware has not arrived on time for the past week, and I'm of the mind I will be forced to rectify the matter with her.' He ran his fingers through his thick hair, his face flushed. He realised I was waiting to speak to him, and he shook his head as if to clear his thoughts before straightening up and regaining his composure. 'Now, how can I assist you?' he enquired, the familiar twinkle back in his eyes.

'In the contract, it states something about hotels, and the only hotel I know of is the one here. Hotel as singular. Is there more you need to tell me, Mr Malcolm?' I asked suspiciously. He glanced down at his desk, a habit I had noticed he displayed when he was embarrassed or uncomfortable.

'It's not anything I know for certain, and it's nothing I have been able to confirm yet,' he replied, pausing for a time. 'I have been told by several sources that at least one other Delmont Hotel is under construction as we speak. There is nothing in my instructions about these hotels, as I was left to oversee the building of the London hotel only. The rumours are there is one in Melbourne, and I can understand the Geelong solicitor would deal with this if it were true. If they exist, the others should be handled by me, as they are rumoured to be in Paris and New York. I will make further inquiries into these unconfirmed reports and advise you of the outcome, Miss Delmont.'

He was obviously upset he had not been advised of my wider business interests. As I was getting to know him better, I could see he, too, disagreed with how the Will was being administered and was still upset I had been abandoned to grow up in poverty in an orphanage.

'Thank you, Mr Malcolm, for everything you have done. I will go and join the others.' I excused myself, feeling terrible for upsetting him with my question. He didn't understand either why he wasn't handling all my business dealings or why I was forced to travel to Australia to resolve a second part of the Will when it all could have been finalised in London. I rose from the chair and prepared to leave.

'Miss Delmont, I will make one promise to you, and that is I will always do what is best for your trust fund and the income of your business interests, and ultimately you, with the greatest of concern and care I would show to my own child.'

'Thank you, Mr Malcolm. I do not doubt for a moment you are doing everything you can to benefit me. I am truly grateful.' I stood at the door while he remained standing politely behind his desk, waiting for me to leave him to his work. 'And, by the way, I would like to add a further pound per week to your fee if that is all right with you.' He nodded and smiled as I took my leave. When I entered the waiting room, Bessie and Polly were chatting quietly as they patiently waited for me while Miss Delaware had arrived and was sitting at her desk, trying to look busy.

'Hello, love, and how are we today? I've just arrived. I hope the Mister didn't notice,' she whispered, appearing concerned. I mentioned nothing regarding her employer's complaint, deciding it was safer to remain silent as I bid her farewell while Polly and Bessie prepared to leave.

As I descended the front steps and climbed back up into the carriage, I wondered what kind of morning Miss Delaware had in store for her. I well understood Mr Malcolm's frustration with her, as well as his strong desire to avoid conflict at all costs; however, I could not stop smirking as I adjusted my skirt and made myself comfortable while I waited for the others to join me.

The carriage stopped in front of Madame Felicity's brightly coloured shop front, the street bustling with well-heeled people who all appeared to be of some importance compared to the three of us. Women who came from nowhere and belonged to no one now bonded together. Although I now knew my origins, I was still unwanted and unloved by those connected to me by blood. The blood had drained from Polly's face, and she appeared nervous, wringing her hands in her lap as she stared out onto the busy street.

'It's fine, Polly — everything is going to be fine, I promise you. Felicity is lovely, and she takes care of her customers. If you are going to travel to Australia with me, you will need decent dresses and shoes to take with us on the ship, and you need more nightgowns, too,' I told her gently before helping her down from the carriage; while Bessie remained where she was, muttering to herself. I guided her inside, the bell tinkling above before the door closed behind us. Madame Felicity sauntered over to greet us, recognising me immediately from my previous visit.

'So, new dresses for you now, too. Are you sisters?' she asked, her beady eyes flitting from me to Polly, then back again.

'Yes, we are,' I replied quickly. Polly's face broke into a smile, relief washing over her as she reached across and discreetly took my hand in hers, squeezing tightly.

'At least this sister can be fitted from my ready-to-wear range, as she is of normal size, is she not?' She gazed at Polly, her eyes moving slowly from her face to her feet and back up again, a look of satisfaction on her heavily painted face.

'Yes,' I replied quietly, my face becoming warm. It would be my burden to bear, always having to have my clothes made especially for me. I could never walk into a shop and buy dresses from the few seamstresses who offered ready-made gowns. It had recently become fashionable to stock gowns that only required minor adjustments that took hours, rather than waiting weeks for a fitted and finished gown. I sat down on a small velvet stool, staring after Polly as she followed Madame Felicity into the fitting room, several dresses draped over the seamstress's arm. She promptly returned, leaving Polly in the hands of her assistant.

'Madame Felicity, are you able to make her clothing slightly bigger? She has recently lost a great deal of weight but should soon be back to normal.'

'How much bigger do you hope for her to get?' She raised her eyebrows, appearing mortified, her eyes widening before she shook her head in disbelief, clearly surprised anyone would want to be fatter than they were. I ignored her and rose to my feet, determined to convince her to carry out my wishes. I described Polly's body how it had been the day she left the orphanage, the Madame remaining silent before nodding once, unable to hide her reluctance to comply with my request. 'As you wish. I know precisely what to do.' She hurried away to join Polly in the fitting room. I could hear her muttering to herself, then addressing Polly. 'Yes, you are this size here; no, the blue dress, not that one. These two will do until you gain weight. Now I will go and find some dresses in your future size and put these five that don't fit you back on the racks.' I cringed. I wished she wouldn't speak so harshly to Polly. She was abrupt and bossy, and I was starting to dislike her.

I heard the tiny bell over the door tinkle again as Bessie entered the shop, her feet bare. She had remained inside the carriage due to a broken strap on her shoe, which had snapped as we were leaving Mr Malcolm's office. She had been so excited she skipped down the stairs, missed the last three steps, and had fallen flat on her face. No harm was done except for the damage to her shoe and the bruise to her pride. Her skirts had flown up over her head as she sailed past Polly, landing with her bottom in the air and showing her bloomers to everyone on the busy street. It took all my strength not to laugh once I knew she was unharmed in body, but unfortunately, it had damaged her vanity. She had looked hilarious, flying through the air, showing the world what she had to offer.

'How can I help you now, Miss Delmont?' Madame Felicity asked as she marched towards us, catching sight of Bessie standing close to me.

'I require some uniforms for Bessie here. Can you show us your designs and the colours you have available?' Bessie glanced at me, appearing surprised.

'Do they really have different styles and colours in uniforms?' she asked, raising her hand to smooth her already immaculate hair.

'Yes, we do, and I will go and retrieve the uniform books for you,' Madame Felicity replied haughtily, then disappeared into the back room of her store. When she returned, she led us over to several chairs where we could sit and decide what uniforms we would order.

'Bessie, I want you to pick what style and colours you like, and I want you to have lightweight ones and winter ones. I have heard summer in Australia is like being in a furnace, no different from hell itself. Winter is said to get so cold, there is frost on the ground,' I advised her with confidence, sharing information Richard had imparted to me during our conversations yesterday.

'Are you certain, Mistress? I wouldn't know what to choose,' she replied, her face flushed as she looked away.

Impatient, Madame Felicity turned to me. 'I must say, only the finest of families dress their servants from my collections. You will be more than happy with anything you choose for your maid.' She stood over us, glaring down as she crossed her arms against her ample chest. 'Just one more thing — how many dresses do you require for your sister?'

'The same number as I have ordered for myself, in day and evening dresses, if that's all right?' I watched as she calculated the cost of each dress in her mind, adding them up until her face broke into a bright smile.

'Oh, my dear girl, it's more than all right.' I hadn't seen Madame Felicity smile so wide, or look as friendly as she did at that moment. I assumed these dresses were costing a fortune. We flicked through the uniform books, Bessie pointing to several designs she liked. Instead of getting plain black and white, I suggested she order a range of colours, and she would then feel like she was wearing something different every day.

She chose five winter and three summer uniforms, all in different colours and styles, and selected the finest material. I stood and hurried across the room to find Madame Felicity, acutely aware there was one more thing I had to do. I found her stacking the dresses Polly had chosen in a pile while keeping a watchful eye on my sister, who was still trying on dresses.

'Excuse me, Madame, could we trouble you for some help, please?'

'Of course,' she replied, indicating nothing was too much trouble now.

'I would like my maid fitted with five of the most flattering and fashionable dresses to wear when she isn't working.'

'I will have to make them?' She stared across the room at Bessie, gazing up and down her body disapprovingly. 'I think you need to be aware it is not normal to provide a servant with one of my couture designs, let alone five of them. No one from the highest level of society, or who comes from any family of value, would even think of asking this of me. I am offended.' She glared at Bessie, pointing a shaking finger in her direction.

'Madame Felicity,' I purred calmly, 'with the greatest of respect, I don't care for what is normal in high society, and as your customer, I am asking you to make five dresses of the highest standard, with hats and reticules to match. If this request indeed offends you, I will have no choice but to cancel all orders I have placed with you and seek the services of a kinder dressmaker. One who sees only loveliness in all the shapes and sizes beautiful women are packaged in through no choice of their own. In all kindness to you, of course, Madame.' She glared at me long and hard, my face blank of emotion as I stared back, placing my hands on my hips and tapping my foot as I waited for her to respond; my chin jutted out in defiance.

'I will happily make the dresses, and I assure you they will be the most flattering fit and style for your maid's body in the most fashionable material,' she spat, barely able to hide her resentment. She promptly took Bessie's measurements and selected the designs for her dresses, her face showing no emotion. I nodded my head and thanked her, then requested Polly's dresses be delivered to The Delmont, along with the dresses ordered today. I assumed it terrified her people may hear she had made couture dresses for a maid and would be shunned by society. I could think of worse things.

We returned to our suite to find Richard waiting for us, laying on the lounge with a cushion behind his head while holding up the newspaper as he read the front page. 'How was the shopping, ladies?' He folded the thick newspaper and placed it on the table. I told him how Madame Felicity was reluctant to design clothing for women in service, but later relented, rolling my eyes as I described the battle I had to convince her. 'Well, you do know, Abigail, she is right?' He raised his brows, widening his eyes to make his point. 'Maids have their place, and if you treat them as equals, they won't respect you and will then become lazy and won't carry out their duties to the full extent they are able, or paid, to do.'

'Oh, that's horseshit, Richard, and you know it. There is nothing wrong with giving someone something dignified and treating them like a human being.'

Richard flushed slightly and sighed. 'Abigail, despite your personal beliefs, there is a class system in place that has been there for centuries, and you will not change it overnight.' His face softened as he sat up and patted the seat next to him, indicating for me to sit. 'I agree with you, but you have to realise there are many others who wouldn't, and you are now of a social standing where there are certain expectations of you. If you don't follow them, they will judge you harshly and shun you from society. I would hate to see that happen.'

'Richard, surely you don't believe that; you couldn't, deep down in your soul?'

'No, I don't,' he replied. 'But what I think or believe doesn't matter. I'm only trying to warn you of the repercussions if you continue to push against the boundaries. I want what's best for you, Abigail, nothing less. Because of my friendship and affection for you, I must be honest even if it upsets you, and I feel it is now my responsibility to protect and guide you to the best of my abilities.'

I crossed the room and sat down heavily next to him, listening intently as he explained how the class system functioned in this day and age compared to a century ago. He was such a nice man, and he did have my friendship, which I believed would be a long and close one. I trusted him, but we would be forced to agree to disagree when it came to the difference in our beliefs and values regarding class.

'Anyway, I have something planned for you ladies today and tomorrow.' He relaxed back in his seat, smiling secretively, his hands behind his head.

'What is it, Richard?' Polly and I yelled in unison.

'I plan to take you to the London Library this afternoon and out to dinner this evening. Then tomorrow, we will go to the Zoological Society of London to observe all the rare and exotic animals it holds. Then, because it's been only mildly cold lately, we'll have a picnic in the gardens.' Polly and I jumped on him, bouncing him up and down on the lounge as we screamed in excitement. 'Get off me, you big oafs; I can't breathe.' He shoved us off, Polly landing on her backside, while I fell forward, raising my hands to protect my face from the table, rolling, eventually landing on my back several feet from them.

'You two are like five-year-olds. You get so excited over the smallest things.'

Richard was becoming a big brother to both Polly and me, and the three of us were so comfortable together we had started to tease one another. I found it fun, as I hadn't spent time in the company of boys growing up. I found men interesting and lovely to be around. Polly and I giggled as we lay on the floor, Richard struggling to his feet before assisting us up.

Several maids entered unannounced, quietly placing the food on the table, abruptly leaving as we made our way to the table. We ate lunch while chatting and laughing, the friendship between us all only growing stronger. Finally, we prepared ourselves to leave, all of us in high spirits, following Richard to the door before taking the stairs down and out to the carriage.

Richard spoke quietly to Mr Miller, who helped us up into the carriage, requesting he take us to St. James' Square, where I presumed the library was. We talked and laughed on the ride there, with me teasing him about having a sweetheart. Richard blushed but denied it profusely.

'I think you protest too much, Richard. Come on. Tell us about her. You can trust us,' I teased him. He looked down at his hands, appearing embarrassed as he shifted in his seat.

'All right. There is someone, and I think she is wonderful. The problem is, I don't know what she thinks of me. I have known her for years; she is a family friend and the most beautiful woman I have ever had the fortune to meet. Present company excluded.' He chuckled, appearing relaxed the more he spoke, his eyes filled with love as he spoke of her. 'Her father is best friends with my father. Her name is Jasmin Butler, and she has hair the colour of wheat, eyes the colour of the ocean, and the prettiest face the heavens could have bestowed on her. It's not only that or the reason I'm drawn to her — she is kind and gentle, generous of spirit and fun. The fact we get along well is only another reason I care so much for her. We have a shared history, as we have been friends since childhood. I don't know how to show her or tell her how I feel, and I'm not sure the timing is right yet. I must complete my studies before I have anything of value to offer, and I must be confident I can provide her with a decent life.' We sat in silence, the carriage rocking back and forth, the clip-clop of the horses echoing through the narrow ally before we slowed to turn onto the main road.

'Richard, any woman would be privileged to have you and would take you as you are now if they could see what Polly and I see in you.' I reassured him. Richard appeared touched and nodded, a grin spreading across his face.

'Maybe one day I will have the courage to tell her, but not yet.'

The carriage slowed, then stopped, Mr Miller jumping down to assist us. We thanked him before slowly ascending the steps that led to the imposing library. Although not as grand compared to the buildings of importance I had observed around London on my travels, it was a large building. I was not overwhelmed by the exterior, but by the thousands of books and journals inside that held so much information and knowledge. We stepped through the door, and I stopped, Richard and Polly going ahead of me. I closed my eyes and inhaled deeply, feeling I had died and gone to heaven and hadn't even noticed until this very moment. After several minutes, I opened my eyes to find several people glaring at me, appearing concerned I had recently escaped an asylum close by and sought refuge here among the sane. I hurried over to a large shelf and started to browse, my face hot as I wished the ground would swallow me whole. I reached for several books, flicking through them before making my way towards one of the comfortable lounges and settling in to go on an adventure. Polly and Richard were wandering around, pulling books from the shelves, flipping through the pages and putting them back. They did not share my passion for the written word, and after some time, they looked bored.

'Why don't you go and have afternoon tea somewhere and collect me here when you are finished?' Relief washed over Polly's face, promising me she would bring me back a cake before skipping off to find Richard. She knew I had no control when it came to anything sweet and was confident she could get away with anything if she bribed me with sugar. They departed, and I settled back to soak in the exciting escapades of characters who were unfamiliar to me; however, I was confident in no time, they would feel like family. It seemed such a short time before they returned and complained and whined until I agreed to leave. I reluctantly put my books away, following them back to the carriage, muttering things that would send me straight to hell.

Polly carried a small parcel with her. She told me it was a surprise when we returned to the street; however, I grunted loudly and ignored her. Mr Miller helped us into the carriage while Richard thanked him before easing himself in beside us. They seemed to have had a wonderful time together and were teasing each other on the journey home. I sat back in silence, observing their playful interactions, resisting the urge to pinch both of them on the nose for ruining my afternoon. I felt tormented. I had not found out the ending and vowed to return to finish the novel that now haunted me. This was Polly's first healthy friendship with a man, as it was mine, and she radiated happiness as she settled into her new circumstances, completely ignoring my black mood.

I had calmed down significantly by the time we arrived back at our suite. I relaxed in the sitting room, kicking off my shoes as Polly joined me and handed me the parcel. I unwrapped it, feeling terrible for hating her only minutes before, finding a sticky, sugary cake with syrup. I could smell the heavenly aroma of cinnamon, closing my eyes as I inhaled deeply. I placed it on the plate she had brought from the buffet and cut it into three, offering a slice to each of them. We sat and ate together in silence, and I enjoyed every sticky mouthful. Richard excused himself and bid us farewell to allow us time to change for dinner, leaving to arrange a Delmont carriage to take us to the restaurant. Polly and I walked side by side to our bedchambers and selected the loveliest gowns we owned, assisting each other to dress before fixing each other's hair. We met Richard down in reception, where he was sitting drinking a whisky.

'You both look lovely. You lied when you said hats don't suit you. I believe you both just don't enjoy wearing them.'

'Where are we going, Richard?' Polly enquired, appearing not to have heard a word he said, her eyes flitting nervously around the large room to ensure no one present recognised her.

'I'm taking you to a place called Pagani's. The patronage is mainly artists and musicians, and I believe you will enjoy the atmosphere. You just haven't dined in London until you have been there.' He looked handsome in his evening suit, a cravat tied neatly around his neck that complimented his hat.

We arrived near Queens Hall in Langham Place just after seven o'clock. The restaurant, with its beautiful entrance, looked inviting. We were seated on the first floor in a pretty dining room with blue paper on the walls, soft, indigo curtains that framed the pane-glass windows and shaded electric lights. We ordered borscht soup for our appetiser, and Richard chose calf brains as his main meal. I opted for a fillet of sole and Polly potato croquettes. For dessert, we had decided on the chocolate soufflé, which was said to be the best in London.

'So, Richard, do you plan to visit Abi and me in Australia?' Polly asked. Richard gazed at both of us, unable to answer. He had just taken a spoonful of his beetroot soup, which I thought now was the only way to eat beetroot.

'Yes, of course,' he replied, after swallowing and dabbing his lips with his napkin. 'As soon as my studies are finished, I plan to take ship to see how you are faring in your new home. I feel I have an obligation to you both now, as you are my friends. What they initially forced on me — to be Abigail's chaperone — has turned into an enjoyable experience, and I value you both as if you were my younger sisters.'

'What a lovely thing to say,' we heard, turning to find the woman at the next table smiling at us as she listened to our conversation. We smiled back and continued to eat our soup. He was one of the nicest people I had met so far, but so were his parents, so I could understand why he had turned out to be the man he was. They brought our main meals to the table, each of us devouring the delicious morsels Polly and I had never had the good fortune of experiencing. I looked at Richard's calf brains and thought they looked like white worms — not something I would ever be eager to try. We waited for our dessert and chatted about the future. I noticed the other patrons were brightly dressed and looked different from people I had seen on the street. Some women wore scarves in beautiful colours tied around their hair or waists; long, dangling earrings; and colourful makeup on their faces. Their conversations with dinner friends appeared animated. Our dessert arrived, and I could smell the chocolate wafting up my nose. God, I hoped they had chocolate in Australia. I had become so addicted to it.

A man strolled over to the fireplace with his guitar, sat down, and strummed a tune. As we ate our soufflé, we listened to him sing about a girl he loved but couldn't have, and I thought what a magnificent voice he possessed. I was having a thoroughly enjoyable evening, and I thanked Richard for bringing us here.

'It is my pleasure, and I am looking forward to spending the day with you both tomorrow.'

We returned to our suite, the three of us collapsing onto the lounges, or settees, as the posh people liked to call them. I always referred to them as lounges, as it was by far a more simple term, often used by the lower classes. My stomach was so full; I thought I would burst. Richard struggled to his feet, bidding us goodnight, and I thanked him again for being such a wonderful chaperone.

'I will leave you ladies in peace and return home. I want to be refreshed tomorrow.' He bent down, embracing us warmly. I groaned as I rose, accompanying him to the front door, bidding him farewell and safe travels before closing the door and making my way into the bedroom, where I found Polly laying on the bed, holding her stomach as she moaned.

'I can't move, Abi; my belly is so full. I never knew what it was like to have a full stomach before you found me, and it's not a feeling I enjoy as much as I thought I would.' I giggled at her, helping her to her feet to prepare for bed, wanting to sleep so tomorrow would arrive faster. I soon drifted off to sleep, dreaming of a muscular black horse, a fishing boat, and a block of limestone.

Chapter Fifteen

I WOKE EARLY, FULL of anticipation for the exciting day ahead, but for some reason, a heavy stone sat in my stomach, and I couldn't shake the feeling of dread that had started to bubble up inside me. I glanced across at Polly, still sleeping soundly, and fear engulfed me. I tried to catch my breath, a thousand thoughts racing through my mind. What was wrong with me? Polly was here and safe, and there was no reason for me to feel this way. I pushed the thought to the back of my mind, which I often did when I thought or felt something that made me upset or uncomfortable. Finally, I turned over in the enormous bed, reached over, and touched her shoulder, finding her still curled up asleep.

'Come on, Polly, wake up. We have so much to do today.' I jumped up, bouncing up and down on the bed to rouse her.

'Abigail, you can be so annoying at times, just like the little ones at the orphanage.' She smiled sleepily at me. She had such a pretty face, especially when she was happy. We lay on the bed and chatted, waiting until we would eventually be disturbed, which was inevitable in this hotel.

Our stomachs had recovered from last night, Polly and I enthusiastically sitting down to an enormous breakfast of eggs, bacon, kidneys, along with tomato, sausages, and toast with big dabs of butter. Bottles of juice and hot, creamy coffee were laid out before us as if we were feasting at the palace with the Queen herself. Bessie was her usual cheerful self, chatting away while we ate.

'How is your training progressing, Bessie?' I asked between mouthfuls.

'It's hard work, Mistress, but I love it.' She moved swiftly about the room as she tidied up after us. 'I never realised all the things you had to do to keep someone happy, but mind you, the ladies I have been attending to are nothing like you. They are very formal, extremely demanding, and they rarely talk to me other than to order me about or complain I haven't done something right — or completed a task fast enough. I'm trying my best, and I hope by the time we sail, I will be just as good as the other ladies maids, and you will be satisfied with me.' I gazed across at her, realising she experienced self-doubt and nervousness under her extroverted exterior, just as I did.

'Bessie, I am more than happy with how you are now, and you will never disappoint me, so please relax and enjoy your last weeks in London,' I advised her gently. 'I want you to be happy, too, and remember — this is also a new start for you — not just Polly and myself. We are all in this together and finding our way as best we can. You are part of this — we are all family.'

'Thank you, Mistress, as I feel the same way towards both of you.' She busied herself in our bedchambers, selecting our dresses and undergarments and organising us for the day ahead. Polly followed her in to dress first while I finished my breakfast. I crossed the room and walked through the door, throwing myself on the bed to wait until it was my turn. After what felt like an eternity, Bessie helped me don a beautiful peacock blue dress with bows on the bodice and shoes to match. I pondered whether to wear my hair up or down today. I left it down, and Bessie tut-tutted in disapproval at me, all the while pinning my matching hat to my head. One thing I could count on was Bessie would always make her opinion known, whether I liked it or not, and it was up to me if I listened to her or made up my own mind. I could see we would have our battles in the future, and laughed aloud.

'What are you finding so funny?' She narrowed her gaze suspiciously, jabbing the last pin into my hat a little too hard.

'Nothing, Bessie. I was just thinking of something that happened a long time ago,' I fibbed and smirked at her while she eyed me sceptically. I genuinely liked Bessie and was coming to love her — which I would have done had the golden aura not surrounded her. I knew she was special and would play a significant role in my life; however, I was more confused than ever about the golden glow. I was questioning more each day why some I had met and liked did not have it, such as Mr and Mrs Malcolm, or several of the Sisters who had cared for me, or the lovely new people I was meeting every day?

I hoped Bessie would be happy working for me and would stay a long time, not only as my maid, but also as my friend. Finally, I set my thoughts aside, aware Polly was now ready, her hair pinned up under her hat, and she looked very much the lady she was. I was proud of her for surviving what she had endured and how far she had come in such a short time. We were just getting our coats when Richard knocked on the door.

'Is everyone ready to see the animals?' he shouted, causing us to scream in excitement as we jumped up and down.

'Yes,' we shrieked again as he raised his hands and covered his ears for a moment. Then, he grinned widely, and I thought this Jasmin he'd mentioned would have rocks in her head to reject him when he finally revealed his feelings for her.

We picked up our reticules and set off to Regent's Park to visit the Zoological Society of London. I was looking forward to seeing animals I had only ever seen in books, although I hoped they couldn't escape their enclosures, as I didn't feel the need to be face-to-face with a lion or a hippopotamus. Nevertheless, there were some first experiences in this new world I could happily live without.

Even in winter, Regent's Park was beautiful. Polly and I gazed around in awe at the giant trees as Richard paid our entry fee before the three of us walked in together. Polly and I were like five-year-olds wanting to run ahead to see everything.

'Ah, to be gambolling in the sunshine with not one, but two lovely ladies on my arm makes me feel like the most important man here,' he teased. We strolled with our arms linked, Polly giggling at him while she looked around, wide-eyed, as we approached where the animal enclosures stood.

I enjoyed the feel of the winter sun on my face and felt my excitement building about seeing the exotic creatures I had only appreciated in books. Richard had arranged for Mr Miller to meet us at lunchtime with refreshments and food, leaving us several hours to explore the grounds, which thrilled me. I wanted to spend as much time as I could studying every animal to see how they moved and what sounds they made, things books never could truly describe.

We entered a heated building with a very high ceiling, and I could not believe my eyes at what stood before us. Two giraffes stood proudly, their baby at their feet, while they chewed the leaves from some very tall trees. I felt my mouth drop open, Polly gasping beside me in surprise as one giraffe moved closer, while Richard watched our reaction smugly, as though he himself had created the magnificent creatures that stood majestically before us. They were truly beautiful, and I stood gazing at them for the longest time.

'What do you think? Can you imagine seeing them in their natural habitat in Africa?' Richard asked, his voice low. 'I'm not the adventuresome type, so I will never do that, but I imagine you two would go and try anything, the way you behave like naughty schoolgirls sometimes.'

'I think it's amazing. I want to go in and touch them, but they're so big,' Polly replied before we moved on to visit more of the magnificent animals I had only imagined from images in books. Every creature I saw fascinated me, including the hippopotamuses, elephants and lions, one of which roared directly at me.

We spent a long time in the zoo, enjoying all the things Polly and I had only ever seen in books — and the books had left a lot out. There were animals here from all over the world I didn't even know existed, and I memorised each one. Then, finally, Richard looked at his pocket watch, turning towards us and grinning.

'It's time to collect our lunch from Mr Miller. Why don't you two girls come with me, and we can go and eat by the river?' We eagerly agreed, and each took one of his arms, leaving the animals and, much to my relief, the reptiles behind, strolling through the grounds to meet Mr Miller outside the zoo's entrance. He was smiling broadly when we arrived, as always, while holding a large basket and a blanket. We thanked him before parting and moving towards Regent's Canal, a tranquil river running through the park. Richard spread the blanket and opened the basket. There was roasted chicken, hard-boiled eggs, potatoes chopped up in a creamy sauce, and salad with tomatoes, onions, carrots, and lettuce. The sweet pastries were freshly baked and still a little warm.

'Where did you get all this, Richard?'

'Our cook prepared the basket this morning for us, and I asked her to include something sweet, as I know you have a fondness for sugar, Abigail,' he teased before inviting us to join him on the blanket.

We ate with enthusiasm, enjoying the scenery and chatting between mouthfuls. I pondered on how fortunate I was and, despite people bossing me around, my life was turning in a direction I had never considered possible. 'Richard, thank you for being such a great friend, as that is what you have become, and so quickly, too.' The fact he had the golden glow had only made me feel closer to him almost immediately.

'Well, I feel the same about you, Abigail. And you also, Polly.' He bit into an apple, crunching and chewing before he swallowed and continued. 'It's been wonderful spending so much time with you both, and Abigail.' He waited until I gave him my full attention before continuing. 'You haven't driven me insane yet, as my father warned me. However, he did say you are feisty and strong-willed and will stamp your foot and jut out your chin when you get upset and argue your point. He seems to have had a great deal of experience with you in such a short amount of time.' Polly giggled while I poked my tongue out at him, rolling my eyes.

We were having a wonderful time, but I still couldn't shake the vague feeling of dread that had hung over me all day. I would occasionally experience feelings I could not explain and made no sense, later finding it had been a warning of some sort I had not understood at the time. I pushed it to the back of my mind, deciding there was nothing I could do when I did not know why I felt the way I did. I helped Polly pack everything away while Richard gazed out over the river before rising to his feet, collecting the basket, then throwing the blanket over his arm.

'I will return this to Mr Miller. Don't wander too far away,' he warned, while we nodded obediently. Soon after he left, Polly and

I went back to the animal enclosures to await Richard's return, confident he would find us.

'Are you enjoying yourself?' I asked, slipping my arm around her frail shoulders. She stared up at me, her eyes shining.

'Oh, yes, Abi.' She smiled to herself as she gazed across at the silverback gorilla, who appeared larger and heavier than a man. 'This is one of the best days of my life. I never knew a person could be so happy and feel so at peace without a worry in their mind, but that's how I feel. All my problems have dissolved since we met again, and now I know for certain we will have the life we always dreamed of.' She embraced me, and I hugged her back tightly, the gorilla turning his back on us and bending forward, parting his buttocks before slapping himself on his behind and making loud, unfamiliar noises. We held each other up as we laughed, our bodies shaking before moving on to the next enclosure. We held hands, gazing across at the ostriches, finding gloriously enormous creatures with large, brown eyes, beautiful feathers and the longest legs I had ever seen on a bird. I had read they were native to Australia, only they were called emus there and differed slightly from the ones before us, leaving me giddy at the prospect of seeing them in their natural habitat.

'They are taller than me when they put their necks up,' Polly remarked, appearing intrigued. I watched the gigantic birds closely, just as fascinated as Polly, when I noticed a man and his family standing next to us and turned to observe them. For some reason, they bothered me. I glanced away, finding the well-dressed man staring at Polly intently, and I felt my stomach drop. I glanced at her, my heart racing, to see she was frozen where she stood, and the colour had drained from her face.

'Polly, what's wrong?' I whispered. She remained silent, unmoving; her face turned away from the man while her body trembled. Richard snuck up behind us, placing his hand on my shoulder; however, I ignored him as I stared deeply into Polly's terrified eyes.

'Abi, please, I have to get out of here,' she whispered, her voice so low I could barely hear her. She had turned from white to grey, her entire body shaking so violently, Richard rushed to her side to support her. I glanced back over my shoulder to find the man was still staring at her, then focussed his attention on Richard and me. Polly kept her back towards him and attempted to walk away, appearing to stumble before Richard slipped his arm around her waist, and I hurried to her side, her legs having turned to jelly. We held her up and hurried away, turning down a path lined with small bushes, hiding us from his sight. I turned and took her by the shoulders, forcing her to look me in the eye as she gasped for breath, tears flowing down her cheeks.

'Polly, what's happened? Please tell me,' I begged, shaking her gently. She returned my stare, her face blank as I gently shook her again. Richard stood close, remaining silent but leaving his hand on her back should she collapse.

'Did you see that man?' she asked, her voice shaking. Richard and I both nodded, concern crossing his face. Her bottom lip trembled, and tears continued to flow freely down her face. 'He is friends with the boss of the tavern. We must leave before he tells them I'm here. Please, can we go?' She began to sob hysterically. while Richard quickly slipped his arm back around her waist, leading her carefully towards the entrance, murmuring to her in a soothing tone. I held her hand as we walked as quickly as we could to the carriage. I had glanced across several times at the man standing with his family before they forced us to leave, finding it strange he had made no move to approach us or talk to Polly. I wondered if he had recognised her at all, given she looked completely different now.

Mr Miller was true to his word and was waiting in the same place he had left us this morning, shouting out greetings as we arrived. He stayed perched upon his seat while Richard helped us into the carriage, instructing Mr Miller to ensure we were not followed.

Although Mr Miller appeared concerned, he didn't ask any questions and immediately smacked the horses with his long reins to move them forward at great speed. Once we had settled ourselves in the carriage and had calmed a little, Polly sniffed, wiping her face with a clean handkerchief before blowing her nose. 'That man visited me twice a week at the tavern. He will not hesitate in telling the boss he saw me, where I was and who was with me. Leroy will know within the hour.'

We sat in silence, not knowing what to say. Her past was haunting her, and she clearly felt she would never escape it. I held her as she cried the entire way back to the hotel, attempting to soothe her, but there was no consoling her. When we arrived, Richard quickly ushered us inside and up to our suite, informing us he was leaving to meet with his father. He felt he needed to tell him, given the sudden and concerning events that had occurred, reassuring us that Mr Malcolm would know how to keep Polly safe before embracing us and bidding us farewell.

Polly and I sat side by side on the couch in silence, the door closing behind him.

'Please don't cry, Polly. No one can harm you here.' I grasped her hand in mine. 'We weren't followed, so if he recognised you and says something, it can only be that he saw you out today. He knows no more than that.' She sat up abruptly, pivoting her head, then stared directly into my eyes.

'Abi, you don't know these people. You have only been out in the world for less than two weeks and, although you are the smartest person I know, I have experienced the darker side of life and know more about these things than you do, for which I am grateful. I could never have lived with myself if this had happened to you. That's why I don't want you involved. These people will find me and hurt me for running away.'

My heart pounded as if it would burst through my chest while my hands trembled. I was frightened and couldn't imagine how Polly was feeling, given I was not the one they were trying to find; or control, possess, and beat into submission.

We talked of the abuse she had suffered at the brothel and of what she had experienced. It felt as if hours had passed when Mr Malcolm and Richard arrived, hurrying through the unlocked door to find Polly drinking a cup of tea while I sipped my coffee in silence. Mr Malcolm appeared to have been informed of what had happened, the lines on his face appearing deeper, and he looked much older than he did the last time I had seen him. He sat down next to Polly and reassured her she was safe, that everything would be all right.

'Ladies, unfortunately, this changes everything.' He grimaced, as if in pain, before continuing. 'You can no longer leave the hotel, Polly. At least until you sail. It is far too dangerous for you. They might find you and take you by force. We will do our best to ensure that doesn't happen; however, you must take heed and listen to me; and you must agree you will stay here from now on without exception.'

Mr Malcolm's face appeared grave, as did Richard's, who was quietly sitting by my side, gazing across at Polly. Polly nodded her head, tears streaming down her face.

'It's all right, Polly, I will stay with you until we sail,' I said gently, forcing a smile as disappointment hit me, the realisation I could not see as much of London as I wanted to, leaving me feeling deflated and selfish. I could forgo seeing London if it meant she would be safe, which I knew she would be at the hotel. Even if they discovered she was here, there was no way they could take her by force without being stopped by the hotel employees.

'I'm such a burden, Abi, and now you have to be locked up here with me instead of enjoying London before we leave, possibly forever. I'm so sorry I have brought my troubles to you. It's not fair.'

She struggled to get the words out as Mr Malcolm reached across and patted her hand, attempting to comfort her.

'Polly, this is no one's fault, and we have to do what we can to keep you girls safe,' he said gently. 'We will not leave you alone; I give you my word and solemn promise. Richard will be here every day, and I will visit often. Additionally, you have the employees here around you; and of course, you have Abigail.'

Polly had started to calm, and her tears had ceased. Mr Malcolm stood and offered her his hand. 'You need to go to your bedchambers and rest.' He helped her to her feet, embraced her quickly, then led her to the door, waiting in the entrance to the suite until she had climbed under the covers fully dressed. He returned to the lounge and sat with us in silence for a time, each pondering the situation and what it now meant for everyone involved, not only Polly. Finally, Mr Malcolm abruptly rose to his feet, bending down to pick up his leather case.

'I will see you both tomorrow, and of course, you will have Richard calling on you each day.' He frowned before continuing. 'I cannot emphasise any more than I have the importance that Polly must not step out of this hotel and is to have someone with her at all times. I will speak to the manager and explain I want Bessie to spend her entire working day here in the suite with you for company, attend to your needs, and run any errands for you. Anything you require, please, you only have to ask.' We nodded silently, waving as he called out his farewells while making his way to the door.

'Richard, can I ask you an embarrassing question?'

'Of course you can. But first, who will be embarrassed? You or me? If it's me, I may not answer,' he replied as he laughed out loud.

'Definitely me.' I smiled to myself as I reminded him again how I didn't understand money or its value. I told him of my angst at being forced to trust the shopkeepers and vendors, which bothered me, as I was not confident everyone was honest.

'I will be glad to teach you. I know you mentioned this the first night we met, but it slipped my mind. We have over four weeks, and you will learn in no time. There is no need to feel embarrassed. How could you be expected to understand money when you have never had to?' He smiled, his handsome face now starting to relax. 'Should we start now?'

'I would love to.' We set to work, leaving Polly in bed, her soft snores echoing through the suite. I checked on her as she slept, returning to sit with Richard, who had notes and coins already sitting on the table in front of him.

'All right, give it your best shot,' I challenged him. 'I can't promise I will understand straight away, but I will eventually get it, even if it kills me.' He chuckled and began to explain everything I needed to know that no one had ever taken the time to teach me.

Chapter Sixteen

I WAS LOSING MY mind trapped in the hotel suite. It felt like Polly and I had been taken prisoner, even though we had no official captor. Of course, I was free to leave and go about my business; however, I felt that would have been a betrayal to Polly, leaving her alone in the room with nothing to do and no one to talk to. Although Bessie had been instructed to stay with us by Mr Malcolm, she was in training, and there were expectations placed on her by the hotel management she could not evade. I knew how I would have felt had our situations been reversed and Polly abandoned me to go out and do fun things. Today, though, I just needed to have some alone time somewhere other than in these rooms. Not that Polly bothered or annoyed me. On the contrary, I loved spending time with her, and we always got along, but staring at four walls day after day for just under a month was becoming unbearable.

'Polly, I'm going out for a little while today, if you don't mind?' They had laid breakfast out on the table only moments before we sat down to begin our favourite task of the morning. Eating. One of the few pleasures we could look forward to day after monotonous day.

'Good. I've wanted you out of the suite for a long time, but you wouldn't go.' She burst into giggles, nearly choking on her food, which made me laugh as I pounded her on the back. I had been planning to go to the library we had visited when I first arrived in London, a day I had thoroughly enjoyed that now felt so long ago. Spending even a short amount of time sitting in the peace and quiet, reading wonderful novels, history books, and science tomes indeed excited me more than diamonds and pearls ever would.

I closed my eyes as the carriage rocked back and forth, a sense of freedom washing over me and a deep yearning to be aboard the ship and among people again — one more week. I felt prepared for anything we might find in Australia. I knew at the very least we had a house to live in. I didn't know how big it was, but I knew it would easily accommodate the three of us, and I could afford Bessie and several employees to help me. Polly and I were old enough to look after ourselves and even planned on finding jobs.

It didn't matter after that. Polly and I would have a comfortable lifestyle with Bessie. Given we all came from orphanages and had no one but each other, we could start new lives together; to become the family each of us had yearned for since we were small. I was certain Mr Malcolm would send me money if I needed it until I could access my trust fund when I turned thirty; he had promised me I would never go without. I would pay Bessie's wages as of next week from the money he had given me the first week I had arrived; until I found out what awaited us in Geelong.

The carriage pulled up outside the library, and I quickly stepped down without assistance. I thanked the driver, arranging a time to collect me, before climbing the library stairs. It was my second visit, but I still felt overwhelmed stepping into a building so full of learning and the ghosts of the great minds that had entered before me.

I had already decided I would finish the book I had started, so I scanned the shelves until I found it, then made my way to a comfortable chair and began to read. When I finished the last page, I sat back and sighed. Would I ever find that kind of passion? I wanted to meet someone who would sweep me off my feet and find my own happily ever after. Yet did life ever truly go that way?

I spent the morning enjoying several more novels, moving on to a range of books, from more romances to philosophy. All this new information intrigued me. Since coming to London, I had read more books than I had read in my entire life, but what I had wanted most were experiences. Unfortunately, I hadn't been able to explore the city for the past three-and-a-half weeks due to the threats Polly faced, and I was sinking deeper and deeper into melancholy each day that slipped past.

I found I missed interacting with new people, but I would now have to wait until we boarded the ship before I could truly relax and socialise. Of course, Richard and Mr Malcolm had been wonderful, visiting every day, with Richard sometimes staying from morning until evening. Besides books, he would bring all sorts of savouries and desserts from all over London. The best part had been the sweets. Polly and I would indulge in them after he had left for the day.

I stood up from my comfortable chair, smiling to myself, put another finished book away, and left the library to find something to eat for lunch. Halfway down the street, I stumbled across a restaurant called Lebrina, which appeared cosy and inviting, sitting just inside a small laneway. I stepped inside, inhaling the heavenly aromas, wondering what I would order while taking in the elegant décor and upper-class people who were dining there. I stood at the entrance feeling self-conscious as I waited for someone to assist me. When the server approached, I noticed she had the largest bust I had ever seen, and thick, black, curly hair pulled back tightly from her face. She was pretty, but unfortunately, she had the biggest nose I had ever laid eyes on. She showed me to a small table by the window, the grey sky casting a dim shadow on the wet streets outside.

'Good afternoon. My name is Antonia. Do you know what you would like to eat or drink?' She cleared her throat twice, quickly scanning the room before focusing her attention back on me.

'Hello. I am Abigail. What would you suggest?' I felt my awkwardness creeping up again. I couldn't stop looking at her enormous nose.

'What do you enjoy?' Her mouth twitched in amusement as she waited patiently, my mind racing as I tried to focus. She would barely have been eighteen, and I wondered if I would enjoy being a server as much as she appeared to. You certainly would meet many people of all shapes and sizes.

'Anything. I love all food,' I replied, feeling self-conscious. She smiled and suggested several options, noticing me screwing up my face at each one, as I found I had to be in the mood for certain foods.

'I would suggest the steak and gravy with roasted vegetables, and if you like dessert, the apple pie with cream and custard.' I let out a deep breath. That sounded perfect. I had again navigated a bumpy road with this lovely young girl's assistance. I nodded my head and thanked her profusely as I caught sight of a tall man whose nose resembled my server's. I assumed he owned the restaurant as I watched him standing behind the counter talking to a woman who appeared to be his wife. She had black, curly hair and an equally large bosom as the polite young woman who had taken my order.

I wished Polly and Catherine could be here with me. I noted the other patrons glanced at me oddly at times, then spoke to each other in hushed tones. I wondered what I had done wrong this time. Finally, Antonia returned with my meal and placed it in front of me.

'I hope you enjoy the steak. My father is the cook here and, although I am biased, they say he's one of the best in London,' she said proudly. I watched her attend another table and then looked down at my meal. The steak was so large it covered half the plate, and the vegetables were brown and crispy. I cut into the meat and placed a piece into my mouth. It was flavourful and crisp on the outside, the meat so tender it was like cutting butter, and the gravy was like nothing I had tasted before.

Soon my mind wandered to Catherine. They would still be on the ship, but at least by now, they would be in warmer weather and nearing the end of their journey. London had been cold and dreary with sporadic sunshine, and I hated it, just like the weather in Scotland. I knew I couldn't live here. I wanted to be somewhere where the sun bathed my skin, and I could be outdoors enjoying everything life had to offer. I finished my meal and made my way to the front counter, paying my bill before thanking them profusely. I stepped out onto the street and hurried back to the library. I promised myself I would read just one more book and then return to the hotel. I felt guilty about leaving Polly alone for so long; however, the desire to be back in that grand room surrounded by books was far too strong.

I opened the door and walked towards the sitting room. Polly usually yelled out as soon as she heard me, but the room was silent today. I searched the remaining rooms, then walked into the washroom. There was no trace of her. Her clothes were still there, and I noted everything was in its place as I went through her wardrobe. Maybe she had gone for a walk, feeling shut-in like I had, and would return soon? If I went to look for her, she might return of her own accord, and I would walk the streets for no purpose. I decided the best course would be to wait for her here.

Hours passed, and I was afraid. I had checked with the hotel employees during the afternoon and evening, but no one had seen her, and Bessie was nowhere to be found. The only people Polly knew, outside of myself and the Malcolm family, were the awful people at that tavern; and they would hurt her if they ever found her or she returned there. She knew better than that. I felt in my soul something terrible had happened to her, and I just knew it had to be tied to that damn tavern.

As I placed the shilling in the hand of my coach driver, who had delivered me safely to the docks, he thanked me, climbing back up to his seat. 'Do you want me to come with you, Mistress? It's no place for a lady to be walking around alone at this time of the evening.' I had never seen him at the hotel before tonight. He was a tiny young man whom I doubted could protect himself, let alone me. If he accompanied me, I would more than likely be obliged to defend him.

'Thank you for your kindness, but I will be fine. I will return shortly, so please wait here for me. I am only going to collect a friend.'

'Thank you, Mistress. I will be here,' he replied, staring at me, his eyes vacant and his face blank, causing me to wonder if he was drunk. I turned on my heel and hurried determinedly toward the tavern where Polly had worked. The docks were a bustling place, even at night, and all the taverns were full of people, mainly men, often spilling out onto the street, intoxicated and obnoxious. As I moved down the dark street, a large man approached me from a darkened doorway.

'How much, luv?' he slurred, a scar from long ago running from the corner of his eye down to his lip.

'More than you can afford. Go away, you pig. Fuck off,' I yelled at him and attempted to pass. He tried to grab me, but I avoided his grip and started running. The sounds of his angry taunts faded in my ears as I reached the tavern. I stopped outside to catch my breath, then peered through an unwashed window. I couldn't see Polly anywhere, but I recognised some women I'd seen the last time I had visited the premises. I pushed open the door and entered, finding my way through the rowdy, smoke-filled room to a table, ordering an ale from the server to calm my nerves. I maintained my outward composure, but inside I was shaking. I watched the women with deep sadness as they lounged along a wall where men chose their prize, paid the owner, and took them upstairs for sex. I saw several women who had been upstairs earlier circulating in the centre of the tavern and talking to the customers, a routine Polly had told me they were required to do. When a short blonde woman walked past my table, I gently tugged at her sleeve.

'Excuse me. Do you have time to sit with me and talk?' I asked politely, taking a quick sip of my ale. She looked me up and down in surprise.

'Luv, I 'ave all the time in the world, but it'll cost ya,' she replied with a grin, and I could see she had few teeth left. The few that remained were black and rotten.

'Please order a drink and sit with me,' I offered, at which she raised her eyebrows in amusement.

'It's not often I get sweet, young girls wantin' ta pay me for me services.' She laughed at her own joke. A weak smile was all I could manage in response. She sat down opposite me and told me her name was Mary, which I didn't believe for a minute. Soon, after downing a whisky I had ordered for her, she told me her life story. She said she had been working there since she was thirteen, adding how her mother had sold her to the owner, leaving her to pay off a family debt. She appeared to be in her thirties; however, her eyes were hard, and her face sunken and hollow with a yellow tinge. I wondered how many more years it would take for her to get over her mother's betrayal — that was, if she ever could.

Finally, I summoned all the courage I had in me. 'Do you know Polly?' She stared at me, showing no emotion, but didn't answer or move. I knew I would have to be gentle with this woman — although I felt like screaming and shaking her until I had the information I needed. 'I am Polly's best friend. I saved her from this place a month ago, and she has been staying with me ever since, but she has disappeared, and this is the only place she could be, willingly or unwillingly. I have to find her.' Tears sprang to my eyes, and I quickly wiped them away. She continued to stare, her eyes cold.

'So, it was you that took 'er. The boss an' Leroy were plenty mad. Oh, God, yes, there was a big ruckus 'ere for weeks, I'm tellin' ya, lady. Ya caused a lot of problems for us 'aving ta put up with their foul tempers 'cause of it.' She glared hard at me, cursing under her breath before leaning back in her chair and sighing deeply. I remained silent, not knowing what to say anymore. Not that I regretted the trouble I caused them, even for a moment. 'So, ya really saved 'er? Ya looked after 'er an' provided for 'er 'cause she's ya friend?' she asked quietly, and I nodded.

'I need her back, Mary. She is all I have in the world, and if anything happens to her, I don't know what I will do.' I couldn't stop the tears flowing freely down my face. She looked at me again, not without sympathy, then leaned forward.

'Ow much ya willin' ta pay ta get information?' she whispered, her eyes darting around the room. I reached into my bag, finding what I needed.

'How much do you want?' I asked directly, as I would have given her everything I had.

'One pound, take it or leave it.' She crossed her arms against her ample bosom, leaning back in her chair with a determined look on her face. I took out several pound notes and handed them across to her discreetly so no one else could see. Her eyes went wide as she hid them in her undergarment. 'Ya must really love Polly. Yes, I know 'er, an' yes, she's back 'ere. They brought 'er in, kickin' an' screamin' this afternoon, an' dragged 'er down ta the cellar. That's a place ya don't wanna be. I spent a few bitter days down there once when I 'ad trouble meself with the boss — no, lady, ya don't wanna go down there. That's all I know, luv. 'Aven't seen 'er since.' She rose unsteadily to her feet, indicating our conversation was over.

'Wait. Tell me, before you go, how do I find the cellar door? Please. I'm desperate to find her,' I begged, grabbing her hand before she could stand. She leaned down so close to me I could smell the alcohol on her breath mixed with a foul, decaying odour that made me want to gag.

'See that door at the back? Go through there an' keep walkin' 'till ya see a corner on ya left. Turn, an' you'll find some stairs leadin' down. Can I go now?' she asked impatiently, snatching her hand away. I nodded and thanked her, which she ignored and walked away without looking back. I studied the door at the back of the room, waiting for the right time to make my move.

I crossed the room and weaved my way through the crowd, slipping through the door unnoticed. The hallway was dim, and it took a moment for my eyes to adjust, but much to my relief, there were stairs to my left. I stopped to catch my breath before slowly descending, wincing each time the boards creaked under my feet. Forced to take two at a time, I finally stepped into a large room, finding large, wooden barrels stacked to the ceiling and the smell of rum intoxicating. There was an enclosure with bars around it, a single iron bed with a thin, dirty mattress, and a bucket inside. Huddled in one corner was Polly. Shock overwhelmed me for a moment before relief washed over me. She was still alive.

'Polly, what has happened?' I ran to her, sobbing loudly. She slowly lifted her head, and I could see her tear-stained face as she recognised me.

'Abi, thank God you found me. I thought you would believe I had run away and would sail without me. I'm so sorry I left the room, but I just had to get out in the fresh air, and they caught me.' She stood and came to me, and, with tears running down our faces, we held hands through the bars.

'Polly, it's all right. Everything will be okay. But you must tell me where the keys are.' Polly slumped on the small bed, placing her head in her hands in despair.

'The boss has them on his belt.' I shook the door, but it was far too strong to break open. I took out one of my hairpins, bent it a little, inserted it into the lock, and jiggled it around.

When we were at the orphanage, I would break into Sister Monica's office with my hairpin at night so Polly and I could read of the bad behaviour and sins of the children in the Bible of Punishment. I believed she kept it as it was a reminder of the penances she so enjoyed carrying out on the vulnerable, frail and defenceless children in her care.

'It's not the same kind of lock you used to open at the orphanage, Abi.' She struggled to her feet and pleaded with me to go before someone discovered me.

'I will not leave this terrible place without you, Polly. I don't care what you say.' Her eyes went wide, and she began to tremble. The colour drained from her face, and I thought she was going to be sick.

'So, this must be ya little friend who stole ya away?' I heard a deep voice and turned to find a solid man, taller than me, with dark hair and a mean, unattractive face, standing behind me. He stepped forward, grabbed me roughly by both arms, and shook me sadistically, making my teeth clatter, my head rocking back and forth violently. 'You're goin' in with 'er. I think you'll make me a pretty penny, too,' he growled as I tried to kick him. He opened the door of the enclosure and threw me in, shoving me hard. I fell on the dirty floor, hitting my head on the corner of the bed as I landed. I raised my hand to my head, the warm, sticky blood oozing down my face and covering my fingers.

'You bastard,' I screamed. I struggled to my feet, my body shaking, as he rushed forward and threw me against the bars, hurting my back. He bent down and picked me up by the hair, holding me by the throat with his large hand against the bars.

'You listen to me, ya little cunt. You'll do as I say, an' you'll shut that fuckin' big mouth, or I'll 'urt ya like no one 'as ever 'urt ya before. Let me see what standard of meat I 'ave 'ere, just so I know 'ow much to charge.' His eyes glinted dangerously as he aggressively pushed his hand up my skirt and shoved his finger inside my private parts, making me gasp in horror as Polly lay sobbing on the bed, unable to stop him. No man had ever treated me so violently or touched me in this way. I felt completely violated and burst into tears. He loosened his grip on my throat so I could breathe, but he refused to let go.

'You bastard,' I gasped.

'Well, well, well, we 'ave a fresh one 'ere. Still intact, 'ey? I can sell a woman like you to a wealthy gentleman for a lot of money. I'm a lucky man to 'ave a lady like yourself come to me so easy. You were stupid to show up 'ere. No friendship is worth that, 'specially with this wee trollop, but it'll be to me good fortune,' he sneered, gazing intently into my eyes, his face only inches from mine as I continued to gasp for air, my body screaming in pain. Thoughts of my impending death filled my mind before he suddenly let me go. I dropped to the floor, stunned, panting hard. Polly was screaming but unable to get up from the bed. 'Shut up, ya whiner,' he growled, bending down and slapping her with such force, she fell back onto the mouldy mattress, her hands going to her face where he had struck her. She whimpered, trying hard to stop herself from making a sound. I was still on the floor as he locked us in and climbed the stairs. I joined Polly on the small bed. It was filthy and, ironically, had only a thin blanket for warmth.

'Abi, I'm so sorry for what he did to you. This is all my fault. I wish you'd never seen me again.' She sobbed as we held each other tight, our hands clasped together as we sat side by side on the filthy bed.

'Polly, it's no one's fault but those evil bastards. We must keep our wits about us. Tell me — what happened today?' I sniffed before wiping my face on the bottom of my coat.

Polly sighed deeply before relaxing back on the bed. 'I left the hotel shortly after you did. I only walked for a few minutes when a carriage jerked up beside me, and two men I had never seen before grabbed me and threw me inside.' She quickly brushed away a tear before continuing. 'I thought I would be safe in broad daylight, but they didn't care who saw them. I was kicking and screaming, and no one came to help me. They brought me back to the tavern and took me straight down to the cellar.'

I burst into tears when she told me how the boss of the tavern had come down to her prison cell and smacked her in the face, telling her she would be sorry when Leroy arrived and would hand out her punishment for running away.

'Until you showed up, I'd been sitting here alone, just waiting for them to hurt me.' She gave me a half-hearted smile that broke my heart into a million pieces.

'What's going to happen to us?' I asked, feeling frustrated as well as frightened. Polly had calmed down significantly and explained to me as best she could how things worked here and who was who, so I knew how to protect myself.

'They will keep me down here for a while to make me suffer, and they will beat me and starve me, then they will send me back to work.' She gazed down at the floor, a fresh bruise swelling near her temple. 'It's you I'm worried about because now he knows you are a virgin, he will sell you to the highest bidder, and it won't be anyone from the tavern. He will look among high society to get the most money he can. That will take time to organise, maybe a few days, so you are safe for a while. They shouldn't harm you physically, as they wouldn't want you to be marked if they expect good money for you. Some of the upper-class men I have been with have black souls, so I fear for you if they do not rescue us.'

'That will be soon, Polly. I left the driver of the carriage at the docks and told him to wait for me. When I don't come back, he will report me missing to the hotel, and I am assuming Mr Malcom.'

I was not at all confident the driver would act on my behalf, thinking I had found my own way back to the hotel. I was kicking myself for not sending word to Richard before charging off like a raging bull. I felt so cross with myself for not even leaving a message with the hotel, aware of the danger I was placing myself in by coming here alone.

'I'm so sorry, Abi,' Polly said again, her legs trembling as she sat on the edge of the bed, staring down at the floor. She appeared so tired and beaten down, almost like she had been when I first found her. 'If you had never seen me again, you wouldn't be in this situation. I'm nothing but trouble.' She started to cry again, and I slipped my arm around her slight shoulders.

'We are going to get out of this, Polly, and we will start a new life in Australia,' I reassured her, patting her back in an attempt to soothe her. 'This is not your fault, so stop blaming yourself. We need to be strong until they rescue us. Let's try to get some sleep, so we have strength enough for what tomorrow brings.' I kissed her on the cheek, then stood up and took off my coat. Polly did the same. 'We can sleep together under our coats and stay warm,' I told her, and she nodded, smiling weakly at me.

We lay down together on the tiny bed in our dresses and pulled the coats over ourselves. The cellar smelled strongly of rum and wine, while the air was frigid. We lay cuddled together for the longest time, but neither could sleep. I couldn't help but listen for footsteps coming down the cellar stairs, wondering if someone would come before terrible things happened to us.

I had faith Richard would do everything in his power to find us before it was too late. I finally fell into a troubled sleep, where I dreamed of a shovel, an island, and a striking man with sandy blonde hair.

Chapter Seventeen

I GROANED, AWAKENED FROM a tormented sleep as something rattled nearby, a key turning the lock on the heavy steel door to the prison that confined us. The tavern owner stood aside, and an enormous man strode in, his ebony skin glistening in sweat.

'So, you have returned, my dear?' Leroy asked Polly, who struggled to open her eyes, still half asleep as he loomed over us, gazing down with a crooked smile on his face. He spoke in an accent I had never heard before. Polly had told me he had travelled to London from America, where he was born; however, I knew very little of him, as it pained her to speak of him. 'Stand up and let me look at you,' he ordered politely, a look of surprise crossing my face, but not Polly, who obeyed him immediately. She struggled to her feet, looking up at him, her eyes full of fear while her face remained blank. 'Now, come to me.' She reluctantly took a step forward before he swiftly raised his arm in the air and smacked her hard in the face. Her head jolted back as she attempted to remain on her feet, her nose bleeding before she dropped to the ground heavily. He reached down and grabbed her by the hair, pulling her upward as she screamed, clutching her tightly by the throat as he shook her violently. His voice, deep and eerily calm, terrified me. 'Now, I want you to listen to me and listen well. If you ever run away again, I will kill you — do you understand me?' Polly cried out in pain, fear overtaking every part of me as he shook her sadistically again by the hair with each word he spoke.

'Yes, I understand, Leroy. I'm sorry. I won't do it again — if you would just let my friend go. You have me back, and she has nothing to do with this,' she whimpered, tears streaming down her face while I silently hung my head and cried. Leroy smiled, his white teeth shining in contrast to his dark skin. In his tailored navy suit and immaculate blue hat, he dressed like a gentleman, his brightly coloured cravat tied neatly around his thick neck; but in no way did he behave like one.

'You think you can ask me for favours after what you've done, girl?' he scoffed. 'Maybe I need to put you into the asylum for a while to teach you a lesson. You'd be insane to think I'd do anything you ask of me now. You're going back to work today, and I'll be escorting you to the room where the client will be waiting. Later, I will escort you back here and repeatedly do it until you've learnt your lesson and I can trust you again. It's up to you how long you stay in this cellar, Pollyanna. After you start behaving yourself, you'll be able to return to your room and be with the other girls when you work each day. I see you are both dressed expensively, so if I find out you're working for another man, I'll track him down and destroy him. I blame your friend here for what you've done. You never would've left me, but she'll pay in her own way.' He turned his stony gaze from her to me, releasing his grip on Polly before brutally throwing her on the bed, then stepped towards me. I cowered, not only because of his frightening size but the fact I had witnessed his brutal treatment of Polly, who he supposedly loved and cared for, confirmed just how dangerous this man was to a stranger. He smiled, his face only a whisper from mine, before he drew back his muscular arm and punched me hard in the stomach. I doubled over, unable to breathe. Tears welled in my eyes as I gasped for air. No one had ever scared me as much as this man or had purposely hurt me in this way before, and it overwhelmed me with terror. 'I hear you're a virgin and going to make old Robbie and me here a lot of money,' he sneered. 'Don't worry. After the first time, it won't even bother you if you do what you're told and please the clients. Have I made myself clear to both of you? If one of you tries to escape or gives Robbie or me any trouble, I will hurt the other one, and you will feel pain like you have never felt before.' Polly whimpered in fear as she watched me from the bed.

I continued to gasp for air, my hands clutching at my throat, still feeling his touch and could only nod my head. Leroy grabbed Polly roughly by the arm and dragged her out of our prison cell — my screams echoing through the cellar. Robbie, the tavern owner, quickly locked the barred door before I could run after her. I screamed out to her as she was taken away and forced up the stairs. I felt sick over what they would do to her and helpless I could do nothing to prevent it. All I could do was wait.

I estimated an hour had passed before I heard footsteps. Leroy re-emerged from the tavern above, stomping heavily down the stairs while holding Polly's arm tightly, appearing furious as he dragged her across the room. Polly had blood on her face, while her left eye was swollen shut. Her lips were split and engorged, and her dress torn and splattered in blood. He unlocked the door to our cell, cruelly shoved her back inside before slamming the door closed and turning the key, the lock clicking loudly in the silent cellar. I glanced down at her to ensure she was breathing, finding her huddled on the floor crying quietly. He left without saying another word. I helped Polly to her feet, sitting beside her on the rickety old bed, holding her in my arms as we both sobbed, her despair palpable. When she finally was able to talk, she pulled away, wiping her tear-stained face with the skirt of her torn and grimy dress.

'They took me to my old room, where a man was waiting for me. He was awful, Abi. They left me alone with him, and when I refused to let him kiss me, he beat me.' Her voice broke as she hung her head, tears streaming down her face. 'He raped me, then beat me some more, before raping me again. Leroy waited on the other side of the door and heard my screams.'

Polly stared at the wall, no longer showing any emotion — her voice flat and monotonous — rocking slightly back and forth before I wrapped my arms around her. We lay together on the bed, and I told her a story I used to tell her at the orphanage that would help her fall asleep when we were small. It was all I could think to do to comfort her at that moment, finding I had no words of reassurance or comfort I could speak without being untruthful. As she lay limply in my arms, I listened as her breathing slowed into a deep, regular rhythm as time passed; how much time I was uncertain. We remained huddled together and silent until Robbie stomped down the stairs with a loaf of bread and a bottle of water. Polly sat bolt upright, shrieking, as he rattled at the cell door, immediately ceasing her terrified screams and going silent as she realised where she was; and they would hurt her or me if we made a fuss. He placed the bread and bottle on the floor, just inside the cage door.

'Eat quickly; another man is waiting for ya,' he ordered sharply, his eyes narrowing as he stared at us. 'You 'ave 'alf an 'our before I come and get ya. This time, ya better be friendlier and be'ave yerself, Pollyanna, or you'll receive the same treatment ya got before. Leroy 'as given 'is permission to any client ya 'ave they can use force if ya don't cooperate.' Polly trembled uncontrollably, nodding her head in defeat as he walked away, climbing the stairs before disappearing from our sight.

When he returned, she showed no resistance. The bread remained untouched, as did the water. I lay on the bed, crying for my Polly, picturing in my mind what they were doing to her in the tavern above. Someone would have noticed we were missing from the hotel and must have begun a search. I was not confident they would find us in time, and my hopes were gradually diminishing.

Polly remained upstairs as the hours slowly passed. I nibbled some bread and drank some water, leaving her half, although my stomach churned, and I felt ill. It felt like days had passed before I heard footsteps above, abruptly turning towards the old, wooden staircase to see her being marched down the stairs, Robbie holding her firmly by the arm. Although he seemed less violent than Leroy, I believed he was equally dangerous. He unlocked the door silently, and Polly stumbled in as though in a trance. She sat on the bed next to me but didn't utter a word. There were no tears, only a blank stare.

'Polly, you must eat something, and you need to drink.' When she did not respond, I broke off some bread and tried to hand it to her; and when she still didn't react, I fed her each piece, holding the water bottle to her lips between each bite. Finally, she lay on the bed again, broken and battered.

We spent the day waiting to be rescued, waiting to know if our lives would be normal again. Robbie would return and take Polly upstairs throughout the day, leaving me alone for long periods; until they brought her back, more withdrawn than before, breaking my heart anew. It made me want to kill every man who had ever touched her. I glanced across at the small vent that shone dimly into the musty, dark cellar, noticing it was getting dark outside. Polly had been gone for a long while, and I was becoming frantic. I lay on the bed with my eyes closed until I heard familiar footsteps above, remaining still in an attempt not to provoke our captors.

'Stand up,' Robbie barked. I did as I was ordered, feeling fear rise in me. He stood next to a man I had never seen before. He was tall and well-dressed, looking as normal as Mr Malcolm. My mind raced as I wondered if I was to be taken now and defiled by this unknown man, feeling I would vomit at any moment.

'I have to say, Robbie, she is a beauty,' the man remarked. 'She's the best one I've ever seen — look at that body and hair. And you say she is a virgin?' He glanced across at him, appearing suspicious, before he looked me up and down again, fixing his gaze on my breasts.

'I promise ya she'll bleed, an' if she don't, I'll return yer money to ya.' Robbie's eyes were also fixed on my breasts before I twisted away. They began discussing business between themselves, their voices low, speaking as if I weren't even in the room.

'Write down what ya willin' to pay, as I 'ave more gentlemen comin' tomorrow to look at 'er; an' I'll inform the 'ighest bidder the day after tomorrow ta come and complete the transaction,' he told the man, who refused to take his eyes off me.

'What about if I give you the money for Polly and me?' My voice broke as I sat down on the bed, placing my head in my hands. Robbie laughed — a low, evil sound — and I summoned all my strength and rose to my feet, slowly approaching the bars.

'Now, that wouldn't be as much fun, would it?' He chuckled to himself, guiding the potential customer back up the stairs while they both laughed loudly. I was alone again.

I heard the cell door open — the hinges screeching as I sat bolt upright, waking immediately — my heart in my throat. Leroy stepped inside the cell, ignoring me as he roughly grabbed a sleeping Polly by the arm and pulled her from the bed, standing her up while staring at her face.

'This is not good for business, Pollyanna,' he murmured sweetly. 'The more you fight, the more you'll be hurt. Go back to how you were, and all will be right again. You know I love you, and you will only have to do this a little while longer, then we can be together.' He stroked her hair soothingly as I watched her hesitate, confusion crossing her face. He bent forward and kissed her, and I could see she kissed him back. He still had a hold over her. I could see that now, the way she looked at him despite his cold, cruel treatment of her. I glanced over at the vent, the light brighter than before we had fallen asleep, confirming it was now early morning. My mind wandered to what Robbie had said to that man last night.

Men would come to look at me today, and tomorrow one of them would come back and take my virginity by force. I felt sick to my stomach and sat down on the bed as Leroy locked the cell door and guided a silent and obedient Polly upstairs. I lay back on the bed to await my fate, a stray tear trickling down my cheek.

One after another, seven men had come and gone throughout the day to view me as if I were in an enclosure at the London Zoology Park. All wrote down what they were willing to pay for me, handing their envelopes to Robbie before hastily departing, the brims of their hats pulled down low over their faces. Polly hadn't returned once throughout the day, despite my prayer to any God that would listen to me. I hoped they had at least given her something to eat, as I was starving and had eaten nothing since the bread yesterday. The hours had passed so slowly, and as the sun faded, I worried this time someone had really hurt her, maybe even killed her.

I felt relief wash over me as loud footsteps echoed above; however, the thought of my impending rape made me dizzy. I felt sick, not knowing if Polly would be returned safely to me or those evil men would be at the cell door within moments to lay hands on me. My heart beat faster when I summoned the courage to open my eyes to find four police constables entering the cellar, their loud stomps as they rushed down the stairs music to my ears. I jumped up from the bed and ran to the bars, holding my hands out to them, bursting into tears of relief.

'Are you Abigail Delmont?' asked one of the coppers, who stood at the door of my prison in his immaculate uniform.

'Yes. Yes, I am. Please help me,' I cried out as the constable took my hand in his, trying to comfort me. 'They have my sister, Polly Delmont, upstairs in one of the rooms.'

The Sergeant turned and walked back up the stairs, leaving the three constables to stand guard over me. They stared at me, a mixture of pity and sympathy in their eyes, as if believing they had defiled me. Within minutes, Richard and the Sergeant returned with the key to the cell door. He turned the key and swung the door wide before I rushed into Richard's arms, unable to stop the sobs of relief that wracked my body.

'Are you all right? Did they hurt you?' The fear and pity in his eyes was almost too much to bear.

'It's P-Polly,' I stammered. 'They took her again this morning, and they have been hurting her. I don't even know if she is still alive.' Richard held me tightly, stroking my hair as he murmured in my ear.

'It's all right. We found Polly upstairs in a room. She's bruised and battered, but she's alive. I escorted her to the carriage and now we need to get you out of this place and back to the hotel.'

Richard supported me up the stairs and into the tavern's main room, where the police had Robbie handcuffed and standing against the bar. I pulled away from Richard and stopped, turning around. I pulled myself up to my full height and jutted out my chin before I strode across to Robbie, smiled widely, then kicked him as hard as I could in the testicles with my knee. He screamed, dropping to the ground as he writhed in pain — the sound of several people laughing ringing in my ears before Richard led me away to the waiting coach.

Exhausted, I tried to focus on Richard, who was doing his best to explain why it took him so long to find us — the carriage rocking back and forth as the horses trotted through the narrow streets and alleys.

'I arrived at the hotel yesterday in the early morning to visit with you, only to discover you missing.' He explained he had immediately advised his father, who initially assumed we had run away, having changed our minds about immigrating to Australia — but Richard knew better. He had insisted that the hotel manager allow him access to our suite, where he discovered nothing was missing and I had left most of my money behind. Suspecting we hadn't gone of our own free will and had met with foul play, he interviewed every employee of the hotel who would speak with him — including Bessie — who was frantic to know what had happened to her Mistress. He continued on, informing us one maid reported she had seen me leave in a carriage alone the night before, but she didn't know where I was going; however, I appeared to be in a hurry. He then spoke to the carriage drivers along the street, but no one remembered taking me anywhere that night. He consulted with the police, but they would not act unless he had some evidence that something sinister had happened, so he had gone to the tavern last night to ask the girls if they had seen us.

No one had — at least, that was what he was told. Today, he had returned to the hotel and spent the day talking to the employees again and re-interviewing the carriage drivers. He finally found a slow-talking young man who remembered taking a pretty lady to the docks. He informed Richard that she had asked him to wait, but she never came back; and he had returned to the hotel, thinking she must have found another ride. He did not mention this to anyone, as these things happened all the time. The next day, he was off work and stayed home, tending to his plants, unaware of the danger he had left me in. Richard returned to the police and presented the evidence he now had that something sinister had occurred to us, and they had agreed to accompany him to the tavern to conduct a search. They arrested Robbie for running a brothel from his tavern. Leroy, however, was nowhere to be found.

As the carriage came to a stop in front of The Delmont entrance, Richard informed me that a doctor was on his way to examine us and ensure that we were both unharmed. I nodded before carefully climbing down from the carriage while Richard assisted Polly, slipping his arm around her waist. The hotel employees stared as we limped through the grand reception and climbed the stairs to our suite. I knew we looked a sight, with Polly's injuries and torn clothing, my soiled dress, and our hair not brushed for days. Within minutes of arriving in our room, Bessie burst in and tearfully embraced us both.

'Oh, my dear girls, I have been sick with worry for the both of you,' she said, her voice breaking. 'I only left to do the laundry before having to carry out other duties for the hotel, and suddenly you are both missing when I returned with your dinner. I went to the hotel manager and told him, but he refused to believe anything was wrong. I wanted to send for Richard the first night you didn't return; however, I was threatened with the sack if I disturbed him during the night. I didn't sleep a wink and found him here the next day looking for you. I have done nothing but blame my wretched self since it happened.'

Stifling her tears, she offered to draw us a bath. I asked her to let Polly go first, as she was shaking and injured and needed to be cleansed more desperately than I did. She took Polly gently by the arm and coaxed her into the washroom, closing the door behind them. Richard sat with me, shifting in his seat, appearing uncomfortable.

'Did they hurt you, Abigail?'

'Not really, Richard. They punched me in the stomach, but that was all. They were trying to sell me to the highest bidder, and if you hadn't found us tonight, I would have been harmed come tomorrow. Polly is a different story. They hurt her and made her go with men who beat her and forced her ...' my voice trailed off into silence; however, I knew Richard understood as he nodded silently. He crossed the room to bring me a fresh cup of tea, returning to his seat beside me. I told him of Polly's abduction and how I went looking for her later that night at the tavern, what they did to us, and how I was kicking myself for not sending word to him before I rushed off.

'Don't worry about that now,' he reassured me, relief crossing his face. 'You are both safe, and I will make sure it stays that way until I see you safely aboard the ship.'

Polly limped out of the washroom in her dressing gown, her hair in a towel, looking much better as she smiled weakly, managing to walk unsupported. Although covered in bruises again, I knew they would fade in time. It was the emotional scars that worried me. I hoped and prayed she would recover from those. Bessie stepped out of the washroom, Polly's ruined clothes bunched up in her arms.

'Should I mend this, Mistress?' she asked, holding up her tattered dress.

'No, Bessie, throw out everything she was wearing, and the same for me. We don't want memories of this whenever we see those dresses.' She nodded and placed the offensive garments in a heap near the door.

'Come on, you — it's your turn,' Bessie called out, motioning me towards the washroom. I stood and slowly crossed the room, stepping through the door to find a warm bath waiting that smelled of roses. Bessie stripped me, then gathered up my clothes while I relaxed in the soothing water, taking everything downstairs to be burned. When she returned, she gently washed my hair and scrubbed my body. I felt so much better. Just having her massage my head as she put the conditioning paste through my hair comforted me, and I knew I was safe again. Wrapped in towels, then dressed in my nightgown and dressing gown before returning to the sitting room, someone already tucked Polly up in bed. She snored softly, while Richard prepared to leave. I hugged him, thanking him again for everything, and nodded when he said he would see me in the morning. Given Leroy's whereabouts were still unknown, the police had stationed an officer at our door.

I slipped into bed beside Polly while Bessie showed the doctor to our room and then left him to examine us. He possessed a kindly face, explaining gently that I was uninjured other than the bruises on my stomach, reassuring me it would heal quickly. It would take longer for Polly, however, given the seriousness of her abuse. Nothing was broken, he found and advised us her black eye, cuts, and abrasions would disappear in time.

He administered laudanum for the pain and to help her sleep, then quietly left the room. I rubbed Polly's hand to keep her awake while waiting for Bessie to return with our food. I knew we would be all right once we got away from London and that Polly could start her life again fresh, without having to worry about the hideous abuse she had endured, leaving it all in the past the minute our ship sailed. Once again, we were safe, warm, and — most important — together.

Chapter Eighteen

I T WAS BARELY DAYLIGHT when I was woken by several loud knocks on the front door. I cursed under my breath as I slithered out from under the covers, quietly rising to my feet, slipping my dressing gown over my shoulders, before making my way to the door. Mr Malcolm and Richard stood before me, alongside the constable, who had remained outside the door of our suite through the night to protect us. I invited them in, following them into the sitting room as a maid hurried past, carrying a tray with a fresh pot of coffee and a plate of toast. We sat down on the lounges as she placed the tray in front of me, pouring a cup for each of us. I wondered what had happened for them to call upon us so early in the morning; however, I knew for certain it must be important. It was clear by the look on Mr Malcom's face; this was not a social visit.

'I have been thinking a great deal about your situation, and I have reached the conclusion that you are not safe here,' Mr Malcolm explained, averting his eyes from mine. 'I hardly got a moment's rest during the night — thoughts of what happened to you girls ran rampant in my mind. What could have happened had Richard not located you last night makes me feel physically ill. I am mortified by what you and Miss Polly have endured while under my care. I have let you down greatly, Abigail, and I wish to make amends for this. However, there are only four days left until you sail on Monday morning, and we would feel far more comfortable if you would accept our hospitality and stay with our family for the rest of your time here in London.' Mr Malcolm appeared concerned as he sat back, gauging my reaction. I felt he was merely stating a fact and not seeking my permission, but I knew he viewed me as a daughter and was only trying to take care of us.

'That's a very kind offer, Mr Malcolm,' I replied, raising a silver cup to my lips and taking a sip. 'I'm sure it would be lovely to spend the little time we have left in London town with you and your family. When would you like us to come?' I smiled at him graciously. It really would be nice to spend our remaining days at their home. They had treated me like family since I had arrived nearly six weeks ago, a lost puppy who knew hardly a soul in the world.

'Well ... now, actually,' he replied before pausing. 'As soon as you are dressed, I will have your things brought to my house. I will station the police officer outside our home to continue protecting you.'

'Yes, we would be honoured to be guests in your home, Mr Malcolm, and would appreciate your hospitality and protection.' He seemed relieved I had agreed so quickly and smiled. He finished his coffee and picked up some toast spread with butter and marmalade jam, demolishing it within moments. He possessed a healthy appetite, but mine was no less. He would often admonish me that it was unacceptable for ladies to eat their food the way I did or consume the amount of food I could in one session.

'We will take our leave and wait for you in the reception room while you ready yourselves.' Mr Malcolm finished another piece of toast before smiling again. 'There is no need to bring anything other than your personal items, as everything else will be delivered to my home this afternoon. I have arranged for Bessie to end her employment here today and join you so that she also has time to finish the last-minute things that are required before you sail. Given today is Thursday, we only have a few days to ensure you have everything for your voyage. Our family is looking forward to spending these last days with you both and hearing of your plans for your new life in Australia.' He looked fondly at me, both elegantly rising to their feet, preparing to leave. As I walked them to the door, Richard turned and embraced me tightly.

'What was that for?' I laughed, holding back emotions that were bubbling up to the surface.

'I am just so relieved that you are both safe and back where you belong. I don't know what I would have done had we not found you, or if something dreadful had happened to you ...' His voice trailed off, realising that something dreadful had indeed happened to Polly. 'She will heal in time, Abigail, with the love and care that only you can give to her,' he mumbled, obviously remembering the bruises and cuts on her face. He winked at me before turning and stepping out the door, hurrying to catch up with his father.

Polly and I strolled arm in arm into the sitting room, the maid who had assisted us in dressing scurrying behind us. She offered us the breakfast she had laid out on the table, which we politely declined, aware we must make haste. She helped us place our personal possessions in my calico bag, which I had kept, despite now owning numerous trunks made of beautiful timber. I had vowed to keep it as a reminder of Emiliani House and never forget where I came from, what it was like to be hungry and cold and to have no control over your own life. We met Mr Malcolm and Richard in the grand reception room, the hotel busy given it was still early. Mr Miller was waiting outside, leaning on a carriage wheel while he drew on his pipe, inhaling deeply. In her weakened state, Richard supported

Polly, his arm wrapped around her tiny waist as she limped towards the carriage, still weak and suffering immeasurable pain. Mr Miller appeared shocked when he caught sight of her, sadness darkening his lined face as he helped us into the carriage; however, he remained silent. Once settled and the carriage was moving swiftly through the streets, I turned to Mr Malcolm, who appeared distracted.

'How does Mrs Malcolm feel about us coming to stay with such little warning?'

Mr Malcolm chuckled. 'My dear girl, she has wanted you to stay with us ever since you came to dinner, but I didn't ask you because I felt it was better to give you the freedom to do as you wish. Don't misunderstand me. You will still have your independence, but unfortunately, in the confines of my home.' He was right, and it would be better than being confined to a hotel suite day and night. 'I have arranged a bed in the servants' quarters for Bessie. I relieved her of her duties until you sail. She may like to spend time with friends she has made in London before saying goodbye.' I was pleased and nodded gratefully. I didn't want her leaving London with any loose ends or regrets and admired and appreciated just how very kind Mr Malcolm had been to us all. I glanced at Richard, his face pale and drawn, his head resting back on the wall behind him, his eyes closed but his body rigid. The events of the past few days had taken their toll on him, more than anyone had realised, including me. I knew I must find time to sit and talk with him later, to make sure that he was all right. It touched me how deeply he cared for Polly and me and I wanted to thank him privately. The horses slowed as we drew up to the front of the elegant double story house. Mr Malcom assisted us inside, finding Mrs Malcolm waiting in the hall.

'Oh, my girls. I am delighted to welcome you to our home. Anything you want or need, you only have to ask.' She embraced us both warmly, tears welling in her eyes when she saw Polly, who looked as if someone had smacked her with a lump of wood a hundred times over. Her left eye was swollen shut, her cheekbone had turned black, and her lips were split in several places and swollen far worse than they had been yesterday.

Mrs Malcolm, who reminded me she would prefer to be called Jenny, showed us through the house. It was a stunning residence — not grand compared to the mansions I had seen in books and certain parts of London, but decorated beautifully down to the finest detail. She led us through the parlour, then on to the sitting room, guiding us past an office tucked away at the rear of the house. Polly gasped when we stepped into the dining room: however, I had become accustomed to the grandeur of the room, having dined there before. She ushered us quickly through the kitchen, and servants' quarters, allowing us to slow down once we had reached the stairs that led to several bedchambers and a washroom. We were shown two rooms, and I could see by Polly's face that she didn't want to sleep alone.

'Would you be offended if we asked to share a room?'

'Of course not, Abigail. Whatever makes you both more comfortable here during your stay is acceptable to me. I want you to treat our home as your own. Richard still lives here with us, and my elder two sons, Johnathon and George, are married and have their own homes. You will meet them on Sunday with their families for lunch.' She obviously loved her family deeply. I wondered what it was like to have a mother like Jenny, who loved you fiercely. 'I will go and organise your breakfast with the cook; I heard you haven't eaten yet. Come to the dining room when you are both ready.'

Jenny turned and hurried away, leaving us alone in the bedroom to unpack what little we had brought with us. The room was large, with a four-poster bed and nightstands on each side decorated in dark shades of blue. I expected this had been one of her son's rooms before he married and moved away. The room smelled of lavender and was quite lovely. Polly sat down on the bed and let out a loud sigh, her shoulders slumping as she hung her head. She had hardly spoken a word this morning, and I was worried about her.

'Don't give me that look, Abi,' she said sharply, continuing to stare at the floor. 'I'm fine, I promise. I can cope with the pitiful looks I am getting from everyone else, but not from you, so can you just stop it? You seem to forget what I endured over the past few days I was accustomed to experiencing daily, so I will be all right again. I put it behind me when you first found me, and I will do it again, but please don't look at me with pity in your eyes. I can't stand it!' I looked away, feeling terrible. I had hoped she wouldn't notice my anxiety when glancing over to ensure she was all right, believing I was maintaining a blank face.

'All right, I won't. It's only that I worry about you, Polly, but....' She cut me off immediately, raising her head and glaring at me.

'Well, stop it! It's irritating,' she snapped. I stared back at her, knowing how strong she had always been and obviously still was. If I had been through what she had, I didn't think I could cope and would feel truly crushed, but not Polly. 'I need some time to myself, so you go down to breakfast. I'm going to go back to sleep,' she ordered sharply, standing abruptly to undress. I thought it best to leave her be, quickly helping her undo her laces, then slip the nightgown over her head before hurrying to the door.

'I will bring you something to eat later. Sleep now, and you will feel better.'

'Abi, just go and leave me alone, please.' She pulled the heavy, blue coverlet up over her head as I left the room without saying another word and made my way downstairs. I knew it wouldn't matter what I said. When she was in a mood like this, you just had to wait for her to return to normal — how long that could be — even I was uncertain.

I entered the kitchen to find a tall, thin woman in a black uniform and white apron, a lace cap atop her tightly bound grey hair, who immediately caught sight of me and turned around.

'Good morning to you, child. Which one are you, Polly or Abigail?'

'I'm Abigail. I am pleased to meet you.'

'I am Mrs Shank, and I am very pleased to meet you, too. I am the cook here in the Malcolm house and have been since they married and had the children. Is Polly coming down to eat?' She glanced across at me, a large bowl on the bench in front of her she was whisking rapidly, her face flushed from exertion. I pulled out a chair and sat at the kitchen table to chat.

'No, Polly has gone to bed. She is not feeling well. I will take something up to her when she wakes.'

'Well, I will arrange that without a bother. You need to relax before your journey. Have you ever been on a steamship before?' she enquired, placing a glass of juice on the table in front of me.

'No, I haven't. I've never been on a boat — even a little one.'

'Oh, my dear, you will enjoy it very much. I once went with Mr and Mrs Malcolm to New York with the children, acting as their Nanny, and it was wonderful. Being on the ocean and looking out over the deck to see nothing but water and sky, the wind in your hair, is the greatest feeling I have experienced. And there is so much to do on a ship. They have games, a swimming pool just for the ladies, and dinner parties every night. You will meet many new people, and I am sure you will love every minute of it.'

'I am looking forward to it, Mrs Shank.' She served me two boiled eggs in their shells, both sitting in tiny cups with toast cut into strips, crispy bacon sitting on the side of the plate. She showed me how to take the top off the eggs and dip my toast into the creamy yolk. Just when I dug my toast into the runny egg yolk, Jenny walked through the door, her eyes widening in horror.

263

'Abigail, you are our guest and are to eat in our dining room. Mrs Shank, I would have thought you at least would have known that.'

'Oh, Jen, stop trying to impress the girls. Abigail felt comfortable in here, so this is where she ate. I will make you both a nice cup of tea.' I smothered a smile, Jenny's eyes now even wider as a result of her cook's admonishment. They had obviously known each other forever and were comfortable speaking their minds. Jenny joined me at the table, appearing defeated as she sat down heavily beside me, then smiled at me as we waited for our tea, deciding to take it outside to the garden to enjoy.

As we strolled among the barren flowerbeds, she chatted continuously, telling me of her love for her family and how proud she was of Johnathon and George. They were both qualified solicitors who worked in their father's practice; however, Richard was of great concern. He had mentioned to his parents only two days prior that he did not want to follow his brothers into the family business. He expressed his desire to go out on his own and become a great criminal barrister, which displeased his father immensely. Mr Malcolm had envisioned all three sons working beside him until his retirement, when he could confidently hand his practice over to them.

The thought of telling his parents had tormented Richard for weeks, uncertain if he should admit the truth and suffer the consequence of his father's wrath, or let him continue to believe, for the next two years until he qualified as a solicitor, he would join the family firm. I had strongly encouraged him to tell the truth now, so his parents could get used to the idea. It seemed he had followed my advice; however, had forgotten to tell me.

Jenny confided they hoped he would change his mind before he completed his law degree and, although worried, had accepted his decision at this point, not wanting friction or discontent within the family. We continued to stroll through the garden, stopping several times to gather the blooming primrose that grew abundantly, despite how frigid the weather was and had been for months now. Jenny held the flowers in her hand, smiling as she opened up about her sons.

She explained Jonathon was their eldest and married to Isabelle. They had a small son named John and lived close to the family home. George had married Georgina only two years before, and she was pregnant with their first child, due to be born in the next few weeks. Jenny spoke fondly of all her sons and their wives and spent a great deal of time with them. She filled her days running the household, managing their servants, and meeting her friends for luncheon often and her daughters-in-law once a week.

Jenny had met her husband when she was seventeen through her father, a Barrister who sat in the Old Bailey as a judge in his later years. Mr Malcolm had been employed at his law firm as a junior solicitor, newly graduated from university. As soon as she laid eyes on him, her heart was his forever; however, it took some time for him to realise because he didn't want to be accused of furthering his career by marrying his employer's daughter. Nevertheless, Jenny had finally convinced him he was destined to be her husband, and they were married shortly thereafter. Before he had time to change his mind or even really know what was happening, he was standing in front of a priest, saying his vows. As the years went on, their love grew intense, and now she loved him more than the day they had married.

We sat on a bench under a leafless tree, sipping our tea. 'Enough of my rambles. I can be a sentimental old woman at times, but only because I adore every one of them.' She reached across and took my empty cup from me, placing it on a small wooden table with her own. 'Tell me of the sights you have seen since arriving in London.' I told her of the places I had been before they forced us to remain inside for our own safety. 'You actually went to restaurants and dined alone?' she asked, her eyes wide, disapproval crossing her face.

'Well, yes, I did.' I felt the blood rush to my face before quickly turning away and gazing out across the lawn.

'It is unheard of for a lady to dine on her own in public. I am surprised they even served you. I could not do anything like that. I would be too worried about what people would think and how they would gossip.'

I sighed deeply. 'I'm not too concerned about that, Jenny. I want to experience everything, and if it goes against other people's expectations, then that's their problem, not mine.'

'Do not misunderstand me, Abigail,' she replied, shifting in her seat before taking my hand in hers. 'I think it's refreshing you don't mind what other people think, but believe me, sometimes in life you must conform, or it only makes it harder than it already is.'

In her mid-forties, Jenny was a petite woman with golden hair that had streaks of silver running through it, pinned up on the back of her head. Blessed with porcelain skin, she wore nothing on her face — only a touch of lip paint in a soft, pink colour. I thought she was lovely. I could see why a man like Mr Malcolm would be taken with her and imagined how fetching she was as a young woman.

'If you don't mind, Jenny, I need to return inside and check on Polly.'

'You really love her, don't you? Henry has told me of your circumstances growing up, which grieves me greatly, but I am thrilled you found each other again. It does amaze me you were raised in Scotland, yet you speak like an Englishwoman. Polly sounds Scottish through and through, yet you grew up side by side. Go to her. I will meet you later in the parlour.' She sat back and smiled, waving me inside while she remained where she was, enjoying the crisp, fresh air.

I climbed the stairs, relieved Mr Malcolm had confided my situation to Jenny, leaving me unburdened with no need to explain anything to her about my past. It was a subject I did not want to discuss with those who had grown up with a family. Polly snored softly when I entered the room, making my way over to the bed, before slipping in beside her, fully dressed. I stroked her hair as she slept, knowing in my heart she wasn't really cross with me, only feeling closed in, like I was, and noticing that everyone was feeling sorry for her, which they were, and she hated it. She refused to wake, so I silently rose and crossed the room, hurrying downstairs to find something to read in the library. I found a copy of Vanity Fair, written by William Makepeace Thackeray, the plot centreing around a crafty spitfire named Becky Sharp. How differently the life of that orphan turned out.

We sat together, deep in conversation, at the elaborate oak table in the very formal dining room, waiting for dinner to be served. I wondered if my new house in Geelong had a formal room like this or a regular kitchen with a table, which was my preference. It was all lovely; however, I liked to take my meals in a casual setting. Mr Malcolm was at the head of the table, with Jenny sitting next to him, gazing up at him adoringly. I thought it darling they were so in love. I watched him place his hand on hers and squeeze it lightly, smiling at her with his eyes twinkling even brighter than usual. That's what I wanted — to marry for love, and love that person until the day I died. But first, I wanted to grow up and create my own life before having to join the life I made for myself with someone else's, aware I'd be forced to make compromises. Jenny had explained this was imperative to ensure you enjoyed a long and happy marriage, which was not something I was prepared to sacrifice quite yet.

Polly sat on the other side of Mr Malcolm, with Richard sitting next to her, while I was comfortable beside Jenny. The dinner conversation was cheerful and loud, with Richard and Mr Malcolm discussing their day and Jenny chiming in every so often. Polly and I talked about our impending travels and the few items that still required purchasing before departing. Richard kindly offered to collect the last-minute things we needed, given that neither of us could leave the house. As I finished the last of my dessert, Mr Malcolm requested to see me in his study after dinner, to which I agreed. I followed him to a large room lined with books. It held a desk more intricate than the one at his office, with a high-backed leather chair behind it. He motioned me to a smaller leather chair, and I sat down.

'How are you and Polly settling in, Abigail?' He took a cigar from a wooden box, quite similar to the mysterious box that had turned up at the orphanage, which now felt like a hundred years ago.

'Very well, thank you, Mr Malcolm. We would like to thank you for your generous hospitality.'

'It is our pleasure to have you here and to spend your last days in England with us. How is Polly faring?' He lit his cigar and settled back in his chair, inhaling deeply before blowing the grey smoke towards the ceiling.

'She looks worse than she feels and hates anyone pitying her, so at least once the bruises fade, I am confident she will return to the old Polly,' I told him, hoping he would discreetly tell the others.

'That's good to hear. I do pray she can put this dreadful mess behind her.' He picked up some papers on his desk, nodding his head before staring across at me. 'Now, let's attend to business and get that out of the way for the night. I have two letters here; one addressed to you from a Sister Josephine and one to me from Mother Bernadette.' He handed me the unopened letter from Sister Josephine — my heart leaping as happiness enveloped me. This was the first personal letter I had ever received from someone I knew and loved. I could hardly wait to tear it open when I was alone and read every word: however, I restrained myself and placed it on a small table beside me. 'The letter from Mother Bernadette states they are extremely grateful for your offer of financial help,' he began, looking up from the document to ensure I was paying attention. 'They give their consent and agree to meet all the conditions attached to the contract, including removing the Sisters you have elected should not be at Emiliani House. Instead, they will return to the Mother House in Inverness and be pushed into retirement. Mother Bernadette intends to send seven younger Sisters and several postulants to Emiliani House once the renovations are complete. She states that the offer of two thousand pounds in the first year will make significant changes for the better for all the children in the orphanage and ease the worry and constraints on the Sisters who care for them. The letter goes on to thank you many times over for your kindness, etcetera. I will personally make a monthly visit to the orphanage to ensure the work on the building is carried out promptly, and the children have all they need. If I believe increased financial assistance is required as the years go on, are you happy for me to approve this?' I nodded, relaxing back in my chair, smiling across at him.

'Of course I am. I want them to have everything they need.'

'Good. That will save me the bother of having to write to you each time and wait months for your response; however, I will correspond with you often and send progress reports.' He nodded his head, shuffling the papers in front of him before continuing. 'When you find out the terms of the Will from your Geelong solicitor, I need you to write to me immediately, as I do not know what financial arrangements have been made for you there. In the unlikely situation there are none, I will arrange to send you money from the interest of your trust fund every three months. You will be able to live quite comfortably for the rest of your life on that alone, so take that worry from your mind.' His confidence was evident as he puffed away on his cigar, although the heavy smoke made it hard for me to breathe. I smiled anyway, breathing through my mouth due to the vile smell.

'What do you believe are the terms and conditions of the Australian Will?' I felt anxiety rising inside me again, as it did every time I thought about what lay in store for me.

'To be honest with you, Abigail, I don't have a clue. Having met your great-aunt Isabelle, it could be anything. She was quite the old eccentric, and who knows what weird and wonderful plans she had for you? You must admit, though, it has all worked out well for you so far, has it not?'

'Well, yes, it has, but she was certainly a controlling woman. I mean, I'm not ungrateful, but I feel like I'm a puppet, and she is pulling my strings from the grave. So why not just leave me the money to do with as I pleased?' I valued his opinion since he had met her personally, while the woman was a stranger to me entirely.

'Maybe she thought you would be too young and immature and would need some guidance to help you find your way,' he replied, chewing thoughtfully on a piece of liquorice, offering one to me.

'Yes, that could have been a concern, but even after death, she seems quite controlling, and is forcing me into a life that I may not want, despite being in her grave for close to fifteen years.' I straightened in my chair, jutting out my chin. 'I didn't necessarily want to immigrate to Australia, and here I am, being forced to do so. I have become accustomed to the idea now, and I am feeling some excitement toward the journey, but if I dislike the conditions of the Will once outlined to me by the Geelong solicitor, I will walk away from the money, Mr Malcolm. I will get a job and create my own life.' I crossed my arms stubbornly while he looked at me for a long time, silence hanging over the smoke-filled office while the wood in the hearth burned warmly, casting a romantic light across the room.

'I don't doubt that for a moment, Abigail, but I would hate to see that happen to you. I want you to have the best life possible, and this inheritance will ensure that for you — and Polly, too. I want you to write to me and discuss this before you do anything, one way or the other. Please promise me you will do that?'

'Yes, I will. I promise.' As he stood to dismiss me, I indicated I had one more question. He sat back down, waiting patiently; although I could hear his foot tapping under the desk. 'Is there any way you can find out the names of those men who placed bids on me at the tavern? The owner had them written on papers that the police could have seized. Although I memorised their faces, I would like to know their names on the off chance I run into any of them someday.'

'Well,' he paused, sighing deeply, 'it isn't exactly ethical, but I will see what I can do. I'll include any information I find in my future correspondence with you.'

I thanked him before he escorted me to the sitting room, my favourite place of all the rooms in the house, given it was the least formal of all. Polly and Richard were playing cards — or more like Richard was trying to teach Polly how to play cards, while Jenny looked on, laughing quietly to herself.

As the night drew into the early hours, Mr Malcolm and Jenny retired to their bedroom, bidding us all a good night. It had been lovely to watch them together — he brushing her hand, their legs touching for a moment as they sat together on the lounges, and the looks that passed between them filled with love, longing, desire. I thought it the most marvellous thing and again wondered if I would ever find such intense love, and would I have to stop believing in the golden glow?

Richard had proven I wasn't attracted to every man surrounded by it; however, it had drawn us together like brother and sister. I desperately wanted the kind of love I had read about in books and what I had witnessed tonight. The deep, uplifting understanding and support; the passion; the lust; the compatibility — I wanted all of it, and I would not settle for anything less.

Chapter Nineteen

THERE WAS A KNOCK on the door, a young maid entering with our breakfast on trays, pushing the small cart towards the bed. I assumed the family did not take their morning meals together, which eased my mind that the house was not as formal as I had feared. Polly and I quickly sat up, placing several pillows behind us before leaning back, the maid placing a tray in each of our laps before hurrying away. We chatted while we ate, concluding that we loved the Malcolm family. I told her of Sister Josephine's letter, which I had devoured with my eyes, heart, and soul last night, and had tucked away in my bag to read again when I wanted to feel close to her.

After we had finished and helped each other dress, we made our way downstairs together, her hand tightly in mine. We entered the parlour to find Mrs Malcolm looking immaculate, as she did each time I saw her. The instant she caught sight of us, she waved us in.

'Sit, my dear girls, sit.' She appeared upset as she gathered her things, placing them in a large carpetbag. 'I have been waiting to speak with you both. Unfortunately, I must go out for the day, and I wanted to assure you that you will both be safe. The constable is guarding the front door, but he does walk through the grounds every hour to ensure there are no trespassers, and Richard will stay with you and not leave the house until I, or my husband, have arrived home. I do apologise. I feel like such a terrible hostess; however, I have been called away to my sister's house regarding an urgent matter. I cannot tell you any more than that, as that is all I know. I apologise again for leaving you both on such short notice.'

She gazed down at us, her face filled with concern — so much so, I believed she knew more than she was telling us. We wished her well and embraced her warmly before she ran to the carriage where Mr Miller waited, hurrying away at great speed on her errand. Polly and I stayed in the parlour waiting for Richard, who appeared after fifteen minutes.

'Good morning, my dear friends. How are we this lovely morning?' he asked cheerily. Polly giggled when he bowed as low as he could, stumbled, and nearly fell sideways into a table.

'We are well, our dear friend, Richard,' Polly replied, bowing to him in return. We laughed as Richard sat down, leaned back on the lounge and placed his hands behind his head.

'Have you had a proper tour of the gardens?'

'I went outside with your mother yesterday, but no, we haven't looked around,' I replied, still smiling. He certainly knew by now that I was inquisitive and would want to explore the house and see everything. We pulled on our thick, woollen coats, then followed him through the kitchen, where Mrs Shank took a wooden spoon to Richard's backside.

'This is not some alley down a side street, you cheeky boy. Use the right door.' Richard only laughed, kissing her on the forehead as she smacked him again on his backside with the large, wooden spoon, continuing on and leading us out to the grounds. The air was cool and crisp, stinging my cheeks, but the sky was clearer than I had seen it since I had been in London. The large home sat on an undulating plot of land, and the grounds were quite extensive, given it was on a suburban block close to the centre of London. My eyes widened in surprise to discover a large stable at the rear of the property, barely visible because of the trees and shrubbery surrounding it.

'I never imagined city people would keep horses behind their houses,' I remarked, Polly snorting in amusement beside me.

'So, where did you think Mr Miller kept his horses and the carriage?' he teased, raising his eyebrows at me.

'Don't treat me like I'm stupid, Richard. I never really gave it a thought. I assumed that Mr Miller lived on a farm.' I felt the blood creeping up my neck, my face now hot, and no doubt, the colour of beetroot, shame filling me as I realised I had yet again made a fool of myself. Richard reached across and touched my nose before lifting my chin to look into my eyes, his tone reassuring and gentle.

'No, Abigail, he lives here in the grooms' quarters above the stables, and there is no ignominy in asking. If you do not question what is around you in this great world, how will you ever grow and learn and become the woman you are meant to be?' He let his hand drop to his side before guiding us towards the stable door. 'Mr Miller rises before dawn and prepares the horses by six o'clock in the morning, spending his days driving people around for my father. But, of course, he takes my parents everywhere they need to go as well. I will show you through.' I felt the tenseness leave my body as we entered the stables. It smelled sweet and earthy, the odour of horse manure mingling with fresh cut hay and the smell of leather, and I was surprised to find it quite pleasant. Richard led us past several stalls, pointing out feed bins and harness boxes. I noticed a ladder and strolled away from Richard, running my fingers over the smooth wood, while Polly had taken the opportunity to explore the bluestone building on her own.

I was curious, gazing up into the loft where the ladder led. 'What's up there, Richard?'

'Mr Miller's quarters. He sleeps up there and comes inside to have his meals with the other servants.' Before he had time to react, I lifted my skirt and started to climb. I wanted to see how Mr Miller lived. 'Abigail, come down now.' Richard stood at the foot of the ladder, holding it firm as I ignored him, stepping into the small room. 'Mr Miller doesn't like anyone in his stables, let alone spying on his quarters.' His warning floated up into the quiet room; however, it was too late. I was already up in the loft, slowly making my way around, picking up objects and studying them before gently placing them back down exactly how they were. The room was neat and clean, a wooden, single bed pushed up against the wall under the one window in the room, a small table sitting next to it. A hard wooden chair and a chest for his clothes in one corner completed the furnishings in the sparse room. On the table sat a small, well-worn Bible and a brown-tinged photo of an older woman, possibly Mr Miller's mother, in a tiny brass frame. I felt a pang of emotion as I found myself surrounded by the invisible aura of this plain but kindly man, whom I would never forget. Richard's head soon poked up from below, calling out I needed to return down the ladder immediately. As I descended the ladder, Richard grabbed me by the waist and placed me on the floor.

'God, you're impossible, Abigail,' he complained, hurrying me towards the stable doors while Polly giggled, the icy air hitting me in the face as I was pushed outside, the door behind me slamming shut.

Polly and I spent the afternoon talking and playing games in the sitting room, waiting impatiently for Mr and Mrs Malcolm to return. Richard had left several hours before to purchase the last of the items we needed before we sailed. Hours passed before Mr Malcolm arrived home in a friend's carriage, just as the sky darkened into evening; however, there was no sign of Jenny. The evening turned into night, and she still had not arrived. We remained with Mr Malcolm until Polly's eyes started to droop, and I reluctantly rose to my feet, taking her hand and helping her up. We bid him goodnight, leaving Mr Malcolm staring into the fire, his brow creased in concern, while fear reflected in his eyes as he waved us off, requesting we close the door behind us.

We woke early the following day, the first thought in my mind being Mrs Malcolm. I quickly threw on my dressing gown, hurrying through the door and downstairs to ensure Jenny had arrived home safely the night before. I left Polly sleeping, her soft snores diminishing as I stepped down into the hallway. The more she slept, the stronger she became after our ordeal, and I wanted her healthy and ready to enjoy our voyage. I found Jenny in the parlour by herself, lost in thought. I sat down opposite her, remaining silent as I leaned back in my chair, swallowing hard before licking my dry lips.

'I don't know what's wrong, and you don't have to tell me.' I cursed myself for not stopping in the kitchen to at least drink a glass of water, my throat dry. 'I only wanted to let you know I hope you're okay.'

'Oh, Abigail, I don't know what to do anymore. If I share something with you in the strictest confidence, do you promise me you will keep it a secret?' Tears began to fill her eyes as she spoke.

'Of course, I will.' I struggled to my feet and crossed to her side, settling myself next to her on the lounge, reaching over and gently stroking her hand.

'All right, because I need to talk to someone, and I trust you.' She paused to wipe away tears before continuing. 'My sister, Martha, is married to a man who hurts her. He has beaten her for the twenty years they have been married. To cope, she gets drunk every day on hard liquor. All her children left home early because they couldn't stand it any longer, and now live with my parents, who are elderly.

Yesterday, my father summoned me to the house, as he suspected my sixteen-year-old niece is pregnant. She confirmed it when I spoke to her. The baby's father is long gone, and we do not know what to do to help her. This will bring shame upon her and our family — she plans to keep the child, with no husband beside her.' I didn't know what to say. Even I knew it was unheard of for an unmarried woman to have a child and keep it, especially when you were from a respectable family. 'I talked to her throughout the day and into the night, but she won't budge. She is determined to keep the child, no matter what anyone says to her or the humiliation she will bring to our family.' Finally, she hung her head and began to sob, tears welling in my own eyes as I patted her hand some more.

'Will your parents cast her out?'

'No, they have already told me they won't, but they're so old I'm frightened that this will kill them. They will be shunned and cast out from society, and there is nothing anyone can do now to prevent it.'

I passed her my handkerchief, in which she buried her face, trying to stifle her sobs. I was starting to learn there were so many situations in life that money could not fix. I would give her any amount from my trust fund to solve this problem for her family, but nothing would. What was done was done, and there was no going back. One bad choice could affect your entire life and those around you forever. Polly, I knew, was another perfect example, although I was doing everything in my power to help her change her destiny and would continue until I took my last breath.

Richard, Polly, and I spent the day eating and talking — eating some more and talking — laughing and eating and talking. By the time I was ready to retire, my stomach was so full I could feel it bulging, but I felt relaxed, happy, and loved. I truly looked at Richard as an older brother, and I felt he would be in my life forever. I was amazed to have met a man with the golden glow, even though it hadn't felt the way I expected it would.

My thoughts on the matter were muddled. I wanted to know what it meant when I saw these beautiful, golden outlines around people. I realised I couldn't dismiss a man who didn't have the golden glow and I must attempt to get to know people for who they were. But, on the other hand, I was confused about the ramifications of the auras only I seemed able to see and the people I loved who possessed them, along with the people I loved who did not. I was unsure if I would ever come to understand the meaning of the auras I was cursed to see.

I lay in bed, tossing and turning, a thousand thoughts running through my mind. Then, finally, sleep claimed me, and I dreamed of a feather, a headstone, and an imposing, black-haired man.

I stretched in the big, comfortable bed, feeling my joints click as the morning light filtered into the room. I arched my back and stretched my legs, squeezing my toes hard, lifting my arms above my head and pushing them up as far as I could; my hands tightened into fists. It was heaven sleeping in this bed, the soft bedding filled with the scent of lavender, the heavy quilts providing their comfort and warmth right down to my bones. I would have given anything to have been born into this family.

Today, Polly and I would finally have the pleasure of meeting the rest of the Malcolm clan at their family lunch. I felt today would be a last farewell between us all; although we would not sail until tomorrow morning. I felt a sense of disbelief that the time had finally arrived. Tomorrow, we would board a ship with hundreds and hundreds of people we had never met before. Whose paths might we cross on the voyage? I believed it was fate that you met certain people who become part of your life. They may play a starring role from beginning to end or limited to a short walk on part, crucial to the story of your life, before bowing and exiting the stage after only a moment, each being as important as the other. Whether they stay forever, or just fleetingly, to teach you what you needed to know, it made no difference, as long as you learnt the lesson they were sent to give you. I was looking forward to meeting the people who were fated to be in my life.

As the luncheon neared, I could hardly wait to see what Richard's brothers and their wives were like in character and appearance. I had chosen one of my best dresses to wear and shoes to match. The shoemaker, Mr Higginbottom, had done an excellent job making them. They moulded to my feet, with only the tiniest heels, and I found them extremely comfortable; so comfortable, I imagined I could walk in them for days. The colours he had chosen were magnificent: white, pink, blue, scarlet red, ochre, black — nearly every colour in the rainbow, and more. I had never realised what a difference it made to have comfortable shoes, having to suffer for years wearing ill-fitting pairs that sometimes had the toes cut off.

Our dresses and gowns had arrived a week ago from Madame Felicity's, including Bessie's couture dresses and the extra dresses she had convinced me to order. Before we had completed payment, Bessie had advised me we had forgotten the most essential item — plain, everyday house dresses. She explained they were worn around the house when you wanted to be comfortable and intended to stay home for the day, although I found them respectable enough to wear in the street. I had ordered five each for Polly, Bessie, and myself in different styles and colours, and Madame Felicity had been true to her word — not one of them was the same. All fifteen dresses were of different fabrics, styles, and colours, most with a Bertha neckline, which I loved. Despite her poor attitude, Madame Felicity had a talent for creating dresses that best enhanced the women's bodies who would wear them.

The housedresses were plain and made of the softest materials. Each came with a simple bodice, the folds of fabric falling to the ground in a lovely, long skirt that was easy to walk around in and do your chores. They were all we had been wearing since they were delivered to the hotel more than a week ago.

Bessie and Polly were overly excited when they could finally try everything on, helping each other dress, then parading around the room for each other's entertainment. Bessie had tried on her uniforms, a white apron pinned to the front of each dress that looked very smart. She looked like a proper ladies' maid; although not dressed in the traditional black and white.

Polly, Richard, and I waited patiently in the sitting room, all dressed in our best for the much-anticipated lunch. Richard leaned back on the lounge and yawned before smiling across at me.

'When my brothers and I were growing up, our parents always made sure that they were together on a Sunday for lunch. They would attend church in the morning and, upon arriving home, we would find the dining table full of lamb and pork, along with beef and chicken, all slowly baked until they were dark brown and oozing sweet stickiness onto the roasting plate. There was always lots of gravy. The crunchy, roasted vegetables, along with the boiled peas, carrots, cauliflower, and beans, were always gone by the end of the meal.' His eyes were shining as memories of long-gone lunches flickered through his mind. 'The tradition has carried on, even after Johnathon and George left home, so now they bring their wives and children. No one has ever missed a Sunday lunch.' I smiled across at him, believing this to be the loveliest ritual I had ever heard of, vowing to myself that when I had my own family, I would do the same for them. No matter how old my children were, I would insist those I loved the most gather together for Sunday lunches each week.

A tall, handsome man, who looked strangely familiar, strolled into the room. He looked like an older version of Richard, with thick brown hair, sparkling eyes, and a gorgeous face. He introduced himself to Polly, then turned to me and did the same before shaking our hands politely. A small boy ran in behind him, grabbed him by the right leg, not letting go, and stared wide-eyed up at us.

'Pappa, Pappa. Up, up,' he demanded, raising his arms to his father, who swiftly picked him up and placed him firmly on one hip.

'And this is little Johnny.' He wiped the little boy's nose with his handkerchief and placed it back in his pants pocket, his son screwing up his face for a moment. They clearly adored each other. Then, a small, elegant woman entered the room, whom Johnathon introduced as Isabelle, his wife. She possessed a birdlike face, with beady eyes that darted quickly around the room and a large, pointy nose that somehow seemed to look down on me, despite her being small in stature. Her brown hair was tightly pulled back into a bun, enhancing her birdlike appearance, her shoulder blades and hip bones jutting out sharply in her tightly fitted dress. I wondered how such a tiny body could have carried a child, watching intently as she took Johnny from his father to change him before lunch.

I had started to doubt the affection and love some couples displayed, and I wondered how happy Johnathon really was. He sat beside me, talking animatedly to Polly and Richard, and from what I could see, he was just as sincere and friendly as Richard. A man with a moustache, whom I assumed to be George, entered the room and smacked his brothers jovially on the back, greeting them warmly. He was slightly smaller in stature than his brothers and a little less handsome, his hair as light as his mother's.

After introducing ourselves, Jenny clapped her hands together, calling out cheerfully for all to make their way to the dining room to be seated. She had placed me next to Johnathon, with George's wife to the other side of me; her stomach so large she could barely sit close enough to the table to eat. Georgina was a pleasantly plump girl of medium height, with brown, curly hair that kept breaking away from their restraints, causing her to appear unkempt all the time, no matter how hard she tried. She had an unremarkable face but a warm and genuine smile.

The large dining table was covered with their usual fare, platters of roasted meats, baked vegetables, alongside crusty fresh bread straight from the oven, gravy made from the juices of the roasted meat and a variety of boiled vegetables. I smothered a smile as I listened to Richard and his brothers tease each other, finding their banter not only amusing but comforting. As if I were part of a family, something I had never felt before.

'Do you think you will be able to lose all that weight after the baby is born, Georgina? Of course, you know you must eat less than you do for that to happen. But, goodness, look at your plate,' Isabelle remarked, her tone icy. All eyes went to Georgina's plate, which did have large, healthy portions of food on it. She averted her gaze, while all present looked away, some attempting to resume normal conversation and break the awkward silence that now hung over the room like a black cloud.

I lifted my plate and piled it with more food, heaping it high, then turned to Georgina, her eyes lighting up before she returned my smile. I felt so sorry for her. I knew what it felt like to want to eat everything placed in front of you, and she was obviously not a naturally thin woman, and it would be difficult for her to lose the excess fat. Isabelle knew that too, and we all knew that she knew that. But, with her eyes darting from person to person, she took great pleasure in putting her husband down in front of everyone. I did not like this woman and decided without delay; she was the only thing stopping this family from being near perfect.

Overall, I enjoyed the conversations and observing their interactions with one another. Once the servants had cleared the table and we had finished our dessert, we retired to the sitting room. Again, the mood was festive as everyone talked at once, conducting conversations with one person, while the next was shouting across the room to someone else. I hoped one day that the children in the orphanage would experience the same feeling of family that I was enjoying so much, and the orphanage would be a safe, warm environment where they would feel they were wanted and loved. I felt like a sister to the Malcolm siblings, appreciating them even more for ensuring Polly and I were welcomed and included, making us feel for the first time in our lives we belonged.

Johnathon Malcolm

When my brother told me he was showing one of our father's clients around London, I never suspected it would be this stunningly beautiful creature. Despite being married to Isabelle, I felt an immediate attraction to her. I felt such a strong connection between us; I had no choice but to befriend her, even though she would leave tomorrow to live permanently in Australia. I would more than likely never lay eyes on her again, but I was inexplicably drawn to her. Richard had kept this quiet, obviously wanting to keep her to himself — the shite.

No woman had ever caught my eye as she had. She was beautiful, with her exquisite face and enormous eyes that sparkled like emeralds, boring deep into your soul. Her glorious hair billowed down in waves to her waist in the most extraordinary shade of red I had ever seen, frequently changing in colour, depending on the light. She was tall and slender, with a body I couldn't help noticing, but also friendly and kind, making her even more attractive, given the vindictive woman I had the misfortune to marry.

I watched Abigail from across the room as she relaxed back in her chair, talking animatedly to Georgina, who clearly liked her too. When I approached her to strike up a conversation, I found my throat had gone dry, choosing to make my way to the kitchen first for a glass of water, possibly something stronger to calm my nerves. I strolled in to find Mrs Shank listening to Isabelle's complaints, smiling kindly at her while remaining silent. I muttered under my breath as she stopped talking and fixed me with a hard stare.

'We are leaving now, Johnathon,' she spat at me. 'I will not be made a fool of in your parents' home. Go and get Johnny, and we will say our goodbyes.'

I raised my eyebrows, sighing deeply, knowing what was to come. 'What's wrong with you now?' She turned her head abruptly, her eyes wide, placing her hands on her hips, rage engulfing her as her face darkened to a mottled purple, startling me.

'You really think I am stupid, don't you? You have not taken your eyes from this Abigail since we arrived. Do as you are told before I cause a scene and embarrass the both of you,' she hissed, causing me to step back, finding her a little frightening at times.

Abigail hadn't done anything wrong, but I certainly didn't want her embarrassed because Isabelle had noticed my attraction to her. She had spoken to George and me in the same polite way, so she certainly hadn't flirted or committed any sin against Isabelle for her to behave in such a hateful manner. I was well aware Isabelle would indeed follow through on her threat if I refused to do as instructed. I made my way upstairs to collect Johnny, wishing I had made different choices in my life once more. I entered my parents' bedroom, picked him up in my arms as he slept, and made my way back downstairs, cradling him close to my chest. Isabelle was waiting at the bottom of the stairs. I silently followed her into the sitting room, unable to look anyone in the eye.

'We are leaving,' she announced sharply. I saw the disappointment in my mother's eyes; however, despite this, she smiled, as did our guests and the rest of my family, all rising to their feet to embrace us and bid us farewell. Of one thing, I was certain: I would meet Abigail Delmont again one day and find out precisely what it was about her that had drawn me to her like a magnet to steel.

It disappointed me I could not spend more time with Johnathon to become adequately acquainted; however, it appeared unavoidable, given they had been in a great hurry to leave. The day had passed quickly, and I yawned, hastily covering my mouth, before going around the room and embracing my new family. Polly and I called out our goodnights to Mr and Mrs Malcolm, and Richard, who had been deep in discussion with his father, before making our way to our room. We assisted each other to undress, then slipped on our thick nightgowns, climbed into the gigantic bed, and held hands under the covers, waiting for sleep to come. It did not take long before I was dreaming of a small island, a stable, and a woman's hand.

Chapter Twenty

I WAS NO LONGER alone in the world. Polly had returned to me. I had made many new friends, including Catherine and Richard. I also knew now what it was to have all the luxuries anyone could want, yet still be scared and miss people from my old life at the orphanage. Mr Malcolm, Jenny, and Richard rode with us in the carriage while Bessie sat with Mr Miller in front as we travelled through the busy streets towards the docks.

'Promise me you won't forget us.' I leaned forward and took Richard's hand in mine, a slow smile touching his lips.

'Abigail, how could I forget either of you for a moment? You are family. I will write weekly; I give you my word. The very moment I have completed my studies, I have every intention of taking ship to Geelong; and I promise to send you all those sweeties you adore, just in case you cannot find them in Australia.' I squeezed his hand before relaxing back in my seat, Polly beside me gazing out the carriage window in silence.

The carriage slowed, the crowd thick, a street urchin darting out in front of the horses, causing Mr Miller to curse loudly while pulling sharply on the reins; the carriage halting so abruptly, Polly and I tumbled forward onto Richard and Jenny. Mr Miller continued to curse, jumping down from his seat, while not taking his eyes from the child as he weaved through the crowd, his tiny hand relieving many of them of their week's wages, with no one taking notice. Finally, Mr Miller opened the carriage door, helping Jenny down before Mr Malcolm jumped out and turned to assist Polly and me. Richard soon followed, closing the carriage door behind us. We pushed through the crowd towards the first-class boarding gate, Mr Malcolm and Richard clearing a path as best they could amongst the hundreds of people who seemed determined not to let us pass. Bessie appeared overwhelmed as we turned a corner, and she caught sight of the enormous steamship, gasping, her hand going to her throat as she stopped where she was and gazed up in awe. I completely understood why the RMS Majesty took her breath away; it was magnificent, three towering smokestacks looming above, and I could see the different decks as they wound their way around its smooth curves. I was concerned Leroy, or his revolting friends, could be loitering nearby and attempt to kidnap Polly again, and although I knew we were safe, it did not stop my hands from trembling and my heart beating slightly faster than usual. We continued to move through the crowd until Mr Malcolm, Richard, and Mr Miller were standing together at the bottom of the ramp that led to the first-class entrance of the ship. Several police constables stood discreetly nearby, possibly having the same thoughts racing through my own mind. Hundreds of people swarmed around us, blocking me from seeing anyone other than those surrounding me, my anxiety creeping up slowly, a lump lodging in my throat.

'It is time to board,' Mr Malcolm announced, his eyes shimmering with unreadable emotion before he embraced me warmly. Richard moved to my side, hugging me tight, while I held him just as tightly, tears stinging my eyes.

'Thank you for being you, Abigail.' He held me by the shoulders, pushing me back slightly so he could study my face. 'I will truly miss you, and I hope to be reunited with you and Polly soon. Good luck with everything in Geelong, and safe travels. I love you, my little sister.' He pulled me back into a tight embrace, his voice faltering, while I held him, not wanting to let go.

'I love you too, my big brother, and thank you for everything.' He released me, and I stepped back, but not quick enough, Richard reaching up and swiftly yanking my hair before moving a safe distance away next to his father.

'Ouch. Did you really just do that?' I called over to him, shaking my head in disbelief as he grinned back at me, nodding enthusiastically.

Jenny stepped forward and held me tight.

'I see my son is treating you like a real sister, the fiend.' She smiled, quickly brushing a tear that had escaped her swollen, red eyes. 'I promise that we will visit when things have settled here. I have an enormous burden to bear regarding my family over the coming weeks and months, but I want you to know that a piece of my heart travels with you, just as it would had I given birth to you myself. So go with God, my girl, and please, keep yourself safe and always be sensible.' I nodded as she stepped away, tears trickling down my cheeks as she turned and hurried to her husband's side. Mr Malcolm strolled over to me, leaving her with Richard, who slipped his arm around her trembling shoulders as she cried quietly into her handkerchief. He offered me his hand to shake, appeared to change his mind, then grabbed me, embracing me for the longest time.

'I couldn't be prouder had you been my own flesh and blood.' He continued to hold me to his chest as he stroked my back. 'Please write to us as soon as you can find the time.' His voice faded as I nodded my head, reluctantly letting go of his embrace, the lump in my throat making it impossible for me to speak. He had acted as a father to me in the time I had known him — the only father figure I had ever had. I found him exceptional, not only as a wonderful role model for all fathers, but also as an extraordinary man in every aspect of his life.

He had made me feel safe and cared for, and I would truly miss him. Mr Miller waited a short distance away, his pipe between his lips and appearing distracted. I approached him, leaving Polly and Bessie with the Malcolm family to say their goodbyes. I stood silently in front of him, waiting for him to speak, as it was clear he had something on his mind. Finally, he met my gaze, smiling shyly.

'Well, Lassie...' his voice wavered for a moment before he sniffed loudly and returned my gaze. 'This is goodbye for us unless you ever decide to venture back across the water to visit. In the last six weeks, I have seen you go from a scared young girl to a confident young lady, which has made me very proud. I want to thank you for treating me so kindly, Mistress. You never looked down your nose at me and always treated me as an equal, and I thank you for that. I will never forget you.' He sniffed again before averting his eyes. 'May God be with you on your travels, and may the angels always be by your side to protect you, my girl. The golden light will always guard you.' He extended his hand to shake mine; however, I took a step forward and wrapped my arms around him, his little body tense at the shock and surprise at my inappropriate display of affection. Within moments, he embraced me back tightly, but for only a fleeting moment before turning away to return to the carriage without another word; nor did he even glance back as I wiped the tears from my face with my handkerchief. I strode back to the Malcolm family, who stood close together with Polly and Bessie, fussing over them and freely giving them both last-minute advice they felt we should know.

I embraced them one by one for what I felt was the last time, turning to walk towards the small bridge that led over the water and up to one of the ship's passenger entrances. I climbed the steep platform and stopped several yards from the door, Bessie and Polly behind me, and turned to wave goodbye, unable to stop the tears that streamed down my face. I scanned the crowd to wave to them one last time, finding they were in the same place we had left them, my heart leaping in my chest when I noticed standing not far behind them was Leroy, his evil gaze fixed on us. Polly and Bessie felt they had said enough goodbyes and were impatiently waiting for me to move forward, both focussing on the ship in front of them. I remained where I was, allowing them to push past me, both muttering under their breath. Leroy casually leaned against a cart, chewing a piece of straw between his lips, staring up at me, his face void of emotion, while certainly not appearing like a man that was too worried about the police finding him. I ran back down the platform, gathering all my strength.

'Leroy is behind you, Mr Malcolm,' I screamed into the wind. Mr Malcolm smiled up at me, his hand cupped to his ear while shaking his head, appearing confused. I realised it was useless and turned, slowly climbing the ramp again, deciding to stop further up to scan the crowd again for Leroy. I was hopeful the police standing nearby had noticed him; however, I was disappointed to find he had disappeared. I continued up the ramp to find Polly and Bessie waiting for me, chatting quietly between themselves, while they patiently stood outside the door that allowed us entry to the ship. I turned around and gave one last wave, gazing directly at Richard; his face filled with sadness as he waved back.

I then turned to start my new chapter, leaving them behind, just for a while.

We strolled across the expansive deck, stepping into a beautiful reception area. I stared across at the grand staircase that led up to the higher decks, finding them exquisite. Lit with chandeliers and sculptured sconces on the walls, they cast a romantic glow throughout the room. I stepped forward to speak to a man in a crisp, white uniform who stood behind a large, polished oak desk. I slipped the tickets across the counter, smiling brightly at him.

'Good morning, ladies. I hope you enjoy your voyage aboard the RMS Majesty. If you have any questions, you need only to ask, and we will do everything we can to answer them. Now, you are all in our very best stateroom. Come along with me, and I will accompany you to your suite.' I was surprised by how young the man was, given how efficient and professional he appeared.

We obediently followed him up the stairs and along a short hallway toward the bow of the ship. We stopped in front of a white door, waiting in silence while he took out his keys, Polly and Bessie appearing as nervous as I felt.

'Now, this stateroom is the most luxurious and envied on board the entire ship. There are three bedrooms off the main sitting area.' He smiled as the key clicked in the lock, swinging the door wide before ushering us inside, following us in before gently closing the door behind him. 'Through this door, just past the bathroom, you will find your private outdoor balcony with a private dining area. Here, let me show you.'

He guided us through the elegant sitting room and out to the balcony, the ocean winter wind hitting me full in the face, stinging my cheeks and causing my swollen, red eyes to water. I gazed around at the white wicker table and chairs, and two wicker lounges, along with artificial trees and plants that sat in small buckets, providing a tropical feel, despite the frigid weather we were currently experiencing in London. I hurried back inside to explore the rest of the suite, pleasantly discovering each room was comfortable, although not overly large. The sitting room was modest, and although lavishly decorated, the comfortable room possessed everything we could want and more — finding, to my great delight, a bookcase containing numerous volumes that piqued my interest. I knew at that moment I could happily stay here for weeks; even months would not be difficult.

'When you require a maid to attend to you, press this button here, and she will arrive shortly after to take care of your every need.' He reached across and touched a black button, directing our attention to a small, circular knob set into the wall near the front door. He politely bowed before he bid us farewell and departed, closing the door quietly behind him, the room silent as we absorbed the grandness of it all and the good fortune that had smiled down on us.

'Come along, girls, we've found it,' I called back over my shoulder. We pushed our way through to the railing until we could see the crowd on the docks below. I immediately spotted the Malcolm family and waved to them, calling out as loudly as possible, appearing to offend an aristocratic-looking woman standing beside me. She glared at me as though I were on the wrong deck of the ship and certainly of the wrong class. I ignored her and continued screaming, frantically waving my arm in the air to attract their attention. They were looking up, scanning the crowds at the railings; however, they could not find us. I shouted out again as loudly as my already hoarse throat would allow, the sour woman beside me raising her hands to her ears while screwing up her face in disdain. I continued to thrash my arm around above my head, leaning as far over the railing as I could, exhaling in relief when Jenny finally saw us.

We waved madly before there was a long blast, shattering our eardrums, followed by another, the three of us cringing as we covered our ears. A small tugboat had begun to tow the ship forward, away from the dock. I could still see Richard smiling up at us as he became smaller the further away we sailed, waving until all he became was a blur among a large crowd of miniature figures. Many of the first-class passengers surrounding me made their way inside the ship, while Bessie and Polly took a walk on the now-empty deck. I remained for a long time leaning against the rail, watching the docks become smaller and smaller until the shores of England had disappeared from my sight, possibly forever. I thought of Sister Josephine, wishing that she were here with me, tears stinging my eyes for the hundredth time this morning. I took her letter from my pocket, raised the paper she had made with her own hands to my lips, and kissed it.

My dearest Abigail,

I hope this finds you well, mo luaidh. I have been praying for your soul, as I do every day, and have done since the day I first held you in my arms. I cannot describe my joy and relief in receiving your letters and found great comfort in the news they contained.

First, to discover you are an heiress is more than I ever dreamed for you; however, that does not mean it is any less sweet. Now, I can rest well at night knowing you are safe, warm, and have a full tummy. Second, I was saddened by the news that you must immigrate to Australia. I always believed somewhere deep in my heart that I would see you again.

This belief has now disappeared, and the hope of holding you in my arms again has faded. I must find peace and acceptance that my place is here at the orphanage, and your future lies elsewhere, and although we will be parted, you fill my heart no matter where you are in the world, and I will always hold you close.

Finally, I must mention I was pleasantly surprised to find you now know you are the great-great-niece of Lady Isabelle Delmont. I knew her well throughout my youth, as she was a dear friend to my mother. It brings me great joy to know you have been told of your blood relatives, and with them comes a wealth of history and a family with whom you belong. Even if you choose not to find them, I believe you should know the

Howard family, your family, has lived in York for many generations and is a prominent aristocratic clan.

I must thank you on behalf of the Sisters and children at Emiliani House for your kind and incredibly generous donation. The day we received the official letter, the house was in a festive state, everyone feeling we had been sent a reprieve from God himself.

My dear lass, please write to me regularly of your travels and situation, so my mind may be at peace. I pray for your safe passage and that only wonderful things lay ahead. I love and miss you so very much and, until I hear from you again, will re-read your letters many times over. God bless you, Abigail. Please look after yourself, and I will continue to pray every day we will meet again. I will not lose hope.

Love always,

Sister Josephine.

I gazed out over the open ocean, tears streaming down my face. She missed me, and she loved me. She had hopes of seeing me again in the future, as I did with her. I would make sure, no matter what happened, that I would return to Scotland one day to see her again. I would continue to write to her every second day while on the ship, posting the letters when I arrived in Melbourne. I didn't want her to miss out on anything I was experiencing, knowing it would bring her great excitement while reassuring her I was safe and happy.

I dried my face with my handkerchief, slipping it back into my pocket and inhaling the salt air deeply, my eyes closed. I slipped the letter back into my pocket before making my way inside to join the others.

I pushed open the door to find Bessie and Polly had made themselves comfortable on the lounges, appearing extremely happy and excited,

talking animatedly to each other as I stepped into the room. I smiled at Polly, who sat up, her face lighting up at the sight of me. Her bruises had faded, and although still prominent, the swelling in her eye was slowly receding each day. I wanted this to be a new beginning, to leave all the problems, heartache and angst we had experienced in England' to start again fresh in a new place where we could be whoever we wanted to be. Bessie had chosen a pale blue uniform today and, with her neat, white apron and small, white hat, looked like a maid from a grand estate, except for the fact she was lounging on the lounge as if she were the duchess of that grand home. She smirked as she noticed me eyeing her uniform.

'The beauty of this, Mistress, is it hardly creases, and when I finish work, I can remove the hat and apron and wear each uniform as a dress. I find them so comfortable and feel like the Queen of England herself in them.' I smothered a smile as I sat down next to Polly, her face glowing as she reached across and took my hand in hers.

'I feel as if a heavy burden has been lifted from us, and I can finally breathe without a care in the world.' She lay back down, appearing relaxed, and indeed the happiest I had seen her since she had left the orphanage. I squeezed her hand, deciding to change the subject.

'Bessie, can I ask a favour of you, please?'

'How can it be a favour when I work for you? I am here to do all your bidding, Mistress.' She struggled to her feet, smiling to herself.

'I purchased a pair of diamond earrings as a present for myself. It was my first week in London before I met Polly again. I wondered if you would mind piercing my ears?' She looked up sharply from smoothing the skirt of her uniform, her eyes wide.

'Oh, Mistress, why did you have to ask me that?' She frowned, reaching out and placing her hand on the table to steady herself. 'I faint at the sight of blood. I know how to do it, and I could find all you require, but Polly will have to do the actual piercing. I'm so sorry.

The one request you have of me on my first official day of work, and it's a task I can't do.'

'Bessie, please, it's fine. You can help Polly by just telling her what to do. Is that all right, Polly?' Her eyes were closed and remained so as she opened her mouth to speak.

'Of course, Abi. I'm not scared of blood, especially yours. I've seen enough of it before.'

Polly was clearly referring to my clumsiness throughout childhood that had led to many injuries and much blood loss, along with the times I was reprimanded that caused severe injuries to my hands. She had often helped wash my cuts and abrasions and patch me up. I rose to my feet and crossed the room to press the button, surprising me within moments when I heard a knock. I opened the door to admit the youngest-looking maid I had ever seen. She was barely four-and-a-half feet tall and possibly weighing as much as a sack of potatoes. Her silky blonde hair, tightly pulled back and bound at the nape of her neck, accented her friendly, pale blue eyes. She wore a black uniform with a white apron and hat and appeared not a day older than twelve.

'Good morning, Mistress. My name is Mary. I will be your maid for the length of your journey.' I introduced her to Bessie and Polly, who both shook her hand. Bessie beckoned her, smiling warmly when she obeyed and arrived beside her.

'We need you to collect a few things for the Mistress, who has requested we pierce her ears.' Mary nodded, her face a slight pink. 'I need you to bring a bowl of vinegar, some ice, a cork from a bottle, a candle and a large darning needle. Oh, and some cloths to stop the bleeding.' Mary nodded again, remaining silent while appearing bemused.

I swallowed hard at the thought of that massive needle going through not one, but two, of my ears, and wondered if I should go ahead; knowing I was committing a sin. Sister Josephine would quote to me when she felt I was getting too big for my boots, "excessive pride in, or admiration of, one's own appearance or achievements and boasting of it is a sin, Abigail. The sin of pride, resulting in vanity, and that is not who you are, my sweet girl." Oh, but the thought of those two beautiful diamonds struck me — how they shone and sparkled in the light — and I knew for certain I wanted them sparkling from my earlobes. They were the first item of actual value I had bought for myself, but not the only precious item I possessed. I had hidden the emerald necklace away in my trunk, as it wasn't something I felt comfortable wearing. From what Mr Malcolm had told me, the stone was priceless; the jeweller who had examined it reporting he had only ever seen one stone similar and that had belonged to Queen Victoria. He had estimated the necklace was made in the late eighteenth century; however, the stone was far older, and he believed someone had removed it from a crown and reset it into a necklace. I had already put it away for my future daughter when she came of age or a daughter-in-law if blessed with children.

Mary hurried across the room without making a sound to seek out the items requested, closing the door behind her. I sensed she possessed strong opinions but held them close, as she was trained to do.

'She's tiny, isn't she?' I remarked as Polly giggled to herself while Bessie narrowed her gaze, watching us like a hawk.

'I had a powerful urge to pick her up and cradle her in my arms, and I'm not maternal like you at all, Abi. I find the bairns so annoying,' Polly replied as we collapsed into laughter, Bessie placing her hands on her ample waist.

'Stop it now, the both of you. She was likely deprived of nourishment as a child and didn't grow as she should have. You may have been raised in an orphanage, but you seem to have already forgotten where you came from.' She shook her head in disgust as I averted my gaze, lowering my head in shame. 'You are only as tall as you are, Mistress, thanks to Sister Josephine providing you with extra food, which I'm sure you shared with Polly. Pull yourselves together and stop being cruel before I smack you both on the backside.' She spun on her heel and marched into the washroom, slamming the door behind her. Polly and I sat silently, side by side. I felt as if Bessie had walked over and smacked us anyway, feeling sick to my stomach.

'Oh, everything offends Bessie. But, not to worry,' Polly sang out cheerfully as Mary returned, greeting us before placing the items Bessie had requested on the table, then stepping back and waiting for further instructions. 'You can stay and help if you like, Mary,' I offered, knowing she was curious but too shy to ask. She nodded, her eyes darting around the room, then down at the floor, her only response.

I stood, hurrying to retrieve my diamond earrings from the trunk. I tipped them out of their small velvet bag in the palm of my hand, admiring the two perfectly round stones that sparkled brilliantly as I held them up to the light. I decided the pain would be worth it before returning to the table and sitting down heavily in the high-backed chair. Bessie fussed around me, pushing my head down on a towel she had lain on the table while Mary held a shard of ice to my earlobe.

'There, that's all I can do,' Bessie informed me. 'Now, come here, Polly.' Bessie held the thick needle to the flame of the candle before handing it to Polly. 'Take the cork and put it behind her earlobe. Yes, like that. Now, I'm not going to watch this part, but you put the needle here where I marked the spot and push it through quickly. Then slowly take it out and put in the earring — which I have soaking in this bowl of vinegar — straight back in through the hole. Do you understand?' Polly nodded before Bessie turned away, the colour draining from her rosy cheeks.

'Yes, thank you, Bessie. I'm pretty sure that I can do this. Are you ready, Abi?' Polly's hand trembled slightly, causing me to question the hastiness of my decision, and I firmly pursed my lips.

'Yes, but do it quickly before I change my mind.' I gritted my teeth, gasping as searing pain went through the lobe of my ear. I lay still while Polly fitted the earring, then turned my head for her to do the same to my remaining ear. I found it was all over within moments and not as painful as I had feared.

'Thank you, my dear friends.' I embraced Polly, then Bessie, feeling like an adult all of a sudden. Mary swiftly cleaned up the site of this dramatic operation, then politely nodded her head at me.

'Would you like your luncheon brought to your suite, or would you like to eat in the dining room, Mistress?'

'We will go to the dining room, Mary, as we have been confined for far too long eating in our suite.'

'We have plenty of time before luncheon, ladies, so I can give you a tour of the ship if you'd like,' she offered kindly. We nodded excitedly, Polly clapping her hands and jumping up and down in excitement.

Mary led us down the hallway to the stairs, leading us down several flights until we arrived at the elaborate dining room. I stared in awe through the door into the large, empty space that could easily hold two hundred people at one sitting at the elegant tables and chairs that filled the room. Mary hurried us along past the smoking room, where women were not permitted, along with several salons and parlours on board that catered to men only. Next, we took in the games room, finding a piano and space for dancing, along with a billiard table and lounges in one corner. Next, we moved on to a swimming pool that looked like the Romans had built it — possessing numerous white pillars, along with sculptures of lions throughout the marble room. The pool itself was square, and carved marble stairs led down into its unknown depth. I leaned down and ran my hand through the water, deciding it was warm enough to swim in when the climate improved as we sailed south. Mary described the activities available onboard while Bessie and Polly listened, appearing fascinated. Finally, Mary drew Bessie aside to speak privately, then politely excused herself with a nod and a curtsy, leaving us to wander back to our suite without her.

We relaxed in the sitting room before lunch, or luncheon as many passengers on board referred to the midday meal. Bessie turned, focusing her attention on me.

'If you don't mind, Mistress, there are certain things I need to know, given it's my first proper day with you. My training has taught me I must behave professionally when in your presence, not speaking unless spoken to, and minding my tongue, which I find difficult, and never questioning or complaining under any circumstance. I need to know your expectations of me so I can avoid losing my job if I make you unhappy.' I watched as relief washed over her, appearing calmer now she had spoken her mind.

'Bessie, I expect you to do the job I employed you to do, and do it well in every way to the best of your ability, just as you have done every day since I have known you. There is no harm in us talking and having a laugh, even being friends, while you carry out your duties.' She nodded, arching her eyebrows for a moment.

'Am I expected to be by your side at all times?'

'Of course not. I am happy for you to have time off throughout the day and at night. Go where the other servants go and make new friends. I want you to have fun here, too, while we are on the ship.'

'Thank you, Mistress. I talked to Mary, and she told me that the servants go to the steerage deck at night because they have music and dancing and alcohol. I may go one night with her and see what all the fuss is about.'

Time passed quickly before Mary stepped into the room. 'It has come time for you to attend luncheon in the dining room,' she announced, ushering me to my feet and guiding me to the door, her hand planted firmly on the base of my spine and appearing to now also be the boss of me.

We made our way down several flights of stairs to the dining room, cheerful banter passing between us, while Polly and I strolled arm-in-arm under Bessie's watchful gaze. She had almost immediately noticed that young men were paying us a considerable amount of attention while we toured the ship this morning. Several of the handsome young men had approached us, only to be shooed away by Bessie, swatting her apron at them as she chased after them until they were a distant memory and no longer in our sight. Finally, we had dragged her from the suite to dine with us, forcing her to remove her apron and hat. She followed behind us, muttering under her breath.

'It's just not right is what it is.' Her voice was so low I could barely hear her or keep the smile from my face. 'I should be eating with my own kind in the servants' quarters, not with the likes of the passengers in first-class who stare through me as if I am invisible.' We turned a corner, her voice rising slightly. 'Just because you are stubborn and won't take no for an answer, using the excuse you paid the same amount of money for my ticket as your own. I don't need to eat the same food as you,' she complained loudly as we arrived at the door to the dining room. As we entered the large room, a waiter, who glanced down at the paper in front of him before turning his attention back to me, immediately greeted us.

'I am truly sorry, madam. Unfortunately, there seems to be a slight problem. We have reserved only two seats in the first-class dining room for the guests in your suite. I understand this is your ladies' maid, and unfortunately, we cannot accommodate her here, but I will have her accompanied to where the other servants take their meals.' He smiled politely, waiting for Polly and me to pass; however, I refused to move. I lowered my voice, moving nearer to him and bringing my face close to his.

'I will make a scene, one like you have never witnessed before in your brief life if Bessie is not permitted into the dining room to eat with us.'

He quickly stepped back, fear filling his eyes for a moment. He abruptly turned his head before hurrying away to speak with his superior, who stared over from a distance, then leaned down and spoke quietly to the waiter.

He returned with a smile, advising us it was necessary to move us to another shared table where he had accommodated the additional member of our party. He picked up three menus and guided us through the grand room until we arrived at the new table allocated to us. I jumped as if an electric current had just run through me, unable to believe my eyes. Sitting at the table was a young man with the golden glow surrounding his body — and I felt immediately attracted to him, an intense feeling of familiarity and deep, deep emotions of love and affection drawing me to him. At the same table was another young man who was identical to the first, also surrounded by a golden aura.

The waiter pulled out our chairs in turn for us to sit down, Polly introducing Bessie and me to our new companions, a middle-aged woman and her two sons, along with her daughter. I was seated next to the young man who had awoken feelings in me I had not known were there, while his mother, Mrs Harriet Makenzie, sat on the other side of him. I couldn't help but discreetly glance sideways at him to confirm I wasn't seeing things or going mad. He did indeed have that same beautiful golden glow radiating around his body as Polly and Bessie possessed, as did his brother. In stark contrast, his sister had another kind of aura radiating around her, one I was trying to ignore, wanting to bask in his beauty until I took my last breath. He glanced back at me, sending tingles through every part of my body.

I attempted to concentrate, listening as Mrs Makenzie warmly welcomed us to the table. After spending the first few minutes engaging in polite small talk, Mrs Makenzie took a small sip of her wine, placing it back on the table before turning her attention to Polly, then smiled across at me.

'We are travelling to Australia to reunite with my husband. He took ship just over two years ago to start a cattle station just outside of a town named Geelong. He sent word for us now he has completed our home and is ready for us to join him.' She appeared outgoing and friendly and was English, despite her surname. It was apparent she had been raised to be a lady and came from a background of privilege. So far, I liked her, feeling my body relax slightly.

She introduced her daughter, seated by her side and who hadn't uttered a word since we had sat down. Jemima, who appeared to be around seventeen years old, was extremely pretty, wore an expression on her face like butter wouldn't melt in her mouth, and I didn't trust her for a moment. The grey aura surrounding her, a colour I had only ever seen around Sister Monica, disturbed me deeply. Jemima's aura was the colour of clouds when a storm was brewing, just before turning to black, no different from Sister Monica's. I couldn't take my eyes from her, greeting her politely, suspicious of the insincere smile that touched her lips for only the briefest of moments.

Mrs Makenzie proudly turned towards her son, whom I felt intensely attracted to and couldn't understand the powerful connection drawing me to him. She introduced the handsome young man as Hamish, continuing on to Angus, his twin, who had not taken his eyes from Polly, explaining they had just turned twenty. Seated next to his sister, Angus rolled his eyes as his mother continued to talk without stopping to take a breath. They were both broad-shouldered, with thick, curly, black hair, and possessed the most handsome faces I had ever seen. Hamish wore his hair long and tied back at the nape of his neck, while Angus's hair was short and curly. I glanced at Angus, then at Hamish, deciding that Hamish was so much better looking than Angus, despite being identical. I gazed for a moment into Hamish's dark-brown eyes, framed with black lashes and a strong, straight nose, before quickly turning away, my heart fluttering.

'Tell me, how did three young girls like yourselves come to be on this ship without a chaperone?' Mrs Makenzie asked, picking up her glass and taking an elegant sip.

'I am immigrating to Australia with my sister, Polly, and my ladies' maid, Bessie.' I smiled weakly at her, feeling the blood rush to my face. 'We will also live in Geelong.' I observed Angus and Hamish exchange a look, one I didn't understand, despite it causing my stomach to flip.

'How wonderful and what a lovely coincidence! It will be a comfort for me for my children to have company, even before they arrive in Australia.' She leaned forward and lowered her voice to a whisper. 'You mentioned Bessie is your maid. Without sounding snobbish, which I assure you I am not, may I ask why Bessie is here dining with us?' I forced a smile and explained my reasoning, Hamish laughing aloud while Mrs Makenzie sat back in her chair and stared at me thoughtfully. 'I understand your point; however, I'm not one of those ladies. You will find many on board who think far too highly of themselves because of the men they married. Maybe we should keep it between ourselves.' She leaned forward and lowered her voice to a whisper. 'My sweet Abigail, should any of the other guests find out, they will surely complain.' I nodded politely before she turned her attention to Polly, who appeared to be mesmerised by Angus. He gazed back at her, their heads close together, murmuring between themselves as if all others in the room had vanished. 'My dear Polly, what happened to your poor face?'

'I was walking in London when I was set upon and robbed. They never did catch the perpetrator, but I'm feeling much better now, thank you.' Polly smiled at her, but only had eyes for Angus. They appeared animated as they discussed different breeds of dogs while I sat in silence next to Hamish, his attention focused on the smoked ham and pea soup placed in front of him.

I admired how resilient and kind Mrs Makenzie seemed. She freely gave up everything she had in England, and then Scotland, where she made her home as a newlywed, to be with her husband and start a life in a new country that would provide opportunities to her children unavailable in the motherland. I believed she was the type of woman who accepted whatever circumstances arose, good and bad, and just got on with things. We chatted amiably throughout lunch — all except for Hamish, who remained silent and ignored me completely, despite the fact the mere sight of him sent my heart racing.

Mrs Makenzie continued to speak of their life in Scotland, her eyes glistening as memories overcame her. She talked of just how excited they were to be starting a new life in a country they had heard enjoyed a much warmer climate with beautiful landscapes and many opportunities they did not have in their homeland. Although she was decades older, I enjoyed her company and hoped that we would be friends by the time we arrived. Time flew by before we said our farewells, thanking the Makenzie family for their company. Then we began the arduous journey back to our suite, my heart and mind racing at the thought of Hamish. I could not shake the feeling that I knew him, despite knowing for certain we had never met. Not in this lifetime.

Chapter Twenty-One

I FOLLOWED BESSIE INTO our suite, Polly immediately throwing herself down on the lounge, a dreamy look in her eyes as she stared at the ceiling.

'Oh, Abi, isn't he beautiful?' I settled myself down next to her. 'His lovely brown eyes, which somehow look deep into my soul, give me tingles.' She shuddered, turning her gaze to me before smiling sweetly. 'I love the way he talks about his hopes and dreams and of the things he wishes to achieve, and he's Scottish, just like us. Well, half. They were educated in England, he told me. I cannot believe it, but he's my perfect match. I think I'm in love.' She sighed deeply and closed her eyes while I shook my head in disbelief.

'Polly, you only just met. How can you tell?'

'Abi, when it happens, you just know. I can feel it, and he asked if I could meet him in the games room this afternoon.' She giggled, her feet kicking in the air as if she were running. Bessie glanced at her disapprovingly from the doorway before stepping into her room.

To see her so excited brought me great joy. She was slowly returning to the Polly who had lived and grown alongside me at the orphanage, teasing and joking and always laughing and making fun of the Sisters, despite our heavy-handed treatment until the day we could leave.

She had almost returned to a healthy weight, and her dresses fitted perfectly. The black shadows under her eyes and the gauntness of her face had virtually disappeared. Although her bruises were still noticeable, she appeared healthy and happy; and that brought joy to my heart and soul.

'I'm tired, Polly. Do you mind if I leave you to take a nap?' She shook her head, smiling as she shooed me away, then closed her eyes. I could hear Bessie rummaging around in her room and muttering to herself; I assumed unpacking her new wardrobe. I strolled across to my room, stepping inside and closing the door behind me, before stripping off my house dress and slipping in under the quilt in my shift. The bed was soft, moulding to my body, as did the pillows. The quilts were heavy and warm, pulling me down into a deep sleep and into a land where everyone had soft beds, food to eat, and the sun shone above soft, white clouds, and the rainbow contained colours I had never seen before.

I woke abruptly to hear the girls talking in the sitting room. I stretched, yawning loudly, not bothering to cover my mouth as I struggled out of bed and slipped on my dressing gown.

'Well, you're finally awake, sleepyhead,' Polly teased as I entered the room.

'You look like you're in a fine mood. I take it that the meeting with Angus went well?' I replied, yawning again as I settled down beside her.

'I must make haste and ready an evening gown for you to wear to dinner tonight. I have organised Polly but haven't even unpacked your dresses, thanks to you sleeping the afternoon away,' Bessie grumbled, placing her needlework on the table before hurrying to my room and loudly closing the door behind her.

'Oh Abi, he is the perfect gentleman,' she exclaimed as soon as the door clicked shut. 'We talked and talked, and there was never an awkward moment. He held my hand and helped me down the stairs. I wanted to kiss him, but I remembered what you said about no kissing for at least a week, so I didn't. Come to think of it, he didn't even try. Do you think he might not like me?' Her face fell as I smothered a smile.

'I think he likes you just fine.'

'Yes, you're right. He really does, and I like him so much, too, Abi. There is no one else I want now, or ever. If I can't have him, I don't want anyone and will die an old spinster; with you beside me, of course.' She nodded her head adamantly, as if making a promise to herself. 'He invited me to walk on the deck after dinner.' She hesitated for a moment, glancing at my door, before lowering her voice. 'I've accepted his invitation, but do not tell Bessie. Promise me now.' I nodded, pulling a thin woollen blanket over our legs, feeling the chill in the air. 'I noticed his brother said little to you at lunch.' I felt my stomach lurch again at the thought of the dark, brooding young man.

'More like said nothing.' I frowned, the idea of having to sit next to him tonight no longer appealing. I hated the effect Hamish had on me when he clearly showed no interest in even making polite conversation with me. Despite Angus being identical in appearance and, although funny and friendly, I found I was not drawn to him in the least, despite the glow that also surrounded him, confusing me completely. It made little sense. Hamish had not spoken to me, other than a few words in greeting; therefore, I had learnt nothing about him. I knew a lot more about Angus, who had revealed a lot about himself during lunch, appearing to be a friendly and open person, nothing like the severe and distant Hamish.

Polly paused for a time, staring out towards the balcony.

'Hmm, Angus told me he has never seen his brother so quiet. He believes it was because of you.'

'What do you mean?'

'Well, he believes Hamish likes you. He told Angus he finds you beautiful,' she teased, her mouth twitching.

'You wouldn't know it by the way he acted, Polly. You and Angus talked right from when you sat down together, and he would not say one word to me. To be honest, I think he's rude.'

'Just give him a chance, Abi. Maybe he's just shy, although Angus says he's not.' I nodded, although I was unconvinced.

'Which evening gown has Bessie picked out for you tonight, Polly?'

'It's the most beautiful thing I've ever seen. It has embroidering covering the entire bodice and is the most amazing shade of purple.' She darted into her bedroom, quickly returning with the dress in her arms. The gown, made of heavy silk, shimmered as the fabric caught the light. We were both admiring its charm when Bessie called for me to dress.

She had chosen an emerald-green gown with beads of crystals, with additional crystals scattered throughout the material that skimmed my hips, the soft material dropping to the floor, the skirt full and heavy. I had never worn an evening dress before, tolerating the torture of her trussing me up in a corset just to have the experience of wearing what I considered a piece of art. Bessie helped me into the gown, fiddling with the tiny buttons at the back until they were well secured.

'Sit down. I am ready to do your hair,' she instructed, muttering to herself under her breath. I quickly obeyed, lowering myself down onto the stool that sat in front of my dressing table. I had promised I would allow her to style it however she liked, but only half the time. It had been a battle of wills before she reluctantly agreed, knowing I wouldn't let her touch my hair at all if she didn't concede.

I watched in the mirror as she pinned my long curls up on top of my head, leaving several tendrils that fell around my face and the back of my neck. She hurried over to the bed before returning with a green, feathered headpiece, gently clipping it to the side of my tightly restrained curls, motioning for me to stand before she made several adjustments, then nodded her head, appearing satisfied.

We entered the sitting room to find Polly pacing up and down, dressed in her gown and not a hair out of place. She ran to my side and grabbed my hand, dragging me out into the hallway while Bessie followed, locking the door of our suite behind us. I held tight to Polly's hand to prevent her from running ahead while we walked side by side to the dining room, Bessie taking her time. Finally, we stepped into the dining room, and a young waiter accompanied us to our table. Hamish and Angus immediately stood and pulled out our chairs for us, while Mrs Makenzie smiled brightly before taking a large sip of her wine. Hamish cut a handsome figure in his dinner suit, as I expected he would, and I quickly glanced away, willing my heart to stop racing like I had run ten miles with someone chasing me.

Mrs Makenzie greeted us warmly, as did Jemima, while Angus and Polly were already in a world of their own, talking in hushed tones, their heads close together so we couldn't hear a word. Our server brought our hors d'oeuvre, leaving Bessie and me chatting with Mrs Makenzie while Hamish and Jemima concentrated on their food. Course after course of delicious food was served and devoured, the conversation light and cheerful. Finally, Hamish turned to me as I swallowed the last of my dessert, amusement in his eyes as he studied my face.

'What?'

'I was just wondering how such a tiny lass like you can hold that much food. You eat like a man. If any other girl consumed that amount of food, she would be the size of a house.' He smirked before turning back to the table, and picking up his full glass of wine, drained it within moments.

'I advised the last man who made negative comments about my appetite where to shove his opinion, but in your case, I'll wait until I know you better. Besides, I'm not that tiny.'

'You might be tall for a woman, but your body is small, except ...' he trailed off, his face turning a slight shade of pink as he looked away from my breasts. His words had stung me like a bee, so I picked up my glass of wine and took a deep drink. 'I admire a woman who can eat,' he continued, appearing to have noticed his faux pas. 'So many of them sit through a ten-course dinner and nibble only a morsel, and you wonder if they are truly starving inside. Why can't they just eat their fill? I'm sure many of them go home and eat alone in their bedchambers, with only their ladies' maid knowing their secret. No, I think it's good that you are comfortable eating in front of others and don't seem to care what anyone thinks; or how fat you will become.' My eyes went wide before I looked away, shaking my head in disbelief. Was this man trying to hurt my feelings or pay me a compliment? I was uncertain if he even knew.

The music started, and I relaxed back into my chair, gazing across as several couples walked towards the hardwood floor in front of the musicians; the lights dim and the mood serene as the glorious music filled my ears.

'Would you like to dance with Angus or Hamish, Abigail? They are dancing the Schottische, a very old-fashioned dance these days. Oh, it just brings back so many memories.' I shook my head before Mrs Makenzie gazed across at the couples, her eyes glistening, while many more had joined them, all appearing to have a wonderful time. She leaned forward and lowered her voice to a whisper. 'I heard even before we stepped foot on the ship that Dame Nellie Melba is on board. Apparently, she is returning to Melbourne in secret to reunite with her family and introduce the Duke of Orleans. I will not even speak of the scandal surrounding her, given her husband, Charles Armstrong, has recently filed a petition for divorce on the grounds of adultery. It has been clear to all who mix in the same circles as Nellie and Philippe they have been romantically involved for quite some time. I am uncertain if she will perform for us, but if she does, it will be an experience you cannot miss.' She sighed deeply, appearing to be a thousand miles away as she continued to watch the other passengers dance.

'I'm sorry, but I don't know how and I would trip over my own feet.' Confusion crossed her face for a moment as she clasped her hands together on the table and leaned forward, lowering her voice.

'We will have to remedy that.' She stared across at her sons expectantly, glancing from one to another as they both shifted uncomfortably in their seats.

'I have never learnt to dance, either, Mrs Makenzie,' Polly added shyly, glancing across at Angus.

'Well that is easily fixed. Hamish and Angus will teach you the art of dancing in the games room each morning after breakfast. Be aware it is an art, my dear girls, and one you must master. You cannot go out into society, even in the colony of Australia, without the ability to dance, or you will never find a decent husband.' She nodded, appearing satisfied, while Hamish looked away as if he hadn't heard a word. Angus agreed immediately, turning back to Polly and grinning widely, her face flushed with excitement.

Bessie rose to her feet, smiling down at me before politely bidding all at the table goodnight, hurrying away to join her new friends. I remained where I was, conversing with Mrs Makenzie and Jemima while Hamish listened silently. The dishes had been cleared away; the servers going from table to table pouring wine and offering the men spirits while the music played on late into the evening.

Polly and I stepped into our suite, finding Mary on the lounge in the sitting room.

'I am so sorry. I shouldn't be sitting here like the Queen herself, but I'm waiting for Bessie. She is just in her room changing her dress as we are going down to steerage to enjoy the first night of sailing and to celebrate the new life that awaits her.' I crossed the room and sat down next to her, the suite door clicking shut behind Polly as she made her way up to the deck to meet Angus.

'You are very welcome here, Mary, whether you are working or not.' She nodded shyly as Bessie stepped out of her room and smiled.

'So, you finally decided to return? Unmolested by those enormous boys who remind me of the old Scottish warriors of years past, I hope.'

'Take a breath, Bessie. Those warriors you speak of do not even know I exist.'

'Ah, well. That's for the best, in my opinion. Hurry up and go to your room so I can get to where I'm going.' I bid Mary goodnight as I rose to my feet and obediently followed her. Bessie had me undressed and in my nightgown in record time before sitting me down at my dressing table and plaiting my hair. 'Off to sleep now,' she ordered, hurrying me along as I shuffled to my bed and slipped in between the crisp, ironed sheets. I felt so comfortable in my new nightgown as I snuggled under the heavy quilts and soon drifted off into a deep sleep. I dreamed of dancing in a tavern, enormous ocean swells crashing on a rocky shoreline, and a baby with black, curly hair.

We stepped into the games room to find Angus and Hamish relaxing back on the lounge while a man I had never seen before was quietly tinkering with the keys on the piano. Polly ran to Angus and sat down next to him, moving close as he took her hand in his, while

I hesitantly walked over to the opposite lounge and sat down across from Hamish.

'Thank you for taking the time out of your day to teach us,' I said as politely as I could, feeling resentment rise in me that Hamish was clearly only here at his mother's request.

'It's a pleasure, and I can't say that enough,' Angus replied, not taking his eyes from Polly for a moment. She gazed up at him adoringly, so tiny compared to him; not a difficult feat, given he was one of the largest men I had ever seen. In fact, they were both enormous and stood a full head above me, a rare occurrence when most women barely averaged five feet tall. Most men were not much bigger, particularly those who were not affluent and had suffered from poor nutrition in their childhood. Hamish stood and approached the piano, requesting a song I had never heard. He returned and offered me his hand, which I reluctantly took before he helped me to my feet. I jumped as a strange sensation raced up my arm; I imagined no different than if a bolt of lightning had struck me, the feeling spreading through my body at his touch. I wondered what was happening to me, attempting to catch my breath and maintain my composure before swallowing hard. I stared up at him, searching for any recognition on his face that he had felt the same jolt I had experienced; however, his large brown eyes revealed nothing. He led me across to the small, square hardwood floor a few feet from the pianist, who hadn't uttered a word to anyone other than Hamish.

'Now, I must put my arm around your waist, Abigail. Is that all right?' I nodded silently. He obviously had not felt the same electric charge that had set my heart racing and jumbled my thoughts completely; there was only detached friendliness on his face as I stared up at him. He stepped closer and encircled my waist, taking my right hand in his. I felt as if I were enveloped in a large blanket that filled me with warmth, sending tingles all over my body. Damn it. Despite my previous disdain and humiliation, resulting from him behaving as if I were invisible, I liked this man. I found myself overwhelmingly attracted to him, but to have such a physical reaction caused by another person was shocking to me. It had never happened before with anyone, with or without the golden glow. 'What you are learning isn't difficult at all, and it's a matter of remembering the steps as I teach them to you. Now, watch my feet, Abigail.' I obediently looked down at his feet, much bigger than mine, which instantly made me feel better. I watched and followed along as best I could; however, he constantly berated me, demanding I concentrate. He failed to notice I was distracted by his beauty and couldn't stop staring up at him, forgetting all the steps he had just taught me.

He held me at a respectable distance from his body, whereas with Polly and Angus, you could not see a sliver of light between them as they danced. Polly continually stepped on his toes, causing them to laugh loudly and start again. Angus stood a foot and a half taller than Polly, who was only five feet tall, taking all the strength within me not to laugh aloud as they danced together, given his height and breadth and her petite frame. I tried to focus on what I was doing and found it easier the longer we danced.

'Will you dance with me tonight after dinner, now that you have mastered your first dance?' He looked down at me, his gaze so powerful, I was forced to look away.

'Yes, so long as you promise to not step on my toes.'

'I promise.' He smirked, glancing over at his brother for a moment before approaching him, Angus and Polly still dancing despite the music ceasing long ago. He grabbed his brother by the shoulders and pulled him away from Polly, who immediately appeared forlorn. 'Come on, lovebird, we have to be going,' he told him, laughing loudly as he dragged Angus out the door and onto the deck, Polly and Angus continuing to call out to each other, making plans to meet later in the afternoon. I smothered a smile, standing next to Polly at the door as we watched them argue and push each other while making their way to the stairs.

'Oh, Polly. Stop acting as if he has died, and you are his grief-stricken widow. It's only for a few more hours, and then your hearts will be reunited once again,' I teased her, bursting into giggles as she gave me a dark look. She moaned all the way back to the room about how she missed him and couldn't bear to be parted from him. I rolled my eyes before opening the suite door to find Bessie at the sitting-room table, closing holes in her stockings with tiny, professional-looking stitches that were almost invisible.

'What happened, Bessie?' I asked, crossing the room before sitting down beside her.

'When I went to steerage, it was wonderful, but I was dancing with my shoes off, and the bottoms of my stockings got caught on the wooden floor,' she replied, chuckling to herself. 'I think I had the most fun I have ever had last night. Everyone is so friendly and not fancy at all like the ones I have to put up with in that dining room I have no right to be in.' She glanced up at me, rolling her eyes before returning to her work. 'I even had a nice man pay me some attention. He is immigrating from Ireland and hopes to buy some land and build a house. He would make some lucky woman a decent husband, of that I am certain.'

I kissed her cheek and left her to her business, crossing the room and lowering myself onto the lounge, reflecting on my reaction when Hamish had touched me. I was not acquainted with the man at all, and the little I had heard him say so far hadn't impressed me; however, I could not deny there was a powerful attraction, although it was clearly one-sided.

We walked side by side down the hallway, Polly's hand clasped in mine despite her loud protests, as it was all I could do to prevent her from running down the hall and stairs to get to the dining room ahead of us. Finally, we stepped into the dining room and made our way to our table to find Mrs Makenzie looking lovely in a gown of magenta, as did Jemima, resplendent in a soft yellow dress. Hamish and Angus stood to pull out our chairs, Angus assisting Bessie first, before smiling at Polly as she sat down next to his empty chair unassisted.

'How did you enjoy your lesson this morning, Abigail?' Hamish asked, raising an oyster shell to his lips and sucking into his mouth what looked to me like a large piece of snot.

'It's wonderful to know at least one dance step, and I really must thank you for your time this morning.' I took a long drink of water before smiling shyly at him.

'I enjoyed it, too. I haven't danced since I was in school. It's not something that I have ever really enjoyed before.' I nodded as our entrées were placed in front of us, glad the canapes were gone.

'So, are you going to watch every morsel I put in my mouth, then make comments at the end of the meal about me?'

'Probably. That depends upon how much you ingest.'

We both laughed, the tension between us easing slightly as we chatted through lunch, Hamish appearing far more relaxed in my company than he had been this morning. We talked until the dining room was empty, all except for the employees. Bessie stood, indicating for Polly and me to do the same before we excused ourselves and bid them a warm farewell, arriving back at our suite, full and content. Polly had every intention of meeting Angus and spending the afternoon with him, while Bessie had more clothes to unpack and items to store. Given I knew no one else on the ship intimately enough to spend time with, I decided to go to my favourite place in the world — bed.

I made my way to my room and slipped under the covers; still fully dressed, my shoes kicked off at the front door the first chance I had. I thought about how the Makenzie family would reside in Geelong and what a coincidence it was we had been seated at the same table. Finally, I drifted off to sleep, dreaming of a child with blonde hair, a dinosaur, and a tall woman with emerald green eyes and a golden glow surrounding her.

'Wake up, it's time for dinner,' I heard, slowly opening my eyes to find Bessie standing over me, gently pulling the covers back and holding up my dressing gown. I struggled to my feet with her assistance as she slipped the dressing gown over my shoulders, yawning widely and forgetting to cover my mouth. I staggered to the sitting room to find Polly fully dressed for dinner and pacing impatiently, ready to leave. I clearly was not prepared to go as I returned her stare, struggling to keep my eyes open as I yawned again, still half asleep.

'Abi, come on. You should be dressed by now,' she snapped before throwing herself down on the lounge in despair. I scowled, strolled over to the lounge opposite her, and sat down heavily, narrowing my gaze at her.

'Polly, this is getting ridiculous between you and Angus. I don't mind if you want to spend all your time with him, but when it comes to our group plans, he just has to wait, and you have to shut up about him. You have known him one whole day.'

'I know it's fast, but I promise you, Abi, he is the one for me. He is going to be my husband. I can feel it in my bones.' I yawned again and rolled my eyes at her, but it was clear she would stubbornly stick to her opinion on the matter while I would stick to mine.

I returned to my room to find Bessie had readied my clothes and was making my bed. She hurried me over to the wardrobe and helped me into a golden evening gown that was a delightful surprise. I had barely looked at any of the dresses that were packed away before we embarked on the ship. Polly and Bessie had tried all theirs on when they had been delivered to our hotel room a few weeks before we departed London, while I had only briefly glanced through mine, tried several of them on to ensure they fitted and had them packed away in the trunks again. Of course, when you had grown up with only two dresses to choose from, you learnt to live sparingly, and I found all this changing a little ridiculous.

Jenny Malcolm had warned me we would be required to wear a different gown each evening on the ship and change several times throughout the day. She had explained to Bessie that she felt it was her role to ensure we would do only the things expected of us as young ladies, and Bessie had given Mr and Mrs Malcolm her word she would do everything in her power to make sure we behaved as expected. Now that I was getting used to having someone assist me with everything from getting dressed to bringing me food and ensuring every want and need was attended to, I didn't know what I would do without her. She had taken Polly under her wing, just as she had done for me, and was acting as our unofficial chaperone, taking her role quite seriously.

'I think you will blow someone's eyes out of his head tonight, Mistress,' she remarked, picking up my hairbrush as I sat at the dressing table.

'I take it you mean Hamish?' I replied, smirking slightly.

'Well, it wouldn't be Angus, now would it? What with him and Polly all over each other like grizzly bears? Of course, I mean Hamish. I see the way he looks at you.'

'I am warming a little towards him, I must say. I didn't like him last night at all, Bessie.'

'He's a fine-looking man — strong and tall, and he looks like he would work hard. I think he suits you, Mistress, but just remember you are still so young.'

'We will have to wait and see.' I watched her reflection in the mirror as she finished my hair, abandoning me to prepare herself for another dinner with our new friends.

Hamish stood as I approached my chair in the grand dining room, politely pulling it out for me. I noticed his mother smile to herself, appearing pleased.

'So, Abigail, where do you come from? You have hardly said a word about yourself, and I have wanted to ask from the moment we met why you are unchaperoned?'

'I'm from Scotland, Mrs Makenzie, and my parents are dead; thus, the reason Polly and I travel alone with our ladies' maid and without a male chaperone. Our London barrister sent us to Australia to look at the new home secured for us in Geelong and to meet with our new solicitor concerning business matters regarding our parents and our inheritance,' I replied, having rehearsed this moment a thousand times in my mind.

'Oh, my dear girls, I'm so sorry for your loss. To lose your parents so young and have only one another brings tears to my eyes, especially when I look at my children, older than you, who have both parents. I would never have known you are from Scotland, Abigail, although Polly has the Scottish brogue. You speak like an English aristocrat.' I felt my face flush; memories of Emiliani House and the constant teasing I had suffered my entire childhood because I did not speak the same way as those around me flooded my mind. I swallowed hard as they started to fade, Sister Josephine replacing them as I remembered how confused she had been when I first started to talk. Mrs Makenzie wiped her eyes before returning her attention to Polly, then to me. 'I'm so sorry you lost your parents, girls.' She wiped her tear-stained cheeks with her handkerchief before discreetly slipping it back into her reticule, gazing across at us both, sadness in her eyes, before she picked up her glass of wine and took a long sip. 'Are you connected to The Delmont Hotel Delmonts'?'

'Yes, we are, Mrs Makenzie,' Polly replied immediately, causing me to cringe while leaving me feeling exposed. I had tried to avoid providing too much information, but enough to satisfy their curiosity. I had become aware since leaving the orphanage just how prominent the Howard and Delmont families were, which was confirmed every time their names were mentioned.

'I find it painful to speak of my family,' I remarked quietly, casting a sidelong glance at Polly, who nodded slightly.

'I am sorry, dear. We must move on to a more pleasant subject.' Mrs Makenzie smiled before continuing. 'I've noticed you have met no one on the ship as yet, well, except for us.' I nodded, chewing a tender piece of lamb, reminding myself not to talk with my mouth full. 'All the ladies meet for afternoon tea on the deck. If you would like to meet me tomorrow and join us, I can introduce you. Unfortunately, I can't promise The Dame herself will be there, as it appears she has chosen to take her meals in her suite.' I considered her invitation for a moment, knowing I should make an effort to meet new people and overcome my shyness. Nearly everyone I had met so far had been lovely; therefore, I was certain I had nothing to lose and everything to gain.

'It would be my pleasure, Mrs Makenzie.' She smiled, appearing quite satisfied with herself. We chatted through dinner, the mood light and cheerful, Hamish occasionally glancing at me when he thought I wasn't looking, although he remained relatively quiet and was not as talkative as his twin. From the little he told me about himself and his plans when he arrived in Australia, I found him even more interesting. The evening passed quickly, Polly and I dancing for hours with Hamish and Angus, Mrs Makenzie watching intently from the table while talking with two women with whom she had been acquainted in London. The night seemed to disappear within minutes, and I soon found myself tucked up in my comfortable bed, thoughts of Hamish filling my mind.

I eventually drifted off to sleep, content that all was well in the world, dreaming of a dolphin, a pickle, and a tree weeping at the edge of a wide river.

Chapter Twenty-Two

I FELT SAD FOR Hamish as I lay in my big, cosy bed, thinking about the evening before and how he had so formally said goodnight after we danced. Angus and Polly had snuck out to meet on the deck after dinner, leaving me wondering if she had returned safely as I stretched my limbs, hearing several loud cracks. Finally, I rose to my feet and slipped on my dressing gown to ensure she was indeed in her own bed. I crept through the sitting room and quietly opened her door just a crack, relief washing over me as I listened to her soft snores. I quietly closed it again and made my way to the lounge; a tray with a pot of fresh coffee sitting on the table. Thanks to Mary, bless her. She was well aware the first thing I did when I woke was have my morning coffee, which I had come to believe I could never live without.

I reflected on Hamish and Angus's upbringing and how they were raised by nannies' and then lived at a prestigious boarding school in England from a tender age until they graduated at eighteen. Hamish had confided in me during one of our many dances that as long as they were together, they did not mind being away from home or their parents and found they were happier living at the school, anyway. Due to their size, no one ever picked a fight with them, and anyone

that wanted to always knew the other brother would be close behind
to defend his twin.

His father had purchased five thousand acres near Geelong to run
Black Angus beef, which he believed was the best meat you could eat,
and he planned to sell it all over the country. Hamish appeared to love
and respect his mother, but when it came to his father, he did not
seem to be close to him at all. I had enquired why his mother had not
gone to be with her husband earlier, like the way of so many families
immigrating to Australia — at least that was what I was noticing
more and more each day. He had alluded to the fact that his parents
did not get along and, although they conducted all the formalities for
everyone's benefit, behind closed doors was another matter. I leaned
forward and poured a cup of coffee, picked it up and relaxed back on
the lounge, sipping it slowly; my eyes closed as I inhaled what smelt
like heaven and tasted like a tonic for the soul.

Polly and I had arrived at the games room far earlier than required to
attend our dance lesson with Hamish and Angus. It had taken all my
strength to prevent Polly from leaving an hour earlier than we had,
finally giving in fifteen minutes before our agreed appointment. We
sat side by side at the piano, tinkering around, when Jimmy, the piano
player, strolled into the room and smiled at us.

'Hello, ladies. If you prefer certain music or a particular song, just
ask, and I will arrange it for you.'

We quickly stood, stepping away from the piano to allow him to
sit, making our way over to the lounges in the corner of the room.
Shortly after, Angus walked in, his eyes darting around the room
until they stopped on Polly, their eyes meeting as they both smiled
adoringly at the other. Angus rushed over, pulling Polly to her feet
and up into his embrace, lifting her from the ground as she squealed

in delight. I knew they had gone as far as holding hands and Polly was determined to put her past behind her, only sleeping with him after they were married. I admired her for that. I found it amazing that she could put a section of her life in a box, seal it up, and put it away forever without thinking about it again. She had put her memories from the orphanage behind her before I found her, the sight of me reminding her of those difficult times once again, and had done the same regarding her time spent with Leroy. I hoped it didn't come back to haunt her in the future and ruin whatever life she had made for herself.

I couldn't help but notice her eyes were shining as she gazed at Angus. I shook my head, hoping I would never let myself become a blithering idiot when it came to a man. I would shoot myself first. I barely noticed Hamish standing in front of me, saying something I could not hear due to being so intensely focused on my imagined self-obliteration at the thought of acting as strangely as Polly.

'I'm sorry, Hamish, what did you say?' I apologised, trying to focus my attention back on the present.

'I said, good morning, Miss Abigail. Are you ready to dance?'

He offered me his hand and helped me to my feet, and there it was again — that feeling of warmth, sudden and unexpected, jolting up my arm and into my body. It was not unpleasant; in fact, it was the opposite. He led me across the room to begin our lesson, holding me closer than he did during yesterday's practice, where he had kept me at arm's length the entire time. I found him to be a gifted dancer and felt comfortable in his arms.

Seeing him again up close, I couldn't help but be overwhelmed by his beauty. Those big, brown eyes that stared so deeply into your own that you thought you would die, and his lovely face with that wide, friendly smile — yes, I could have pretty children with this man. The way he made me feel when he brushed against my body was something I had never felt before. I hadn't touched many men in my life; however, there was the odd occasion where a man would take my arm, and nothing happened. Richard had touched me all the time, and I never felt a quiver. When I thought of Hamish, I would get butterflies in my stomach and feel strange sensations in my body, let alone what I felt like when he touched me; no matter how lightly or innocently. I wondered if this was the start of what it felt like to fall in love. The speed at which Polly and Angus were going would have them married before the voyage was over, from what I had witnessed so far, bringing a smile to my lips.

'What's so funny?' he asked, grinning down at me.

'Oh, it's nothing, Hamish. I was just thinking about Polly and Angus.'

'Yes, I think they have found that thing called romantic love that you only read about in storybooks,' he remarked sarcastically while continuing to hold my gaze before he leaned forward and lowered his voice. 'Do you think you will ever find it, Abigail?'

'I'm not sure.' I glanced away, unable to bear the intensity of his stare. I had never had a man look at me the way he looked at me before, leaving me nervous and feeling awkward.

'I think I know what it feels like,' he remarked as he swung me around in time with the music. 'When you see that person, your face lights up without you wanting it to, and you feel nervous around them. You want to touch them, to kiss them, but you don't know how to start. They make you laugh, and you feel you are friends already.' He paused for a moment, pulling me back into his arms. 'Well, that's what I think, anyway.' He looked away as we continued to dance, each lost in our own thoughts.

'Have you ever been in love, Hamish?'

'No, and I never did believe in it. You see it all the time, people falling in love and getting married before the season has changed, then as the years go on, they no longer sleep in the same room, and they hardly speak to each other, just like my parents. I think I will just change women every few years, so I don't end up like that.' I lightly smacked his arm, his face lighting up in a mischievous grin. All I knew was that I was feeling things I had never felt before and, given I had never experienced romantic love and wasn't confident I would recognise the signs, I was unsure if I was in love and didn't even realise. 'Would you walk the deck with me after dinner tonight? I would like to speak to you in private, with no one around to listen to our conversation.' He looked slightly flushed, and his hands had suddenly turned cold and clammy.

'Of course, Hamish. I would love to.' He pulled away, wiping his hands on his handkerchief before we enjoyed one last dance. I swore he was sniffing my hair as he held me close to him, but I could not tell for sure. If this was how love began, I was enjoying it already.

Mrs Makenzie led me out onto the deck and towards a large table, preparing to introduce me to her new friends. I noticed from a distance the ladies sitting together and taking tea were in their finest clothes and hats, and I felt like an imposter in my burnt orange dress and matching hat, despite outwardly appearing to fit in. My shoes were of the same colour as my dress, made from the softest suede as promised. They were flat and comfortable as I had requested — how Mr Higginbottom had made them so fashionable was beyond my comprehension, having only ever suffered the privilege of ill-fitting shoes.

'Good afternoon, ladies. I want to introduce Abigail Delmont, who dines with my family each day. She is from the Delmont Hotel Delmonts,' Mrs Makenzie announced loudly, puffing up like a mother hen beside me and making me cringe. Our server pulled out my chair, and I quickly sat down, my face becoming warm.

'How do you do?' They greeted me warmly, and as the afternoon tea progressed, I learnt a great deal in their company, gradually relaxing and enjoying the stories of where they came from and where they were going. Mrs Dana Shannon was in her early fifties, possessing bright orange hair and a painted face that made her look like a doll. She was tall and attractive, informing me she was travelling with her daughters, Charlotte and Victoria, who were also present at the table. She had left her husband in England, a very wealthy man, in the dead of night, taking her belongings and those of her daughters' and sneaking away to London, where she had emptied his bank account. They then took ship to Australia, where she planned to file for divorce, live a genteel life, and search for wealthy husbands for them all. I smiled at her cunning plan, and she smiled back, exposing beautiful, straight teeth. I could barely breathe as I gazed at the golden glow she was surrounded by, feeling intensely drawn to her, as though we had known each other long before even a word had passed between us.

Charlotte and Victoria favoured their mother in looks and personality. They had inherited her hair and voluptuous body, their faces only younger versions of their mother. All of them were extroverted and friendly. It wouldn't take any of them long to find husbands, I was sure, as they all seemed like amiable people — except for the stealing part — and they were quite beautiful.

Mrs Amelia Johnson was a young woman in her early twenties. She had confided she was travelling with her baby and had left England to meet her husband in Melbourne, who had left England sometime before. I noticed how quiet she was and how she did not join in when our companions gossiped about the other passengers. She was small, with brown hair that had golden streaks throughout, and was exceptionally well dressed. She had quietly told me her baby, Mathew, was on another deck with his Nanny getting some sunshine, and she was enjoying the break and some time to herself. She appeared sad, as if she had something on her mind taking up so much of her energy she had none left over for a conversation. I made a mental note to have tea with her alone in the future.

Elizabeth Christy and her sister, Tamara, were travelling to Australia to join their parents, who had left them in England, just as Catherine's parents had done. Tamara was nineteen, and Elizabeth, seventeen. Their father had started up a large sheep business just outside of Melbourne, where he had built a mansion for his family of four. Their mother had decided she could not be parted from him and left alongside him a year-and-a-half ago to build their fortune and ensure everything was ready for the two girls to come out in society and make suitable matches.

I glanced around the table at my new acquaintances and realised five of the eight women were looking for husbands. I hoped I didn't get pushed down that road. I wanted to have time to myself, get my bearings, and find what the Sisters would refer to as my calling. I was happy being with Bessie and Polly, and soon Catherine and her family, without a husband, but I undeniably enjoyed Hamish's attention and company. I liked these women and could see myself becoming friends with each of them in time.

Bessie stood as soon as they cleared the last dish from the table, and the orchestra was preparing to play, excusing herself, as was her usual practice every night, to meet Mary and their new friends in steerage. Jemima had retired to bed with a headache halfway through dinner while Mrs Makenzie was organising herself to return to her suite. Angus and Polly had left long before dessert arrived to walk the deck.

'I will escort my mother to her quarters and then collect you from your suite, if that is acceptable to you, Abigail?' Hamish asked politely, winking at me discreetly, and I nodded slightly.

I silently climbed the stairs, not another person in sight, feeling as if I were floating on air. The hallway was quiet as I made my way to our suite, wondering if he would hold my hand or would even try to kiss me. Despite all the lectures I had given Polly about guarding her honour, here I was contemplating letting a man touch my lips with his, despite the fact he did not believe in love and intended to throw over his women every couple of years.

I hurried inside and quickly removed my hat, leaving it on the table before painstakingly unpinning my hair. I retrieved my hairbrush from my dressing table before returning to the sitting room to brush my hair while waiting for Hamish. I relaxed back into the plush lounge, noticing a fresh box of chocolates on the table, so I decided to have one. I sat back with the box lying on my stomach and continued to eat while pondering my situation. He really was beautiful on the outside and, although I had sensed that he was a good person, I really didn't know him at all. I heard a loud knock at the door, startling me from my thoughts.

'Come in. It's open,' I called out as I placed another chocolate in my mouth. Hamish slowly opened the door and stuck his head in, his eyes wide in disbelief.

'Are you coming out? I'm not allowed to be in your room, so hurry up, Abigail. If we get caught, it's my head.' He stepped back, looking up and down the hallway before his head reappeared.

'Yes, but my reputation,' I shot back at him and giggled.

'Did you eat all those chocolates by yourself after you ate everything at dinner?' he asked incredulously as he stood waiting impatiently in the doorway.

'Yes. I was filling in time, and I just felt like having one, which turned into three, and so on. So who are you, anyway? The chocolate police?' I placed the empty box on the table and donned my long coat over my dress, hurrying to the door.

'I have never seen a woman eat as much as you do. I'm sure you could eat me under the table.'

'Probably.' I brushed past him, the door clicking shut behind us as the sound of his deep laughter filled the hall.

I stepped up onto the top deck, Hamish not far behind me, the wind blustery and cold as it stung my cheeks and whipped my hair out and around me, causing me deep regret that I hadn't listened to Bessie and left it how it was. I could see Polly and Angus huddled together on an outdoor lounge in the distance, talking and holding hands. Hamish led me to the opposite end of the deck; however, it was extremely windy, and we couldn't hear a word no matter how loudly we yelled. Finally, I motioned for him to follow me back to my suite as I found the situation impossible. He nodded obligingly, leading me back to the stairs we had only climbed minutes before.

'I'm sorry it didn't work out.' He stood in the doorway, about to take his leave.

'No, you are not going anywhere,' I replied with authority, running my fingers gently through my hair to untangle the knots before throwing myself down on the lounge. 'Come inside. No one will know, and we will just sit and talk. Bessie and Polly will be home soon. Please, Hamish. I don't want to sit up by myself waiting for them.'

I looked forward to spending time alone with him and didn't see the harm in us talking in the sitting room. He gazed at me for a moment, glanced up and down the hall, then ducked in and quickly closed the door. I opened a bottle of wine and filled two glasses, then sat back on my lounge, waiting for him to say something.

'I've told you a lot about me, but you haven't told me anything about you. Real things, I mean.' He made himself comfortable at the end of the lounge, turning towards me as he waited for my response.

'Hamish, there is a lot to tell, and you're right; I haven't been entirely honest, but I need to tell it to you in my own time. When I'm ready, if that's all right?' I asked, meeting his gaze. He moved closer, clearly able to see the sadness on my face. The kindness of his action caused me to burst into tears. I hated having secrets and didn't understand why I had to hide my upbringing in front of people like Hamish and his family when I hadn't caused it or committed any sin — nor had Polly. We had been the ones abandoned and left at the mercy of an orphanage. I didn't feel we had anything to be ashamed of; however, Richard had been clear that we could not change our story or tell anyone the truth, no matter the circumstances. He believed we would risk being the subject of ridicule and could be shunned by society. Hamish lifted me into an embrace on his lap, and I burrowed my face into his neck as he stroked my back, making soft, comforting noises and trying to soothe me as I sobbed. Then, after some time had passed, I sat up on his knees and wiped the tears from my face, hiccupping loudly.

'Hamish, I really like you, but you must warn me of your intentions. You are so nice to me, and I feel things I've never felt with anyone before you, so please be honest with me.' He flinched, turning away for a moment before taking my hands in his, meeting my gaze.

'Abigail, I don't know what to tell you.' He shook his head, a nervous smile touching his lips. 'I'm unable to express how I feel about you in words. I'd only embarrass myself if I told you the things I think an' feel about you directly as when I try, the words get stuck in my throat.' He stopped, swallowing several times before tightening his grasp on my hands. 'I have had many women since I was sixteen, so I'm worldly in these matters compared to you, but I have been somethin' of a bastard, too. There are things you should know about me when it comes to women, an' you've a right to know before we go any farther.' My heart pounded hard in my chest, and I was certain he could feel my hands trembling in his. 'I've always been the type of man who gets what he wants, then moves on to the next conquest until I am bored with her. Then I repeat the pattern. That first night I saw you walkin' towards our table, my heart started racing, an' I thought you were the most beautiful girl I'd ever laid eyes on. I couldn't speak to you — I was worried the words would come out wrong, an' they did for a while, but now I'm gettin' used to you.' He smiled and gently kissed my hand. 'No woman or livin' creature has ever had that effect on me, so yes, I know this is special. I don't know what it's goin' to turn into or what'll happen, but I know in my heart, an' I state this with every fibre of my bein, I will never leave you. Not ever.'

He reached up and placed his hands on my cheeks, pulling me towards him. As his mouth closed over mine, I felt sensations I had never experienced or imagined possible. He ran his fingers through my windblown hair, drawing me into him, his hand tightly around my waist, and his mouth on mine. I could have stayed locked in his embrace forever, but I could hear voices coming down the hall.

'The girls are back,' I warned him and quickly pulled away, jumping from his lap and over to the other lounge. By the time Bessie, Mary, Polly, and Angus entered the room, we sat on opposite seats, drinking our wine and talking. Mary excused herself for the night, obviously a little worse for wear, Bessie deciding she would escort her back to her quarters just to ensure she was safe.

'What have you two been up to?' Polly asked, narrowing her gaze at me as she threw herself down next to Hamish and made herself comfortable.

'We saw you up on deck, but it was too windy and cold, so we came back here to have a drink and talk while we waited for you,' I replied, narrowing my gaze back at her.

'You were in here alone?' Angus shook his head in disbelief, his eyes wide as he lowered himself down onto the lounge beside me, glancing across at his brother, clearly shocked at his lack of decorum.

'Nothing happened. We only just got here ourselves, Angus. If you tell mother, I will belt you so hard you won't know your own name for a week, at the very least.' Hamish and Angus exchanged smiles that confirmed in my mind they were thick as thieves. I doubted that either told on the other, ever, no matter what the circumstances. I admired how they still feared and respected their mother; a good sign, I believed, given they were both adults and strong-willed men.

'I'm going to marry this one,' Angus blurted out next to me, my head turning sharply in his direction. 'I asked Polly tonight, and she said yes. I wanted you to be the first to know.'

He moved to her side, pushing Hamish further down the lounge, and pulled her close, holding Polly's hand while she looked up at him adoringly. I silently wondered how his family would take the news, but then again, Polly was one of the Delmont Hotel Delmonts. I smothered a smile, knowing nothing I could say would change her mind, even though I wanted to. Finally, the door opened, and Bessie stepped inside, taking a moment to catch her breath before raising her eyebrows at me.

'What are you smiling at, Mistress? I shudder at the thought of you two young girls here with these two young men and no one to chaperone. Look at the size of them. They are filling up this room, and I'm not ready to be allowing anyone to court you girls, as you are far too young. If I can't keep you away from them, from this minute forward, when you are with Hamish and Angus, I will need to be there, whether you like it or not. Be forewarned; I will come down on you like a ton of bricks if you even think about disobeying me. Do you all understand?'

She stopped again to catch her breath, her face pink after her speech, and I suddenly felt like I had a mother. I may not like what she was forcing me to do, but she was doing it because she loved me; and I truly believed now that Bessie did, profoundly and with a fierce loyalty that would keep me safe as long as she was by my side.

'Bessie, I think that's a wonderful idea, as long as you don't mind. Of course, it would mean you wouldn't have a lot of spare time for your dancing below deck and such,' I teased. She glared at me suspiciously, placing her hands on her ample waist.

'Now, don't you be worrying about that, Mistress. I have all the time in the world,' she replied, smirking wickedly before ordering the twins to leave, bidding them farewell as she pushed them towards the door, Angus and Hamish calling out goodnight and promising to meet with us the following day. Feeling tired, Polly and I embraced before I made my way to my room, Bessie helping me undress and slip into my nightgown. She tucked me in, said a silent prayer over me before making her way across the room and turning off the lights, appearing relieved she could finally rest as she closed the door behind her.

I lay in bed reflecting on the day and how quickly things could change your life. Finally, I drifted off to sleep, dreaming of a mammoth black horse, a bullfrog, and a wide, open landscape leading to the sea.

Chapter Twenty-Three

I SAT ALONE AT our usual table, arriving early to see if I could catch Mrs Amelia Johnson on her own. I enjoyed the women's company yesterday and was surprised I liked each of them. As luck would have it, Amelia arrived not long after I had been seated. Within moments, we were chatting about the ship, how we had settled in, and her blonde, blue-eyed son, Mathew.

'So, tell me more about yourself, Amelia.'

'Oh, I'm not that interesting, Abigail,' She shifted uncomfortably in her seat before elegantly taking a sip of her tea. 'My father is an Earl and demands respect and obedience, despite having none of those qualities within himself. He forced me to marry a man who I don't love and never will, the match justified by my parents only because his father is wealthy and powerful, forming an allegiance with my own.' Her eyes glistened, tears threatening to spill over as she quickly wiped them away. 'I left the man I deeply and desperately love back in England. My parents would never agree to the match, and now I am joining a man whom I don't even like, let alone love, in a place called Melbourne, apparently building tanneries on a large scale, and that is the only information I have.' I reached across and took her hand in mine.

'How long has he been gone?'

'He left for Australia months before our son was born, and Mathew is three months old now. I don't even know the man, and the little I have seen of him so far does not impress me in the slightest. The sight of him makes my blood run cold.'

I felt sorry for her having to leave her true love behind, tearing her heart out. The only thing that came close for me was losing Sister Josephine. Luckily, I had not experienced romantic love; however, that could change depending on how close I would allow myself to get to Hamish until I could trust him not to return to his old ways.

The ladies had joined us, all of them greeting each other warmly and talking animatedly about the events of the day. Mrs Makenzie was in deep discussion with Charlotte and Victoria regarding the current fashions, while Amelia silently listened to them, smiling shyly at me occasionally. Mrs Shannon was seated beside me, sipping her tea as she listened to the numerous conversations, all as interesting as each other.

'How are you, Mrs Shannon?' I asked politely.

'Call me Dana, sweetie. I am having a wonderful time, all on my husband's money. I am rich beyond belief.' She threw her head back and laughed loudly, the people nearby staring and whispering behind their hands. Personally, I liked her cheerful, robust laugh that made you know that she really meant it.

'What will happen if he sends the police after you, Dana?' I asked her quietly. It was fine to laugh and joke, but the reality was he would try to get his money back at some point in the near future, and Dana would be charged with theft.

'Well, that's the trick. You see, I know all of his personal habits and business affairs,' she replied, winking at me while I stared back at her blankly, not comprehending at all to what she was referring. 'Honey, I know all of my husband's secrets. If they were revealed, it would destroy him, and he would be imprisoned. You don't think

I'm stupid enough to do this without some form of insurance now, do you?' I shook my head, deciding it was time to change the subject.

'Do you know where you are going to stay in Melbourne until you buy a home? I heard you were unsure of where you will settle.' She remained silent for a moment before clasping her hands in her lap, a slight smile on her lips.

'Yes, it is true; we don't know where we will end up. I keep hearing talk on the ship about a place called Geelong, and I heard that's where you and the Makenzie's are going.' I nodded, a bubble of excitement starting to rise in my stomach.

'I know nothing about the place myself, but I do know I have a house there.' I picked up my tea and took a sip, mimicking the ladies at the table to ensure I fitted in before taking a cucumber sandwich from the platters set out on the table before us. 'What type of house, I do not know, and I'm unsure what awaits me, so I would be the last person to seek advice from.'

'Until we decide, we will stay at The Delmont Hotel. Stop by if you are in Melbourne.'

'You said The Delmont Hotel?' I asked, my eyes widening as the sandwich stuck in my throat for a moment.

'Yes. It's a brand new one right in Swanston Street, behind the church. Has everything you ever imagined and more. I can't wait to get there.' She stopped, watching as I took a long drink of water before clearing my throat. 'What's wrong, sweetie? You look a little surprised.'

'No, I am perfectly fine. I do apologise. I wasn't concentrating.' I cleared my throat again, my appetite vanishing within moments. 'So, do you think you may try Geelong, given you know so many people going there now?' I felt relief wash over me. She hadn't made the connection yesterday when I was introduced to her by Mrs Makenzie, the memory causing me to cringe once more.

'I'm uncertain as yet. I will discuss our options with Charlotte and Victoria when we arrive in Melbourne, but it certainly has given me something to consider. At least the girls would know all of you young people before they even arrived. Yes, I may like that very much.' I smiled before turning towards Tamara and Elizabeth.

'What are your plans when you arrive in Australia?' They stared back at me silently, both appearing puzzled.

'What do you mean by plans, Abigail? The only plan we have is to meet our future husbands, as that's what our parents have asked us to do — and they assure us they have made good matches for Elizabeth and myself,' Tamara explained patiently. I immediately felt concerned, unable to stop the words that erupted from my mouth.

'What if you don't like each other? What if he's old and fat or ugly? He may have not a hair on his head, or he may like the drink and leave you and your babies to starve. What if he has no teeth and smells bad?' Elizabeth jumped in fright, Tamara gently placing her hand on her shoulder as she murmured in her ear before turning her attention back to me.

'Abigail, we trust our parents' judgment, and if they say they have matched us with good men, then I believe this to be true.'

I didn't want to shatter her dream, but couldn't she see they would match her with the wealthiest partner who would provide them with opportunities to climb the social ladder first, rather than one who shared common beliefs and, at a minimum, found each other attractive? That's what Catherine had told me a lot of wealthy families did. That, to me, was the same as selling your daughter, and I was relieved I didn't have parents who would dictate a similar path for me. I took several deep breaths, deciding to say no more on the matter unless it was supportive and positive.

'Tamara, you must be right. I am sure your parents have provided you with the best potential matches they could arrange. I wish you both all the happiness in the world.' Tamara smiled back at me, continuing to sip her tea elegantly. I knew I would rejoin the group tomorrow. I had started to feel a kinship with these women, no matter their backgrounds or where they would end up in the future. I knew that I would have contact with each of them in the new world somehow, and it was not my place to judge any one of them, even the ones who could end up marrying unfortunate-looking men with unbearable personalities.

Everyone seated at our table in the elegant dining room was silent, most choosing to concentrate on their food and avoid the topic of Angus and Polly's recent engagement. Mrs Makenzie, who had not uttered a word since hearing of the impending nuptials, had pushed her food around her plate, not tasting a morsel. Once dessert had been served and consumed in record time, the dishes were cleared away, and we were offered a small glass of sherry. We relaxed back, enjoying each other's company while chatting quietly as we watched the other passengers dance, the glorious music filling my ears. Time passed, and the guests started to retire to their suites for the night, several of the ship's employees hurrying around the room and collecting any dirty dishes that had been overlooked, removing the soiled linen tablecloths, while several others swept the floor. Bessie had ordered us to remain in the dining room until the dancing had finished and the musicians were packing up, allowing her time to spend with Mary and her friends. Bessie had advised us she would not suffer because we could not be trusted, and she would collect us from the dining room each evening to ensure Hamish and Angus were in their own beds and we were safely tucked up in ours. Alone.

Given Bessie had named herself head chaperone for all to obey, one consequence was Hamish and I would not have a second alone to repeat last night's kiss. Polly and Angus did not care who saw them kiss, and there was nothing anyone could do to stop them, so we had all given up trying. The fact it would cause a scandal didn't bother them, and they were blind to the withering looks directed at them from the women gossiping behind their fans with scandalised looks on their faces. At that very moment, I wished I were more like Polly.

Bessie held the door open and ushered us into our suite, Hamish and Angus politely waiting for Polly and me to enter first before following us in. I lay down on the lounge, making myself comfortable before Hamish joined me and lay behind me. Bessie opened her mouth, then promptly shut it, while Hamish looked back at her defiantly, his eyes twinkling.

'Bessie, you are chaperoning us. What can happen? Abigail and I are not acting like Polly and Angus over there.' He nodded towards the opposite lounge, where Polly sat cuddled into Angus, his arms around her as they kissed and murmured to each other.

'Well, you will be soon if that lot keeps going at it like this. I am taking these girls to Australia as the virgins they are, and anyone trying to hinder that process has to go through me,' she snapped, her hands planted firmly on her hips.

Polly froze, and I realised why within moments. How would she explain to Angus on their wedding night that she wasn't a virgin?

Hamish sighed deeply, moving closer and breathing in the scent of my hair, whispering in my ear. I hoped he was being entirely truthful and not bearing me false witness. A small part of me felt relieved we were being chaperoned, as this would give me time to get to know him and observe how he behaved in Geelong once we arrived. However, given his history with women, by his own admission, I felt I had every right to be concerned his head would be turned by another woman as soon as we docked. All I could hope for was that Hamish had a genuine heart and was a man of his word.

Polly and I walked side by side on the deck, Bessie following close behind, grumbling to herself. I gazed up at the indigo sky and inhaled the fresh, clean air, tasting salt before I stepped into the games room for our dance lesson. Over the past two weeks, we had learnt many dances: some fast, while others slow and romantic — I loved them all. I had discovered I loved to dance and enjoyed myself immensely; the fact Hamish was a dedicated teacher had only made the experience all the more pleasant. Within an hour of practising a new dance, I found I had mastered it. For someone who didn't like to dance, Hamish appeared to enjoy the experience just as much as I did; and he taught me well.

The expensive boarding school fees had paid off — at least for Hamish. Angus was less interested in dancing and more interested in romancing Polly and spending every waking minute together. After two days of chaperoning them around the ship, Bessie had put her foot down and demanded they were to stay with her each day and go where she went according to her schedule, which they agreed to without argument — as long as they were together.

I had drawn the line with Polly, who wanted the captain to marry them; however, I insisted they have a church wedding in Geelong, with an engagement party held before the wedding. She had reluctantly agreed after many arguments between us. After the initial shock had passed, Mrs Makenzie was kind and welcoming to Polly, taking her under her wing, just as she had done with me. It was a comforting feeling, knowing you had that person on your side to call on for help or favour and to whom you could show kindnesses in return. I believed that we now had that in Mrs Makenzie, who had offered us both friendship and respect in the short time we had known her.

I thought she would be a wonderful mother-in-law, or at least the positive mother figure that Polly had never experienced. The idea of Polly belonging to someone, to a family, to people who cared about her made my heart soar, and again I thanked the universe for letting me find her. She would lead such a different life now from the one that had seemed her destiny on the dirty streets of London.

Polly and I debated for days what to tell Angus about the inevitable fact that he would soon find out she was no longer a virgin. I had suggested we remain true to every detail leading up to Polly's employer taking her by force, resulting in Polly fleeing into the night to London. I had felt it more palatable to say that I found her soon afterwards begging on the streets and avoiding her time at the tavern altogether. Although she felt she was being deceptive and worried her marriage would be doomed if started with a lie, Polly had reluctantly agreed.

We had told Angus and Hamish the truth about our childhoods and that we were not siblings, nor was Polly an heiress. Angus and Hamish accepted our history without question, and Angus did not waver once in his love for Polly. He didn't care where she came from, and he didn't care that she wasn't wealthy, impressing me greatly. Hamish had been a little more cautious.

'Good morning, ladies,' Hamish called out from across the room, bowing slightly as laughter bubbled up inside me. Polly had run to Angus, who picked her up and swung her around as they laughed loudly. Bessie sighed deeply before finding a chair and sitting down heavily, reaching down to find her needlework to keep her occupied for the next hour, her mood far from pleasant this morning. Finally, the music began, and I stepped forward into Hamish's warm embrace.

We sat together on the lounges drinking lemonade and trying to catch our breath while Bessie and Jimmy talked in hushed tones as she sat next to him in front of the piano. Although I couldn't hear what they were saying, they laughed loudly, and Bessie appeared to be having fun, softly punching him on the arm.

'There is a couple to watch. Maybe she will stop looking at us and leave us in some peace if she's getting some loving herself,' Hamish remarked, his face relaxing into a smile as he gazed into my eyes. 'Abigail,' he whispered in my ear. 'I want you to know how much you mean to me. I have never felt this way about anyone in my life. I know you are the woman for me, the only woman destined to be mine. I will make you my wife one day when the time is right.' He kissed me gently on the earlobe. 'I feel like I have known you for years, that you are the missing piece of the puzzle in my life. You are not only the most exquisite woman I have ever laid eyes on, but you are beautiful inside, too, and have a generous heart. You are sweet and lovely, and I need you by my side forever.'

He gently kissed me on the mouth; Bessie, still absorbed in her conversation with Jimmy and paying us no heed, while I slipped my arms around his neck and embraced him. He always said the loveliest things to me and was so sweet. Unfortunately, he didn't show many people the gentle and loving side to him, coming across at times like a spoiled little boy who knew no other life than a privileged one.

'Hamish, I care about you too, but I'm not ready to marry. Give me a couple of years to grow up more and adapt to my new life; then, if I should marry anyone, it would be you.'

'You love me already,' he declared far too loudly. Bessie turned her head sharply, suspicion filling her face. She waved her finger at us from across the room, then turned back to her new friend, Jimmy, and resumed their conversation. Hamish lowered his voice, his mouth close to my ear. 'I can feel it between us without you or me saying a word. I don't care if you have money or not, Abigail, as I have my own from my grandfather, who left me a large inheritance. I want you for you alone and for you to make a life with me. I want you to be the mother of my children.'

'How do you know I even want any?' I teased.

'Because I've seen you up on deck with your friend Amelia's child, and I could tell immediately that you adore children by the way you're always holding him and talking to him. You are a natural mother, and I think you would be a very good one.'

'Yes, I do want lots of children. How many do you want?' I discreetly kissed him on the cheek, pulling away before Bessie caught me.

'Eight. Four boys and four girls,' he replied immediately, my loud giggles once again attracting Bessie's attention.

'Well, that's very specific. I don't know that you can order babies just like that.'

'Well, no, but one day we will have eight of them running around.' I smiled up at him as he chuckled, placing his large hand on mine. 'I know I'm a jealous bastard, and I haven't been very nice when other men have paid you attention, but I cannot help it. I can't stand them near you.' His eyes misted over as I leaned in and whispered in his ear, raising his eyebrows in surprise as he listened intently. 'You're pulling my leg? So, I have no reason to be concerned at all?'

The more time I spent with Hamish, the more he surprised me. I could see he was a deep thinker and generous of spirit, while also possessing a sensitive and loving heart, even though he pretended he didn't care about many people at all. He was close to Angus and his mother; however, not his sister, Jemima, which didn't surprise me, given she was a complete bitch. I found her demanding and rude, not only to her family but also to the servants on the ship, which disgusted me. I would never dream of speaking to anyone the way she talked to her mother. I was still confused by her grey aura, feeling our dislike for each other was somehow connected.

Bessie clapped her hands loudly from across the room, ordering us to prepare to leave. She turned back to Jimmy and bid him farewell as Angus pulled Polly to her feet and hurried across the room to Bessie. Hamish reluctantly stood, pausing for a time as he stared down at me before offering me his hand. Unlike the others, we took our time joining them as we strolled hand in hand, speaking in hushed tones, all the while Hamish doing everything in his power to delay the inevitable and spending the day under Bessie's supervision.

That night, as I lay cosy and warm in my enormous bed, I drifted off to sleep. I dreamed of a proper English butler, a stable filled with black horses, and an enormous building made of bluestone filled with strangers.

Chapter Twenty-Four

I STROLLED ALONG THE upper deck, the sea breeze on my face, keeping an eye out for Amelia. I came upon her as I turned a corner to return to our suite, having given up. She pushed her son in his perambulator, cooing softly to him as she walked across the deck. We embraced warmly before I leaned down and touched little Mathew's cheek.

'Pick him up if you like.' I bent down and gently wrapped my arms around him, lifting him to my chest. His eyes were the bluest of blues, with hair so blonde it was almost white.

'Your husband must have the most beautiful eyes and hair if Mathew favours his father like I believe he does.'

'He does not. My husband has black eyes and dark hair and possesses a soul the colour of jet.' She hung her head and began to cry. 'I can't bear the thought of that man. He makes me feel physically ill.' I quickly passed her a clean handkerchief I kept up my sleeve for emergencies and led her off to the side where we could not be overheard. 'Oh, he is so horrible, Abigail. The thought of him haunts my dreams. I don't know if I will cope even being near him, let alone allowing him to touch me.' Her tears soon turned into sobs. I gently placed Mathew back down in his perambulator, turning to embrace

351

her until she could calm herself. She pulled away, wiping her face with the handkerchief before sniffing daintily, ignoring the passengers who stared rudely in our direction as they strolled past us. 'Do you know, Abigail, you are the only person in whom I have confided? My parents know my true feelings, as does the man who will always have my heart, but they made sure they separated us as soon as I told them of my love for him. They would not listen to my protests and forced me to marry a cruel-hearted man.' Tears again spilled down her face while she raised her hand and placed it on her heart, pounding her chest hard several times as though she were in physical pain. 'I cry for Tom — my Tommy — every night, and I know what awaits me at the end of this voyage. He will have me pregnant again in no time, I'm sure, and dressed like a doll every day to attend his parties and his galas with all his people around him all the time. He would die without someone around to dress him, feed him, and wipe his arse.' She screwed up her face in disgust, holding onto the wall as she tried to catch her breath. A tiny, dark-haired girl approached us, asking if Amelia would like her to take Mathew. She was familiar to me; however, we had not been formally introduced, despite meeting several times. 'That would be wonderful. Thank you.' Amelia bent down and cooed softly to her son before she handed him over to her competent Nanny. We strolled along the deck, talking quietly between ourselves, slowly making our way to the opposite side of the ship to share afternoon tea with the other women.

I enjoyed their company more than I had first believed I would, finding them all wonderful in their own magical ways. They brightened my day, all in interesting and exciting ways. I had become friends, of sorts, with Tamara and Elizabeth, despite our backgrounds and values being poles apart. I understood they were conservative in their ways because of the upbringing they had both experienced.

They had been almost entirely raised by nannies, no different to Hamish and Angus, and only trotted out to see their parents at breakfast; however, they did not eat with them. They would be taken to eat their own meal separately in the nursery. Their parents permitted them to dine in their company at night, as long as they did not speak out of turn or misbehave. I was beginning to understand why some people were the way they were, just like Tamara and Elizabeth, who automatically felt entitled, because that was all they had ever known. I couldn't dislike someone simply because they hadn't been taught the things I thought were important, just as I wouldn't expect someone to dislike me because of my background — even if they did.

Charlotte and Victoria had also become close friends; however, they were far more relaxed and open in my company. Both possessed the wickedest sense of humour I'd had the privilege to encounter, just as their mother did. They were attractive girls, with statuesque figures and bright orange hair, always coiffed perfectly by the ladies' maid they shared. I loved being around them; they were warm and friendly towards me and didn't seem to mind me stealing their mother away to be my own personal friend and mentor.

Dana was a spitfire, and I admired her greatly. She said what she thought, meant what she said, and didn't care what people thought of her. I admired her strength and sass, so much so that I wanted to be like her. From the moment we met, she took me under her wing and treated me as a friend and daughter. It melted my heart that she could be so generous. Amelia was the saddest woman I had ever encountered, looking sidelong at her as we arrived at our table, our new friends all present and waiting for us. We greeted each other before I slid into the chair next to Mrs Makenzie, who appeared tired, prompting me to ask if anything was wrong.

'No, my dear, I'm perfectly fine, I promise you. I am not sleeping very well over the Angus and Polly situation, but I must thank you for getting them to slow down by agreeing to a wedding in Geelong. I love Polly dearly, and I only want them to be happy, but I feel they are rushing into things. They will have known each other only seven or eight weeks by the time we arrive in Geelong. And how long does it take to plan a wedding?' I stared back at her, my face blank, while she appeared slightly puzzled.

'I'm not sure.' I felt the blood rush to my face, hoping no one noticed my embarrassment. Neither Polly nor I knew how to plan even a small party. In fact, neither of us had attended a wedding before. I decided to talk to Dana and ask for guidance regarding what they expected of us and what we would need to do, as she was a wealth of information on every subject I had raised with her so far. I felt relief wash over me, realising that being forced to learn how to plan a wedding before actually planning Polly's would slow down the nuptials even further.

I knew Polly wanted her wedding day to be perfect, just like out of the fashion magazines and in the shop windows she had passed by in London; however, I knew she would soon come to realise that everything took time. She would need a gown made, organise where to hold the event, notify the guests they would like to have present — and I imagined these were only some tasks that must be attended to. Given we didn't even know where we would live yet, as Geelong was a vast place with many farms on the outskirts of town, it would be foolish to undertake such a complicated project until after we had settled. I really knew nothing about my future situation, although I was praying it would all work out. I realised at that moment; I didn't even know if Polly and Angus were of the same faith.

'What religion are you?'

'Catholic, my dear girl. Why? What are you?'

'Oh, I'm sorry. It's just that sometimes when things pop into my head, I say them without thinking. For example, it just occurred to me I would need to know Angus's religion to organise a proper church wedding. Polly and I were both baptised Catholic.'

'Well, at least that prevents any confusion,' she remarked, rising to her feet and asking if I would join her outside for a few moments until they served tea. We stood at the ship's rail in our coats, the wind blustery and cold. 'I don't know how my husband will accept the news when we arrive, as the boys won't give me any time to warn him.' She stood, staring out at the horizon, her voice barely audible. 'Angus plans to walk right up to his father and introduce Polly as his fiancée. I am hoping my husband does not make a fuss in front of everyone. He does things like that, which embarrasses me greatly. I have never told you this, Abigail, however, I trust you, and it is important you know, as you and Hamish seem to be drawing closer. My husband is a troublesome man and not a likeable one most of the time. He has always been extremely hard on the boys, and they do not get along with him. He has never treated me well and steps out with other women, expecting me to remain silent, which I always do. He is not a man you speak up to.' She paused for a moment before smiling sadly. 'I want you to know that my sons are nothing like him — they are gentle and kind and respect women very much. Hamish has been a bit free with the girls in his twenty years on earth, having many come and go, just like his father. He has a soft heart, though, which he chose to give to you, my darling girl. Since meeting you, Hamish has changed, and I see how much he cares for you. He is thoughtful and sweet, and I have never seen him act this way with any young woman. It lifts my heart, as I thought he might go the way of his father if he were not careful. I am so worried about my husband's reaction. He is an explosive man with a nasty temper. Please talk to my sons and ask them to give me a few minutes alone with him first to explain the engagement, as that is all I require? I'm begging them, through you, to give me that chance.' Her eyes glistened, the deep pain she felt clearly visible.

Hamish had spoken very little of his father, and that had not been complimentary. I felt deeply sorry for her, married to and living with a man who betrayed her publicly. A man who didn't seem to care how much he humiliated or hurt her, despite her being a loving wife and the mother of his three children.

'You shouldn't have to beg.' I squeezed her hand reassuringly. 'Of course, they will give you as much time as you need to speak with your husband. I will make certain of it. Do not concern yourself with this anymore now. Please try to get some rest. You are looking so tired.'

'I think you're right. I will go and rest until dinner. Give my regards to the ladies and tell them I will see them all tonight.'

I watched her trudge down the deck to her suite and hoped she soon was asleep, dreaming of weddings, babies, and white clouds shot through with the happiest of rainbows.

'I'm getting bored,' I complained as I lay on the lounge, my belly full from the lavish dinner we had consumed. 'I would really like to be doing something other than the same things over and over each day.'

We had been on the boat for over four weeks, and the days were becoming monotonous, the initial excitement now waning and ready to disappear completely. Even poor little Mary had taken to cleaning rooms and items she had only just cleaned hours before, purely for the lack of something to do and the boredom that had settled over us all.

'Why don't you come along with me to the steerage deck?' Bessie suggested. 'It's a lot of fun, everyone is friendly, and I will be there to watch over you.' I abruptly turned to stare at her, as did Polly, while Angus and Hamish appeared just as surprised as I was. Not once had Bessie invited us during the entire voyage to accompany her to steerage, where she could be found every night since we sailed.

'Yes,' Polly and Angus yelled in unison, jumping to their feet and hurrying to the door. Hamish nodded; however, he remained seated, clearly thinking of more exciting places he would rather be.

'What do we wear, Bessie? Is this too fancy?' I looked down at my beaded evening gown, Bessie casting her eyes over me briefly before nodding her head in agreement.

'Put on the plainest housedress that you have, and you should blend in well.' She turned her attention to Hamish and Angus while Polly remained at the door, ready to leave. 'You boys only wear your simple shirts and trousers. We are lucky we have come into warm nights now.' With Bessie at my heels, I hurried to my room to choose a housedress, feeling quite excited. I had not worn them on the ship, given how formal everything was in first class. We were fortunate that Mr and Mrs Malcolm had taught us which knives and forks to use when dining and all the simple things we didn't know. I picked out the dark bronze dress that highlighted the copper glints of my hair and brought out the green in my eyes. Bessie helped me disrobe and slip into my plain dress, which I found much more comfortable than what I had been forced to wear since leaving the orphanage. If only she let me go without a corset, I would have been in heaven.

'You look lovely. I must say, I'm gladdened by the fact you are taking this new romance with Hamish far slower than those other two fiends. I know I am driving him mad, but at least it keeps him honest.' She threw her head back and laughed, her eyes twinkling as she led me to my dressing table.

'He is coping just fine, and as far as Angus and Polly are concerned, they pay you no mind anyway,' I teased.

'And you think I can't see that for myself? Every time I look around, they have their hands on each other, and they unashamedly refuse to stop kissing, even in public. It is a disgrace, is what it is. They are shaming the Makenzie family and tarnishing our reputation all because they are like two rabbits at breeding time,' she spat as I burst into giggles.

'They're not doing anything of the sort, and I know that for a fact. What you see them doing is as far as they go, given they are never alone.'

'Well, I don't trust either of the little shites, so I refuse to turn my back on them. I pull them apart when I feel the need, which upsets them greatly.' She grinned at me wickedly, undid my hair, and brushed it into shiny waves.

I would be forever grateful that Bessie had come into my life and little Mary now, too. I had convinced her to work for me as a maid, cooking and cleaning and doing light household duties when we arrived in Australia. Mary was working her passage across and had planned to get a job in one of the large city hotels, but now she was eagerly looking forward to starting her employment with us. I really had no right to employ anyone, not knowing my circumstances, but I was hoping I could at least utilise Mary in some way; she was such a sweet girl, and she, too, was alone in the world. I was determined to find out her actual age once we arrived, while vowing to myself that I wouldn't employ anyone else until I had spoken with my solicitor.

Hamish and Angus had returned by the time I stepped back into the sitting room, both now dressed casually, while Bessie hurried to her room to organise herself, allowing us to relax and drink the rest of the wine while we waited. 'What will we drink at my wedding?' Polly asked, her eyes shining.

'Something with lots of alcohol, Polly, now let's go,' I replied as Bessie returned. At that very moment, I would do anything to get out of discussing wedding preparations with anyone.

The passageways down to steerage were narrow and dark. As we descended the last flight of stairs behind Bessie, I held Hamish's hand to steady myself. She opened the door to a large room containing wooden tables and chairs, two men in a corner with a guitar and a harmonica, and more people than I had seen in the entire first-class dining room. Some were standing around drinking and talking, while others were sitting at the tables, watching the passengers dancing. Bessie led us to the table where her friends sat, proudly introducing us to several men and women who invited us to join them. Hamish and Angus pushed through the crowd towards the barkeep, a man as tall and broad as them, to order our drinks while we became acquainted with Bessie's new friends.

'So, it's not long now until we arrive. Have I behaved well enough to be considered a serious suitor yet?' Hamish placed a large glass of beer before me and sat down. I wanted to say yes, but the words stuck in my throat. True, he had behaved impeccably so far, but I had not seen his interactions out in the real world. There were plenty of women on this ship looking for husbands, and some were very attractive; however, Hamish had paid them no attention nor spoken out of turn to any of them.

Hamish and I had spent the past four weeks getting to know each other on a deep, emotional level. He knew everything about me, and I knew everything he had told me about himself. Despite Bessie chaperoning us, we had sneaked several intimate moments together. We would lie on the lounge, talking and laughing, while she looked on to make sure all was appropriate. I knew I was falling in love with him, but I didn't shut out Polly or Bessie, or any of my friends for that matter, unlike Polly. I went about my usual daily breakfast routine in the suite with them, then our dancing lessons with the boys, lunch with Hamish, taking time for myself before dinner, and then seeing him in the evening.

I would attend afternoon tea with my new female friends and spend some time with Bessie and Polly alone, talking about the only subject that mattered to Polly, which was driving me to drink. Polly happily came back to the room each afternoon after I had met with the ladies for tea, and the three of us would engage in meaningless gossip.

I sat quietly beside Hamish, observing the passengers and embracing the cheerful atmosphere, while Bessie spoke animatedly to Jimmy and Danny. I had noticed the moment she had stepped into the room; neither had taken their eyes from her. Both were nice-looking men who appeared to be in their early thirties. Danny possessed brown hair and a pleasant face, a face that broke into an easy smile, especially when Bessie was near. Jimmy was a little shorter than Bessie and, although I had thought him nice from our daily interactions, I preferred Danny's demeanour and quiet manner. He sat opposite me, with Bessie next to him. Jimmy sat beside her, not appearing cheerful like the majority present, albeit some merrier than others, depending on how much they had imbibed. Hamish slipped his large arm around me as I leaned back comfortably against his chest.

'So, tell me, why Australia, Danny?' He grinned at me before taking a large swallow of his ale.

'I was a farmer back in Ireland, helped me old Da from the time I was knee high to a grasshopper.' Sadness crossed his face for a moment before he shook his head and took another large swallow of his drink. 'Me Da fell ill one mornin'. Three days later, he died in his bed. Me Ma went to be with him six months later, the angels taking her within days just as they did me Da.' Bessie patted his hand sympathetically, encouraging him to continue. 'Me brothers have their own plots of land to work an' families to provide for, an' as for me sisters', they're all married to good men who I know will always provide for 'em. As for me, I was alone.'

'What attracted you to Australia? The gold rush ended decades ago, and you're not a redcoat; they left long ago too,' I joked, a wide grin spreading across his face.

'Ah, it was the luck of the Irish itself that caused me to remember a newspaper article I'd read months before me Da passed. I was out in the field, breakin' me back when it dawned on me I'd spend the rest of me days doin' the exact same thin' while never bein' able to pay off the enormous debt I inherited from me parents; God bless 'em.' He winked at me before continuing. 'I decided to try me luck in this new land; although, I will let you in on a little secret, Mistress Abigail. Some of me ancestors were quite familiar with Australia, particularly Botany Bay an' Van Diemen's Land — or Tasmania as they call it now. Their old bones now lay deep in the soil of a place they could not return from. Me hope is I have a very different experience. Me original plan was to go north, but since meetin' certain people here on the ship, me plans have changed.' We smiled at each other, and he winked at me again. I believed Bessie was the perfect age to find someone to love, get married, and start a family if she wanted to.

I glanced at Jimmy, talking animatedly with Bessie, before they started jumping up and down in their seats, Bessie clapping her hands in delight.

'Jimmy is going to jump ship in Australia and come to Geelong to find work,' she exclaimed, Danny flinching slightly before regaining his composure. I knew without a doubt that I would not need the services of a piano player, leaving no fear I would offer to employ him. Bessie glowed, basking in the attention of the two men, who both seemed to be in love with her already. She was still her short, plump, glorious self, and I thought she looked the prettiest I had ever seen her tonight. Her face had become slightly flushed while talking to them, splitting her attention between them equally. She was truly beautiful.

'It's so nice to sit with you like this while Bessie is so involved with her own romantic conundrums,' Hamish whispered before kissing my neck, sending shivers up my spine.

'I am having a wonderful time with you, Hamish. I do seriously consider you as my suitor, or I would not be sitting so close to you in public. I just need to be certain. You are the one who warned me in the first place that you are a womaniser, causing me to be cautious of who I give my heart to,' I reminded him.

'That was before I met you, Abigail. You've changed all that for me. I have never actually wanted to stay long term with anyone until I laid eyes on you. I know you're young, but I will marry you, an' not long after Angus an' Polly. I am not lettin' you get away from me because I've been an idiot in the past. I cannae tell you what changed, but somethin' shifted inside me, an' I feel I am different since meetin' you. You're the sweetest an' loveliest woman I have ever met, an' I know, for some reason, you'll be in my life until I take my last breath. I'm not going to propose an' make a fool of myself like my brother — not until we have known each other for an appropriate amount of time — but if I could put all that aside, I would marry you tomorrow.' He stared into my eyes, and I did believe him. He had been cold and distant when we met; however, now he seemed able to talk to me about anything, and I felt I could do the same, as I trusted him more than he probably deserved.

'I love being with you, but let's just get through Angus and Polly's wedding first. By then, we will have known each other for a few months, and I will be settled in my house.' I placed my lips on his, running my fingers through the loose, black curls that fell to his shoulders. He held me in his arms like I was going to break and kissed me back, his fingers caressing my hair and moving down my back. I heard several loud coughs, and I quickly pulled away, glancing sidelong at Bessie, who did not appear impressed.

'What? You're still chaperoning, so nothing is happening,' Hamish called out to her over the noise, smirking as he kept his arms wrapped around me. Hamish grabbed me by the hand and led me toward the music, acutely aware that Bessie's eyes were boring into the back of my head. This was not the music I had danced to before or had even heard. People were dancing a jig in a large circle, laughing and holding each other's hands. Hamish told me it was Irish music and to watch them for a while, and I would get the hang of it. He was right. As we joined in, I found the steps very basic and repetitive, and I loved it.

When the dance had finished, another began; the women passed from one man to the next after a brief dance with each. Hamish and I joined in, and I was soon handed to a young man who had consumed far too many whiskies and then on to another man, who asked if I would drink with him. As the dance continued, I relaxed and enjoyed meeting, no matter how briefly, the many men taking this voyage alone, leaving me wondering if there would be a shortage of women in this new country. I admired their strength and determination to start a new life with practically nothing.

My dance partner, a small, withered little man, smiled before bidding me farewell and passing me to my next partner. I stepped back and gasped before regaining my composure and introducing myself. He was bathed in the golden glow, so bright it was blinding me. He smiled, his beautiful face lighting up as if he knew me. I stepped forward as he took my hands in his, introducing himself as Leonardo. In the brief time we danced, he told me he was originally from Italy but had found work as a chef at one of the most exclusive hotels in London.

'Would you join my table after this dance has finished?' I asked him, aware we were about to part.

'I would be honoured to sit with the most interesting looking woman here. Some of them are so unfortunate in their appearance; most present here tonight appear to have been beaten with the ugly stick. More than once.' He waved goodbye before pulling the next woman into his arms, laughter bubbling up inside me. I continued dancing until the music stopped, Hamish hurrying to my side and taking my hand in his before leading me back to the table. Within moments of sitting down, Leonardo approached us, his gaze lingering on Hamish for the longest time.

I found him to be a handsome man, tall and powerfully built. He had been highly effeminate when in my company alone; however, when he shook Hamish's hand, he appeared as masculine as the men who had assembled around our table. I had never met a man before who had girlish attributes, but I had heard terrible things about men like that.

'Here, come and sit next to me,' I offered, to which he quickly obliged. Hamish sat to my other side, attempting to get my attention, while this bright young man slipped into the vacant seat beside me. Something I could not explain drew me to him; whether it was his flamboyance, sense of humour, or simply the fact that he had the golden glow, I was unsure. What I did know for certain, with nothing to base it on other than how he made me feel, was he would be important to me in some way. Leo relaxed back in his chair, picked up a glass of ale, and drank deeply. He told me he had been a cook in Italy for many years, having left school at fourteen, but his greatest desire was to become a famous chef. He had travelled to London, working his way across Europe to England by cooking in restaurants, where he often was offered permanent work but declined.

When he arrived in London, he took a job at a mediocre restaurant while submitting applications to the ones where he dreamed of working. He finally secured a position at The Rialto Hotel, where he worked for a time until a love affair turned sour. The person he was in love with had been indiscreet, and when Leonardo let himself into their house, he found his lover in bed with someone else. Leonardo couldn't cope and fled, boarding our ship just before it sailed with only the money he had in his pocket, a small bag that contained his most treasured possessions, and only one change of clothes.

He had no plans for what he would do once in Australia, but believed he would find something suitable. I liked him intensely and invited him to stay with us until he could find a job and somewhere to live. Hamish pinched me on the leg hard but dropped his hand once I had made the offer.

'I really don't know you well enough to make that commitment. You could be a black widow for all I know. You do have that look about you. You seem to be the type who, if upset, would bake me a cake filled with arsenic, then tell me it's an almond sponge and to eat every crumb. I will have to think about your offer for the rest of the voyage and will decide once we arrive in that prison without walls.' I smothered a smile as he scowled, clearly not as enthused as his travelling companions.

'So, how has your voyage been?'

'Absolutely horrendous, my sweet little potato. But the good thing is, I might have met my new best friend. Believe me, you have no idea what a privilege that would be for you, as so many women want me; however, not one has caught me yet.'

'I'm not surprised. Let me think about if I am up to the standard you require from your friends, and I will let you know if I will take the position,' I told him, and we both burst into giggles. I didn't know what it was about him, but he was funny and full of himself, but somehow intriguing. Hamish fidgeted, causing me to turn to him before lowering my voice.

'What is wrong with you?'

'You're spending all of your time talking to that stranger,' he whispered back. 'I believe there is something extremely suspicious about him. I am uncertain just what it is, but there is something I don't like about him.' He glared across at Leonardo as I lifted my hand to his cheek and gently caressed his face.

'Come on, Hamish, you're not jealous, are you?'

'No, I'm not jealous. Well, maybe just a bit, but that's because you've been talkin' to him so much. The way he speaks an' behaves, I believe he's a sodomite.'

'Shhh, Hamish. I think they are referred to as homosexuals now and have been since the eighteen-fifties.'

I was astounded he had noticed so much in such a short time, as he had not been privy to our private conversation. I believed Leonardo was a homosexual, and I had been taught to hate them because of the Bible, which preached they were wicked and would burn in the fires of hell. I had long since rejected a lot of what that little book claimed to be true, and I didn't feel I needed to hate anyone.

Hamish nuzzled my neck, attempting to distract me. I held his hand but continued talking to Leonardo, who agreed to meet us in steerage the following evening before rising to his feet and bidding us farewell.

'Can we go now?' Hamish teased, giving me a final nuzzle. 'I would much rather be doing this in your sitting room than in an overcrowded pub.'

'This isn't a pub,' I replied, pushing him away as I laughed.

'Well, it feels like one, and some quiet would be nice now, I think.' He pulled me to my feet, and I realised immediately I had consumed more alcohol than I intended, feeling unsteady on my feet. Hamish slipped his arm around my waist while we waited for Bessie to say goodnight to her two suitors, Polly and Angus emerging from a table that sat in a dark corner of the room, where they had remained the entire time. Bessie guided us towards the door, her face shining while appearing to walk on air all the way back to the suite.

'That was fun, wasn't it?' I remarked, slipping off my shoes and plopping down on the lounge. Everyone nodded tiredly except Hamish, who looked relaxed and happy as he sat beside me, his arm around my shoulders. Polly said goodnight to Angus, walking him to the door then quietly closing it behind him. Within moments, she went to bed, citing she felt drunk and exhausted, embracing us both before hurrying to her room. Bessie followed her, leaving us unchaperoned while she readied Polly for bed.

The moment Polly's bedroom door clicked shut, Hamish grabbed me and pulled me on top of him, my face level with his. He began kissing me passionately on the mouth, his tongue demanding more, and I could feel the effects he was having on my body. I felt tingles everywhere and a deep longing inside my belly. Bessie re-entered the room, shaking a warning finger at us, and we stopped as suddenly as we had started. She then went into the washroom and drew my bath, and we reclined on the lounge again. I was confused by my body's reaction to him, not knowing why sometimes I seemed to ache for him, deep inside, and I did not know why. No one had ever explained sexual relations between men and women, although Bessie had sat down with me a week ago and answered some of my questions. She didn't know all the answers and was embarrassed by what I had asked her. I planned to ask Dana, as I imagined she would be comfortable with anything I brought up.

'I can't wait until I marry you,' he whispered, causing me to jump. 'Now, don't react like you've just seen a spider. I know you are going to be my wife one day. I just have to prove myself, and it hasn't been hard. You are all I think about and the only person I want to be with, so you can put fifty girls in front of me, and all I see is you.'

I sat up and turned to him. His beautiful eyes stared into mine, and I could see he was telling me the truth as he knew it, but I needed to see for myself if he could abstain from other women before I could decide. The way I felt now was I would indeed marry this man one day — not as soon as Polly's wedding, but one day not too far in the future. However, I was feeling inebriated, my thoughts scattered and fragmented.

'Do you mind leaving so I can retire for the night?'

'Can I sneak into your room and hold you until you go to sleep?' he teased, rising to his feet before pulling me up into his arms.

'Oh, sure, why not? I'm sure Bessie would be happy to find you in there,' I replied sarcastically, holding him in a tight embrace. 'Go on, get out of here.' I shooed him out of the sitting room toward the door. As he swung the door wide, I reached up and slipped my arms around his neck, kissing him long and hard, showing him the promise of things to come.

Chapter Twenty-Five

THE OCEAN BREEZE GENTLY touched my face; the sun warming my skin as I listened to the ladies' gossip. I reached across and placed a small slice of Madeira cake on my fine bone china plate before taking a sip of my tea. I leaned in close to Dana, lowering my voice to a whisper.

'May I speak with you in private when you have a spare moment, please?'

'Of course you may. Would you like me to visit your suite?' she whispered back.

'Yes, thank you. After our tea, if that is alright with you?'

'It will be my pleasure.' She took my hand in hers. She had not only become a mother figure to me but a best friend also, and I trusted her completely.

Tamara and Elizabeth were acting oddly of late, seeming to worsen the closer we sailed to Australia and towards their future husbands. I had overheard the captain speaking with Dame Nellie herself, assuring her we would arrive at the port of Melbourne in a week. We were all suffering, feeling closed in and bored, and I was certain I was not the only person who would be relieved to set foot on solid ground after what had seemed like months.

'How are you, Tamara and Elizabeth? Are you eager to see your parents again and meet your betrothed?' Tamara smiled sweetly, Elizabeth grunting at me before turning away.

'Oh, yes, we are,' Tamara replied, elegantly sipping her tea.

'I am worried that he will be old, or fat, or both, like Abigail said, and with no teeth.' Elizabeth scowled at me as though I were somehow to blame for her situation. I choked on my tea, splattering it all over the table, much to my horror. The ladies exchanged knowing smiles; they were getting used to my gaffes after all the time we had spent together. I picked up a napkin and soaked up as much of the brown liquid from my clothes and the table as possible while trying to catch Elizabeth's eye.

'Come on, Lizzy, it's not that bad. As you both have said in the past, your parents would not make a terrible match for you.'

'Oh, hush, Abigail. You make everything worse,' she snapped.

It had been an effort to feel sympathetic towards them at times, and I did hold genuine sympathy for them, despite their holier-than-thou attitude when we first set sail. Now that time had passed, it seemed the reality of their situation was dawning on them. Going to bed with someone you hardly knew and doing things you may not want to do, while being expected to slave away for a husband who would demand dinner on the table when he arrived home from work, along with sex every night, did not seem to have occurred to either of them. Despite their misgivings, I could see that neither girl even considered changing her mind.

At my invitation, Leonardo joined us for afternoon tea most days, despite it being only for the ladies, and today was no exception. No one complained. It seemed the other passengers had decided to embrace my idiosyncrasies, such as bringing my maid to meals and ensuring they provided her with the same quality of food as the other first-class passengers; or having my male suitor join us at times for our afternoon get-togethers, and now considered my dissimilarities to themselves as charming.

I had become increasingly frustrated the more time I spent with aristocrats and 'people of good breeding,' as Polly liked to say. Sister preferred to call them the 'upper crust' of society, sitting down with me and telling me the history and meaning of the phrase. I preferred to call it what it was: rigid and segregated. Men were permitted to do as they pleased; whereas, their wives were forbidden to be seen in certain places and had little freedom, expected only to present themselves appropriately in public and forge as many powerful connections as possible for their husband. Even their children were isolated, shut away, and raised by nannies, who ironically were the ones expected to teach them how to behave in society when most of them came from poverty themselves.

Leonardo was his fine, charming self, as always, and I thoroughly enjoyed his company. He had been coming to first-class as my guest since the night I met him, and we had taken a shine to each other. All the ladies loved him — he brought so much gossip about the latest fashion trends and the secret to making the perfect sponge cake. He gave them all his hints and tips, and they enjoyed his company as much as I did.

Leonardo would often keep me company in my suite, painting my toenails with something called French polish yesterday while telling me stories of his trips to France with his lover; and all the splendid memories he had of their time together. He had sworn me to secrecy and told me that his lover's name was Alex and that he was one of the hotel owners where he had worked in London. Once he had found Alex in bed with another man, who also worked at the hotel, he knew his career and life as he had known it was over.

Given he knew not a soul in Australia, he had decided to travel to Geelong to seek work; although I had my doubts a highly trained chef — who thought far too much of himself — would find suitable employment there, believing he should try his luck in Melbourne first. I had offered to help him as much as possible until he found work, his own home, and hopefully a better life than the one he had left behind. I worried for him. The world was not kind to effeminate men — especially if it became common knowledge that they were homosexual. The fact was, I thought of him as part of my growing family that had enveloped me, and it pleased me he would live close to me.

Danny, and the Makenzie family, were also planning to settle in Geelong, which pleased me greatly. I had every intention of remaining in contact with the ladies, and Catherine and her family, once they were all settled in Melbourne. Everyone had welcomed Leonardo, except for Hamish, who was still suspicious of him. Hamish was not happy that we were spending so much time together. I did not tell him that Leo slept with us in our suite most nights or that we snuck him into my bedchambers after Bessie had gone to sleep, as Hamish was already of the opinion Leonardo was in love with me. This had caused many tense moments and flare-ups between us, and I was getting sick of his jealousy. I didn't know whether he was irritating me more now because we had been together for weeks on end, or I was seeing a side to him I didn't like.

Once we had finished our afternoon tea, Dana, Leonardo, and I excused ourselves, embraced each of them before departing, calling out our farewells. We strolled side-by-side down the expansive deck towards our suite, where Polly and Bessie were waiting.

'So, what are we doing that's so secretive and exciting, sugar lips?' Leonardo asked me as we ambled along, then stepped into a wide hallway, nodding politely at the passengers who greeted us as they passed.

'I just need to talk to Dana about something.'

'You know I don't like secrets unless I am told every detail. Why can't you talk to me about it, Abigail?' he whined.

'For the same reason you're not married with ten children. That's the way God wants it, and she knows what's best.' I stopped and leaned over, holding the wall as we both laughed loudly, Dana waiting at the end of the hall tapping her foot, amusement in her eyes.

'I'm meant to be your best friend out of everyone you know, so I should automatically be the one you come to now. Stop being so selfish and only thinking about yourself. You know I can't stand secrets. Especially when no one will tell me what they are,' he squealed, startling Dana, who flinched, quickly placing her hands over her ears.

'Calm down and stop screeching at me in that voice. It's nothing you would be interested in any way,' I replied, smirking sidelong at him, confusion crossing his face.

Once we entered the suite and made ourselves comfortable on the lounges, I decided to get straight to the point. 'Dana, the reason I asked you here is that there are some intimate things that Polly, Bessie, and myself need to know, and you are the only person we trust enough to ask.' She smiled knowingly, while Polly and Bessie looked as embarrassed as I felt, my face already burning. She glanced across at Leonardo and raised her eyebrows questioningly. 'Ah, yes.' I rolled my eyes, choosing my words carefully. 'Leonardo, you do need to excuse yourself. Can we meet tonight after dinner in steerage?'

'Well, I must say, I'm not overly feeling the love, being thrown out of here onto my derrière, but of course I'll meet you tonight, my little cat's bum.' He flounced across the room, straightened himself up, and attempted to assume a more masculine personality, which was more of an attitude than a look. Finally, he blew me a kiss, closing the door quietly behind him.

'Abigail, you do attract some interesting friends,' Dana remarked, smiling to herself.

'What are you talking about? You're one of those interesting friends.' I giggled, Polly and Bessie joining in. She smiled fondly at me, her eyes shining as she relaxed back into the armchair.

'What would you three lovely girls like me to tell you?' Bessie and Polly stared wide-eyed, remaining silent, while my hands trembled slightly.

'We want to know about sexual relations. All of it, no leaving anything out, even the dirty bits.' I felt like my face was on fire, and Bessie and Polly did not look much better, their faces a slightly different shade of purple, but both clearly embarrassed.

'Well, that's the most interesting question I've been asked on this journey — or any journey — I have to tell you, Abigail.' She laughed until tears streamed down her face, her body trembling. Then, when she had blotted them away with her handkerchief and managed to contain herself, she leaned forward, resting her elbows on her knees and her chin in her hands. 'Fire away, girls.'

We shyly took it in turns to ask questions, and she provided the answers, in graphic detail, answering everyone without any shame. She told us everything she knew, from how it felt to lose your virginity to what you could do to enjoy relations with your husband. She spoke of the pain of childbirth, but how, when it was all over, it felt like the best thing you had ever achieved, going on to speak of ways to avoid becoming pregnant, which she felt was the most important for us to know, being so young.

Dana reflected on her own marriage and explained that in the beginning, she and her husband couldn't keep their hands off each other — until the children came along. Something changed in him then; his eyes started to wander, and she didn't know what to do to get him to take notice of her again. He began to spend a lot of his time at his club with his manservant, and she noticed how, more often than not, he slept in the guest bedroom. It went on like this for many years, until one day, she walked into his dressing room to find him and his valet engaging in homosexual acts. Disgusted, she cast him from her bedroom permanently and confronted him, only to find that this behaviour had been taking place during the entire course of their marriage and for years before that.

Given they had Charlotte and Victoria to protect from the scandal a separation would cause, they came to a mutual arrangement, where they lived in the same house but kept separate bedrooms and lives. Dana took many lovers after this and told us of her affairs with sixteen different men over the years. She described the things they had taught her, which she was now imparting to us.

I was relieved I had asked a woman who so obviously enjoyed having sex for guidance, as we listened to her as if she were a high priestess imparting sacred knowledge, taking in every word she said. I liked her enormously, and I would miss her and our daily chats dreadfully when we were forced to part.

I had learnt a lot from her — how to run a grand house, not that I thought I would need to. I expected mine would just be cosy compared to hers. She had even taught me how to apply a small amount of make-up on my face when I had a special event to attend. At least I knew she was staying at The Delmont for an indefinite period and could contact her there once I knew where I would be.

After giving each of us a hug, she excused herself and returned to her suite to have a nap. That sounded delightful to me, and I struggled to my feet and made my way to my room, calling out farewell to Polly as she stepped out into the hallway to meet Angus. Bessie undid my buttons, and I was in my nightgown within moments. I slipped under the heavy quilt, snuggled down into the soft mattress, cosy and warm in my bed, thinking of Leonardo. It was comforting to have another person to sleep beside and hold you through the night, leaving me wondering if that was what it was like to have a husband.

I slowly drifted off to sleep, dreaming of Hamish's naked body; however, shortly thereafter, I was screaming like I had never screamed before, looking down at the child that had just left my body, confused as to why he resembled a watermelon.

The Makenzie family greeted us warmly as we joined them in the dining room. We arrived late because Bessie refused to dine with us, ordering us out of the suite and locking the door behind us. Mrs Makenzie looked radiant and was slowly becoming accustomed to the idea of Angus and Polly marrying in the near future. She had confided in me that, although she still felt slightly nervous about her husband's reaction, she was confident that she could speak up for her son and Polly.

Jemima barely acknowledged me, which was not uncommon. I glanced across at her, listening to the cheerful conversations around me, choosing to eat rather than speak to her. From the moment I had laid eyes on her, I had felt uncomfortable in her presence. The grey aura that swirled around her had confused me, and we already had an unspoken dislike of each other.

During the voyage, I discovered she was nothing more than a gossip and was constantly causing trouble, manipulating her mother on a daily basis while being disloyal to her brothers. While they were friendly and charming and made people feel at ease, Jemima had thorns.

I swallowed the last of my dessert as Hamish lowered his voice and leaned in close. 'Would you consider walking the deck with me?' I nodded, wiping my mouth with a napkin. I would consider anything, as long as it didn't involve being in the same room as Jemima.

We stepped out onto the highly polished, wooden deck and into the blustery wind, Hamish leading me by the hand towards the stern of the ship where we would be alone. He embraced me tightly while opening his coat and wrapping it around me, the heat from his body warming me inside and out. He pulled me closer, not once taking his eyes from mine, before gently kissing my forehead, then my cheeks, and then my lips. We sat down to shelter behind a large crate that seemed to have been forgotten by the crew.

'Only a week now, an' we'll all meet our fate. Are you nervous?' he asked, gently unpinning my hair, the soft curls falling loosely down my back. I knew I would suffer for it as soon as I stepped out into the wind again, not to mention Bessie's reaction if she caught me returning to our suite with my hair tangled and looking like a vagrant, as she would often say.

'No, I think I'm more excited than nervous.'

'Seems like it was meant to be, Abigail — meetin' on the ship an' findin' we're destined to be livin' in the same town when Australia is such an enormous country. Bein' with you has been completely different from any of the women I've been with before. None of them behaved like you; they always acted very proper if people were around.' I felt my eyes go wide as I glared up at him, feeling the urge to smack him in the face.

'Are you saying I don't behave appropriately in public?' I snapped, narrowing my gaze at him. He slipped his arms around my waist, chuckling loudly.

'Aye. That's exactly what I'm sayin'. You're far too quick to say what is on your mind. You bring your maid to dine in first-class, you walk around with no shoes under your long dresses an' think no one notices, an' a hundred other things that make me feel the way I do about you. I am deeply in love with you, Abigail, an' I'm not going to let you get away from me. There is no other woman on earth who could take my interest or love from you. I dinnae know why, but I feel we're somehow connected, an' will always be together. I know people believe me to be arrogant an' entitled, an' I'm the first to admit I am, but with you, I'm different. I'm changing my view on the world a little.'

I took his hand, raised it to my lips, and kissed his palm. 'How have your views changed?'

'Well, just as you had a certain way of being raised an' were taught what to believe, I did too. The difference is you formed your own opinions, unlike me, who always believed everythin' my father told me about life an' women. He taught me the fairer sex were just to be used an' enjoyed, then discarded. I realised he wasnae a good man a long time ago due to how poorly he's treated my mother, an' he continues to step out on her to this day. He always told me to marry a respectable woman from a wealthy family to bear my sons an' keep my mistress secret. That's all changed since I met you.'

My heart hurt for him, being forced to endure a cold and distant childhood, and tolerating a terrible example of a father. The more I heard about this man, the more I disliked him for how he had treated his family, people who I had begun to love. Hamish was changing, and even Polly and Bessie could see it. The closer we became, the better I felt about what awaited us. I knew that whatever was to come, we would face it together, along with the support of all the wonderful people I had met.

That night, I dreamed of a river, a village, and — again — a weeping willow tree.

Chapter Twenty-Six

I AWOKE TO SILENCE for the first time in days. Usually, I could hear Polly and Bessie talking over breakfast or arguing about this or that, but this morning, there was nothing. I checked the time and realised I had overslept. I pressed the small button beside my bed, then stretched, yawning loudly, before realising Leonardo had risen for the day and left without waking me. Within minutes, Mary was standing at my door with my breakfast tray.

'I was just bringing you this, Mistress. Last day of full sailing, and we arrive tomorrow. How are you feeling?' She hurried to my side and placed the tray on my lap, fluffing the feathered pillows before placing them behind me.

'I'm more than enthusiastic and very, very happy to be getting off this ship. I appreciate and am grateful that we were comfortable and so well looked after, unlike those in the second and third classes. Having said that, Mary, I have had enough of this ship. I don't mean to sound ungracious, given my surroundings.' Still, I felt churlish within moments of the words leaving my lips.

'I completely understand, Mistress. No one enjoys being cooped up like a chicken all day and night. No, not one person. I will be glad

379

to get off this ship with you.' She glanced at me shyly, then handed me a napkin from the tray.

'I'm beyond pleased you are getting off with us, too. How are you feeling about starting your life in a new country?'

'Oh, Mistress, I'm so excited. Just the thought of having open spaces around me, and the sunshine beaming down on my head, puts me in a glorious mood. Being with you and Miss Polly, with Bessie by my side, is comforting because I thought I would be so alone there,' she replied, tears welling in her eyes. I hugged her, much to her surprise, before she stepped back from the bed and smiled, a smile I returned before digging into my hearty breakfast.

I lay back against my pillows, enjoying every bite. Thoughts of how I would fill my day crossed my mind as Mary bid me farewell. I could hear her chatting with Bessie outside the door, who then entered my room.

'I was wondering when you would wake up,' she snapped. 'It's all this dancing with Hamish and staying up all night that has tired you out, Mistress. We have been up for hours. I woke up and was sure I heard someone sneaking out of here this morning. You just remember I'm watching you and Polly. I don't know if I was dreaming it, so I won't rip shreds off anyone yet; but, if I find out there has been canoodling with those two boys going on behind my back, there will be hell to pay. Hamish is a pain in my you-know-what today. He won't stop coming here to see if you're awake. I've left Polly and Angus with Mrs Makenzie, given they can't be trusted at all, while I came back to attend to you. Every single person is driving me mad today.'

I quickly finished my breakfast and struggled to my feet, obediently going to the washstand where Mary had left a jug of warm water and scented soap. Bessie bent down, opening one of my trunks before rummaging through my dresses, muttering angrily to herself. She had packed away many of them yesterday with her own hands. I was thankful she hadn't caught Leonardo this morning in our suite, given her current mood. He always left before she woke, and she hadn't a clue he was sleeping here every night, or she would have tanned my hide.

'Oh, Bessie, you poor darling. I am so sorry I have left you to watch over everyone. You must have been dreaming, though. The boys were in their suite all night and not here. I give you my word.' I was quite aware that I was lying by omission, a technique I had used with the Sisters back at Emiliani House. I dried myself, remaining silent as she dressed me, then ordered me to sit down at my dressing table. She picked up my brush, styling my hair to perfection; the room so quiet I could have heard a pin drop.

'There you go, Mistress.' She nodded her head in satisfaction, pinning a matching emerald green hat to my hair, then stepping back to admire her work. 'Looking like a proper lady. Just make sure you keep behaving like one. I'm watching how that Hamish acts with you, and I don't mind if you tell him I will rain fire and brimstone down on him if he dares ruin your reputation.' I smothered a smile, staring back at her in the mirror.

'I'll tell him. I'm seeing him in a few minutes.'

'Well, you both better be staying close to Mrs Makenzie until I can get there.' She spun away and stomped out of the room, slamming the door behind her before I could reply. I hurried into the sitting room, calling out goodbye to little Mary, who had returned to share tea with Bessie, then made my way to the deck. Despite my misgivings, the thought of seeing Hamish set off hundreds of butterflies in my stomach. I found him at a table located toward the front of the ship, and I slipped into the chair beside him before he even noticed I was there.

'You look beautiful. That colour on you brings out your eyes even more.' His face lit up with love as he stared into my eyes. He looked incredibly handsome in a casual shirt that fit snugly across his broad shoulders. He smirked, glancing at my breasts, raising his eyebrows before looking back up at my face. His divine black hair was bound back tightly, and the way he stared at me made me want to kiss him across the table; however, I stopped myself, remembering Bessie's admonition.

'Bessie chose it, but thank you very much,' I said. 'By the way, she has a message for me to give you.' I repeated word for word what she had told me, his laughter so loud the surrounding passengers began to stare.

'Really? Fire and brimstone? I've often thought she's the devil incarnate rather than representing the almighty.' I giggled as he gazed over the water, grinning broadly.

'You know full well how much she likes you, and the fact is, we don't behave like Polly and Angus. It's your own fault that she has to reprimand you nearly every day for touching me where you shouldn't.'

'Well, the woman has a third eye. I swear she can see what I am doing even now. She doesn't give me a break, the evil troll.'

'That's her job, and she takes it very seriously. Mr Malcolm gave her strict instructions about how he expected us to behave under her care and what her responsibilities were.'

'And what exactly was that?' He sipped some tea, then placed an entire custard tart in his mouth.

'Keep lecherous men away from me, and to ensure I stay a virgin until I'm married,' I told him. He laughed aloud again.

'Well, my precious girl, she has certainly done that.' Our server brought us a range of delicious cakes while we chatted, along with a fresh pot of tea. Hamish reached across the table, taking my hand in his. 'Have I proven myself to you yet?'

'Hamish, it's not about proving yourself anymore. It's about waiting to see how we all settle first, then talking about a future together.' He annoyed and irritated me, raising the subject yet again when we were having such a great time together.

'It's only that I want to do somethin' tonight, an' I don't want you to get upset straight away when I ask, but to think about my proposal.' I eyed him suspiciously, his face flushing a slight pink. 'I want to sneak into your room when everyone else is asleep, an' I promise you nothin' untoward will happen. I will stay fully clothed, an' I'll not touch you anywhere I shouldn't. I just want to hold you close for a few hours, an' I give you my word I will return to my own suite before anyone gets up.'

He shifted uncomfortably in his chair, averting his gaze. It was difficult not to give in to those big, brown eyes and that adorable face. I knew he wouldn't do anything he shouldn't, but I wondered if I could trust myself with my newfound knowledge on the subject, thanks to Dana. I knew I possessed a great deal of self-control, but that had tended to lapse a bit the more I was around Hamish.

'Let me think about it.' I looked over at the clouds darkening in the distance, the sun now hidden as the storm approached. Polly had surprised me by maintaining her vow not to sleep with anyone until she married, even Angus. They were constantly chaperoned; however, it would have been easy for them to sleep together by sneaking him in at night like I did with Leonardo. Angus had accepted her version of what had happened to her before we were reunited. He felt enraged and wanted to return to her former master's home and apply justice of his own. Of course, that was not going to happen; however, I could see it made Polly feel safe that he had reacted protectively, and she was relieved he did not blame her for any of it.

I continued to hold the belief Polly needed to leave the past where it belonged. She was hesitant about not being entirely truthful with him but remained true to our agreement that Angus never find out about her life before we were reunited at the dockside tavern on that fateful day. I was feeling excited — this time tomorrow, I would be in Melbourne and finally see Catherine again. I couldn't wait for her to meet everyone. I knew she would like them immediately; even little Mary, who never stopped working and would never think to sit down with me and have a drink. It just would not be proper, in her opinion. I snickered to myself, Hamish turning back to me, his eyebrows raised.

'Sorry. I was just thinking how formal little Mary is,' I told him, picking up my china teacup and taking a small sip, regretting not ordering coffee.

'Abigail, when you have servants, you are expected to remain formal with them at all times. It cannae be like you are with Bessie; you must keep your distance. My family has employed many servants over the years, an' I have witnessed what can happen if you become too friendly with them. My mother once had a ladies' maid, who became a close friend an' confidante. Unfortunately, this woman took advantage of my mother's kindness an' slackened off in her work, behavin' as if she were above the other servants. Then, when my mother's jewels started to go missin', my mother refused to accuse Annie out of loyalty, despite us all knowin' she was stealin' from her. The final straw came when my mother found her rummagin' through her jewellery box, placin' items in her pocket, an' my father dismissed her on the spot.' I waited for him to finish, feeling terribly sorry for Mrs Makenzie. 'They were close friends for ove'r twenty years, Abigail, an' look what happened when my mother let down her guard. Annie had been a fine an' loyal maid for many years until that moment when my mother offered her friendship. My mother lost her closest friend in the world, an' she never fully recovered. It broke her heart. I don't want to see the same thing happen to you, Abigail.'

'Hamish, I don't know what you want me to say. I can't change who I am, and what you see is me. I'm not going to mistreat anyone, and if I want to be less formal, I will be.'

'Now, don't go pointin' your chin out at me like that an' gettin' all defensive, my feisty, wee wench,' he teased. 'I only mean that you shouldn't be sittin' down drinkin' cups of tea with them, that's all. Be careful.' The sun reappeared, the clouds moving away, appearing much less threatening than they had only an hour before.

I found Hamish to be a snob at times, given his education and upbringing. He was strong-willed and knew his own mind, which I admired. The problem was that he was that way with me, too. It had been playing on his mind that I was taking things slow, unlike Angus and Polly, and it made him doubt my commitment and love for him. I already knew I loved him, but had no plans to admit that until I was certain he would commit to me, and only me. He appeared far more cheerful than in recent days, and maybe getting off this ship was the best thing for all of us. I had noticed many cranky people on board, and in my suite, over the past week. Hamish and I finished our tea, deciding to walk the deck in the glorious Australian sunshine. It did seem the weather could change quite dramatically in this part of the world, and quickly from what I had witnessed. The ship sailed down the south-east coast of Australia towards Melbourne and Geelong, a place that many of us were pinning our hopes and dreams on. He rose to his feet and pulled my chair out for me, offering me his arm. We strolled down the deck, occasionally stopping to look over the side and down at the white-capped waves.

'Well, hello, lovers. Isn't it a fabulous day?' Leonardo appeared out of nowhere. 'The sunshine is lovely for your skin. I wish I could find a secluded spot somewhere on this boat to lie naked, so I turn brown all over like a coffee bean.' I giggled while Hamish looked at him in disbelief but remained silent as they shook hands. 'Is it all right if I use your suite to have a bath? I desperately need to get clean. I'm really not a steerage person and deserve much better, as we all know. I'm certain I am destined to be extremely wealthy in this new land, with servants of my own and a mansion in hand. Say, that rhymed, and I'm not even a poet. You may both escort me down to our suite now, and you can draw my bath, Abigail, as you don't really do much else.'

I choked, coughing and spluttering as I gasped for breath, Hamish's mouth twitching in amusement as he pounded me on the back while Leonardo skipped ahead of us and out of my sight. Finally, I regained my composure and followed Hamish through the long, endless hallways directly to my suite, laughing as we discussed Leonardo and his odd behaviour. I opened the door wide and stepped into the sitting room, finding Leonardo waiting for me in the washroom. I stood in the doorway, narrowing my gaze as he sat on the edge of the bath.

'Run your own bloody bath. I know you believe you came from royal blood in a past life, but here you will live the life you were given.' I closed the door, ignoring the shrieks that penetrated the heavy door, before returning to Hamish. He grabbed me, pulling me down on top of him on the lounge, gently placing his lips on mine. I wanted to crawl inside him and curl up safe and warm, kissing him back deeply, wanting to stay like this forever, until I heard a grunt... and a door slam.

'What are you two doing alone? I thought you were with Mrs Makenzie,' Bessie snapped as I quickly sat up, straightening my dress, then my hair.

'I was with mother until mornin' tea then, we wanted some privacy to talk, so met on the deck. Nothin' happened, Bessie, I promise.' He grinned at her while Bessie shook her head in disbelief, rolling her eyes.

'Oh, yes, that's what it looked like you were doing when I walked into the room just now, Hamish. You wonder why I'm watching you like a hawk and can't turn my back on you? It's because you can't be trusted, boy, as you have just shown.'

Bessie stomped off to her bedroom to collect an item she had forgotten to mend. She seemed more emotional than usual, concerning me enough to push Hamish away and follow her to her room, closing the door quietly behind me.

I sat down carefully on her neatly made bed, noting she had a place for everything around the room. If I had seen Bessie happy anywhere, it had been here on this ship. Although she took her self-assigned responsibility as our chaperone seriously, she still allowed us to have fun, but today she was having none of it. She stood with her back to me as she packed items away in her trunk.

'Bessie, please share with me what is bothering you. I may be able to help.' She turned slowly, tears welling in her eyes. She joined me on the bed, and I took her hand in mine.

'I think Danny has gone off me. Last night he was talking all night to Leanna, who is moving to Geelong, too. It's made me realise how much I really like him.' She started to cry. Bessie had been dividing her attention between Jimmy and Danny throughout the entire voyage, and this turn of events had not surprised me. We had spent a great deal of time in steerage, dancing to the Irish music and getting tipsy since Bessie had first invited us, and I had always known this particular love triangle would end in tears.

'Maybe he is sick of sharing you with Jimmy. Have you thought of that, Bessie?'

'It's probably too late now, and he will court Leanna instead of me. Why does she have to be half my size and prettier than me?' She hung her head and sobbed, continuing to cry despite my efforts to comfort her.

'Now, Bessie, that's not true. First, she is far too skinny and would snap like a twig if you touched her. Second, she isn't pretty like you at all — she doesn't have your lovely nature, or beautiful heart. She looks like a small, beady-eyed blackbird waiting to pounce on its prey, and that's what Danny is to her — prey. So, you need to get into action and fight for him and tell him the truth. Tonight is your last chance. I will come with you if you would like me to?' Bessie wiped her tears, sniffing loudly, then nodded.

'Yes, I will tell him tonight, and I would appreciate it greatly if you would come to support me.' She wiped her face again, patted me on the leg before rising to her feet and returning to the task of packing her trunk. I stood and crossed the room, embracing her tightly. 'Thank you, Mistress. You never fail to cheer me up. Now, get along with you and back to Hamish. You have five minutes alone until I'm back in there. Now go.' She shooed me out of the room, her melodious laughter echoing in my ear as I ran back to Hamish, ensuring I closed the door behind me.

It was my last afternoon tea with the ladies, and I felt melancholic, my heart heavy at the thought we may not cross paths again. Strong friendships had been forged, and I hoped I would see each one of them in the future. Parting with Amelia was the most difficult, knowing just some of what she was going through; and the fact she was all alone and grieving for her lost love. Tamara and Elizabeth were suffering from stomach problems. They were not eating a great deal, admitting they felt quite anxious vis-à-vis what awaited them once they stepped onto Australian soil tomorrow. I liked them both and truly hoped their marriages would be successful and happy. I admired their strength to embark on a path I would never take and intended to remain in touch.

Dana, Charlotte, and Victoria were eager to disembark, and I was nearly positive they would decide to move to Geelong in the not-too-distant future. Dana had become like a mother to me, telling me things you only would share with a daughter and giving me sound advice. She thought that, given Hamish's past, I was wise to wait and see how he behaved once we arrived, reassuring me I had made the right decision.

Mrs Makenzie was hoping for a double wedding for her boys, which I had gently told her would not occur. She had just smiled at me and said it would happen soon enough if she knew Hamish as well as she believed she did. She was taking care of Polly as a mother hen cared for its chick, and they had begun to build a friendship of sorts. Jemima, however, was not favourable to the match and had started to cause problems between Angus and Polly. She had confided in Polly that she had observed Angus on deck talking to a beautiful blonde woman who held his arm and flirted with him, appearing overfamiliar. When confronted, Angus denied everything and wanted to know who had told Polly, as it was an outright lie. Polly never told on his sister, but I knew what had happened, and it only caused me to take a darker view of her than I already had.

I reluctantly pulled away from the table, the last to stand as my new friends embraced each other, some shedding tears, while others promised this was not goodbye, but farewell for now. Amelia embraced me, whispering that we must stay friends, no matter where we ended up. I agreed, tears streaming down my face as I embraced each one, then joined Amelia to collect her son from his Nanny on the top deck of the ship. I had provided all the ladies with the name and address of my new solicitor, Mr Ian McPhee, allowing them to forward all mail to him until I had a permanent address. I would meet with him the day after tomorrow and find out the conditions of my late great-aunt Isabelle's Will, a meeting I hoped would go smoothly and ease my fears that I was leading my friends into a hopeless or difficult situation. At the very least, we had a house to live in, more than I had the day I left the orphanage. For that, I was grateful.

I lay on the lounge with my head on Hamish's lap, my eyes heavy and my belly full. Polly sat opposite me, Bessie by her side, while Angus stood near the table, studying Bessie's embroidered handkerchief she had recently finished. Finally, I gathered my strength and struggled to my feet, sighing deeply.

'It's early to bed for me tonight. I am so full after dinner that I just want to roll into bed. There's only one thing I have to do, and I will be back.' I glanced across at Bessie, who quickly stood and joined me at the front door, ready to leave for steerage, calling out our farewells as the door closed behind us.

I took Bessie's hand in mine as we made our way down into the belly of the ship, arriving at steerage in record time. I immediately noticed Danny at a table in the far corner of the room, following Bessie to where he was sitting with Leanna, who scowled when she caught sight of her rival. I pulled out a chair next to Leanna while Bessie sat down next to Danny.

'Danny, may I speak with you in private, please?' she asked him, her hands trembling, her face slightly flushed. He grinned at her, but remained where he was.

'What do you need to be saying to me, Bessie?' Bessie opened and closed her mouth several times, appearing unable to speak. I worried she would not go through with it and would soon turn and flee, especially with Leanna listening.

'The girls have told me I have to say exactly what I feel, and what I feel is love. Love for you. If you don't court me, I will die. I feel certain that I have to be with you,' she uttered, placing her head in her hands. His eyes twinkled, offering us both a drink from the glass jug that sat in the middle of the table before he turned his attention back to Bessie, remaining silent as he gazed at her for the longest time. Finally, he slowly turned to Leanna and gave her an apologetic smile.

'How can I not take notice of what Bessie has said when I feel the same way about her? I'm sorry, Leanna, but there is no future for us, an' I hope you find someone more deservin' than me. I must go where me heart tells me to go, an' I cannot apologise to you enough.'

I was overwhelmed with joy. I adored this man and thought him perfect for Bessie. In a split second, Leanna stood up, swung her arm up behind her head, and brought her hand smashing down on his face, shocking him for a moment. Then she threw her glass of ale over him and stomped away, smashing the glass on the floor. We remained silent, not knowing what to say or do.

'She took that news well,' Danny remarked, mopping off the liquid with a rag and rubbing his cheek, a slow grin spreading across his face. I started to giggle, which soon turned into loud laughter. Again, Danny chuckled loudly, throwing back his head and holding his stomach, his body shaking, while Bessie managed to smile ever so slightly. I soon decided they didn't need me around anymore and excused myself, leaving them huddled together, talking. I made my way back to the suite and, as I entered, saw Hamish and Angus were lying on the lounges while Polly sat on top of Angus's stomach reading a book.

'Do you mind if we have an early night tonight, please? I'm so tired.' I lay down again beside Hamish, tucking my head up under his arm and closing my eyes, waiting impatiently for Bessie, who arrived back an hour later with stars in her eyes. Danny had been nothing but a gentleman and walked her to the door, then kissed her on the cheek goodnight, and she was beside herself with joy. She headed for her bedroom, not bothering to chaperone us, only calling out over her shoulder for the boys to return to their suite shortly and reminding us we were to rise before the sun in the morning. She closed the door behind her as Hamish turned to Angus and Polly, lowering his voice to a whisper.

'If I tell you of a plan, will you agree to it an' keep it a secret?' I looked at him sharply as Angus and Polly nodded. I shook my head in disbelief, feeling the blood rush to my face as I closed my eyes again. I cringed as he told them of our earlier conversation and that he needed Angus to cover for him with his mother. Angus and Polly stared at him, appearing shocked.

'So, are you goin' to do it tonight?' Angus asked, narrowing his gaze at his brother.

'No, Angus. What I told you is the truth. Stop lookin' at me as if I'm about to break the law. You get to hold Polly whenever you want, an' I don't get the chance to do the same.'

'Don't give me that, Hamish. You've had the same opportunities as I have, only you chose not to take them,' Angus replied, laughing loudly at his twin.

'Oh, hush. You will wake Bessie,' Polly reminded him.

'I can't help it if I have respect for Bessie's rules, an' you two don't,' Hamish teased them. I rose to my feet, then straightened my dress, yawning loudly.

'Come on, go home, you two. Come straight back, Hamish, just in case I fall asleep. I will leave the door open for you, but please be quiet, for God's sake. You're like a bull in a china shop, always crashing around, breaking things and making noise,' I remarked fondly before kissing him goodnight, for now, at the door.

Polly and I made our way to my room. She helped me undress, loosening the laces of my corset so I could breathe before helping me into a clean nightgown. It covered me from my neck to my ankles and felt soft and silky against my skin. I assisted Polly, stripping her of her gown and corset and helping her into one of my nightgowns that was far too short for me, advising her to keep it as she bid me goodnight and made her way to the door, her hefty gown draped over her arm. I slipped under the heavy quilt and waited, my mind racing. Was he expecting me to be fully dressed as he would be? Finally, I heard the door slowly open as Polly sneaked him through. She followed him into my bedroom, appearing anxious.

'Now, don't get caught and don't do anything you will regret,' she told me firmly, and I nodded. As she closed the door behind her, Hamish crossed the room and pulled back the covers next to me. He sat down on the bed and removed his shoes and socks before turning off the lamp that stood beside him. He wore only a thin shirt and linen pants when he slipped into bed beside me. I felt nervous energy pulsing through my body, along with excitement bubbling up inside me. He lay on his back and made himself comfortable while I placed my head against his chest.

'You know I want to do this every night, don't you?'

'Yes, I know,' I replied, wishing he did not have to ruin the moment by pressuring me into something I wasn't sure of yet.

'An' you don't want to?' He gazed into my eyes, the moon softly beaming through the small porthole, causing his eyes to shimmer as I stared back at him.

'Yes. I mean, no. I am not completely sure. I'm more than halfway there, but just not quite ...' I trailed off when I saw the pain in his eyes. I knew I was in love with him and wanted to be with him, but I did not know how soon I wanted to be married or be obligated to make all the plans necessary for a wedding. I was learning quickly, though, thanks to the mêlée surrounding Polly's impending nuptials.

I kissed him on the cheek; however, he refused to meet my gaze. I snuggled against his body, gently kissing his neck, then his face, then his lips. I felt him soften towards me, then turn and slip his arms around my body. I could feel his hands gliding up and down my back, feeling the silk of my nightgown. He ran his fingers gently down my spine as though trying to familiarise himself with each part of me. He had never touched me without clothes on, with just a slip of material between us, and I knew I must feel different under his hands. I responded by running my hands over his muscular arms and chest.

'You have a lovely, round arse; I have to say, my dear Abigail,' he remarked, kissing me softly on the lips. He was an excellent kisser, and he had taught me well, as I had never kissed anyone before him.

'Well, you have magnificent arms and a pretty nice arse yourself,' I replied, laughing softly.

He kissed me again, then stopped himself, reminding me we needed to sleep; however, I couldn't sleep with him lying next to me. I started to kiss him softly, then passionately, until I was on top of him while he stroked my body through my nightdress, causing every part of my body to tingle.

He grabbed my backside as I moved up and down his body, and we kissed passionately, causing my body to react in ways I had never experienced; all I knew was I didn't want it to stop. I had not encountered such an intense physical sensation like this in my life. He continued to kiss me deeply, touching me in ways that left me unable to think of anything other than my body. I felt an odd awareness of pleasure intensifying deep inside me, until I could no longer stand it, feeling a sudden release and pure euphoria as I cried out, and he held me tightly as he groaned in pleasure. We continued to kiss for a time before Hamish pulled away and relaxed on his back, closing his eyes for a moment while I settled myself close to his side.

'Do you think that happens to every woman? I've never been with anyone that enjoyed me touching them so much.'

'I hope so. I have felt nothin' like that in my life. I have no words to explain what that felt like.' He chuckled and kissed me again. I turned on my side, Hamish moving close to cuddle into my back. Nestled close, we fitted together like two spoons in a drawer. As I drifted off to sleep, wrapped tightly in his enormous arms, he talked of how we would be married soon, the children we would have together, and all the things I did not want to think of. Soon, I was lost in a land of wedding dresses and churches, a black dragon and several kangaroos chasing me into the ocean, the crashing of the waves so loud I could not hear my own screams.

Chapter Twenty-Seven

I SLOWLY WOKE, HAMISH's lips gently touching my own. The sun had not yet risen, the ship gently rocking, tempting me to close my eyes again and remain warm and snug next to him, shutting out the world around us.

'What time is it?' I yawned, stretching my limbs before yawning again.

'It's five o'clock. I wanted to wake you a little early, so I can have some time with you before I return to my own bed.' I lay in his arms, enjoying his warmth and the closeness of his body, enveloping me as I kissed him back, before we both drifted back into a deep sleep, only to be abruptly woken soon after by the sound of Bessie's voice.

'Oh, my God, get in here until I can get rid of everyone.' I jumped out of bed, my heart racing, frantically pointing at the doors to the dressing room as he reluctantly rose from the bed. I slipped on my dressing gown, urging him to remain silent, before hurrying to the door to greet them in the sitting room, hoping no one would find him hiding in there, quickly closing the door behind me.

'Well, a joyous good morning to you, Mistress,' Bessie called out cheerfully as she busied herself packing the last of our possessions, placing as much as she could at the front door to be collected by the ship's porter. She was the happiest I had ever seen her, and her excitement was contagious.

'Oh, I just feel like bursting into song. I cannot believe we have finally arrived.' Polly was fully dressed, not a hair out of place, and her excitement was palpable; however, I was probably the only one that knew her joy came purely from the fact she was one day closer to marrying Angus; and that was all that mattered to her. Bessie called us to the dining table that sat out on our enclosed, private deck, Mary having laid out a lavish breakfast for us to enjoy. We ate in companionable silence while Polly pushed her food around her plate, eager to arrive at our destination and step onto solid ground.

Have you finished packing, Polly?' I enquired, narrowing my gaze at her. Polly shook her head, and I raised my eyebrows inquiringly.

'I'm sorry, Abi, but it's a mess. Bessie promised she would help me after breakfast.' Polly did not know why, but nothing stayed where it should be when she was in the room. She leaned in close, whispering in my ear. 'Has Hamish gone?' I shook my head slightly side to side, not wanting to attract Bessie's attention as she casually flipped through a magazine she had borrowed from Leonardo. Polly nodded before rising to her feet, hurrying Bessie along, before leading her into her room, closing the door behind her.

I jumped to my feet and hurried back to my bedroom, finding Hamish still hiding in my dressing room, silently indicating it was safe for him to leave. He briefly embraced me and kissed me again before I shooed him out the door and into the hallway, making sure that no one saw him leave.

I stood on the ship's highest deck, gazing down and reflecting on our journey halfway across the world. The waves seemed calmer, and I noticed we were sailing through a large bay, with land stretching out into the distance on both sides. What I presumed to be the city of Melbourne lay ahead of us in the distance. I hurried back to the suite, advising Bessie and Polly, who rushed back up the stairs with me to enjoy the view and cast a first look at the country we would call home.

We gathered in our suite for the last time, the mood sombre. Leonardo and little Mary joined us while Hamish and Angus had already disembarked, advising us they would wait on the dock to introduce Polly to their father. Bessie guided us out of the suite and towards the first-class exit, so crowded I waited in the hallway.

With much horn blowing, the ship slowly docked at Port Melbourne. It took longer than expected before we stepped out onto the deck and proceeded down the gangway — beside ourselves with excitement. We were a fair distance from the central business district and would be required to take a carriage; or the train, the station close by, from the docks. Waiting at the bottom of the ramp was an older man carrying a Delmont sign. I approached and asked him to wait a few moments for us. He nodded politely, grinning broadly, before letting the sign drop to his side.

'When you're ready, Mistress.'

I noticed Hamish standing by the ship with his family, a tall man with salt-and-pepper hair speaking with them. I took my time as I walked towards them, feeling like an intruder. Hamish turned and caught sight of me, his face lighting up.

'Abigail, I would like you to meet my father, Mr Colin Mackenzie.' He nodded politely before turning his attention back to his wife. He had passed down his good looks to his sons; however, he did not have a drop of their decency or good manners. In his younger days, I imagined he was quite the womaniser, although things had changed little, according to his wife. I had watched them greet each other from a distance and wasn't surprised at how formal and stiff they appeared in each other's company. He pecked her on the cheek for only a second before stepping away while inquiring if she had enjoyed the journey, turning his back before she could even respond. She only nodded slightly to herself before looking away and silently staring out across the bay.

After being told of the impending nuptials, Mr Makenzie regained his composure and talked animatedly with Polly, appearing quite friendly. I was pleased that he had not rejected her, despite what a fair bastard he was reported to be. Nearby, Amelia stood with her husband, Mr George Johnson, who was bent down over the perambulator, gazing at the baby. I excused myself and approached them, taking a deep breath.

'Hello, I'm Abigail. I am a friend of Amelia's.' I stretched out my hand to shake his; however, he ignored me.

'Amelia doesn't have any friends here, and it remains unlikely she will make any, given how shy she is. She doesn't like to mix with people,' he advised me abruptly, glaring down his pointy nose. He was a short, sharp-looking man who had black hair, black eyes, and a slight build; while Amelia was much taller than he and looked out-of-place standing beside him. I hugged her tightly, promising to write, while pointedly looking in her husband's direction. I left them standing together, tears in my eyes as I returned to the Makenzie's', embracing each of them, all except Mr Makenzie, who only nodded politely. I led Hamish away from the group to ensure we have a little privacy, an almost impossible task in a crowd of hundreds.

'You know I will marry you, Abigail, if it's the last thing I do. I promise you that.' His eyes twinkled as I looked up into his handsome face and smiled, slipping my arms around his massive shoulders. I no longer cared who was watching as he held me in his arms, kissing me. Finally, his father came over, barking that it was time to leave and that they must return home before dark. Hamish gave my hand a last squeeze, then winked at me before following his family into the crowd and disappearing from my sight within moments.

Hamish

'So, how was yer voyage?' my father asked, moving his gaze to Angus, then Jemima, the carriage rocking back and forth as the two black horses trotted through the streets towards the centre of Melbourne.

'Oh, Daddy, it was dreadful. Those awful women the boys met are so common. I cannot understand what they see in them.' She smiled sweetly at him before he reached over and affectionately touched her cheek. My sister was a first-class bitch, and always had been from the moment she realised how to get her own way since she first began to talk. She was our father's favourite child, and nothing Angus and I did was ever good enough, while she could do no wrong. I glanced across at Mother, sitting beside him, staring out the small window, deep sadness in her eyes. I had wished since I was a young child that she would leave him, or he would go away and never return; however, she had stuck by his side no matter what treatment she received.

'What's this scaffy about gettin' married, Angus? I must say, the young lady is fetchin'; but I dinnae believe she'll fit in tae our family.' I sat back, turning away to look at the houses we passed, while I silently listened to them argue. Mother ignored them both, Jemima constantly interrupting and offering her own uninvited and unhelpful opinions on the matter, causing the argument to escalate even further. It felt like an eternity before our father ended the

401

discussion and focussed his attention back on Jemima. I continued to look out the carriage window, thinking only of Abigail. She had touched my soul and taken my heart without warning, but I knew I loved her deeply and ferociously and planned to spend the rest of my life with only her. I hadn't believed in love before or that I could ever feel the way I felt about her, but she had completely changed my life.

My father turned to me, raising his eyebrows. 'So, who was that red-headed bit o' fluff? I wouldnae mind becomin' more intimately acquainted with that one meself. Naw, I wouldnae mind at all. She's bonny, with eyes like emeralds an' the face o' an angel, an' that body an' hair. Maybe when you've finished with her, Hamish, ye can pass her o'er tae me.' I felt fury rise inside me, wanting to kill him where he sat. Angus placed his hand firmly on my forearm, noting the dangerous glint in my eye.

'If ye ever speak about Abigail like that again, I'll hurt ye so badly you'll scream for death to take ye,' I warned him calmly, surprising even myself.

'Aye, I'm sorry, lad. I dinnae know this one means anythin' tae yer.' He shrugged his shoulders and dismissed me with a wave of his hand. I resisted the overwhelming urge to punch him several times hard in the face, first for shaming my mother and then for even thinking about Abigail in a sexual manner. Instead, I ignored the old bastard and resumed looking out the window as the carriage took us through the busy streets of Melbourne and down Swanston Street. My thoughts turned back to my beautiful girl, who I knew would accept me in the near future; what with the deep connection and love we already had for each other, there was no other outcome for either of us. I was more than confident no other woman would ever catch my eye or capture my heart once I had Abigail as mine — nor would any other man gain her attention or affection while I was nearby — and all she could see was me.

Also By

J L MARTIN

NON-FICTION
Sunshine After the Storm — Finding Joy after Trauma

FICTION
SAMSARA- The First Season
That Fated Night- A Short Novella of Love and Loss
The Golden Glow
Unexpected Beginnings
Torn in Two
Loss of Innocence
Unconditional Love
Returning Home
Letting go
Soul Connections
Healing the Heart
Legacy and Love
Leo- Back to me!
Lilith- Utopia

SPAWNED OF SIN- Trilogy Series
Through Windows in the Sky I Fall
Tainted Blood, Poisoned Soul
The Ties That Bind Behind Me

A Personal Note from the Author

I ASK THAT YOU leave a review for each book on your chosen platform. You can find the links on my website www.jlmartinauthor.com. This not only helps authors become more visible in the enormous world of publishing — it helps readers just like you discover books they never would have found. Thank you, and I really hope you enjoy your journey with Abigail, her friends, and the family she chooses for herself. If Samsara is not the series for you, I wish you well in finding novels that bring you joy and thank you for the time you invested. We cannot be everyone's cup of tea — or coffee, in my case — and life is far too short to drink dregs or read bad books. Much love to all, and I hope you enjoy Samsara xx.

www.jlmartinauthor.com

SAMSARA

THE FIRST SEASON

Unexpected Beginnings
Volume One Book Two

What if you could remember a past life?
Or worse, what if you couldn't?

Abigail's journey to Melbourne, Australia, has blessed her with friendships that will last a lifetime — but has left her even more confused by the auras she has seen since she could first remember. Finding the further she travels from home, the more common they become, and she cannot confide in another soul for fear of retribution. Feeling even more alone when she arrives in Geelong, Abigail finds all is not what it seemed or was promised. She faces an impossible choice that will impact her future — a future she feels she has no control over that leaves her torn between two very different men — forced to make a choice that will change her destiny in ways she could never have imagined.

Join Abigail on her journey through the first season of 'Samsara' and find out what thousands of readers are talking about.

"*That Fated Night- A Short Novella of Love and Loss*' — eBook available free from jlmartinauthor.com and all online bookstores. Available to purchase in audio and paperback where 'Samsara' is sold.

Want to stay up to date and be the first to hear about Samsara? Go to jlmartinauthor.com to sign up for her newsletter and receive alerts and updates, along with bonus content. Links to social media and bookstores available here too.

www.jlmartinauthor.com

About The Author

J. L. MARTIN LIVES in a quiet country town in Regional Victoria, Australia. In a past life of her own, she spent close to two decades working in the Welfare sector and at the coalface for the State Child Protection AHS Emergency Service as a lead investigator, applicant and expert witness within the Childrens' Court—both in the family and criminal divisions—along with the Family Law and Criminal Court systems, before being forced to retire with cumulative trauma as a result of a final assault sustained in the workplace while carrying out her duties. She holds a degree in welfare and has two adult daughters and four grandchildren — along with several adult foster daughters and grandchildren.

J L Martin's transition to full-time author began in December 2015 when she started writing as therapy to assist in her recovery from PTSD, ultimately leading to her debut series 'Samsara'. Her only non-fiction book, 'A Journey to Finding YOUR New Normal—PTSD, Anxiety and Depression,' was first published in 2018; however, J L Martin recently updated the existing manuscript while adding a significant amount of new information due to several changes that have occurred in a short space of time, not only in her own life but more importantly within the mental health field—along with the irritating fact that the phrase 'New Normal' is now closely associated with Covid-19. The updated edition will be published under a new title, 'Sunshine after the Storm—Finding Joy after Trauma,' and is available on her website and from all good bookstores in ebook, paperback and audiobook from January 2023.

She owns a 19th-Century Coffee Palace & Bookstore with her partner, a creative soul and talented artist in his own right. Their 'Penny University,' stocks only tomes from Indie Authors to show their unwavering support of all writers within the community and around the world — and coffee — they have GREAT coffee. Want to stay up to date and be the first to hear about Samsara? Go to jlmartinauthor.com to sign up for her newsletter and receive alerts and updates, along with bonus content from unpublished volumes. Links to social media and bookstores are available here too.

Go to jlmartinauthor.com

Acknowledgements

F OREMOST, I WOULD LIKE to thank my editor and narrator, Marianne Delaforce. Not only does she polish my words until they shine — without her 'Samsara' would not be available as an audiobook. Thank you, beautiful soul. Not unlike the plot of this series, you entered my life serendipitously and I am grateful to call you a friend. Bless you.

You have a heart of service and a generous spirit, Stuart Grant. For no reason other than that, you helped a stranger. Thank you for designing my beautiful website and teaching me how to use it. Your patience was noted and appreciated. You are seriously my hero and one day; I hope to meet you and your sweet family. I'm grateful.

My book cover designer, Thea, what can I say? You are the most beautiful soul, and your work is fantastic. They say don't judge a book by its cover... but how can you not when they are just so lovely? Thank you. Your talent and generosity is appreciated.

To my dad, the one constant in my life who doesn't see me as weird and supports everything I do. I love you.

To my mum, I love you too.

To Steve, my love, my heart, my best friend and my favourite human. I adore you and love you without limitation or conditions.

413

To Ava, Thomas and Isla... just because I love you, too.

Aurorah, Jakobie, Audrey and Makenzie, I love you to the moon and back.

To my beautiful friends. You know who you are. Thank you for your support in every way, on every level. Without you, I wouldn't have had the confidence to come this far....and you were the ones who took time out of your busy lives to read the series and push me to publish. You are forever loved and appreciated.

To my Beta Readers — Gailene Cuttler, Ruben Panopio, Vicki Howard and Michelle Norman. Thank you for your input and love of Samsara. Your feedback has shaped this series. Much love.

To my loyal readers, old and new. What can I say, other than thank you for becoming so involved and passionate about my series. You encouraged me. You gave me the confidence to believe in myself. You told all your friends about 'Samsara', bringing thousands of readers who connected to the books and characters, embracing them as family. I am grateful for each and every one of you and always will be.

Full Dedication

To my grandchildren,

I have cherished you from the moment you entered the world. You have brought me so much joy and taught me the true meaning of unconditional love in a way I have never known. Be courageous and always choose to stand up for what is right and what you believe in, no matter what those around you think. Live with integrity and be kind to all that cross your path in life, as kindness expresses love. Be emotionally vulnerable no matter how many times people hurt you... and they will. Forgive always as hate and unforgiveness is like drinking poison and expecting the other person to die... but under no circumstance let those that hurt or betray you change the essence of you or the love that radiates from you for others. Believe in your soul you can be anything you want to be in this world and will achieve great things, and dismiss those that think your dreams are impossible kindly and without malice... you will prove them wrong, my darlings. I will always believe in you. Speak up for the underdog, and when you see injustice, fight for change—advocate for those suffering and who are less fortunate than you. We desperately need people like you in this world. Always know your worth and allow no one to

415

treat you less than you deserve, and you deserve deep, authentic love and respect and true happiness and joy. Believe in yourself and accept yourself, just as you are, as this is the only way you can live authentically and reach your true potential, a potential that exceeds even your own expectations of yourself. Know I will always love each of you, and I thank God and the universe for you every day and understand that you will do amazing things in this world.

Always remember, to be truly happy, you need to be grateful for all the small stuff; if you are not happy with what you already have, how will you be happier with more? Happiness comes from the inside, not possessions, power; nor are others responsible for your happiness. That's your job. Choose joy, precious ones. Don't strive for material things; seek true bliss, love yourself exactly as you are, and carry out one selfless act a day. I promise it will make the world a better place and increase the joy in your life. I leave 'Samsara' as a legacy to you with all my love, and it is my hope I have shown you through my own actions you can achieve anything in life if you follow your passion, the unique passion that burns deeply in all of you. I love you to the moon and back a million times over and always will, no matter what choices you make in life. I know you will all have an enormous impact on the world; even when I am no longer physically here with you, you will continue what I have started, and I will always look on proudly. Now you have to believe it because Grandma said it! You will always be my babies, and I love you now and forever. Time and distance will never separate or diminish the love and bond we share. You will always be my little ones, and I will always adore you, no matter where you are in the world.

CPSIA information can be obtained
at www.ICGtesting.com
Printed in the USA
BVHW070020090223
658191BV00023B/509